AKEEMA'S Secret

BARBARA RAWLINS-GREEN

LUNA GLOBAL MEDIA
Suncrest Dv. Melbourne, FL
+1 312 212 3899 U.S.
https://lunaglobalmedia.com/

AKEEMA'S SECRET

ISBN (Paperback): 979-8-9888550-8-8

Printed in the United States of America

GLOSSARY

YAHUAH	THE HEAVENLY FATHER
YAHUSHA	OUR SAVIOR;
	THE FATHER'S SON
RUACH HA-KODESH	HOLY SPIRIT
	THAT INDWELLS US
KADOSH	HOLY, PEACE; HAPPY
SHABBOT SHALOM	HAPPY SABBATH

DEDICATION

To Ed, Bruce Sr., and Loretta…

Sometimes we agree to disagree, but I'm thankful for your love and support that is always there.

CHAPTER 1

In her loud, musical voice, Akeema cried out, "It's noisy time!"

The noise that erupted around her was like a warm blanket of comfort. The class of first grade students yelled, whistled, clapped, and stomped their little feet with glee. For the next five minutes they had permission to break the sound barrier if they didn't break anything or hurt anyone. These tension-release moments were allowed once a day.

Akeema watched the children carefully. When they became agitated, whiny, and antsy, this little naughty break seemed to restore their good humor somehow. Only once had she joined them in an ear-piercing shrill that put her four-octave voice to use. On that day, the kids had refused to settle down when she'd cracked her wooden ruler on her desk. When she'd let out her scream, each child had turned to her with wide eyes and open-and quiet-mouths. Since that episode, the kids were obedient to her requests to shut up!

As she slowly cruised among the little ones, she could see they were wearing themselves out. She bent down to meet those who wanted to hug her, kiss her, or give her a high-five slap on her hand. From the plainest child to the cutest one, they all had one thing in common: missing teeth!

She adored every one of them. A few, she admitted to herself, she loved as if they were her own. Since a car crash had resulted in a crushed pelvis and a hysterectomy, she was destined not to birth any babies of her own. Akeema's fate was to be a surrogate mother to a new batch of children each year. By the time she made it back to her desk, the classroom had settled down to a low hum. She only had to hit the desk lightly to be heard. "Ok, that was fun. Everybody please return to your seats now."

Without hesitation, the children did what they were told. When all of their gap-toothed faces were watching her expectantly, Akeema graced them with a satisfied smile.

"We have about an hour before it's time to go home. Who can tell me how many minutes are in an hour?" Over half of the kids eagerly raised their hands. Akeema was thrilled. Telling time by a clock was no longer part of the schedule, but she was determined to teach them anyway. At the end of each school year, she gave each little boy and girl a watch with hands on it. "Ted, please tell the class how many minutes are in an hour."

The smiling, chubby-cheeked little one proudly announced, "sixty, Miss Akeema!"

"That's right! Exceptionally good, Ted."

She turned to the blackboard, drawing a clock face with chalk. After placing the long and short hands on it, she asked, "What time is it?"

Most of the students chorused, "Three o'clock!"

"Correct!" Erasing the old hands to replace them with new ones, the game continued with satisfactory results. As a reward for having a good day, each student was given an apple on their way out of school. When she was finally alone, Akeema sat down at her desk, looking at all the empty chairs. She felt empty inside. Everyone that made her feel loved had gone home for the day.

Strolling down the hallways, Principal Wilson was astutely checking everything out. Except for the staff and a few students in detention, everybody at Roosevelt Elementary School was gone. At 4:30 in the afternoon, most of his teachers were packing up papers to grade later. They also had lesson plans to get through for the next day's classes. They had, quite literally, homework to do.

Suddenly, he halted. Unobserved, he was free to stare at Akeema with all her loveliness. Secretly, he referred to her as the Nubian Princess. She was alone, regally sitting at her desk, looking straight ahead. She wasn't slouching or slumped in any way. She was sitting like a deity on her throne. He feasted on her every feature: the flawless dark chocolate skin, the large-slightly slanted-dark brown eyes, the high cheekbones dusted with a little color, the plump, beautifully shaped lips with a slight sheen that made them look moist and supple. She was quite tall, with a dancer's body. He guessed she was at least 6 feet since she was taller than his own 5 feet, 10 inches. Today, she wore a long-sleeved shirt that was checkered in shades of blue. From what he could see, her slacks were navy blue. In casual clothes she still managed to look formal and well put together. Everyone in the building loved talking with her. It wasn't just that she made you feel like you had her undivided attention, it was the sound of her deep, sensual voice that was so captivating. By contrast, her singing voice was four octaves high and gorgeous. It was reported to him that her students loved her so much that some of them cried when it was time to go home!

Feeling herself being watched, Akeema abruptly turned her head to the right.

Whoops! He was busted.

Smoothly, he walked into her classroom, smiling as if he intended to talk to her all along.

"Good evening, Miss Sprite."

"Good evening, Sir, and please call me Akeema."

"I will, but only if you call me Derek."

"Ah, but you have the position of authority. I don't know if calling you by your first name is appropriate, sir."

"We don't want to confuse the little ones as we 33 to teach them manners, but, when we're alone, I insist. Drop the "sir" as well. Please!"

With a slight incline of her head, she smiled at him before saying, "At your insistence…Derek."

Grinning broadly, he replied, "Thank you, Akeema."

That said, he turned around to leave the room. He could feel her eyes on him as he made a right turn to remove himself from her sight. He loved the way she said his name. With her hint of an English accent, she rolled the "r" in Derek. Before this, he'd never thought of his name as sexy.

CHAPTER 2

Coming through the front door, Akeema smelled something wonderful coming from the kitchen. "Akeema, is that you, honey?" her Aunt Jean called.

"Yes, ma'am! I'm on my way!"

Putting her purse and briefcase on the hall table, she followed her nose.

Aunt Jean's back was to Akeema as she stirred the contents of a huge silver pot.

"What yumminess are you fixin' for dinner?"

"Jambalaya! It's been a while since we had it, and your uncle put in his request for it."

"Good! Where is Uncle Rick?"

"Gone to get beer."

"Good again. Do I have time to get comfortable before we eat?"

Aunt Jean turned to look Akeema up and down.

"You look plenty comfortable."

"I am, I just want to get out of the clothes I've been working in all day."

Turning back to the work at hand, Aunt Jean said, "You've got about half an hour."

"Great, I'll probably get some work done, too."
"Okay, I'll yell when it's ready."
"Thanks, Auntie!"

Akeema sat in the middle of her bed, surrounded by schoolwork. She wore a comfy sleep shirt with knee-pants. Her stomach growled in anticipation of the luscious meal to come.
"Rick, Akeema! Come and get it guys!"
Her aunt always had perfect timing.

After dinner, Aunt Jean looked at her sister's daughter in amazement. "I don't get it, Akeema. You eat as much as I do, but I look like this, and you don't!"
Uncle Rick listened to the women in his life banter back and forth. To him, each woman was beautiful in her own way. Even with a boy's haircut – that he personally didn't care for – Akeema was beauty personified. He knew that she ate more like a man than a woman, but you couldn't tell that by looking at her. She had ballet training that she maintained with a mania. Most men would die if they tried to keep up with her. His missus was big, bold, and loud. There just wasn't any other way to put it. She was invited to parties because she made them a success. She said what she wanted to say, when she wanted to say it. She was as tall as Akeema, but easily outweighed her by a hundred pounds. She had a full head of natural hair, and the clothes she wore were as colorful as her personality. Jean was a loving

woman who gave her all to whatever – and whoever – was important to her. She was the love of his life.

"You are cordially invited to work out with me at any time. I'll have you in shape before you know it," Akeema promised her aunt.

Without missing a beat, Jean quipped, "No, thank you. I can think of better ways to die." Akeema and Rick laughed, knowing she was only half kidding.

Rick would risk his life to protect the ladies in his house. For Akeema, he already had.

Back in her bedroom, Akeema finished up her work and was now flipping through channels with the remote. Finding nothing, she finally stopped on the game network. She'd exercise her mind by playing along until she was tired enough to sleep.

Glancing around her aunt's guest room, it was hard to believe this was now her home. Her voyage to this place had been a tempestuous one…

…The day that would change her life forever happened three years ago. She was a substitute teacher for the first and second graders by day, and a background dancer for the Royal Ballet three nights a week. She was young and happily busy. She looked forward to the future with all its surprises – or so she thought.

Jake Butler sat next to his mother in the box seats at the Royal Ballet. It was her birthday, and this was his gift to her. His father was too busy climbing the corporate ladder to wine and dine his wife. He was sure that she "understood" his necessary neglect of her. Jake appointed himself as his father's stand-in.

The audience hushed as the lights went down and the curtain went up. This particular night came at no sacrifice to Jake. He shared his mother's love of dance. Watching long, taut muscles contort in exotic movements was beautiful to him. The performers all wore heavy make-up that made them look like dolls, men included. What their faces looked like wasn't important to him. His focus was always on the bodies.

The two lead dancers floated out, meeting each other center-stage. The man gripped her waist, gracefully lifting the woman over his head. Their dance had an erotic quality to it, causing Jake to have forward thoughts. He imagined the female lead laying beneath him. They were fully clothed as she squeezed him with her powerful legs around his middle. It was sexy and painful. Jake forced his mind back to the here and now. He breathed in deeply with his mouth closed, then exhaled with his mouth in the whistle position. There. He was now back in control.

Applause erupted as the duo finished their dance. Nine female dancers took over the stage. Jake gasped. The dancers formed a straight line. Eight women had white, chalky faces with bright red lips. Right dab in the middle was an African Queen who was the tallest on the stage, by far. Jake's eyes were glued to her. She was so dark that her teeth were gleaming with whiteness. Her slicked-back hair made her look bald at first glance. He marveled that she was gorgeous in spite of that.

He was mesmerized by her every movement. When she left the stage, he acutely felt her absence. For the first time that night, he reached for the ballet program that introduced all the dancers. Thankfully, each name had a color photo next to it. Even on paper you could see her regal bearing. Her long swan-like neck curved gracefully with her oval face. Her big, expressive eyes had an outward slant that added to her exotic look. In this picture, her hair fell in gentle waves over her slender shoulders. He had to meet her.

After the show, Mrs. Butler was surprised when her son said, "Let's go meet the dancers, Mom."

"Excuse me?" Jake smiled at her as he held her by the elbow, guiding her to the reception line. After each night's performance, the dancers lined up to meet and greet. Usually, the real fans brought their programs to have the pictures in it autographed. Jake and his mother had never stayed around at the end. Until now.

Mrs. Butler went to the line where the lead dancer stood. Jake made a beeline to the supportive cast. Everybody had heavily made-up eyes and lips without the pasty white faces. Except her, Akeema Dawn.

She was even lovelier up close and personal. Her dark, ebony skin was flawless. Her high cheekbones and lips had a deep berry color on them. From what he could see, her beautiful eyes had mascara on thick, real eyelashes, not false ones. At last, he was standing before her. She looked him straight in the eyes, as if he was the only one in the room. When he grasped her outstretched hand to shake it, he wasn't surprised at the softness on the top of it, but he was caught off guard by the callouses on her palm. "Good evening, sir," she said. "I hope you enjoyed yourself this evening." How delightful, Jake thought. She had a deep, smoky voice that was all woman. An added bonus was an accent that was barely there. What was it? Australian, British?

Giving her his best smile and charm, he replied,

"I did indeed. I found that you were brilliant."

He caught the flick of her raised, shapely eyebrows. She didn't think his compliment was sincere.

"Thank you, sir. I hope the rest of your evening goes well."

She was dismissing him! He felt shocked and challenged. Jake was accustomed to having women under his thumb. He was determined that she wouldn't be the exception to his rule. "Please allow me to introduce myself, Akeema." Again, the upraised eyebrows. "I'm Jake Butler, and as of tonight, I'm your biggest fan."

She blessed him with a small smile. "My family would challenge you on that one."

Quickly, he assured her, "Understood. That makes me the first among the non-biological." Never breaking eye contact, she smiled.

A discreet clearing of a throat behind him, reminded him that they weren't alone.

"Regretfully, Akeema, I must move along." She nodded. "Goodnight," she said promptly.

"Jake," he emphasized.

Wanting him to move on, she responded, "Good night, Jake Butler."

He grinned so hard his face nearly cracked. She remembered his last name!

This time when she offered to shake his hand, he kissed it instead. He didn't care how many people shook her hand before his lips touched it. He would gladly receive her germs.

His mother was quietly watching their exchange. She knew her son was a womanizer. Not only had she received reports from her friends, but she'd also heard him share his conquests with her husband. She felt sorry for the beautiful black woman who had his rapt attention.

For the next month, Jake made sure that Akeema saw him three days a week during each meet and greet after she performed. As part of his manipulation to pique her interest, he never asked her out. He did, however, continue to kiss her hand. It became obvious to one and all that Jake was there to see Akeema. He was always first in line at the meet and greet, and the only dancer he talked to was her. As he planned it, it was Akeema who made the first move.

At the end of their meet and greet he was about to reach for her hand when she said,

"The only woman I've seen you with is your mother. Aren't any of your dates interested in the ballet?"

Gotcha! He thought. "Nope, not a single one is in on any of the fine arts. I go alone or with mom." He made sure his voice had a sad quality to it, even though he was celebrating inside.

"What do you consider to be the fine arts?" she asked.

"Besides the Ballet and Opera, I also enjoy going to museums and live stage plays. What are your interests?"

"The same things you mentioned. Every now and then a movie will come out that I'll go see. I'm busy so I don't have much time, I'm afraid."

"Oh," he said – his voice dripping with disappointment.

Looking concerned she asked, "Is something wrong?"

Looking down at his feet, in false humility, he replied,

"I've been trying to get up the courage to ask you out, but you just told me you're too busy. Oh, well." The last word he said with a sigh.

"If we can synchronize our schedules, I'd love to go out with you," she said simply.

"You would?"

"Yes."

"Except for the meet and greet, I have no way of contacting you."

"Give me your program."

Jake promptly did so. He watched as she wrote her cell number next to her picture. Akeema handed it back to him with a smile.

This was the beginning.

From then on, Jake made sure that when Akeema had free time, so did he. He made sure she knew when he was rearranging his schedule to accommodate her. His plan was to prove his devotion to her, seduce her, then move on. He didn't know that his obsession with her would grow into something all-consuming. The control that he so coveted, had slipped away. Before it was all said and done, Jake would discover that he was unwilling to live without Akeema Dawn – or let her live without him.

Akeema was living in a fairy tale. She was living smack – dab in the middle of a storybook romance. She knew and understood that nobody was perfect, but Jake Butler was closer to it than she'd ever seen! She thought he was a beautiful man, inside and out. She was 6 feet tall in her bare feet, but she had to look up at him as he towered over her by at least 5 or 6 inches. His shiny light brown hair was the exact color of his eyes. He was saved from being too pretty by his chiseled jawline. He was slender, but his long, toned muscles kept him from looking too thin. He had a dancer's body, even though he didn't dance. They slow danced together in perfect rhythm, but when they moved separately, he was the typical gangly white boy on the dance floor. When she poked fun at his moves, he'd laughed right along with her. However, he assured her that he would keep right on making a fool of himself as long as it gave him the opportunity to hold her close to him. Sigh.

He was a very successful investment broker with travel often on his agenda. He looked very dapper in his custom-made suits. People often thought he was a model, and he got a kick out of that. Like clockwork, he called her three times a day, even when he was on the road. Akeema started each day with his voice in her ear before she even got out of bed. At lunch, they talked again, often smacking food as they ate and spoke at the same time. Finally, even on performance or date nights, the last voice she heard before falling asleep was Jake's.

She was the envy of all her friends. They were sad to learn that, like herself, he was an only child. Most women complained that the men in their lives were so self-involved that they only wanted to talk about themselves and their own interests. Jake was interested in every aspect of her life. Unless Akeema asked him a direct question, Jake rarely talked about himself.

To top it all off, the man had major skills in the art of love making. Akeema didn't have a lot of experience, but for the first time in her 27 years on the planet, she knew what it was like to be horny. She thought she knew what it was like to have satisfactory sex because she had always enjoyed it. What Jake did to her was something else altogether. He had given her an orgasm so intense that she feared it was killing her! He did so many wonderful things to her that she felt inadequate. Except laying there and enjoying herself, she really didn't know any special things to do. When she'd timidly asked him to teach her how to do the things that pleased him, he'd let her know that he was glad she wasn't an expert sex kitten. He loved knowing that he wasn't coming behind a lot of other men. That night, she climaxed so hard and screamed so loudly that she didn't recognize her own voice!

Thinking of their intimate time together caused an involuntary shiver to course through her body. This wasn't the time or place to be having erotic playbacks. She was sitting in front of a huge mirror applying make-up before a dance performance. Only the lead performers had their make-up professionally applied; everyone else had to do their own. The large dressing room was buzzing with chatter, stretches, and wardrobe changes. The energy in the room was electric.

"Delivery for Akeema Dawn, delivery for Akeema Dawn!"

In the mirror behind her, she could see the young ticket taker holding a huge bunch of pink flowers. Lifting her arm and snapping her fingers, she called out, "I'm here!"

As he walked toward her, the teenager gulped his dry throat several times. He had a huge crush on the statuesque dancer. He didn't know any black people up close and personal. He thought Akeema was the most beautiful woman he'd ever seen – in any color!

Speechless, he gave her the pale pink tulips that blended with the color of her costume.

"Thank you," she said politely.

He smiled and nodded, red-faced. When he turned to leave, he stumbled over his own feet, causing his face and prominent ears to blaze a hotter red.

Several of Akeema's work buddies surrounded her. They were excited for her, and all talking at the same time.

"Oh, how pretty!"

"What does the card say?"

"Are they from that tall drink of water you've been seeing?"

"I didn't know tulips came in pink!"

Akeema laughed. "Ladies, ladies, give me a break! Let's read the card together, okay?"

As she opened the unsealed envelope, she prayed that her lover didn't write anything naughty on the enclosed card. She lifted it in the air so that everyone could see it. Together, they read it in unison.

"Break a leg! Love, Jake."

They all got the joke, enjoying Jake's sense of humor. When the stage manager yelled, "Ten minutes until showtime!", everyone scurried around in high gear.

After the meet and greet, Akeema was invited to a late supper with her friends. When Jake was in town, her world revolved around him. She hadn't had time with the girls in months. She decided to make the most of her free time.

It was after midnight by the time she made it back to her car to head home. The first thing she noticed was her cell phone on the passenger seat. She'd been so busy having a good time she hadn't even missed it. When she'd checked to see if Jake had left a message for her, she was surprised to see that he'd called her six times in two hours! Akeema went into emergency mode. Something had to be dreadfully wrong. Quickly, she pulled up her messages. There were two of them. The first was a text that read: 'Must be a long meet and greet. Look forward to hearing your beautiful voice soon. Love, J.' Akeema relaxed a little. There wasn't a problem at this point. Then she remembered why her phone was left in the car accidently. She'd had the phone in her hand to call Jake before going in to eat. Before she had time to call, however, the girls were tapping on her car window to hurry her. Distracted, she must've put the phone down without thinking. Oh, dear.

She had another surprise when she listened to the message he left:

"How dare you disrespect me like this, Akeema! Since when do you not return my calls or texts? You'd better be dying or worse." Click. He was gone.

Her blood ran cold. Her body began to shake without her permission. Was that hard-edged voice, with the harsh words, her Jake? Because he couldn't reach her for two hours, he wanted her very life to be in jeopardy? Akeema opened her car door in order to throw up her dinner.

CHAPTER 3

A keema hadn't seen or talked to Jake for seven days. She accepted the fact that her heart, and body, missed him intensely. She despised what he said, but she didn't hate him. Her actions were prompted by fear and common sense. If Jake could blow a death fuse over something so trivial, things could only get worse. He'd left many messages on her cell, but she hadn't listened to any of them. Now she had a new unlisted number. The timing of their discord couldn't have been timed more perfectly. The ballet season was over, so she didn't have to worry about him showing up there. Since she was a substitute teacher, she went from school to school whenever and wherever she was needed. In addition to that, he didn't know her last name. In her Dancer's Bio, she went by her first and middle names, Akeema Dawn. Her Nigerian father had simplified their last name when they relocated from Africa. She didn't know that 'Sprite' was also a soft drink until she went to school where classmates poked fun at her. She made it a point to try the soda, which she liked. She didn't mind being associated with a soft drink that she enjoyed. The kids left her alone once they saw she wasn't bothered.

She thought about the many things that Jake had asked about her life. She'd shared quite a bit, but soon realized he was reluctant to share certain aspects of his life. She'd backed off a bit, and now she was glad she had. He knew that her parents, and five other unlucky people, had perished in a freak elevator accident where a cable snapped, plunging the elevator to the ground. She didn't tell him that Aunt Jean had stepped in to raise her. She assumed he thought she was brought up in an orphanage. If he tried to find her, he would end up on a dead-end street. So, the first real love affair Akeema ever had was over. Completely. Or was it?

Jake's apartment was a mess. Through a fit of anger at himself, he'd slammed things around all over the place. With his chest heaving, he was gasping for oxygen.

"Idiot, idiot, idiot! You're a fool!" he yelled to nobody but himself.

Where was she? Who was she with? His mother had warned him over and over about his hot temper. Her council had gone in one ear and out the other. If anyone made him angry, usually women, he felt justified to let them know about it. Except this time. Akeema hadn't deserved the hateful message he'd left her. Akeema had left one final message for him at his place of business. He went over it in his head repeatedly:

"Goodbye to you and your death wish. A.D."

This was the first break-up that he didn't personally orchestrate. He always called the shots; he always did the leaving. He wasn't ready to be without Akeema. She was never at home anymore, and the theater was being renovated so the dancers weren't there. He couldn't understand why he couldn't find her in the D.I.S.D. roster. Her name wasn't that common, it should have been easy to locate her. Was it possible that she had lied to him about working there? No, he knew that wasn't her way. He wanted to apologize to her but, in his heart, he thought her partly responsible for their misunderstanding. After all, if she'd returned his calls, all of this could have been avoided. Of one thing he was certain; he was going to find her. Even if he had to hire private detectives to help him.

When Akeema and her Uncle Rick walked into her apartment, she hated the 20/20 vision that was part of her blessing. She hadn't been home for ten days while she strived to avoid Jake. She could see the fine layer of dust on everything. By nature, she was a tidy person, so this really unnerved her. Without being asked to, her uncle carried her belongings to her bedroom. Then, bless his heart, he looked through every room and closet to make sure they were alone. He even opened the blinds to her patio door to make sure nobody was on her small deck, even though they were on the 4th floor!

Only half kidding, Rick said, "You're good to go, sweetheart. Of course, I know you know that if you need me, I'll stay the night with you. You might be more comfortable if you're not alone on your first night back home."

Looking at him with adoring eyes, Akeema walked over to give her uncle a warm hug. She replied, "You are a dear man. Thanks, but I'm okay. Really." She responded to him softly, but with conviction. He knew he was about to go home to his wife.

It was good to be home after a week of traveling for work. Jake had a slice of veggie pizza in one hand, and a pile of unopened mail in the other. He sat down at his large mahogany desk, which he could tell was recently polished. His cleaning service was authorized to come in once a week whether he was in or out of town. Licking his fingers clean, he separated the junk mail from his bills. At the very bottom of the stack was an envelope from Melville Detective Agency. Rapidly, he tore into the envelope that he hoped would tell him where his Akeema was. What? Her last name wasn't Dawn? Sprite? Was that a typo or a soft drink? As he quickly read the report, he saw that Sprite was her last name, while Dawn was her middle one. No wonder he couldn't find her. Her address was the same, there were no other leases or mortgages in her name. Apparently, he was going to take a vacation so he could camp out in her apartment's parking lot. He saw that she traveled from school to school as a substitute teacher. His choice wasn't to confront her at work. He wanted her back, upsetting her around children and co-workers wasn't the thing to do. When he read that ballet season was over, that was regrettable. That was where he could've seen her at the end of her workday. Oh, well. One way or the other he was going to reconnect with her. Of that, he was certain.

After school, Akeema sat at the teacher's desk with a small smile on her face. The assignment she was on was going to last the whole week. The woman she was subbing for had the flu. She liked this school, and she liked the kids. She even knew some of the permanent staff here. She was content. A gentle tap on the door frame got her attention.

"Hey, Akeema! Are you open for church this weekend?"

The pretty, petite Asian woman was smiling, waiting for her response.

"Oh, Suzan, these days I do more home study than anything else but, thanks."

Walking into the classroom, Suzan never lost her smile. When she was standing in front of Akeema, she replied,

"We are kindred spirits, my friend! Our Bible study is done from our homes!"

"Really?"

"Yep. We rotate from place to place each Shabbat, uh, Sabbath."

"I don't think I'd be comfortable going to a stranger's house or hosting strangers in mine."

Suzan nodded. "That's totally understandable. Lots of people share your feelings. We are also available online and on the phone. That way you can study and fellowship from your own home," she said proudly.

This was new to Akeema. "That sounds good. I think I might join you guys this Saturday."

"Great! If you'll give me a pen and some paper, I'll write down my number for you."

"Okay. What time does the study start, Suzan?"

"We start at eleven in the morning. After we study, those who showed up in person have a potluck that we all share. It's a blessing and a good time!"

"Sounds like it. I'm looking forward to it."

CHAPTER 4

Jake was nervously tapping on his steering wheel. Armed with a pair of binoculars, he was parked across the street from Akeema's apartment building. Luckily, his 2019 gray BMW wouldn't easily be noticed among the traffic of cars coming and going at this gas station that also sold beer and hot dogs, among other things. He was confident that Akeema would come home. He had no doubt that he and she would get back together again. He was glad that her bright red car stood out everywhere. He knew he'd run into her here or somewhere. At that exact moment, he saw a red car pull into the apartment entrance. He watched through the magnified lenses as the car went straight for a while, before turning left. That was the direction of Akeema's place. With shaking hands, Jake turned on his ignition.

Akeema had her hands and arms full as she opened her apartment. She hurried to her kitchen island to unload her purse, briefcase, mail, and grilled turkey sandwich. She kicked off her shoes before plopping down on a bar stool. At a glance, she could see that most of the mail was junk, so she tackled that first.

When the doorbell rang, she couldn't imagine who was calling on her. As she got closer to the door, she thought it might be her aunt and uncle surprising her with a home cooked meal for her dinner. She licked her lips in anticipation. She could eat turkey any day. Out of habit, she looked through the peephole. What a good habit that was. With a control she didn't feel, she yelled, "What do you want here, Jake? I already said goodbye."

Jake sagged against the door. It was her voice. She was speaking to him. Kinda.

"I'm sorry, Akeema, I called to tell you that many times. Didn't you hear any of my messages to you?"

"No. After the death wish, I chose not to hear anymore ugliness from you."

She was speaking to him in a calm, emotionless voice. It was a far cry from the affection he was accustomed to hearing from her.

"I deserve that attitude. Please give me a second chance."

"Why?"

"Because I love you."

He heard the words that he'd just said to her for the first time. He realized he wasn't lying to her. Silence and the door separated them. Jake had never felt so helpless in his life. Akeema knew there was a time when she would've sacrificed everything to hear him declare his love for her. Jake felt close to crying – or cursing.

"Akeema? Will you please let me in, or you come out here? We can sit in, or on the car if you would feel more comfortable. I understand if you don't want to be alone with me in your house."

Finally, finding her voice again, Akeema asked, "If you understand that, why don't you get that I've already said goodbye to you?"

Jake moaned loud enough for her to hear him. "Because I'm having a hard time believing that we're about to lose a special relationship because I was stupid enough to make a mistake!" Her words hit him like a bullet to the heart. "I didn't mean it, surely you know that."

"I can't wrap my brain around why you were so upset just because you lost contact with me for a couple of hours."

"Something could have been wrong with you!" he exclaimed.

She pounced on him. "You weren't worried, Jake! You were angry!"

"Yeah, I know, but not for long! If you'd listened to my many messages, I wasn't mad anymore, I was apologizing!"

Akeema took a deep breath to steady herself. "I'm glad you're sorry, so I accept your apology."

Jake jumped up and down before pressing his ear back to the door. A couple walked past him, watching him strangely. He didn't care. Much.

"Thank you so much, sugar."

"However," she added, "I hope you learned from this, so you won't repeat it in your next relationship."

Hopefully, he dared to ask, "Do you mean my next relationship with you?"

"No!" She didn't hedge or beat around the bush.

"Oh." Was all he could think of to say.

"So, goodnight and goodbye, Jake."

"But you said you accepted my apology!" he said desperately.

"I did."

"Then, can we at least be friends?"

A slight pause. "We're not enemies. Let's leave it at that, okay?"

"Actually, no, it's not okay because it sounds like you never want to see me again."

"That would be correct."

"Why, Akeema? If our slate is wiped clean, can't we forget about the negative past?"

"In a perfect world, sure. Sadly, neither the world nor we are perfect. I'm thankful that you came by, though. I wish you no ill will."

Jake heard the finality in her voice. He couldn't let her go like this! "Well, I must say that this surprises me, Akeema."

"What does?"

This was the last ace in his arsenal. "You've always claimed to be spiritual. I guess it's easier to talk the talk than walk the walk, right?"

"Tell me what you mean exactly." It wasn't a request; it was a demand.

Jake smiled without letting it reach his voice. "I did a wrong thing. I apologized. You say that you accept that apology, but it's clear you haven't forgiven me. That's not what Jesus teaches."

"How is it clear that I haven't forgiven you?"

"It's simple. Your words say one thing, but your actions say something else. You want to shut me out of your life instead of giving me a second chance. That doesn't sound like forgiveness to me," he said sadly. Very sadly. He heard her take a deep breath since his ear was glued to her front door.

"Trust is an issue for me with you."

"I get that. I want the opportunity to regain it."

"I never want to hear you threaten my life again. Is that perfectly clear?"

Jake's heart leaped. "Crystal."

"Until I feel safe with you again, we'll take baby steps. We go at my pace from now on, get it?"

"Got it!" He said with sincere conviction.

"I know your number by heart, but I don't feel comfortable enough to share my new cell number with you yet. So, tomorrow, I will get a burner phone for us to talk to each other on, okay?" Although that stung him, he gave her no hint that it did.

"That's cool, babe. I look forward to hearing from you."

"Fine. I'll say goodnight now."

"Instead of goodbye?"

"Instead of goodbye."

As far as the rest of the week went, Jake felt all was going according to plan. His. He didn't badger or crowd Akeema in any way. When she'd declined his invitation to lunch, he'd been gracious about it without asking her again. Although he'd resumed calling her three times a day, he kept it short and all about her. It was her well-being that was important to him. He was consumed with how her day was going. So far, she'd given minimal information, without asking anything about his day. He was patiently waiting for her personal interest in him to resume. He was confident that it would.

Akeema glanced at little Joey Johnson with tender sympathy. His little tongue was poking out as he used the eraser on his pencil profusely. Long division was giving him fits. At his father's request, Akeema was working with him an hour after school. He couldn't see that he was improving, but he certainly was. It was fifteen minutes before his fretting parent would be there to pick him up. She was about to check on his work, when his head snapped up. "I'm done, teacher!" he announced proudly.

"Very good, Joey. Do you have any questions for me?"

Shaking his head, he stood to bring her his paperwork. She took it and signaled for him to stand beside her. Together, they reviewed his figures. Out of eight problems, he'd only missed one. Patiently, they worked it out together. In the end, both Akeema and Joey were happy. Alone in the classroom at last, she kicked off her shoes to let her feet air out. She'd had a busy, yet fruitful, day. She allowed her mind to shift from work to Jake. She had such mixed feelings about having him back in her life. She still had her guard up against him, and she made no effort to hide it. Akeema could tell he was working overtime to make everything up to her. But she was waiting for his next display of bad temper over the simple things. She knew it was only a matter of time before he blew his cool.

That night before bedtime, Akeema was sitting on her bed waiting for the burner phone to ring. She'd just finished filing her nails, when she heard it. Despite herself, her heart skipped a beat.

"How's it going, Jake?" she answered. There wasn't a need to say hello as no one else had her burner number.

"Pleasantly productive," he responded. "How was your day, my love?"

"Oddly enough, the same. What did you have for sustenance this evening?"

"Two fish sandwiches and a sports drink."

"Fried fish with tartar sauce?"

"Exactly!"

"With your diet it's a good thing you work out like a mad man!"

"Everyone can't be as disciplined as you are, sweetie."

"Don't act like I don't enjoy my treats," she chided.

Jake scoffed. "Treats? What do you consider fun to eat, carrots instead celery?"

"You're a funny man," she dead panned.

"No, seriously, what's your favorite treat?" ,

She replied, "Dreamsicle ice cream."

"What flavor is that?" He honestly didn't know!

"Orange sherbet and vanilla ice cream mixed together." Jake was amazed.

"Sherbet is your favorite? Most people prefer the full fat, creamily delicious ice cream, Akeema."

"I guess I'm not most people."

"Acknowledged!"

She smiled to herself. "I guess a dancer's idea of a treat is a little different in comparison."

"To put it mildly. So, what mind-blowing meal did you have for dinner?"

"A huge salad."

Jake laughed. "What was so mind-blowing about that?"

"The gazillion croutons on it." They each got a kick out of that one. Then they chatted, in more details, about their day. Thirty minutes came and went very quickly. Just as they were starting to say their good-byes, Jake dared to ask a question. "Akeema, do you mind telling me where you disappeared to after our misunderstanding?"

Without any hesitation, she said, "Yes, I do mind." Surprised, he wanted to know why. She saw no reason to lie to him. She wanted to see his reaction to not getting the information he wanted.

"It's a safe haven in case things get ugly between us again."

His heart sank. She was waiting for him to fail. Akeema expected them to end. Damn! She waited patiently for him to say something. Anything.

"You won't need a place to hide, my love. Not from me, anyway."

"I hope not."

"I know not!"

"Good!"

CHAPTER 5

Suzan's pretty, smiling face lit up the screen.

"I hope you guys enjoyed us as well as we enjoyed you!"

Akeema and Jake assured her that they did.

"Please feel free to join us again next Shabbat. On Wednesdays we have a few of us that get together for a midweek study. You two are cordially invited to that too!" she enthused.

"We appreciate that, Suzan. Speaking only for myself, I'll join you online again real soon. The study and fellowship were great."

"I'm so glad you were blessed, Akeema. How about you Jake?"

"Like my lady here, I was also blessed. My family chooses the first day of the week to worship, but this was good too."

"The Word tells us plainly that the 7th day is His holy day. However, I feel like there isn't a "bad" day to study. The Bible tells us each to study to show ourselves approved."

Jake didn't know that but, nodded anyway. She obviously knew more about this than he did. He wasn't about to argue with her. Although the study was over, Suzan was in a good mood and not in a hurry to end the transmission.

"So, did anything we teach today stick out as a question to be asked, or a topic for more discussion?" Suzan and Akeema were surprised when Jake spoke up.

"I was relieved to see Jesus show anger."

"Relieved? Why?" Suzan wanted to know. Akeema kept her facial expression neutral.

"I lost my temper in front of a loved one, and I felt like it was a cardinal sin to have done that. I feel better now. If Jesus can have a bad day, I should be given a little grace I think."

Putting on her teacher's cap, Suzan replied, "What our Savior, Yahusha, displayed was His righteous anger. He had every right to be mad at the money changing that was going on in the Kadosh-holy-temple."

"He didn't get upset over something trivial. The men were gambling in His Father's holy place," Akeema added.

Feeling a little misunderstood, Jake hastily added, "I get that. Before this study, I thought anger was always inappropriate. I felt like I had to amp down those feelings because it showed a lack of control."

Suzan was paying attention. This was a couple's problem for Jake and Akeema. Oh, dear.

"Being slow to anger is considered a virtue. All throughout the Word we see where Yahuah, our heavenly Father, was angry over the many sins of people. We see His forgiveness time and time again. However, when He's ready to react in anger, the consequences can be devastating, sometimes to the 3rd and 4th generations." Suzan saw Jake and Akeema nod in agreement. She continued. "When Yahusha saw the people trying to stone the prostitute in the street, I think we can safely say He was mad. Let's face it, with His power He could have killed everyone who was trying to kill her, don't you think?" "The couple first looked at each other, then nodded. "This time He challenged them to look at themselves. To the crowd He told anyone who was without sin to throw the first stone. Nobody did."

"There are no perfect, sinless people down here." Jake said quietly.

"No, there aren't. Yahusha wouldn't have been needed to save us if we could achieve perfection."

"And forgiveness?" Jake asked, "What does the Bible say about that? Is it okay to forgive three or four times at least?"

Suzan laughed. "Except for our Savior, I'd like to meet the person who could manage what the Word tells us on this one."

"Tell me," Jake whispered.

"With the help of the Ruach, the Holy Spirit, we could do it. On our own, I seriously doubt it."

Louder, Jake said, "Tell me, Suzan! Tell us."

"We're to forgive each other 70 times 7 I think it is. I'll look it up for you to get the exact number. But I'm pretty darn close. It's a big number, my friends. That much is true."

"My goodness," Akeema said out loud, but to herself.

Suzan replied, "I hear you, my sister. We must think about it. Our Father demands that we love Him and each other. How can we love and not forgive? How short would marriages be if husbands and wives didn't give each other the grace of forgiving?"

Now, Suzan noticed that Akeema and Jake were not making eye contact with her or each other. Something was making them uncomfortable.

Out of the blue, she felt prompted to say, "Of course, in a world where the adversary does his dirty work, we exist with some bona fide bad people. We are all Yahusha's creations, but we are not all of His people."

They looked up at her. Once again, she had their attention.

"If you are a child of the Most High, He expects you to treat others with kindness and respect. We don't have to accept abusers."

The pair were holding her gaze intently. She asked them, "Do you remember when the disciples were frustrated because people were not believing what Yahusha taught them to say?"

Akeema replied, "Yes! He told them to shake the sand off their shoes and move on…or something like that."

"Yes, you got it. He doesn't want us to stick around for nothing. We all have free choice to believe His word or not. As His people, we are to spread the Good News, but we are not responsible for their choice. Thank goodness!"

Emphatically, Akeema said, "Amen!"

Just then a voice off screen called to Suzan, "Hey, Soos! Do you want me to fix you a plate?" Turning her head to the left, Suzan nodded in that direction – along with a thumbs up gesture.

Akeema was contrite. "Oh, Suzan, don't let us keep you from your meal! We don't want you to eat alone."

"Don't worry about me. I can eat anytime, anywhere, alone or with company. This is more important to me right now. Is there any other topic you'd like to cover today?" she asked kindly.

They both shook their heads.

"Okay then. You guys go eat too, and I will be happy to see you for class Wednesday, or our next Shabbat gathering."

Jake replied, "Thanks again, Suzan. We appreciate the extra time you spent with us."

"I enjoyed our time together too. Shabbat Shalom!"

Everybody waved before the screen went black.

Sitting at her kitchen island, Akeema and Jake were chowing down on big bowls of delicious chicken tortilla soup. When Jake asked what he could bring for their Sabbath meal, Akeema told him to bring the extras to go with the soup if he wanted them: Shredded cheese, sour cream, and tortilla chips. Today, he came with everything except the cheese. Plus, he brought a pound cake that he knew she really enjoyed. All said, they were both pleased with the lunch they threw together.

Slurping from his spoon, Jake garbled,

"This is the best soup I've ever had, Akeema! Thank you for coming home after work last night to cook."

"You're welcome. Please know that I am going to have leftovers for several beautiful days. I love it!"

"Aw, man," Jake groaned.

"What?" She asked between spoonfuls.

"I was hoping to get into those leftovers."

"Don't worry, you moocher. I've already got you a to go bag packed and ready."

Jake gave a gleeful 'whoop' before leaning across the island to give her a quick peck on the lips. It was the first touch of their mouths since reconciling. Neither commented on that fact.

As they continued eating, Jake kept sneaking peeks at Akeema. Finally, she caught him.

"Why are you staring at me?" she asked bluntly.

He shrugged, "I love the way you look, so I look."

"Thanks," she said ruefully.

"I'm serious, Akeema. Look at you. Even dressed casually, you have a regal, well put together air about you."

She looked down at herself to try and see what he was talking about. She had on a forest green tank top with gray leggings, and flip-flops that matched. That's it. Oh, well. What woman could ever figure out what a man really thought when he observed the opposite sex.

"More soup?" she asked.

Jake eagerly passed her his empty bowl.

Once Akeema's back was turned to him, he got a nice eyeful. Her upper arms were so toned they rivaled a prizefighter's. Her leggings fit her round bottom and muscled thighs so snugly they looked painted on. Nothing on her tight body wiggled or jiggled. No dips, no dimples. Nothing.

After refilling his bowl, Akeema nibbled on a salad – something she knew Jake had little to no interest in. They were enjoying a comfortable silence when Jake dared to ask her a question.

"Am I seeing things, or do you have shadows under your arms?"

She laughed, not a bit embarrassed. "Boy, I gave you no credit for noticing black hair stubble under the arms of a dark chocolate girl!"

"Well, if you had it all along, I'm a tad late."

Waving her hand, she replied,

"Not at all. During the ballet off season, I take a break from all the shaving and waxing."

"Am I the only one who noticed it?"

"You're the only one who's said anything about it."

"Sorry," he said sheepishly, hanging his head.

"Don't be. I'm doing what I want to do with my body. The only reason you see it is because I don't have any sleeves on this top."

"How long do you let it grow?"

"I keep it clipped so even short sleeves will hide it."

"Like you said, it's your beautiful body. It's even kinda sexy."

"You think?"

"Yes. Of course, I think everything about you turns me on. I miss our intimate times with each other, Akeema."

Their light-hearted banter was gone. He was serious and she knew it. Although she gave no outward sign of it, her heart was accelerating. She struggled with being honest with him or saying nothing. Lying was out of the question. What Jake saw was Akeema's regal bearing and outward calm. She didn't let him see any of the turmoil that was brewing inside her.

Jake searched Akeem's impassive face for any heat inside of her that matched his own. He found none. "I know it's the Sabbath, so I don't want to be sexy today, but I want to reopen our love life. You haven't even let me kiss you anywhere but your cheeks."

He saw her slight nod, but she still didn't speak.

"Do you miss feeling me inside you, baby?" he asked huskily.

Akeema nodded.

"Can we work on making love soon?"

She shook her head, no.

Controlling his angst, he asked,

"Why not?"

Before the words tumbled out, she took a very deep breath. "Our lovemaking was so great that I went through withdrawal when we broke up."

Akeema saw hope light up Jake's eyes. She didn't let that stop her. "If we start having sex again and we separate again, I don't want to go through that awful feeling again, with its sleepless nights."

"What's the solution? I don't want to be celibate."

"I understand. Since we're just friends now, you are free to find other sexual partners." She couldn't believe she got the words out without choking on them.

He couldn't believe he controlled himself from choking her.

Horrified, he asked, "You want us to have sex with other people?"

"I said you could if you feel you can't wait until I'm ready to."

Jake relaxed. A little.

"Let me make sure that I understand you," he began. "I can have sexual release with others until you are ready to join me in bed again, right?"

Akeema nodded.

"And, since this is your idea, you won't hold this against me in any way, right?"

Another nod.

"And, although I've professed my love for you, and you alone, you'll understand that if I do this, my heart will not be involved at all."

She hesitated for a moment, then nodded.

"Now, last but certainly not least, you won't be having sex with anyone until you and I re-hook up, right?"

This time Akeema spoke. "At this moment, I'm not sexually interested in anyone. So, your statement is true. However, I am a free woman as you are a free man. If I meet a man that I lust for, it will be my choice to have him sexually if I wish."

Jake nearly vomited.

"No deal," he said harshly.

Akeema leaned into Jake without touching him. She hissed, "Fine. But understand this: I might never want you sexually again. I might take another lover. I don't consider us a couple at this point. We owe each other no faithfulness."

Jake swallowed the bile that burned his throat. His hands, out of Akeema's sight, were balled into fists. He wanted to strike her.

CHAPTER 6

To anyone on the outside looking in, Akeema and Jake were a happy, beautiful, mixed-race couple. Only the couple knew the passive aggressive war they were in. Jake's obsession with her had not waned. He meant to have her under his thumb, and under him. He would be her master in life, nobody else could have her.

Akeema calmly and gently antagonized him at every opportunity. She was determined to not be surprised at his next anger eruption. She was in an unspoken war with Jake – and herself. Her traitorous body wanted him badly. Her memories of their intimacy came back to her in X-rated dreams that left every nerve in her body throbbing. She didn't know how long she could hide her desire for him from him. She knew she'd lose all her objectivity if she started sleeping with him again. She took so many cold showers that her skin was drying out. She kept a huge bottle of lotion, in her tote bag, for such emergencies. She felt as long as she kept her flesh under control, she would be able to control the situation.

Jake was about to play his ace card. He and Akeema were sitting in a restaurant after seeing a romantic comedy, performed live on stage. They'd both enjoyed it, talking about it in detail up to this point.

"What are you doing Sunday night?"

Akeema replied, "Nothing special, why?"

"I'd like to invite you to dinner with me and my parents."

He enjoyed the surprise that she couldn't hide on her beautiful face.

Regaining some composure, she asked, "Why?"

"So you can meet my parents and have a really good meal."

"When we were in a closer relationship you didn't introduce me to them. Why now?"

He didn't see this coming. He expected her to feel special at being asked to meet his family. He reached across the table to grasp both her hands in his. "I don't make it a habit to bring people to my parents' house. This is what I want to do with just you," he said only half meaning it.

"Right now, we are just friends. If I go with you, I won't pretend it's anything more." Her calm, brutal honesty never ceased to amaze him, or tick him off.

Akeema watched him closely. He didn't like what she just said, but he didn't show it. She could tell by his touch, the extra pressure of his hands, that he was managing his temper. That was good. She liked when he didn't fly off the handle.

"I understand," he said shortly.

"Then, I'd like to meet your parents and have dinner. What time should I be ready?"

The butterflies in her stomach wouldn't go away. She stood in front of her full-length mirror, appraising her appearance. She had to admit that it mattered to her what Jake's parents thought. Seeing his classy, well-dressed mother at the ballet meet and greet added pressure to what she decided to wear. This plain black dress was her fifth and final outfit. She didn't have any more time to fret. Her date was punctual to a fault, and she never made him wait – something he let her know he loved about her. Akeema had on a simple tea length dress with sheer cap sleeves. Splashes of red from her shoes, purse, and earrings broke the severity of the dress. She took several deep, cleansing breaths to lower her pulse rate. When the doorbell rang, she was ready.

The Butler mansion looked more like a castle than a home. It was stark white with lots of glass and pillars. The curved driveway in front of the house looked so clean that Akeema had a hard time imagining automobiles on it. The well-manicured lawn had flowers of every color and variety scattered everywhere. While Jake and Akeema stood before the front door waiting for it to open, she quickly scanned the expansive porch. The outdoor furnishings appeared to be made of whitewashed stone with chiseled floral patterns decorating it. Since there were no pillows or cushions she doubted if anybody ever sat down, at least not for long. When the door opened, Akeema couldn't believe what she was seeing. Expecting a servant, she was looking at Mr. and Mrs. Butler! They'd actually answered their own door.

Kyle and Lucille were perfect examples of the perfect, successful couple. At 6 ft. 3 in., Mr. Butler was a big man without being overweight. His short, salt and pepper hair was thick and healthy-looking. He had a thick mustache that reminded Akeema of Rhett Butler in "Gone with the Wind." About 8 inches shorter than her husband, Lucille wore a stylish navy-blue pant suit and pearls. Jake had her brown hair and eyes. She was an attractive woman without being flashy. She was groomed as the perfect accessory on her husband's arm. If his father was surprise she was black, he didn't show it. Of course, his wife could've given him the heads up, Akeema thought.

As they were graciously ushered in, Akeema had to stop herself from saying, "Wow!" For a middle-aged couple, they had a very modern house. Impossibly high ceilings, chrome, glass, and glossy flooring was everywhere. They were led into a large dining room with a huge glass table and a dozen white, linen chairs that were comfortable and clean. Akeema lived in fear of dropping even a speck of food on them. Someone had taken the time to pick a fragrant floral arrangement for the table. It was a good thing they were tall, or they would've been lost.

The meal was delicious. The vegetables in the salad were so fresh, they tasted like they had come out of the earth right before being put on their plates. Akeema was surprised again when she was told that Mrs. Butler prepared the baked salmon and rice pilaf herself. Lucille was trashing all Akeema's misconceptions about rich, pampered white women.

Dessert was a divine chocolate mousse – a first for Akeema. She had read about it in books and magazines, but nobody she knew (including herself) had the courage to make it. Only her dancer discipline kept her from asking for a second serving of it.

When it was time to clear the table, Akeema's mouth almost flew open when Lucille started doing it herself! Without hesitation, she stood to help her. Lucille hurried to stop her. "Oh, no, my dear! You're our guest. I've got this covered."

Akeema didn't stop working or acknowledge her words. She was going to help her and that was the end of that.

Left alone, the men went to the drawing room for brandy and conversation. Drinks in hand, they sat comfortably in two huge brown leather chairs before the white fireplace. Jake's father didn't mince any words. "So, is Akeema a business associate?"

"No, Dad. She's a friend."

"We haven't fed your friends since your high school graduation. Why did you bring her here?" Jake tried to appear casual, non-committal.

"She's special."

Skeptical, Kyle asked, "How so?"

Jake shrugged as if he didn't know. Kyle didn't let his son off the hook. "How is she special to you, son?"

"She's…one of a kind."

"As darkies go, she's good looking."

Jake gasped, "Dad, watch it! She might hear you!"

"Relax. I didn't say the "N" word."

"It's still a slur, dad!"

"Not really. They're all too sensitive if you ask me."

"I didn't ask you. Don't mess this up for me, man!"

Pointing at his son, Kyle hissed, "This is my house, young man. You would do well to remember that. I say and do what I want in here!"

The last thing Jake wanted to do was to rile his father. Especially with company in the house.

"Sorry, dad," he said humbly.

Kyle sat back in his chair as he calmed down, finishing his drink.

"What happened to that Asian girl you were dating last year?"

He responded honestly. "Nothing happened to her, Akeema happened to me."

Kyle squinted at his son. Did he sound serious? "I think you're smart not to tie yourself down with one girl. You'll have time for that when you choose a wife and start a family."

Jake's mind drifted to him and Akeema in the future…with a houseful of half-black kids.

"What if I settled down with Akeema? Your grand-kid will be half her and half me."

His father went numb. His son couldn't be serious.

"Don't be a fool, son," he said in an icy tone.

Before Jake could respond, Akeema and Lucille joined them. Kyle gave his offspring a look that said shut up.

With her hostess hat firmly in place, Lucille had a cheerful smile plastered on her face. "So, are you men discussing anything for mixed company?" she asked.

Akeema could feel the tension in the room. The strained looks on the men's faces was more evidence that something was wrong. Inside her, Lucille felt exactly the same thing. Oh dear.

Lucille tried to crack the silence again.

"Well, folks, we have an extensive video collection if anyone would like to see a movie. And, I believe we have every boardgame known to man – or woman. Would anyone like to watch or play anything?"

Akeema came to her rescue. "I'm sorry, Mrs. Butler. I'm afraid I need to call it a night. I've got lesson plans to get through tonight. I don't want to get up early in the morning to do them."

"Why would a ballerina have lesson plans?" Kyle asked.

Jake stepped in. "Akeema is a part-time dancer and a full-time elementary school teacher."

With that said, he downed the rest of his drink before walking over to his date, holding her hand as he stood closely by her side.

Admiringly, Lucille replied, "Beautiful and accomplished. You're a very impressive young lady."

"Thank you, Mrs. Butler."

"Lucille," she stressed.

Akeema gave her a sweet smile.
Kyle Butler looked on, concerned.

"Ok, homeboy, out with it."
Driving to Akeema's place, Jake gave her a sideways glance. "With what?" he feigned innocence.
"What was going on with you and your father?"
"Not much."
"I beg to differ. All I had to do was walk into the room to tell something was wrong."
"You're imagining things. Let it go, Akeema."
She heard the agitation in his voice.
"I enjoyed the food, and I like your mother. Your dad didn't seem to care for me."
She watched his hands grip the steering wheel tighter in response to her words. He remained mute. "I couldn't tell if he was prejudiced against me, all black people, or women. What would be your guess?"
"Since he's always yelling at my mom, for one thing or another, I'd say women aren't high on his respect list."
Now Akeema understood his temper issue, at least in part. The only example he had at being a man was his bully of a father. His idea of a women was his gracious, dutiful mother who took all the verbal abuse that her husband threw at her. Akeema could tell Jake was trying not to be like his father. Usually, he succeeded at that. But, when he didn't – look out!
"Your mother is great. Why do you think she's put up with your father all these years?"
"She loves him, I guess," he said quietly.

Bluntly, Akeema asked, "Is that what love is to you? The little woman taking verbal abuse without complaint?"

"Apparently, it is to my mother," he hedged.

"I didn't ask her, I asked you."

Jake looked straight ahead at the road, silent. She went for the jugular. "Am I the first girl you screamed a death wish at in anger?" She saw his barely there nod.

"Why me?"

"Any other time with any other person, I would just change my phone number and move on."

"Why didn't you do that with me?"

"Besides the fact that you beat me to it, I wasn't ready to say good-bye. And, last but not least, I owed you an apology for my obnoxious behavior."

Wow! Akeema was impressed. For the first time in weeks, she felt Jake was being honest – and unguarded. She felt a fresh blooming of affection for him.

"Apology accepted," she said quietly and really meaning it. "And I'm glad you weren't ready to say goodbye."

He turned to look at her with a wide smile that she returned. This was their new beginning.

CHAPTER 7

Laying sated in Jake's arms after love making left Akeema heavy-limbed and drowsy. With her head resting on his chest, she could hear his regular heartbeats. They still had a fine sheen of sweat over their nude bodies from their sexual exertions. Classical music, her favorite, was playing softly in the background. All was right with their world. Kinda.

For the most part, they got along well. Sexually, they got along great! When they disagreed, they had lively 'discussions' – as Akeema put it. She stood her ground, much to Jake's frustration. He never again uttered a death wish, but he raised his voice when things got on his last nerve. For all his vocal acrobatics, she remained calm, which only served to frustrate him even more. Akeema remained logical under fire, while Jake lost his cool and some of his mind.

Although his mother had extended more dinner invitations to them, he hadn't accepted any of them. He couldn't trust his father's big mouth not to say something insulting to his girlfriend – yes, Akeema was his now. They'd both agreed to date each other exclusively. He didn't want his dad, or anyone else, to mess up what they had together.

"Jake?" she whispered.

"Hmm?" he murmured.

"Since your parents had us over, shouldn't we return the favor?"

He yawned. "How so?"

"We could cook them dinner."

"We who?"

Akeema smiled against his chest. "Alright, alright. I'll cook if you help me clean."

"They don't expect us to do that."

"I just thought it would be a nice thing to do."

"My dad's pretty busy. Except for business, he doesn't go out much.'

"Even if they don't socialize much, I'd be willing to bet they'd make an effort for you."

"Yeah, right."

"Seriously, Jake. How many of your girlfriends ever cooked for your parents?"

"Zero."

"None?"

"Correct."

"Why not, for goodness sake?"

"The women I used to date barely ate. They sure as heck didn't cook!"

Akeema smiled. "Okay, I get that. But you're now with someone who watches her weight and cooks. So, please let me."

He caressed her back lovingly. "I don't stop you from cooking for us. I love what you do in the kitchen." Seductively, he added, "almost as much as I love what you do in the bedroom." By her chin, he guided her to his mouth for a long, lingering kiss. His hands gently probed her favorite places. She forgot all about cooking in the kitchen.

"Why haven't we seen or heard from you, Akeema Dawn?" Aunt Jean demanded.

Whoops. They didn't know she was seeing Jake.

"I'm sorry. I've just been busy. You know I love you and Uncle Rick."

"Your love isn't in question, Miss Thang. Your absence is!"

She knew that if her aunt and uncle knew she was dating Jake, they would fret and worry about her. Their peace of mind mattered to her. She'd involved them in her personal love life in error. Akeema didn't want to make the same mistake twice.

"School is really keeping me busy. I've been at the same place for a couple of weeks now due to a really sick teacher. The kids and I are starting to bond."

"I'll pray for the poor teacher, but I still don't see how your uncle and I got kicked in the dirt."

"Auntie, I'm sorry I've been neglectful. But I've got all kinds of new responsibilities that I haven't had before. Right now, the only free time I have is on Sabbath. If you and Rick want to join our Sabbath, it's an on-line service where we can see and talk to each other."

"Well, that's at least an option," she said grudgingly.

"Just call me any Saturday morning around ten or so, and I'll get you hooked up."

"Okay, but promise that you'll have dinner with us the first opportunity you get."

"Yes, ma'am. I promise."

"Alright then. This officially takes you off my doo-doo list."

Akeema loved this woman!

Jake watched Akeema pick at her salad instead of eating it. He didn't know what was wrong, but he fervently hoped it didn't have anything to do with him.

He attempted to lighten her mood. "Is your liver and onions delicious?" he asked.

"Mmm," she said absently.

Trying his best not to laugh out loud, he choked, "Would you like to order a vomit vanilla shake with urine ice cubes?"

"Uh-uh. I'm fine."

That did it. Jake let loose an uninhibited snort and giggle. Akeema looked up. She looked around to see what had tickled him so much but saw nothing.

"What's funny?"

"Not what, who!"

"Okay, who are you laughing at?"

"You," he spat out before pounding his hand on the table. He was trying not to call too much attention to himself as he smothered his laugh. His eyes were beginning to water.

Clueless, Akeema said, "What have I said or done that's cracked you up like this? I'd love to be having at least half the fun that you are!" There was an edge to her voice. She was a little cranky and she wasn't sure why.

Jake heard it too, but he couldn't resist the urge to poke fun at her. He so seldom had the opportunity.

"Little Miss Perfect who only puts clean food in her perfect body, didn't raise an eyebrow at being offered liver and onions with a vomit vanilla shake with urine ice cubes!"

This time she heard him loud and clear. Black as she was, he could see she was turning pea green with distaste. He howled.

Unfortunately, Akeema Dawn was not amused.

Once he came to his senses, he zeroed in on his lady. She was sitting straight as an arrow, completely still. Her beautiful face was unsmiling as she watched him with daggers in her eyes.

"Aw, come on, Akeema, lighten up! You've been ignoring me all this time, and you don't see me having an attitude about it. Where's your funny side, for goodness' sake?"

In a calm voice dripping with sarcasm, she retorted, "At mealtimes, excuse me if I don't find vomit shakes a fitting and absolutely not funny, subject to talk about."

"The ridiculous thing is often the funniest," he pointed out.

"Like anything else, taste is subjective. This type of humor doesn't reach me – at all!" With that said, she dropped her fork with a clang on her uneaten salad.

She watched the light dim in his eyes. He was losing his good humor, and she was the cause of it. What was worse, she didn't care.

Jake leaned toward Akeema across the table. He hissed, "Since you haven't been paying any attention to me, I found a way to entertain myself. Excuse the Hades out of me for trying to infuse some levity into the evening!"

She watched his face get redder with each word he spoke. This was her fault and she owned it. Akeema wished she could share with him the reason for her distraction. However, she still felt that her aunt and uncle were her secret to keep. If her relationship with Jake didn't work out for the second and final time, she loved having somewhere to go that he knew nothing about. For now, she needed to repair this failing date. She had a visual in her head of grabbing her purse and walking out alone. Right now, this was the last place she wanted to be, and she was with the last person she wanted to be with. Outwardly, she showed none of this. Her countenance was calm, reserved. Teaching children had taught her not to show frustration or panic. She had to be in control in order to have control.

Jake's agitation grew as he observed Akeema's unruffled exterior. This drove him crazy about her. She also had his envy, but only he knew that. He was full of righteous anger. He'd been ignored by her, for reasons he couldn't fathom. His attempt at humor had been coldly ridiculed. He was done.

Akeema knew that if he completely lost his temper, they would be asked to leave the restaurant. The fact that he was a white boy meant no jail time, but people would be looking upside her head. Not only that, cell phone cameras and videos would be clicking away. She didn't want to have to explain to her aunt and uncle a humiliating episode.

Putting all the tenderness in her voice that she could muster, Akeema whispered, "I'm sorry, Jake. This is all my fault. Please forgive me." She wasn't arguing with him. Since they'd been back together, Akeema didn't back down on anything. Jake was being taught the fine art of agreeing to disagree. He hated it. He wanted to be sure that this victory was his.

"Let me get this straight," he said. "You're admitting your fault in this?"

With a nod, she replied, "Absolutely."

The rest of the evening went smoothly. Akeema used all her acting skills to pretend interest in everything Jake talked about.

CHAPTER 8

"**D**on't lie to me, Akeema! I know what I just saw!"

"You need to have your eyes checked," she said curtly.

He exploded. "Don't treat this like a joke! You were openly flirting with that guy!"

Jake was walking beside her, barely keeping up with her long strides. When they reached his gray BMW, he opened the car door with his remote. Akeema put the bag of groceries in the backseat before climbing into the front passenger side. Jake's butt had hardly touched the seat before his rant continued. Akeema successfully tuned him out. She reflected on how positive their evening had begun…

After a torrid lovemaking session, Akeema marveled at her lover's sexual prowess. She always tried her best to please him, but on this night, Jake hadn't allowed her to do a single thing. He had insisted that she just lay there and just **feel**. Within 45 minutes, she'd climaxed 3 times. Later, Jake offered to go out to get them dinner since they were both famished.

A happy and grateful Akeema, offered to cook him dinner. Over time, Akeema had stocked Jake's kitchen with seasonings like garlic, onion powder, and seasoning salt. She made sure that their lingering dates were at his condo, since her aunt had a key to her place, and often visited without calling first. Jake loved her steak and pan-fried potatoes, so it came as no surprise to her when he asked for them on this occasion. She was familiar with the neighborhood grocery store, so she volunteered to do a quick run on her own so he could stay relaxed in bed. However, he'd insisted on driving her to the store while he stayed in the car. So far, so good.

As she efficiently shopped, she literally whistled while she worked. Her sexual satisfaction had her floating on air.

"Teacher Akeema! Is that you?"

She turned toward the deep male voice calling to her. The young man smiling at her was the single parent of one of her students. She'd given his son special attention since the passing of the little boy's mother.

"Yes, Mr. Smith, it's me. How are you?"

"Please call me Joseph. I'm fine, and you?"

"I'm good. Shopping for a late dinner. How's Joey?"

"He's great, his maternal grandmother has him tonight."

"It must be nice to have help. Being a single parent takes some getting used to, I'll bet."

The handsome black man beamed at her. "It's over-whelming sometimes. I try not to whine and complain about it, though. It's nice to hear your understanding about it. Do you have any kids?"

Akeema admitted, "No, that's why I love sharing a little bit of yours with you and the other parents in my classroom."

"You are cordially invited to love on Joey any time you feel like it, and thank you for caring."

"Flirt alert! Flirt alert!" It was Jake's voice behind her. Akeema would have been okay if the floor had opened to swallow her. He seemed to have that effect on her more and more. She didn't turn around, hoping against hope that he'd go away.

"Who's this bozo?" Joseph asked under his breath.

"My date for the evening," she replied. She wasn't about to use the word 'boyfriend' tonight.

"Oh, I see," he said, although he didn't. "Are you okay?"

"I'm going to deal with it," was her reply.

"Do you need me for anything?"

"Are you finished on this aisle?" Joseph nodded.

"I'm not going to turn around to go to him, so, I'd appreciate it if you'd turn around and let me follow you. At the end, you turn right, and I'll go left, okay?"

"Sure, whatever you want. If things get out of hand, just yell my name and I'll come runnin'!"

Akeema gave him a grateful smile. "Thanks, Mr. Sm…Joseph." He returned her smile before turning around to walk away from her.

Akeema let him take four steps before following him. Behind her, she heard Jake's call.

"Akeema, where are you going? Akeema, come here!" he demanded. She was annoyed. Very.

She quickened her steps so that she could make it to the check-out line. Hopefully, Jake would act better when they had people around them. When he walked up behind her, she was second in line.

In a low voice, he asked, "You want to tell me what that was all about?"

"We can talk about it when we are alone, okay?"

"Great," he replied. His voice was low and harsh.

She fought the urge to put the basket down to walk out.

"Was that someone you met in here?"

"No."

His voice raised a little. "You already knew him?"

"Yes." She heard him take a deep breath. "Where did you meet him?"

"In school. He's the parent of one of my students."

"Oh, I see," he said, obviously relieved. He lovingly massaged her shoulders. She made herself be still. His touch wasn't welcome.

At the register, Jake tried to pay for the items Akeema had in the basket, but she stopped him.

"This is my treat, remember?"

"You did the shopping and you're going to cook. I don't mind paying for it."

"I mind." Subject closed.

As they were near the exit Jake asked, "What was that guy's name?"

"Joseph Smith."

"And just how would you know that?"

"I know the names of parents when I work over-time with special kids."

"He's a looker, isn't he? I doubt he'll be single for long."

"He's a widower, so I'm sure he's going to mourn his wife's loss for a while."

"Does he seem depressed to you?"

"No, not really. He seems to be handling her passing very well."

"Does he talk about her?"

"Not to me."

"Are you attracted to him'?"

Uh-oh. Where was he going with this? Carefully, Akeema asked, "What do you mean?"

"I mean do you think he's good looking?"

"Obviously."

Jake stopped walking. Akeema did not. Just as she went through the automated glass doors, she heard his footsteps hurrying – again – to catch up with her.

A little breathless, he shouted, "So, you <u>were</u> flirting with him! That's why you were taking so long in the store!"

Akeema rolled her eyes. "You're being silly, Jake."

"I seriously doubt that."

Her annoyance was growing.

Back in the now, the car was quiet. In the time that Akeema had zoned out, Jake got through his tirade. Good.

"So, you're just going to sit there and not answer me? Just more disrespect thrown my way," he said, seething.

Oh, crap! Akeema realized the car was quiet because it was her turn to speak. There was no way to salvage this. She was headed for more trouble. Best to get it over with.

"I'm sorry, what was the question?"

With both fists, Jake slammed the steering wheel three times. "You weren't even listening to me?" he roared.

Quietly, she replied, "The louder you yell, the less I listen. If you want to keep my attention, I suggest you lower your voice."

Jake looked at her with his mouth open in disbelief. She was scolding him as if he were one of her students! She'd shown him blatant disrespect and he was supposed to somehow be calm about it. And she called him silly!

Jake opened the car door, slamming it so hard the whole car shook. He paced back and forth as he talked to himself. Akeema turned on the car radio, choosing a station that played classical music – some of which she'd danced to, at one time or another. She didn't mind at all that Jake was working out his anger outside the car. It showed her that he was making an effort to spew out his temper in a different direction, not at her.

Finally, he got back in the car with her. He didn't drive off, he simply sat there for a while listening to the radio with Akeema.

"It's getting too late to cook, Jake," she said gently. "If you're still hungry, let's stop and get you something. I'll leave this food at your place to cook at another time, okay?"

He nodded. "Aren't you hungry?"

"I don't eat heavy foods this time of night. When I get home, I'll eat a piece of fruit."

"When you get home? You're not spending the night?"

"No, but thanks for the invite."

Jake didn't say anything. Despite their argument, he wanted her to stay. But he said nothing. He knew he'd messed up. Once again.

CHAPTER 9

With a gentle smile on her face, Akeema sat behind her desk listening to Joey read. He was doing a good job, and she was proud of the progress he'd made. She didn't notice that Joey's father was standing in the doorway watching the pleasant scene in front of him. His son was reading out loud, with a confidence that he never heard before. The beautiful teacher listening to him was to be credited for this achievement. He marveled at her perfect posture as she blessed Joey with her undivided attention. It surprised him when he felt a stirring in his body that had been absent since his wife had died eight months ago. Almost immediately, he felt guilty.

Akeema seemed to feel his eyes on her. Turning her head to the right, her smile widened when she recognized him. When she placed her index finger on her puckered lips, he knew she wanted him to be as quiet as he could. He understood that she didn't want Joey to be distracted as he read.

When the little one was done, he closed the book softly before looking at teacher Akeema for her approval.

Joey was holding his breath. Looking at him tenderly, she said, "Well done, Joey, well done. I'm proud of you and so is your dad!"

Joey beamed at his teacher and his father. They were the people he wanted to impress the most.

Still standing in the doorway, Joseph Smith fought back tears of pride and happiness. It seemed to him that, since his wife died, he cried at the drop of a hat.

"Please join us, Mr. Smith." Akeema beckoned.

"Joseph," he reminded her kindly.

Returning his smile, she reported, "Joey had a good day today!"

Nodding his head eagerly, Joey chimed in, "I had a <u>great</u> day!"

Laughing, Akeema replied, "Excuse me! I stand corrected." Catching Joseph's eyes, she amended, "Joey Smith had a <u>great</u> day!"

"So I hear. Congratulations, son!"

"As a matter of fact, he doesn't have to take any books home tonight because all of his homework is done!"

Joseph whistled his appreciation. "To celebrate, how about going out to eat instead of chowing down on your old man's cooking?"

Little Joey pumped his fist. "Yes!" he exclaimed.

"How does burgers and fries sound?"

"Can I have chicken nuggets?" he asked hopefully.

"Yes, you sure can."

"Alright!" Joey stood up to dance. Akeema joined him, then Joseph joined her. They had no music to dance to. They caught Joey's rhythm, hopping and jumping around to his beat. It was wonderful. So, when Joey assumed Akeema was going with them to eat, she didn't correct him.

Later, at the diner, Akeema watched in amazement as eight-year-old Joey consumed a dozen chicken nuggets, fries, and a vanilla shake. Every bit of it. Joseph got a kick out of her reaction. He had a tiny eating machine on his hands. Feeding his little boy was like feeding an adult. He wished he had his metabolism; Joey didn't have an ounce of fat on him. Joseph had to hit the gym at least four days a week or his mid-section puffed right up. Now that he was up close and personal, he could see that Akeema was in phenomenal shape. Her dark, ebony skin was so deeply muscled that it looked etched in stone. Except for some gloss on her lips, her face was devoid of makeup. He smiled to himself. His deceased wife taught him how to apply her blush and lipstick so that her face was always 'on.' Even at the end of her life, she was concerned about her appearance. Toward the end, her cancer-ravaged body and face were skeletal looking. But, because he knew it was important to her, Joseph made sure she looked as good as she could. This included the many changes of the silk pajamas that she favored. Claire was a loving and giving wife and mother. She took great joy in spoiling her family. Her genuine care of them was sorely missed.

"Daddy, Daddy!" Joey's desperate voice brought Joseph back to the present.

"I'm sorry, son. What is it?"

Excitedly, Joey said, "I ate it all up. Can I go play now?"

Joseph smiled at his boy. From his pant pocket he pulled out eight quarters. "When these are gone, it'll be time to go home, okay?"

Joey nodded happily before hurrying off.

"Who is he going to play with?" Akeema asked.

"Not who, what. They have an arcade here. When he comes back empty-handed, he'll ask for more money."

Akeema shook her head, "As a parent, I'd be a pushover. He'd get more money, I'm afraid."

Joseph confided, "Confidentially, I have two more quarters in my pocket. I can't resist him either!"

They both laughed, enjoying themselves and each other. When Akeema's phone dinged, she saw that Jake was trying to reach her. Quickly, she sent him a text that she was busy tonight, but would call him in the morning. He'd have a fitful night. She couldn't figure out why she didn't care. Finished with her phone, Akeema looked up to find Joseph watching her intently.

"Oops!" she said, "Did you ask me something and I didn't answer? Sorry!"

He smiled, "No, you just caught me appreciating your beauty. I never had a teacher that even came close to looking like you. No wonder my son is crazy about you."

She shrugged, feeling bashful. "I guess Joey might have a thing for tall, skinny girls."

"Well, I'm not sure about that, but he's obviously in on the kind, patient, and smart ladies."

Akeema lifted her hands in surrender. "Stop, stop it! You are going to give me such a big head that I won't be able to get out the door!"

"Every word is the truth, Akeema."

"Well, thanks, but enough already."

"Shall I add humble and modest to the list?"

Exasperated she said, "At the risk of getting your mouth taped shut."

With perfect timing, Joey came back. "Can I have some more quarters, dad?" Sternly, Joseph replied, "What was our deal, pal?"

"I know, I know, but please! Just this once?"

With a twinkle in his eyes, that only Akeema understood, Joseph said, "Here's just two more quarters for you and that's it, got it?"

Happy as a lark, Joey yelled, "Got it!" as he ran off like a shot before any minds were changed.

Joseph and Akeema watched him scurry off with wide grins on their faces.

Wistfully, she sighed, "I'd like to have four or five of him one day."

"Then, one day you will," Joseph said with confidence.

"Nope, I'm afraid not."

"Why do you say that?"

"A car accident years ago that crushed my pelvis and female parts."

"Oh, I'm sorry. You can always adopt, though."

"Yes, I know. But, birthing my babies was my heart's desire."

"It seems our Father has other plans for you." Akeema agreed with a nod.

Impulsively, Joseph reached across the table to cover her hands with his. It wasn't a romantic gesture; it was a compassionate one. She received it the way he meant it. A new friendship was born.

Akeema sat at her kitchen counter, sorting through her mail. She was comfortable in an old sleep shirt, with a few holes here and there. As the pile of junk mail got taller, she reflected on the fun she'd had with Joseph and Joey. It was hard to say goodbye to them when they walked her to her car. Joey gave her a big hug and a promise to mention her name in his prayers. Yes, indeed, this beloved child had a father who was raising him right. Intruding on her thoughts was the insistent ringing of her cell phone. She thought about letting it go to voicemail but considered that to be cruel and unusual punishment.

She answered, trying to sound pleasant. "Hello, Jake."

"Hello, Akeema, are you less busy now?" His words were not combative, but his voice was.

"I'm going through a mountain of mail."

"Does that mean you are still too busy to talk to me?"

"If I was too busy to talk, I wouldn't have answered the phone."

"What were you busy doing?"

"I was having dinner with friends," she replied.

"Do I know these so-called friends?"

"Nope!"

This bone of contention between them needed to be fixed, he thought. "Why don't you introduce them to me?"

"Maybe I will one day."

"Can you take the 'maybe' out of it? After all, I've introduced you to my parents already."

Curious, Akeema asked, "What does one thing have to do with the other?"

"As a couple, we should be introducing our family and friends to each other."

"Why is that?" she wanted to know.

"It shows that our relationship is growing,"

"Does it?"

Tersely, Jake said, "Yeah, it does to me."

"I like that you spoke for yourself and not for me."

"I admit that I hope we are both on the same page."

Akeema shrugged. "Maybe one day."

"Huh?"

"Did I stutter?" As soon as the words were said, she regretted that she said them.

"No, you didn't." he retorted in a hard voice.

"Am I not close enough, or good enough to meet the people in your world?"

Akeema suppressed the frustrated sigh that she felt building inside her. "Sure. But, with my teaching and dancing, I don't have a lot of people in my life who are close."

"Oh, I see," he replied. But he really didn't. Akeema was so personable, she got along with just about everybody. He had a hard time believing she didn't have hordes of friends loving her. Like he did.

Was she being honest with him, or was she lying to him as she lived a whole other life that didn't include him?

Akeema listened to him breathe as he had his private thoughts about what she'd said. She realized, once again, that what he was thinking didn't interest her. She wanted to go through her mail, get ready for bed, and recharge her body for tomorrow's activities. She knew, with blazing clarity, that she and Jake weren't getting closer. It was her body that responded to him, not her heart. Except for mind-blowing orgasms, she didn't need him or want him. She didn't know how long they were going to be together, but their time was limited.

"Akeema, are you there?" She heard the mild panic in his voice.

It annoyed her. "Yes," she replied shortly.

"Did you hear my question?"

Oops. "I'm afraid not."

He paused before he responded, expecting an apology. None came. He pushed his irritation aside. Being angry at her would defeat his purpose. When he spoke, he made his voice husky and low. "I asked if you want me to come…over."

Akeema's private parts twitched in response. She had zero control over her body. "It's late and we both have to work tomorrow." Stating the obvious did little to quell her libido.

"I promise to do everything you like and then leave. I won't linger when it's over. You won't have to ask me to leave, I'll go. Period."

"I'm ready for you," she whispered.

"Is this the way you like it, baby?" Jake panted over her.

"Yes, Jake, yes! You know it is!" Akeema shouted. This ecstasy was making her lose her mind. He played her body to his music. She danced to his beat while flat on her back. Her will was his will. Her body quickened as she neared climax number three. "Now, now!" she screamed while riding a final wave of passion that left her breathless and floating. She held Jake tightly as her body trembled with fulfillment. She didn't loosen her grip on him until her pulse returned to normal. Jake gently caressed her earlobe with his lips, making her giggle.

"Am I leaving you satisfied?" he asked.

"Mmm, yes," she murmured.

"But you didn't let me do anything for you," she complained. "That's starting to be a habit."

"When I make you happy, I'm happy."

She rubbed his bare back. "Then you should be deliciously gleeful!"

He smiled before kissing her cheek, lips, and nose. "Goodnight, sweet lady." With that said, he got out of bed, put his clothes on and left, as promised.

CHAPTER 10

Humming to herself, Akeema stood in front of the floor length mirror to check out her look. She was usually pinned and tucked neatly with tops that matched bottoms. Today, however, her look was festive to match her mood. Over her navy slacks, she wore a pale pink pin-striped long-sleeved shirt. The V-neck dipped into darker pink buttons. Pretty flowers in varying shades of pink, yellow and green covered it – front and back. Akeema let it flow over her slender hips and muscular backside. Seeing her reflection made her smile. Later, as she was about to close her briefcase, the phone rang. When the display showed Jake's name and number, she was surprised. "Good morning. What a surprise."

"Good morning. I had you on my mind. Hearing your sexy voice is a good way to start my day. Do you mind?"

Akeema surprised herself by smiling into the phone. "No, I don't, but I've got to get out of here in about two minutes."

"I'm aware of your famous discipline. I'll not hold you long. Do I get any brownie points for keeping my promises last night?"

"Yes, sir, you certainly do."

Feeling in complete control, he was satisfied with the start to his day.

"Have a good one, Akeema Dawn!"

"Thanks to you, Jake, I will." She meant it. If their relationship was always like this, she could see a long future with him. If…

The classroom was blessedly quiet. Her little ones were laying on individual floormats for rest period. She looked out at them from behind her desk, with a small, contented smile on her face. The mats came in a variety of bright colors. To Akeema, it looked like the children were sleeping on a rainbow.

Her eyes visited each child to make sure that all was well. A couple of them were gently fidgeting as they struggled to get comfortable. Deliberately, Akeema looked at Joey last. When she found him, he was laying perfectly still with his eyes on her. She wasn't surprised. Without saying a word, they knew that they were connected. She knew they were kindred spirits. She loved this little boy as the child she'd never give birth to. He didn't smile at her until she smiled at him first. He was careful about showing her affection around others. Nobody told him that, he just knew it instinctively.

Due in large part to Akeema's tutoring, Joey was doing exceptionally well in school. Her services weren't really needed for him anymore, but nobody, including Joseph, admitted it out loud.

Joseph loved his son like no other. He was determined to be all the parent Joey would ever need. His wife's death had left a hole in the family that had to be filled. Joseph was the only one to take on that task. Akeema admired him for that. She made herself available to help them in any way possible. Both father and son were comfortable with her. She was just starting to realize how much they meant to her. Both of them. Suddenly, a noise from outside distracted her. What was it? All at once she knew, Rain. It was raining! On October the 21st, in Dallas, Texas, it was raining!

Akeema walked to the window, forcing herself not to run to it. She wasn't supposed to open it, but nothing was going to stop her from letting in the cool, fresh, clean air. Nothing smelled, or felt as good, as freshly watered earth.

It took all her strength to lift the hardly-ever-opened pane. When the clean, fresh air hit her face, Akeema smiled broadly. She took a deep breath, enjoying the wonderfulness of it all. She felt Joey standing beside her. Again, she wasn't surprised. She bent down to lift him, placing him securely on her hip. She felt his little arm go around her neck.

"Be real quiet, partner."

He nodded before looking out the window. His gap-tooth grin lit up his face. And her heart.

As Joseph walked down the school hallway, he smiled at the thought of seeing Joey, his son. He carried a picnic basket, hoping that teacher Akeema would join them for dinner. He'd planned to eat at a nearby park, that had tables and benches, but the surprise rain had soaked everything outside. As he neared the classroom, he was surprised when he didn't hear Joey reading. The door was open, so he should've been able to hear anything that was being said. Slowing his pace, he peeked around the corner to see Joey standing next to Akeema's desk, watching her work. He paused to listened for a while.

"Good boy! You did good work. Now what did I write down as your grade?"

Joey squealed, "I gotta hundred!"

"That's right, all of your answers are correct! All of your homework is done, so you and your dad won't have to do any tonight. Congratulations!"

"Thanks, teacher Akeema. Can I tell daddy?"

"Absolutely. It's your good news to tell. Now, can I get a hug? I sure need one."

Joseph heard his son chuckle. He knew they were hugging. He was a little jealous of Joey.

Heavily stomping his feet so they would know he was coming, the pair weren't touching when he entered the room.

Seeing his father, Joey ran to him. Excitedly, he jumped into his arms – or rather arm since the food basket was occupying the other one.

"I gotta hundred on my work!" Joey exclaimed.

"That's fantastic, son! I'm proud of you."

The tot looked from his father to his teacher and back again, beaming.

To Akeema, Joseph said, "I had an evening dinner in the park planned, but I got rained out."

"Oh, I'm sorry. However, if the food is good, you can enjoy it anywhere."

Little Joey exulted, "I smell chicken, Daddy!"

Smiling, Joseph replied, "I have all your favorites because you are doing so well in school these days. Can you guess what else is in the basket?"

Joey nodded happily. "Fries and oatmeal raisin cookies!"

"Very good! Now, what will we have to drink?"

"Pink lemonade!"

"Right again!"

Akeema loved their exchange. "Stop, you're making me hungry!"

"Please join us," Joseph said. "I have enough for us all."

"Oh, that's nice, but I don't want to horn in on your food and time together."

Joey wiggled to be put down. Walking to her, he looked up at her with pleading eyes.

"Please eat with us, teacher Akeema. The food will taste gooder if we all have some."

Smiling gently at him, she said, "The food will taste better, Joey."

"_Better_ food, okay?"

She looked at the cute little one and the handsome big one. "It's kind of hard to say no with the food smelling up the room."

"Then don't say no," Joseph responded quickly. "Please have dinner with us, Akeema." It was nice to hear him say her name without her title in front of it.

"Do you have plates?" she asked.

"Yep. Enough of everything. Where shall we set up?"

"How about laying down a big blanket on the floor so we can spread out comfortably."

"Sounds good. Let's get started, shall we?"

Sitting on the floor with their repast laid out before them, Joseph asked, "Shall we pray over our food?"

Without hesitation, Joey chimed in.

"Can I do it, daddy, huh?"

Looking at him with pride, Joseph nodded.

After all heads were bowed, Joey began.

"Dear heavenly Father, thank You for my best food. Please be nice to my daddy and teacher Akeema. I love You, and I thank You for loving me. In Jesus' name… oh! I forgot something! Please tell my mother that I made a hundred on my paper! Amen!"

Akeema and Joseph chorused their Amens with shiny eyes and mutual lumps in their throats. As they tried to gather themselves, Joey dug in, famished.

Akeema enjoyed the company and the food. Ballet rehearsals would resume in a few weeks when her diet wouldn't include fried chicken and French fries. With this in mind, she ate freely and joyfully.

When the dining was over, Joey excused himself to play with any of the toys he wanted to. Being an only child, he didn't have a problem entertaining himself.

"Thank you for including me in your dinner, it was delicious."

"I'm glad you enjoyed it, Akeema." He loved saying her name.

"In a few weeks it's back to water, soups, salads, and fruits."

Joseph stole a quick look at her taut, muscular body. "There's not an ounce of fat on you. I'd hate to see you disappear into nothing."

She could tell that he meant that, and it touched her.

"It's not about losing weight, it's about health. When I'm dancing and teaching it takes a lot out of me."

"Dancing? You can control how much of that you do can't you?"

"Nope."

"Do you mind if I ask why not?"

"Nope."

He watched her watch him. Silently.

Finally, he said, "Uh, I'm waiting for your answer."

"To what?" She asked innocently.

"To my question."

"I already answered it."

Joseph frowned. "How do you figure that?"

"Well, when you asked if I would mind if you asked me…"

"You said nope!"

Like little kids, they had a good laugh. Joey hurried over to see what was so funny. Joseph saved the day.

"I just told teacher a grown-up joke."

"Do you know a little boy joke, daddy?"

"Uh…"

Now it was Akeema to the rescue.

"I think I have one," she said.

Joey clapped his hands.

"Tell me, tell me!"

"Okay, here goes. Why did the man cross the street?"

Joey gave it some thought. Akeema wanted to be sure he understood the punchline. She waited patiently. Anxious to see his son's reaction, Joseph said,

"It's okay if you don't know the answer cause that's part of the joke. Let teacher tell you the answer." he prodded.

Joey's little face pouted.

"Let me think, daddy! Shush so I can think!" he demanded.

Both Akeema and Joseph were surprised. They didn't know he was going to take this so seriously. Was it possible that Joey didn't know the meaning of the word 'joke?'

The grown-ups each felt an empathy for the child they both loved. How was he going to take it when he came up with the wrong solution? Giving Joey the quiet he asked for, Akeema and Joseph sat silently waiting for him to speak. When he finally did, they were astonished.

"The man wanted to be on the other side." The wise tot said seriously.

The amazed grownups looked at each other, open-mouthed.

Joey was looking back and forth from Akeema to Joseph. "Is that right, daddy?" he asked timidly.

His father made a 'whooping' sound before he gathered Joey in his arms, throwing him in the air then catching and twirling him around. Akeema was laughing and clapping her hands. She was so proud of him. Whoever thought this was a dumb kid was the true dumb one.

Without giving it a second thought, Akeema reached for Joey. Without hesitation, Joseph handed him over. Feeling his little arms around her neck, made her feel like a part of him. She felt like they belonged together.

Watching his son with his teacher, Joseph felt a heart pang. The last time Joey had shown this kind of affection for a woman was with his wife. His loneliness knew no bounds.

CHAPTER 11

The next morning, Akeema slept soundly. After Joey and his father left, she finished up her evening schoolwork in her classroom instead of taking it home to do. The high-fat meal she'd eaten was sitting heavily in her stomach. She not only needed a workout, but she also wanted one. Long ago, Akeema had joined a 24-hour gym that she rarely used. It was going to come in handy now. Her deep slumber was interrupted by the annoying ring of the phone. Moaning, she covered her head with the extra pillow on her bed. It finally stopped ringing but started up again a short time later. She knew who it was. Jake.

Last night, after her shower, she'd planned to call him. She remembered stretching and laying down for a minute. That minute melted into hours. What a way to start the day.

"Hello," she mumbled.

"Well, top of the mornin' to you," Jake said with fake cheeriness.

"Hello, Jake." Akeema sighed.

"I'm not disturbing you, am I?" his voice dripping with sarcasm.

"I was sleeping and you woke me before I wanted to be awakened."

"Well, excuse me for wanting to start my day talking to you. Especially since I only heard your voice once yesterday."

Akeema yawned loudly. "I had a busy day."

"Doing what?"

"Jake," she said wearily, "I wanna go back to sleep. We'll talk later about my busy yesterday, okay?"

"What if I say it's not okay?" He challenged.

"You'll be listening to a dial tone," she replied coldly.

He clearly heard the agitation in her voice. She meant him to. Jake knew he had to back off. Getting her too mad would risk her doing one of her famous disappearing acts. She still hadn't introduced him to any of her friends or family, so she could hide from him in any number of places.

"What are you doing tonight?" He forced himself to take all the edge from his voice.

"I haven't thought about it yet – what time is it?"

"It's almost six."

"What?" Her eyes popped open.

"It's five-fifty to be exact. Why?"

"How dare you call me this early in the morning!"

This isn't how he wanted to start the day. "I wanted to give us time to talk," he replied.

Silence. Uh-oh.

"Akeema? You still there, honey?"

"Yeah," she said curtly. "Let me be clear on this… unless there is a medical emergency of some kind, I don't want to talk to you - or anyone else – this early in the morning. Got it?"

Jake stammered, "Well, uh…yeah, I got it. But…"

"But nothing," she interrupted.

"Am I allowed to be worried about you?"

"Not after midnight."

"But anything can happen!" he exclaimed.

"True, but if you're not with me, there's not a thing you could do about it." she pointed out.

Frustrated and trying to hide it, he replied,

"Well, as far as I'm concerned, you can call me or worry about me around the clock."

"Thank you. Since I'm wide awake now, I'm saying goodbye so that I can make me a leisurely breakfast."

Jake saw an opening. "Since I started your day off in such a crappy way, let me bring you breakfast. My treat."

"Thanks for the offer, but I'm not feeling very social at the moment."

Earnestly, he responded, "I get that, but wouldn't a good breakfast that you don't have to cook for yourself be a good thing?" Since Akeema didn't answer right away, Jake felt a renewed hope. "I'll also add an orgasm to that, if you desire."

To her shame, Akeema's traitor-of-a-body began to moisten her girlie parts. She tried to ignore the sensual feelings spreading through her. She could almost feel him on her, in her. Crap!

Feeling victory swinging in his direction, he lowered his voice, knowing it turned her on. "Your wish is my command, baby."

With a tremble in her voice she said, "I have to be dressed and ready to walk out of her in an hour and a half."

"I can be there in 25 minutes." he promised.

Akeema heard herself say, "Forget the breakfast."

"Teacher Akeema, can we sing a song?"

The request came from sweet little Suzy. With her two blonde pigtails and bright blue eyes, she looked like a living, breathing doll. She was also a talented singer. The other, less talented, students joined in with her request as they clapped and jumped around.

"Okay, that sounds like fun! What song would you like to sing?" Akeema asked.

Quick as a whip, Suzy yelled, "He Knows You Inside Out!" Again, her classmates screamed their approval.

They had toy versions of drums, cymbals, flutes, and violins.

"How many of you would like to play an instrument today?"

Exactly four hands lifted and waved in the air. Good. A person for each item. There would be no hurt feelings for the child left out.

The orchestra was set up in front of her desk. The choir stood to the left and right of the musicians.

Nobody had a problem with Suzy standing in the middle as the soloist. Akeema, of course, was the self-appointed conductor.

The musical introduction was on the pitiful side, but Suzy's voice drowned them out for the most part. She began, "You don't have to be a teacher's pet, don't worry wings won't sprout. Just get smart, He knows you inside, He knows you outside." Then, everyone – even the tone-deaf- joined in.

"He knows you inside out!"

The kids gleefully sang the song several times, each time was louder than the version before it. Akeema's students were happy while she was getting a headache.

When the singing was finally over, the kids were pretty revved up. Their little minds needed more time to settle down before reading and arithmetic could be tackled. Akeema decided to bring out paint and crayons for artwork. This would give the students something to concentrate on individually and quietly. Slowly, she walked behind them scanning the drawings. She could see there were a handful of budding artists in the class. One of them was Joey. His drawing was of a two-story house with shutters at the windows. Lots of trees and flowers surrounded the abode, along with a white picket fence. It was the kind of house Akeema hoped to have one day. Again, she felt the, now familiar, pang of sadness for the youngster who lost his mother to death.

Kneeling beside him, she asked softly, "Is this where you and your dad live?" She saw him shake his head.

"Does someone you know live there?"

Again, no.

"Where have you seen this house, Joey?"

"In my head."

Caught off guard, Akeema responded. "Huh?"

"When I grow up, I'm going to build this house," he said confidently.

Regaining her teacher composure, she assured him, "What a wonderful thing to do! I'm sure your father will be very proud of you."

"Are <u>you</u> proud, teacher Akeema?"

How badly she wanted to hug him. "Absolutely!"

His gap-toothed smile warmed her spirit, and her heart, as usual.

Keenly aware that she should be reviewing everybody's artwork. She gave him a brief shoulder pat before moving on.

She cared about all of those in her care. They got her attention as well, feeling like they were all her favorites.

Joseph Smith was loading fresh bread on the grocery store shelves. He was the shift manager who actively helped keep shelves neat with current merchandise. Lately, he had his son Joey on his mind, as well as Akeema, his son's teacher. His little boy was doing exceedingly well in school. He was repeating first grade and was doing great. He was falling in love with his teacher, so he was trying to do his very best for her. He understood why Joey was fond of Akeema – Joseph was fond of her too. These past months, his thoughts had been about his beloved Claire. The horrible nightmare that ended up taking her life, started with the common cold. She had it for days, weeks, then finally a month and a half. By the time he talked to her about going to the doctor, she had full-blown pneumonia. Claire passed away shortly after being hospitalized. He was holding her hand as he listened to her raspy breathing. Only once had she opened her eyes to connect with him. As she held his gaze, he couldn't believe how unafraid she looked. Her expression said, "I love you," louder than the spoken words ever could have. Claire had gripped his hand so tightly that it almost hurt. Then suddenly, it was over. The room was quiet, and her hand was limp in his. Blaming God for his loss, he'd wept bitterly. He and Joey hadn't been to church since. Joseph had a graveside service for family and loved ones to say goodbye. Slowly, he started saying prayers over meals and at his son's bedtime. But, since being a widower, he hadn't had any heart-to- heart conversations with his Maker. He was still a believer; he was just an angry one. Feeling as he did, he very carefully kept his mouth shut about it. He didn't want Joey to hear anything negative about the God he was brought up to believe in. Joseph was a widower for eight months, when he first met Akeema. His attraction to her made him feel like he was cheating on his dead wife. He didn't care one iota what anyone else thought about it; his struggle was with himself. Except for treating her like his old-buddy-old pal, he showed no outward sign of a romantic interest. This wasn't hard for him because he honestly liked and respected her as his friend. As for Akeema, Joseph knew she was in love with Joey.

Jake was having a great day at the office. A new lucrative client had been referred to him, which meant money in his pocket. This day was great in every aspect. His morning love-making session with Akeema put a smile on his face every time he thought of it – which was often. He was obsessed with controlling her. He was determined to make her as crazy about him as he was about her. He was accustomed to women who groveled at his feet. To say that Akeema kept him on his toes was an understatement. He wanted to be the most important person in her life. Except for her dancing, he didn't want to share her with anyone or anything. Their relationship was paramount to him. He learned how to control his temper – thanks to her.

He still got angry with her when she chose her will over his, but she had a way of avoiding him when he made her angry. He never knew where to find her when she took a break from him, and it drove him mad. Right now, the only area where he held her hostage was carnal. It was the only place where he could exude his power over her. Akeema was strong-willed in every other area in her life. Jake wanted her to be his willing puppet. He wanted her to come running at the snap of his fingers. He wouldn't stop until he had her the way he wanted her. Helpless.

The children were all diligently and quietly working on puzzles. Some were frowning, some rested a hand on a cheek while the dominate hand maneuvered the pieces, while others had little tongues pointed outward as they concentrated with all of their might. Akeema heard the sweet sound of Suzy's voice floating in the air. She couldn't help but smile. She didn't recognize the tune, but she liked it. When her eyes finally settled on Joey, she smiled even more. Her prize pupil had two puzzles in front of him! She watched as he went from one to the other, covering them both. She would love to clone him so that she could have a Joey of her own. Content with how her class was going, Akeema allowed her mind to drift. Of course, her thoughts shifted to that morning's liaison with Jake. The things he did to her made her body scream with pleasure. Just the thought of it made her pulse quicken, as always. She realized something; Just the thought of "it" made her breathless – not Jake! Akeema couldn't remember what they last talked about. She didn't recall their last public date. But she could recall each touch of his hand on her body, his last passionate kiss, his last…

"Teacher Akeema, teacher Akeema!"

Brought back to the present by the desperate cry of little Miranda, Akeema focused on the little one who was holding herself while dancing in front of her.

"I need to wee wee!" she cried.

Quickly, Akeema announced to the class, "Continue with your work. We'll be right back." She scooped Miranda into her arms, understanding that she could be peed on. However, she could walk faster which would get them to the restroom quicker. To Akeema, it was worth the risk.

Mission accomplished; her charge was busy urinating an alarming amount for someone so small. Akeema stood out in the hallway while Miranda did her business. This gave her a perfect viewpoint to see anyone coming or going from her classroom. She could hear her students a little, but nothing was disruptive.

"I'm done teacher Akeema," Miranda called sounding happy and relieved.

Promptly, she cleaned up the little girl and the small amount of dribble on the toilet seat. Once again, all was right with her world.

CHAPTER 12

Driving home from school, Akeema reflected on her relationship with Jake, Shamefully, she admitted that her body was in love with him, but her heart wasn't. Even thinking about their last lovemaking session caused her body to heat up. If she was white, she mused, she'd be beet red for sure. All of this was new to her. She wasn't a virgin when she met Jake, but she didn't have an overly active sex life. Prior to Jake, Akeema had taken only two lovers. Those men were liked and respected by her. They were friends then and now. Although she was having knock-your-socks off sex with Jake, she didn't consider him a friend. Because she'd seen the worst of his temper and tirades, she didn't put her full trust in him – she always held herself back. Akeema saw his attempts to do better. His efforts weren't lost on her. But she felt like he was a ticking time bomb just waiting to explode. She knew that he was going to lose his cool and throw a tantrum one day soon. When that day came, she would say goodbye to him. She hoped. Until that day came, she accepted the fact that she was hooked, not by the man, but by what the man could do. Akeema had always scoffed at the idea of being sexually addicted. Those who really enjoyed the act probably had it more often. To her, that wasn't being an addict – it was being active. But, because of Jake she knew what it felt like to crave sex. To hunger for it. To think about it in public places, around kids. When she wasn't having sex, she was thinking about it and dreaming about it. When she finally called it off with Jake, she knew she would go through serious withdrawal. Last night's love fest came to mind. Again. Right on cue, she felt her body respond. Again.

As Akeema was pulling into her parking space, she saw a car that looked like…no, it <u>was</u> Jake's ride! Gathering her purse and briefcase, she hurried over to the grey BMW to peek in. Sure enough, she saw his mahogany and navy-blue jacket on the passenger seat. She was excited and annoyed by his surprise visitation. Walking to her apartment, she saw him before he saw her. Akeema liked the way he looked. Since he was five inches taller than her, she could wear heels without worrying about being taller than he was. His shiny brown hair was bobbing up and down to the beat of the music he was listening to. In addition to his phone, he was holding a large grocery bag. When he saw her, he grinned ear to ear. Nearing him, Akeema pasted a small smile on her face.

"Hi, Jake, what a surprise."

With his arms occupied, he leaned down to kiss her forehead. "Hello, my lovely. You look beautiful, as usual."

"Thanks." Akeema said politely. "What do I owe the honor of this visit?"

"Dinner!" he exulted.

Her brows lifted. "Are you under the mistaken impression that a very tired me is going to cook for you this evening?"

Jake vigorously shook his head. "Nope. I'm here to cook for you!"

"Really?"

"Yep. So can we take this conversation inside?"

Akeema opened the door, then stood aside to let him enter first. He whistled as he walked into the kitchen. As she closed the door behind him, Akeema thought of the bed that was unmade because of that morning's lovemaking session with him.

Jake cooked while Akeema cleaned. She insisted on eating with plasticware and paper plates. Once she'd washed all of the pots, pans, and utensils that the chef used, no more cleaning would be required.

Akeema found it amusing that he claimed to cook the meal for her, but what he prepared was <u>his</u> favorite meal: sirloin steaks and mashed potatoes. The meal was edible, but her taste buds would have appreciated some brown gravy on the bland potatoes and meat that was a little more on the tender side.

While she was wiping down the island and the kitchen countertops, Jake went into the living room to wait for her.

He loved this room with its lack of clutter. A dove grey couch, two mauve wing chairs, and an ivory and glass coffee table seemed to fit exactly right. A large area rug, that matched the furniture, was covering most of the hardwood floor. On each side of the grey-bricked fireplace were two built-in white bookshelves. Several white framed pictures were scattered among the reading material.

Looking at the pictures, Jake realized that he didn't know any of them. For the first time, he noticed something else that he found strange.

"Hey, Akeema!" he called. "Why don't you have any pictures on your walls?"

Casually, she replied, "I don't like putting holes in the walls."

Jake turned around to look at her, astonished.

"Excuse me?" he asked.

Looking up at him from her task, she sighed.

"I know, I know, I'm a tad on the strange side."

Jake laughed at her understatement. In spite of herself, Akeema smiled as she defended herself. "Not only is it not good for the walls," she continued, "I have absolute freedom in re-arranging my furniture. I don't have to worry about re-hanging pictures because I moved the couch. Ugh!"

Incredulous, Jake remarked, "I can't believe how serious you are about this." She wasn't done.

"And, one day, I'm going to own my own home. When it's time to paint, no pictures will have to be removed or holes patched," she said proudly.

"You've got a point there," Jake admitted.

Akeema nodded. "Don't I always?"

Later, at Jake's request, Akeema made some popcorn to go with the beer he brought with him. She decided on ice-cold cranpineapple juice.

Sitting on the couch, Akeema was scrolling through the cable channels to find a movie they would both enjoy. She preferred the Classics, but Jake liked horror and shoot 'em ups. Most of the time, she was the one to compromise on what they watched together.

She paused when she saw Clark Gable on the screen, not because she hoped to watch the movie, she just liked looking at him.

"Hey!" Jake exclaimed, "Isn't this that 'windy' movie?"

Akeema looked at him like he had two heads. "Its proper name is 'Gone With the Wind.' I can't believe you don't know the name of a classic movie."

"Classic is code for old," he replied.

"it's no secret that the better movies, for the most part, were made back in the day."

"It's a matter of taste, and taste is subjective. This guy Kent Gable, probably wouldn't be the heart throb today that he was back when."

Horrified, Akeema said, "<u>Kent</u> Gable? That's what you think his name is? Really?"

"Isn't it?"

"No! It's <u>Clark</u> Gable, for goodness sake!"

Jake hit his forehead with his palm. "Oh, my bad! I was mixing him up with Clark Kent!"

Now Akeema looked at him like he had warts all over his two heads. "You're confusing a comic book character with an Academy Award winning actor?"

Seeing how irate she was getting, he tried to calm her down. Putting his arm around her shoulder, he pulled her stiff body closer to his side. "Baby, baby, relax. It's no big deal. I admit I'm no expert on Classic movies and their actors. Let's not ruin a good evening over something like this," he cajoled.

Akeema did a silent count to twenty before she spoke in a calmer voice. "Do you still want our relationship to have a long run?"

Confidently, he answered, "I do."

"Then, I'll share something with you. I don't like the horror movies that you do. Period. I only half-like the shoot 'em ups. But, I've been sacrificing my personal taste to spend time with you."

Jake was touched. She'd never given even one hint that she was bored or not interested. "Wow, thank you, Akeema."

"You're welcome – up to now."

"What?"

"From this moment on, I want equal viewing time. For all the movies I've watched and not liked, it's your turn to watch what <u>I</u> want. After this, we'll take turns."

"Okay," he said slowly.

Satisfied, she hit him where it would probably hurt. "We'll begin right here, with Clark Gable."

"Are you kidding?"

"Nope. Just be glad it isn't in black and white. You still have that to look forward to!"

That night, Akeema didn't have to worry about her lustful feelings for Jake. After three hours of the oldie-but-goodie fest, Jake couldn't wait to get out of there!

CHAPTER 13

The next few weeks passed uneventfully for Akeema and Jake. She continued to expose him to classic movies, much to his annoyance. However, they both were faithful to the deal they'd agreed upon. Jake had to increase his workouts since he was drinking more beer to get through classic movie nights. He'd started to get a 'beer belly' that Akeema made fun of without mercy.

He was both pleased and pissed that her long-limbed, tight ballerina body was always perfect, no matter what she ate or drank. This amused her because he 'assumed' she didn't exercise when she wasn't dancing – which was ludicrous. Since he hadn't ever asked her about her workout routine, she was content with his egotistical assumption. He thought he knew her so well when she knew he didn't. His arrogance was just one of many walls that kept them from getting closer. The fall season was upon them, so Akeema's ballet rehearsals were just around the corner. She wasn't tutoring anymore for lack of time. Any student needing extra help had to be referred to another teacher. Joey was doing so well that he and his father decided to discontinue all after class help. She missed them both.

She was on her way to Aunt Jean's and Uncle Rick's for dinner. Her schedule was about to get crazy busy so she wanted to spend some time with them while she could.

Although she had a key to their place, she rang the doorbell instead. The door opened, and before Akeema could even say hello, she was wrapped in her aunt's ample arms. She closed her eyes, inhaled the fried food smell that her aunt wore like perfume, then hugged her back. Once loosed, her uncle stepped in, lifting her off the ground. She loved that he smelled like Ivory soap, so fresh and clean.

When her feet were back on the floor, Akeema finally got a word in, "It's so good to see you guys," she said warmly. "What smells so good?"

In her loud booming voice, her aunt replied, "Fried chicken with rice and brown gravy!"

This was Akeema's favorite childhood meal; she clapped her hands joyfully.

Akeema squealed, "Will there by enough for leftovers?"

Proudly, Aunt Jean responded, "Your doggie bag has already been packed!"

"Woo-woo!"

Uncle Rick attempted to bring order in the house.

"Come on ladies, get in here! You're letting all the air out and the gnats in!"

Akeema sat patiently in the pretty country kitchen as Aunt Jean prepared her dinner plate.

When the meal was placed before her, she laughed out loud. The food wasn't on a plate – it was on a platter! Her aunt huffed. "Laugh all you want to, young lady, as long as you eat every bite in front of you. You know you don't have an ounce of fat on you!"

Akeema sputtered, "That's a bad thing?"

With both hands on her wide hips, Jean was the picture of authority. "When we're sick and can't eat much, it's the fat that our body uses to feed and fuel itself. You don't have enough to keep a small bird alive," she admonished.

"Auntie, I can't have too much fat on me and be a ballet dancer too," she explained. "Not only do I have to float myself through the air, but I'm also often lifted by my partner."

Aunt Jean nodded. "I get that. It's not like I'm trying to make you morbidly obese, honey, I just want to add a little 'healthy' fat to that lean body of yours."

"Healthy and fat. They don't sound like they should be spoken in the same sentence as good things."

"We need fat to live. Granted, not an abundance of it, but certainly some of it."

Akeema raised both her hands in surrender.

"Now, start working that mouth to eat instead of talk. Cold gravy is never a good thing."

Rick watched and listened silently. He loved these two women more than his own life. He felt blessed to have them in his world. After the meal, Akeema was surprised, and pleased, once again. Aunt Jean had made one of her delicious homemade poundcakes!

"I can't believe you cooked and baked for me today, Auntie! Thank you so much!"

"Whoa there, young lady! Don't think for one moment that I'm not gettin' a hunk of that cake!" Uncle Rick hurried to say.

Akeema laughed, "Don't worry, Unc. Even if it was only one piece of cake, I love you enough to share it with you."

Rick gave his round stomach a pat. "I'm a happy, much- loved man."

In unison, the women in his life said, "Yes, you are!"

When it was time to clean up in the kitchen, Rick sent his wife and niece to the living room to spend some time alone. Before Akeema had arrived, Jean told him she planned on asking about her dating life. He figured she'd talk more openly about her private side if he wasn't in the room.

Getting right to the point, Aunt Jean asked, "So, how's your love life?"

Akeema chuckled. The orange and ivory couch that she'd just sat down on was still cool beneath her. The warmth of her body hadn't had time to warm up the checkered material. The pleasant room, with its large wood furniture, and a 25-inch floor model TV, seemed caught in a 1970's time warp. Whenever she was in this house, she felt like she was home.

"My love life is stable right now, Auntie."

Jean eyed her keenly. "Are you expecting it to be <u>unstable</u> for some reason, Akeema?" She'd never lied to her. She didn't always tell her things that would worry her, but whenever her peeps asked her a direct question, she'd always responded with an honest answer.

"I'm dating Jake again. Exclusively."

Jean jumped to her feet. "You're <u>what</u>?"

"Now, now, you calm down. Sit back down and I'll tell you why it happened."

Sarcastically, Jean said, "He must've held a gun to your head." She sat down next to Akeema on the couch. Her usual smile was gone.

"First, Auntie, he apologized profusely."

"And?" It had to be much more than that.

"Then, he threw the Bible at me on the topic of forgiveness."

Jean looked at her crossly before fully understanding what she meant. Slowly, her features softened. It was easy to be preached to, but hard to practice what you preach.

"I see."

Akeema relaxed. "I knew you would. He's got his second chance to do better. So far, we're doing okay."

"How many chances are you giving him?"

"This is it, Auntie. I made it clear that I might forgive him 70 X 7, but I'm only open to dating him this last time."

"I'd like to be a fly on the wall when you guys have your first argument."

"We've had it."

Jean's mouth formed a perfect 'O.'

"We disagreed like sensible adults. It was okay."

"Really?"

"Yep. Do you feel better?"

"Some."

"I understand. I brought you guys into it by staying here – or should I say hiding out – when we broke up before. I shouldn't have done that."

"Nonsense," Jean huffed, "we're your family. You can _always_ depend on us, as we do you. It's your life, and you get to choose who you want in it. With or without our approval."

"I'm working on more _with_."

Jean replied. "Good."

According to the car clock it was 11:15 pm. She was on her way home, but she easily had thirty minutes before she'd get there. After all the wonderful fatty food she'd eaten, a morning workout was needed. She had to get to bed sooner than later. She decided to call Jake to say good night while she was in transit so that she wouldn't have to do it later.

"Good evening, mister. Did I wake you?"

"Hardly." He said sourly.

"I'm on my way home so I thought I might call you before it got even later. How was your day?"

"How do you think?"

Uh-oh. "I don't know, that's why I asked."

"My day was okay for a guy whose lady had a dinner date and didn't include him."

Double uh-oh. "Didn't you get the message I left for you?" Akeema asked.

Jake's voice was low, ominous. "I know you had a dinner date that lasted past eleven. I don't know who you ate with, however."

Guarded, she replied, "You don't know them."

"I know, you make sure of that, don't you? How many guests were there?"

"Three of us," she responded automatically.

"All women?" He prodded.

"A married couple and me. She cooked. I ate."

"So, I could've come. Why wasn't I invited?"

"They always cook me a mega-calorie meal before I start dance rehearsal. It's a tradition for us."

"I like the sound of that. Do they know about me?"

"Yes."

"So, you talk to them about me, but you say nothing to me about them, right?"

Yikes. "Right," she said calmly.

"Why, Akeema, why?" he cried.

She heard desperation, not anger, in his voice. Was this really so important to him? And, if so, why?.

"I've known them all my life, they are family to me. There's not a lot that I don't share with them. You are new in my life. I'm not sure if you have a permanent place in it yet."

She'd just told him the absolute truth, but he didn't know it.

"I get that, and I'm a little jealous of it."

"All the time that I spend with you is time away from them. They understand that you and I are getting to know one another. I see them so seldom these days that I don't think it's fair to make them share me with you on the rare occasions that I'm with them. That's the way it is, Jake."

He was quiet. She took that as a good sign.

"So, if you and I make it, will the people closest to you get to meet me?"

"Yes, if we make it."

"Do you doubt that we will?"

"Sometimes."

"What can I do to give you more confidence in our relationship?"

She knew he honestly wanted her to tell him. That's why she wouldn't.

"Jake, the last thing I want to do is tell you all of my likes and dislikes so that you can mold yourself into the perfect man for me."

This confused him. "Why wouldn't you want me to change into your perfect guy?"

"Because it wouldn't be <u>you</u>! You would be pretending to be what I want, and that would get old after a while. It wouldn't be long before you'd start to resent me. A life that started out good for me would end up being a sucky life for both of us."

"So, tell me in general what you are looking for."

"I'd like it if me and my other half liked ALMOST everything about each other. We'd both compromise for each other to get along better. The two of us would respect each other's careers, especially since I both dance and teach. Since I can't birth kids, he'd have to already have his own or be open for adoption. We'd be comfortable talking about everything, even the things where we had a different point of view. Even tempers and a Holy Spirit belief system are a must. I'd never knowingly date anyone that didn't consider himself a child of the Most High."

"Sounds good to me. Anything else?"

She wished she didn't have to say it, but she did.

"A good sex life."

CHAPTER 14

Akeema's time was no longer her own, and she loved it. She rehearsed before and after school. This season's rendition of the Nutcracker was especially grueling. To get more work done, a full day of rehearsing started on Sunday. On school days, when the alarm on her phone ended nap time for the kids, it woke Akeema too. Saturday was her one and only day off to recharge her energy. If Jake didn't join her for on-line study of The Word, he wouldn't see her at all. He called her every day, but it was merely to touch base, they didn't have any quality time together. They weren't even having sex! He was lonesome, horny, and losing control of Akeema. He was trying to act understanding during this hectic time in her life, but his patience was wearing thin. His original plan was to have her under his thumb before she resumed dancing. He was woefully behind with his own schedule. Between the children and the dancing, he was coming in at a distant third place in her world. When he'd dared to share his feeling with her, she'd quickly said,

"I think you are right; I'll totally understand if you decided to find someone else with more time for you." And that, was the end of that.

Leaving school, Akeema pushed open the huge wooden double doors. Going down the stairs, she was stopped in her tracks when she saw Joey and his father leaning against the railing. The little boy ran to her for a hug. She complied while making eye contact with a smiling Joseph.

"Hello, you two!" she said, "What's going on?"

Joseph replied, "Joey wanted a hug, and I wanted to say hi."

The sincerity in his voice and the kind facial expression touched her. She looked from one to the other, feeling her heart swell.

Impulsively, she bent down to scoop Joey into her arms. "You give great hugs," she whispered into his ear.

"That's what daddy says," he giggled.

"He's a smart guy."

Joey nodded, squeezing her neck tightly.

Sadly, she knew she had to break this up. Putting Joey on his feet, she ruffled the top of his head playfully.

Akeema smiled at Joseph. "Thanks for hanging around to say hi. I appreciate it."

"Thanks for making my son feel special."

"He is."

"We found something to agree on."

"You bet."

For a few seconds, they stood there just looking at one another. She had to go.

"Well, fellas, I need to scoot. I've got a teacher that doesn't like it when I'm late."

She gathered up the briefcase and clothes bag that she sat down to hug Joey. She gracefully hurried down the stairs. Akeema didn't look back until she heard the little boy's voice yelling a final goodbye. Never breaking her stride, she returned the waves of Joseph and Joey. Two of her favorite people.

It was finally over. Everybody in the dance hall was leaning on someone or something. Chests were heaving, bodies were sweating, nobody talked. Each and every dancer was exhausted and starving. Barney, their task-master, didn't have a sympathetic bone in his body. At 5'6" and 120 pounds, he was all muscle, He alone was not sweating profusely. He usually wore pink and had yellowish blonde hair. His wide lips were painted red. Nobody made fun of him – at least not where he could hear them. He was a man of few words; he never used endearments. He clearly said what he meant. Tonight, he had on all white, even though it was the fall season. He obviously didn't care what anyone thought about him. The first time he spoke to you was a shock. For those who assumed he had a tenor voice, the reaction to his Barry White – like baritone was comical. In his booming bass, he announced, "Be here promptly at 5:00 am people!" And then he was gone.

A short time later, the hard-bodied dancers regained their breath and their stamina. The only thing left was their appetites.

Kristen moaned, "As my mother once told me, my stomach thinks my throat has been cut. Anybody want to join me for a light supper?"

The pretty blonde, blue-eyed dancer scanned the faces of her fellow dancers. Most were shaking their heads no.

The single redhead of the troop, Chelsea, made a negative face. "I'm much too funky to go out in public. It's home with a can of soup for me, I'm afraid."

Akeema spoke up, "How does fried chicken, rice and brown gravy sound?"

Chelsea rolled her big green eyes in ecstasy. "It sounds heavenly, but we can't eat like that while we are in training."

"I know that's right!" Kristen agreed. "Barney would sniff out the grease coming out of our pores! How can you look as good as you do and eat like that?"

"It's not a usual thing, believe me. My aunt gave me the leftovers. If I split the food with you guys, we'll have a reasonable sampling of the yumminess. Otherwise, I'll end up eating it all by myself. C'mon, help me out. Please!" she beseeched. Kristin and Chelsea exchanged silent looks. Impatiently, Akeema asked, "Do we have a date?"

Smiles and nods followed. Three ballerinas headed out the door for a fatty supper. Life didn't get much better.

Happy and semi-full, Akeema was just shutting her front door after saying goodnight to Kristen and Chelsea. The phone rang, not surprising her at all. She expected his call.

"Hey, Jake," she answered. There was no need to say hello.

"Hey, baby. How's it going?"

"Good. Your timing is perfect. I just said bye to everybody."

"Oh?"

Oops, she needed to explain. His question was a little on the icy side. "Kristen and Chelsea helped me eat up the leftovers I had in the fridge."

"Oh." Trouble avoided.

"So, how was your day?" She asked pleasantly.

"Not bad, pretty productive. Anything unusual with your day?"

"Nah. Just busy, then busier."

"I know that's right. Have you got a little time for your one and only?"

"Yep, I'm giving it to you now."

"What are you giving me?" Jake asked.

"Time."

"Cute, Akeema, very funny."

"I wasn't joking. I have a little time before I go to bed and I'm giving it to you."

"I mean personal time, sweetheart."

"This call is just between you and me. I call that personal." She yawned loudly.

"I hear how tired you are. I can be there in fifteen minutes."

Akeema moaned. "I'm sorry, Jake, I need to wash this stink off me and hit the sack."

"Mmm, I love your brand of stink," he said suggestively. "By the time you finish your shower, I'll be at your door. We'll both feel better after I'm done."

Dang nabbit! Akeema could feel her personal part throb. Because of her two full-time jobs, she had successfully avoided this. Her body was letting her know it hungered for Jake. Now.

"Um, I, uh, really need to get to bed. I'm exhausted."

"Just think how much better you'll sleep after an orgasm…or two."

He heard her quick in-take of breath. He was getting to her.

"I need to go to bed, to sleep," she stressed.

"I know, baby, I know. I'm trying to help us both. If you don't want to see me, I have a plan B."

Despite herself, she had to know. "What is it?"."

"Phone sex."

He constantly surprised her in the erotic zone.

"Phone sex?" How would that work? I don't have any porn here."

He lowered his voice to its most seductive. "We are the stars in our own movie. You're creative and so am

I. My hands will be your hands, and the reverse. Come on, sweetness. Play with me."

As always, his voice and his words had an immediate effect on her body. Her pulse and her breathing sped up. "Okay," she responded hoarsely.

"Let's take off our pants."

With her fingers shaking, she did as she was told.

Slowly, Jake whispered, "That part of me that loves to be inside you is rising to the occasion. You know every inch of it. Can you see it?"

"Yes," she said moaning.

"Is your body preparing itself for my entry?"

"Oh, yes," she replied.

Akeema could hear Jake's breathing hard between his words. Her eyes were closed as her head thrashed from side to side on her pillow. "Jake, Jake…" she whimpered.

"I'm with you and you are with me. Keep me with you, in you, now, now, now!" Thirty minutes later, Akeema and Jake were sound asleep.

CHAPTER 15

T he following day was not an ordinary one for Akeema. Thoughts of the night before had her so distracted that concentration was difficult to prolong. Basically, as long as they were quiet, she let the kids in her class do what they wanted to. She couldn't imagine how she could be this obsessed with a man she wasn't in love with. As thought of him filtered through her mind, Akeema squirmed in her chair as her flesh responded to thoughts of him. She wished her heart would follow suit.

"Teacher Akeema? Teacher Akeema!"

Joey's voice finally got through to her. Apologetic, she gave him her undivided attention. Even with a tooth missing, he was so cute. Although his black hair was shorn short, she could see the side part that the barber had shaved in it. His big round eyes were dark brown with extra-long lashes. The dimple in his chin matched his handsome father's.

"I'm sorry I didn't hear you, Joey. What is it, dear?"

He pulled a neatly folded piece of notebook paper from his shirt pocket. After giving it to her, he didn't move as he patiently waited for her to read it. It was neatly printed from his father:

Akeema, I'd love to join
your Bible study Saturday.
Please write the time and
Phone number that I need
to call. Joseph

Smiling, she promptly did as requested. At the end of the note, she added, "I look forward to sharing the holy day with you."

Akeema refolded the note, then carefully put it back in Joey's pocket. "Thank you, sweetie," she said in a voice that only he could hear. He grinned widely before skipping back to his desk and puzzles. Thinking of Joseph gave Akeema a much-needed break from thoughts of Jake.

Exiting the rehearsal hall, Akeema saw it right away – Jake's BMW. She scanned the area, not seeing him anywhere. He had tinted windows so she couldn't see inside the car. Listening intently, she didn't hear any music either. Although it appeared to be empty, she found herself heading toward it.

As she got closer, she saw the window lower on the driver's side. Jake was smiling warmly at her. She'd been in a state of almost constant arousal all day, so the mere sight of him sent her pulse racing. Walking to his car, she left some space between her and the vehicle.

"Surprise, baby! Give me some sugar…sugar."

Akeema forced herself not to roll her eyes at his lame attempt at a joke. "I don't want to offend you. I need a shower in the worst way."

"I don't care if you just had a shower or if you need a shower. I love all of your aromas," he leered.

With everything they did sexually, Akeema couldn't understand why she was blushing. At least her black skin hid it from Jake.

Trying in vain to change the subject, she said, "I'm glad to see you, but I feel like I'm about to pass out from exhaustion and food deprivation. Were you just in the neighborhood or something?"

"Yep. On purpose. Come here."

His voice lowered to that sexy register that turned her on so easily. She stepped closer to the car. Jake grabbed her by the back of her neck, pulling her head and chest inside the window. His lips were on hers before she could protest. In mere seconds, Akeema's tongue had entrance to his mouth. As she tasted its freshness, she could feel him sucking her tongue in a way that lit all of her fires. When the kiss ended, Jake's lips were mere inches from hers when he ordered, "Get in the car, baby."

Akeema was his puppet. Without question, she opened the back door to crawl in. She placed her gear on the floorboard, then sat patiently as she held her breath in anticipation of Jake's next move.

First, he turned on the radio. Then, he joined Akeema in the back seat. He pulled her closer to him, massaging her back. Expertly, he removed her bra, dropping it on her belongings. Next, he resumed rubbing her back with one hand as he cupped her right breast with the other. When he tweaked her nipple, Akeema felt it harden immediately. Very slowly, Jake began to softly kiss her throat. His lips traveled downward until his mouth replaced his hand on her chest. At first, he suckled gently. Her breathing was ragged as her excitement grew. Suddenly, he began sucking harder. She moaned, holding his back with her hands. "Lift your hips," he ordered.

She did. Jake removed her leotard and underwear. Akeema closed her eyes to revel in all the wonderful sensations he was giving her with his mouth and fingers. On the brink of losing her mind, she asked, "What can I do for you?"

He breathed into her with one word. "Come."

She did. As always.

Later, with their bare bottom halves entwined, Jake held Akeema as she snored lightly. He smiled as he remembered her first climax as he manipulated her body to his will. As she trembled with the first throbbing of her orgasm, he raised himself to kiss her deeply so that she could taste herself. Powerfully, he took her with him as he relieved himself with a shout. He kissed her salty tears that fell down her face to her chin. No words were spoken. No words were needed. Akeema was asleep in minutes. Her last coherent thought was, "If only I loved him the way I love this."

It was 5:15 am according to Jake's car clock. Akeema was sleeping so soundly that he hated to wake her. When he'd changed their position in order to turn the radio off, she didn't rouse at all. He got the blanket from the passenger seat that he'd brought along to throw over them.

Since she wouldn't go to his place or allow him to go to hers, he'd chosen his spacious car as plan C. She was his responsive wanton woman. He had no intention of leaving her – or allowing her to leave him. He didn't know when his feelings for her had changed, but they had. He didn't look forward to telling his mother that she'd have a black daughter-in-law one day.

It was Saturday so neither of them had to go to work. He could let her sleep until she was ready to wake up. But, he knew how important her Bible class was to her. She'd never forgive him if he let her oversleep.

He kissed her forehead once, twice. Nothing.

Looking down at her pretty dark features and full lips, he kissed her mouth. A soft smile parted her lips.

"Good morning, Black Beauty," he whispered.

"Mmm, am I dreaming?"

He kissed her lips again, lightly. "You're the dream, sweetheart."

He saw her smile before opening her eyes. It took her a while to focus. He watched her expression turn to shock as she realized where she was and why.

"What happened? Did I nod off?"

Jake chuckled. "No. You passed out."

"Oh, my goodness. I've got to get home." She sat up, seeing the blanket that covered their nakedness. Akeema flushed with shame. It was her first experience with car sex. Was there nothing she wouldn't do sexually with this man? She faced the reality that she was open to doing any and all things that felt good to her… Dang it!

Jake reached for a thermos. "I know you're not much of a coffee drinker, so I have some of your favorite cranpineapple juice for you."

She ran her tongue over her fuzzy-feeling teeth.

"Thanks, Jake. I appreciate you."

"Back at you, baby."

Her mouth felt dry as the desert. Eagerly, she drank from the thermos until it was empty.

Uh-oh. Now she had to pee!

"Oh crap!" She wailed.

Concerned, Jack said, "What? Was the juice not cold enough or something?"

"The juice was delicious. But now I have to use the restroom."

Playfully, he kissed her nose. "Oh, honey, that's not a problem. The rehearsal hall is open. Go on in."

Akeema rolled her eyes in dismay. "Oh great! Everybody I know will know that I had a sexual assignation in the flippin' parking lot!"

He loved this woman. Who but Akeema would use 'sexual assignation' and 'flippin' in the same sentence! "Calm down, sweetie, there isn't any reason in the world why anyone would jump to that conclusion. It's just your guilty conscious acting up. Here," he said gently, "put your clothes on and get going."

A little calmer, she did as she was told. Fast!

"Don't go in with me," she told him.

"Not a problem. Once you are safely inside, I'm outta here."

"Good. I'll talk to you in class later." She was talking fast as her bathroom date was becoming more urgent.

"I'm coming over with lunch, okay?" Barely hearing him, she said, "Uh-huh," as she dashed out of his car and into the building. Jake watched her until she disappeared. A big goofy smile was plastered on his face.

After her car sexcapade with Jake, Akeema had just enough time to shower, change, and wolf down a bowl of cereal. She hadn't had a morsel of food since lunch yesterday, so she was past ravenous.

Just as she was slurping the milk out of the bowl, her phone rang. She let it ring until the last drop of milk was running down her throat.

"Hello," she answered, licking her lips.

"Hey, Akeema, It's Brett, Shabbat Shalom!"

"Shabbat Shalom, Brett, what's up?"

"We have a couple of visitors today. I wanted to see if you're okay with doing question and answer day."

"I never object to that – if we have enough questions. Sometimes the visitors are shy and quiet. You should be prepared with a lesson plan in case mum's the word."

"Agreed. I've got that covered. We'll start in about ten minutes?"

"Yep. See you then. Bye for now."

"Later."

CHAPTER 16

After prayer, a praise song, and introductions, the Sabbath service was ready to start.

Brett: Since we are blessed with visitors today, we'd like to get to know them better and let them know us. So, we will give testimonies about how Yahuah, our Heavenly Father, got us to this point. Akeema, shall we start with you?

Akeema: I, like most of us, have a Christian background. But there was a time when I let man test my faith. When the Pastor of our church got a single woman pregnant, I was done with the church. I never stopped believing in the Most High, but accepting men as my spiritual leader and teacher was part of my past. I wish I could say that I studied the Word for myself during that time, but I didn't. I bumped into this Bible study and ended up staying. I love studying from the Hebrew root to get a more in-depth understanding of the Word.

I'm convicted that our Heavenly Father led me here." (a chorus of Amens was said by most)

Brett: Thank you, my sister. I understand that one of our visitors is a friend of yours.

Akeema: Yes, a brand-new friend. Right, Joseph?

Joseph: Yes, but you were my son's friend first. Joey let me know that you are more than just his teacher to him. I'm so thankful for that.

Akeema: With little Joey and me it's a mutual love fest. Please share your experience with our Father and His son.

Joseph: Like Akeema I have a Christian beginning. We were 7th Day Baptists.

Amy: I've never heard of 7th Day Baptists, only Adventists.

Jesse: Being in my 70's now, I heard of them. My grandparents checked them out for a while.

Joseph: Except for praising, worshipping, and fellowshipping on Saturdays, the doctrine was Baptist.

Clem: Were the food laws observed?

Joseph: No. To me it was man picking and choosing what felt good to them. When I got grown, I studied the Word for myself and made the choice to leave.

Amy: Your wife was okay with that?

Joseph: I hadn't met her yet.

Amy: Is she with you today?

Joseph: No. She passed away about ten months ago. (Surprised gasps and sympathy platitudes followed. Joseph resisted the urge to leave)

Amy: I'm sorry, Joseph. So you are raising your son alone?

Joseph: Yes, I am.

Amy: That must be hard on you.

Akeema: Joey is a wonderful child. I know how great he is because I'm with him eight hours a day, five days a week as his teacher.

Joseph: Thank you, Akeema, we feel blessed to have you as his teacher and our friend.

Brett: So, did you have a spiritual family to help you through your grief?

Joseph: No, I must be honest and admit that I was angry with the Lord for my wife's death. I took the loss for me and my boy. It's been rough.

Brett: Praise the Most High for getting you here today, my brother!

Joseph: He used Akeema as His vessel to get me here. My trust in her as a person helped me decide to check in on this study. I figured if she was a product of this group, I should at least see what it's about for myself.

Brett: We are thankful to have you with us, Joseph. I pray that your spirit and life will be fed.

Joseph: Thank you. I am enjoying it so far.

Brett: Praise Yahuah! Now, let's see. Mary, you have a guest too, is that right?

Mary: Yes, I do. She's Rachel and she's new to our school.

Brett: Welcome, Rachel! Tell us a little bit about your spiritual journey.

Rachel: My foster parents have me helping with the other eight siblings that I have. After we ate, I cleaned up the kitchen, so I don't have to be back home until 6:00 this evening.

Brett: Do you want to share with us the status of your natural parents?

Rachel: My mother married a man who attacked me. When I told her about it, she didn't believe me! She told me I needed to apologize for the lie against her husband. I refused. Before he could hurt me again, I left home.

Clem: Praise our Father for guiding you here through your fellowship with Mary.

Rachel: Amen! I consider Mary a blessing from our Father. I'm expected to help with my foster brothers and sisters, and I don't mind. I don't worry about being sexually attacked anymore. That's what's important to me.

Mary: I'm one of her first friends. I feel that I'm supposed to be there for her, spiritually as well.

Rachel: I'm busy, but my foster parents also give me private time. I'm expected back at 6:00 pm to help with the preparation of dinner.

Clem: Do you cook, Rachel?

Rachel: Yes, it's a hobby of mine.

Brett: May I ask a personal question?

Rachel: You can ask – but if it's too personal, I may not answer.

Brett: Understood. Did you file a police report against your mother's husband?

Rachel: No. I just wanted out!

Brett: I understand. But, if you ever want to go to the authorities, Akeema and I will work with your foster parents to get that done.

Rachel (bows her head): Thank you, sir.

Brett: You are quite welcome. Please know that each member in our class will keep you in our prayers.

(Rachel nodded and fell silent)

Clem: Does anyone have anything they'd like to share with the class?

(Nobody said anything, but everyone could be seen on screen as they shook their heads no)

Brett: Well, let's have a little Bible fun, shall we?

Mary: Bible fun? Is there such a thing?

Brett (Chuckle): It depends on the person. Everyone has their own brand of humor, of course. Today, we are going to address some everyday issues that some of you might be surprised that the Word tackles.

Rachel: Like what?

Brett: I get a kick out of a problem that Jesse once had.

Please tell the class about it, sir.

Jesse: My missus has gone to glory now, but the sixty-something years we were together were happy ones.

Mary: Married over sixty years? How old are you, if you don't mind my asking?

Jesse: Not at all. I'm 95. (Mary and Rachel were stunned, their mouths wide open).

Akeema (astonished): Brother Jesse, you don't look 70, let alone ninety-five! You are a very blessed child of the Most High.

Jesse (nods): That I am. I take the good with the bad, knowing that I am not in charge.

Akeema: What bad? Are you sick? If you are, you are hiding it very well.

Jesse: For an old codger, I'm doing well. But, I've out-lived my wife and my children. I would have gladly gone in their places.

Akeema (sadly): I understand how you feel. I lost both my parents at the same time. It was rough. If I wasn't a person of faith, I might have joined them by committing suicide.

Jesse: I heard that! I can't tell you how many times I went to sleep at night with a prayer to wake up on the other side.

Mary (under her breath): Are we having fun yet?

Brett (smiles): These testimonials give us an example of the ups and downs in life, and how our Father is with us through it all. (enthusiastic 'Amens' are shouted)

Akeema: I'm sorry for getting us a little off track. Brother Jesse, please continue what you started.

Jesse: Okey-dokey, I'll try to focus on one thing at a time folks. As I was saying, my wife and I had a long and happy marriage. But it was a little bumpy at first while we were getting to know each other.

Jake: I have a feeling we are about to have fun.

Jesse: I admit I have fond memories of making my point by using the Word.

Amy: How so?

Jesse: For starters, I'm a person who is slow to wake up in the mornings. I'm not very people friendly at the start of my day.

Akeema: Lots of people are like that. Why was this a problem for you and yours?

Jesse: I didn't know until our honeymoon that my beautiful new wife started her day with a song and a smile. <u>Every</u> day!

Clem: Uh-oh!

Jesse: Uh-oh is right! We were like oil and water getting on each other's nerves from the moment we woke up. By the time our honeymoon was over, we were considering a divorce!

Rachel: Wasn't that supposed to be a hyper-romantic time for you guys?

Mary: Yeah, man. How do you fix something like that?

Jesse: I prayed, as I'm sure she did. Finally, we stopped feeling ashamed long enough to seek help from our Pastor.

Joseph: Why were you ashamed? During our courtship we got along so well that we ignored the advice to get pre-marital counseling. We were too big for our britches, I'm afraid.

Amy: Did you guys talk about it so that a compromise could be reached?

Jesse: Oh, sure. I asked if she could be a little quieter in the morning, and if she would please not start the day dancing to the loud radio. I was about to rip out her vocal cords by the time we'd only been married for a month!

Brett: What was her reaction to your requests?

Jesse: Maisie let me know that I was being petty, picky, and that I needed to get over it. She told me that she wasn't going to be unhappy every day in order to make me happy.

Amy: Oh, dear.

Jesse: For a while it was like Mission Impossible at our house.

Jake: I'm dying to know how the pastor helped.

Jesse: After patiently listening to both sides, he hit us with the scripture: Proverbs 27:14.

Brett: Let's all turn to that scripture, please. Who would like to read today?

Rachel: I'd love to read, but I'm new to the class so I don't have the Hebrew translation.

Brett: That isn't a problem. Just let us know what version you're reading from.

Rachel: I have the New Living Translation and it reads, 'A loud and cheerful greeting early in the morning will be taken as a curse!' Wow, who'd a thunk it?

Jake: That's hilarious!

Joseph: If I ever get married again, I'm gonna remember Proverbs 27:14, that's for sure!

Akeema: Does that apply to you?

Joseph: It does, but raising a son makes me smother my morning irritation.

Akeema: Being a teacher of little ones put me in the same boat with you.

Joseph: It's nice to know we have that in common.

Brett: It goes to show you that no problem is too small to be addressed in the Word.

Amy: It also shows that humanity is more alike than different.

Brett: Agreed. On that note, let's sing a couple of praise songs. After that, we'll take prayer requests.

After service was over, everyone got off-line except Akeema and Joseph.

"So, did you enjoy the study today?" she asked.

"I did, Akeema. Thank you for inviting me. I'm pretty sure I'm going to join you guys again next week."

"That's wonderful! I look forward to the fellowship with you."

"Me too you. When ballet season starts, how does Sabbath fit in with your performances?"

"My contract gives me that day off."

"Really? When you have the lead, who takes your place on the weekend?"

"I only have Shabbat, Sabbath, off. I dance on Sundays. And, I don't get the lead positions."

"That doesn't seem fair."

"It's the welcome price I pay."

"Isn't it a dream of yours to be out front in the spotlight?"

Promptly, Akeema responded, "My dream is to dance and teach. Through Yahuah's blessings, I'm doing both. To be the headliner would interfere with my Shabbat and my kids."

Joseph shook his head in wonder. "You're something else, you know that?"

"We all are."

"I guess it's how you look at it. Listen, before we sign off, I have a little guy who would like to speak to you."

Smiling, Akeema felt her heart sing. "Alright! Where is Joey?"

"Here I am!" he yelled.

"It's good to see you, partner! Are you having a good day?"

"Yes, ma'am. I'm gonna fix me and daddy a bowl of cereal. What are you eatin'?"

"A friend is on his way over with food. He's going to surprise me."

"Have fun, teacher Akeema!"

"Thanks, sweetheart! I hope you and your dad have a fun day too!"

"Bye!" Father and son said in unison.

Jake looked sullen. Sitting next to each other at her kitchen island, Akeema was perplexed.

The on-line Bible study went well, and the spinach quiche they'd eaten for their late lunch, was simply delicious. She was hesitant to ask him what was wrong because she wanted to secure her Shabbat peace. Rather than argue she chose silence.

Finally, she stepped out on safe ground. She hoped. "Thanks for the quiche, Jake. I really think it's the best I've ever had."

He nodded, saying nothing.

Sighing, she stood to throw away the trash and wipe the counter tops. It was then that she noticed the absence of extra food. Jake always brought more grub for dinner, or for lunch the next day. Something was absolutely wrong. "Do you want to watch some Biblical movies, or do you have other plans?"

S-l-o-w-l-y Jake turned to face her. His glare was ice cold. Her calm holy day was about to bite the dust.

"I don't plan on staying long." His voice was low, ominous.

She tried to get him out of her place without incident. "Okay, then I won't hold you up. Have a blessed day. If you get some free time later, maybe we can touch base again."

She turned to walk to the front door to see him out. He grabbed her by the wrist, stopping her in her tracks.

"We need to talk," he said. His voice was barely above a whisper. She recognized he was exercising his newfound control over yelling at her. It certainly proved to her that he had the ability to threaten her without raising his voice.

Akeema stiffened her spine and lifted her chin. She refused to show him fear. Her eyes moved down to his hand that still gripped her wrist. She remained mute. She didn't look at him again until he let her go. Once he did, she met his steely gaze with one of her own. Game on.

As was her way, she didn't beat around the bush. "What has happened to bring on this frosty attitude?"

Jake looked mildly surprised. "You don't know?"

"Obviously not!"

He stood up to stand right in front of her with his muscular arms crossed over his chest. "What was all that one-on-one visitation with that Joseph guy?"

Puzzled, she asked, "What are you talking about?"

"Part of the class was spent listening to you and your 'friend' have a one-on-one visit."

She relaxed. A little. "Since I invited him to join us, I felt it was my duty to make him feel like one of us. He seemed to feel comfortable."

"Yeah, with your undivided attention."

"That's just how you looked at it. There wasn't a single other person in the class that felt I was favoring him, Jake."

"Is he a dancer?"

He saw the briefest of a smile touch her face.

"No."

"Where did you meet him?"

"He's the father of one of my favorite students. I told you about him. He's the widower."

"Oh, yeah, I remember." He admitted.

"I don't have anything to hide from you where men are concerned."

He heard her. "But, you have plenty of other things that you hide?"

Akeema tilted her head up to meet his gaze steadily. "At this point in our relationship, I've elected not to tell you everything about my life."

"Why?" he dared to ask.

"It's something I've never done with men that I date. So far, when our time together is done, I've been glad that over really means <u>over</u>."

"So, when you start telling me things like who your friends and family are, I'll know you see us as something that will last?"

"<u>IF</u> I start telling you, then yes."

He stepped closer to her without a touch. He could feel her body heat and smell her body freshness that was always a part of her.

"I have a feeling that I see a long-time affair here that you don't."

She nodded that he was right.

"I'll be with you for however long it takes to convince you that I'm your present and your future."

"Wow, that's deep. I'm not feeling any of that."

"You will, trust me."

The confident way he spoke unnerved her. Did he know something she didn't know? She wanted him to be somewhere she wasn't.

"Well, homeboy, I'm bushed. I need a nap in the worst way. I've got six hours of rehearsal in the morning, and this is my only day to recharge my batteries."

"I understand. I know this is Sabbath so I can't grope you in any way. But may I kiss you goodbye at least?"

Akeema took a few moments to ponder this. She knew her attraction to him was massive. But she wasn't about to risk hitting the sheets on Shabbat!

"A smack on the cheek is okay."

"A smack on the cheek? I didn't know you were into that. Turn around."

She looked at him blankly. Akeema was nowhere near knowing what he was talking about.

Jake couldn't hold it in. First, he smiled. Then he chuckled. Finally, he laughed…a long time.

She expected him to tell her what was so funny. He didn't.

It wasn't the first time that Akeema thought he was a strange white boy.

CHAPTER 17

"**1**-2-3 STOP!" barked Barney.

Akeema and the other dancers did as they were told because nobody wanted to die.

"Sway gracefully to the left and STOP!"

Again, the dancers did what they were told. For all of their exertions, everybody barely breathed.

"Ladies, center stage!" Barney watched as they floated into position. Good.

"Everybody else, form your line then circle around them. Listen to the music, people! Watch your timing!"

And on and on and on. By noon, everyone was exhausted and famished. Akeema declined lunch invitations because she desperately needed a shower. She had no desire to sit across from lunch dates who needed the same thing. If she didn't want to smell her workout funk, she sure didn't want to eat while smelling theirs!

Since she needed to go to the store for some salad fixings, Akeema went to the lady's room for a quick spruce up and simple change into a blouse and leggings in a muted gray. She was officially ready for the world.

As she walked across the parking lot to her car, she heard her name being called. Turning toward the voice, she heard, "Teacher Akeema, teacher Akeema!"

Joey!

She heard his footsteps as he ran to her, jumping into her open arms. She whirled him around, loving the feel and the little boy scent of him.

"What are you doing here, honey? Where's your daddy?" "Daddy's behind you, Akeema." Said a man's voice. Transferring Joey to her hip, she turned to face Joseph.

"Hi there! You guys just happen to be passing by?"

Before Joseph could respond, his son exclaimed, "We have a surprise!"

"I see that. You two are the surprise. A really good one," she smiled.

"Are you hungry by any chance?"

"Ravenous, actually."

"Great, because we have food."

"Surprise!" Joey yelled.

Smiling broadly, Joseph said, "Please follow me to our restaurant on wheels."

Shifting a now heavy Joey to her other hip, Akeema obediently followed Joseph to his baby blue van. First, Joseph opened the back passenger door for his son to take a seat. Then, he gallantly opened the front passenger door to help Akeema in – even though she didn't really need his assistance.

Once she settled in, she watched Joseph as he hurriedly walked to the driver's side to sit next to her. Only then did she notice the brown paper bags on the floor-board next to his feet.

Looking over his right shoulder, he asked Joey to give him the tray laying on the seat next to him.

Joseph heard Akeema's surprised gasp when he pulled out the biggest salad known to man or woman. He even had a choice of three different salad dressings for her to choose from. In the back seat, an excited Joey said, "Me and daddy got you the hugest salad we could find!"

Akeema laughed. "I can see that!" She looked at Joseph. "Is there meat in it?"

He nodded. "Yes, and I remembered you eat the clean foods, so I asked that they replace the chopped ham with turkey. Is that alright?"

Akeema's mouth watered. "It's perfect. Let me at it!"

Joseph complied. He and Joey had tuna fish sand-wiches and potato chips. Everybody had cranpine-apple juice to drink. Akeema suggested that Joey say grace over the food. The little boy was thrilled that she trusted him to do it.

"We thank You, Father, for this food. We love You because You take care of us. Please say hi to my mommy for me, in Your perfect Son's name, Amen!"

Both Joseph and Akeema had to choke back tears.

Only half-kidding, Akeema asked, "What's for dessert?"

Little Joey had a BIG voice. "Apples! We have lots of apples!"

After her ears stopped ringing, she asked for hers. She loved watching Joey chomping on an apple with his snaggle-tooth.

The grown-ups let the little chatterbox have the floor. They heard about his pet frog that he named Roscoe, and that Joseph knew nothing about. Appalled, Akeema asked what Joseph couldn't find the words to say. "Does your frog live in the house?"

"Of course not!" he scoffed. "Only me and daddy live in the house. Roscoe lives outside on the patio."

Akeema saw a relieved Joseph hold his forehead in his hand. She managed to contain the giggle that was trying to come out.

"Does Roscoe have a family?" she asked. Her imp was alive and well. The panic on Joseph's face was priceless.

"No, teacher Akeema. He hasn't got a wife yet!"

"Silly me. I wasn't thinking. Thanks for bringing me up to date. Please say hi to Roscoe for me the next time you see him."

Joey bobbed his head up and down. "I will! I told him all about you!"

"You did? What did you say about me?"

"I said you're nice, pretty, my teacher, and that I wish my daddy would marry you!" he said as a matter of fact.

Joseph moaned loudly. This was the first time he'd heard any of this. He doubted that Akeema would believe him. If the ground opened to swallow him, he'd be okay with that.

When Akeema spoke to Joey, her voice was gentle.

"Thank you, sweet boy. Those are nice things to say about me. I like you a whole lot too."

"Do you like my daddy too?"

"I sure do. I consider the two of you, my friends."

He clapped his little hands with joy. "Did you hear her daddy? She's our friend!"

"Yes, son, I heard her. Teacher Akeema is our friend, and we are her's."

"God gave us to each other, right?"

"I believe He's glad we're friends."

"Will you marry her so that we can live together?"

"Uh…we're just friends, buddy. We're not boy-friend and girlfriend."

The tot frowned, confused. "Don't you want her to be your girlfriend?"

"Well…she and I would both have to want to be together as more than friends."

Joey was a quick study. He immediately turned his attention to Akeema. "Teacher Akeema, would you like to be my daddy's girlfriend?"

Akeema hedged, "Maybe one day. But, right now, I have a boyfriend."

"Can daddy be your boyfriend too?"

"Joey," Joseph started to warn, "It's not polite to…"

"That's okay. He can ask me anything. I like it like this."

"Okay, if you're sure."

"I am."Turning her attention back to Joey she said, "I only like one boyfriend at a time. And I like for my boyfriend to have only me as his girlfriend."

Joey frowned. "It's like having only one wife at a time?"

Akeema nodded. "Yes, as far as I'm concerned."

"Me too," Joseph chimed in.

"If you and your boyfriend stop choosing each other, will my daddy get his turn to be with you?"

Akeema answered him as she and Joseph locked eyes.

"Yes, if he wants a turn."

"He does, Akeema," replied Joseph.

Gazing at each other, Joey's dad and Joey's teacher realized they each meant it.

Before she could put her key in her front door, Akeema heard someone call her name from a distance. Jake.

She was still basking in the 'Joseph and son' glow. She wasn't ready for it to end.

Looking toward the parking lot, she saw him coming her way. Akeema put a smile on her face that she didn't feel.

When he reached her, she opened the door for them to walk in. Her plan to shower and nap was dead. Walking behind her, Jake said, "I've been here for a while. Did rehearsal last longer than usual?" For a second, she considered lying.

"It was long enough, believe me." She groaned while stretching her long, toned limbs. "We were all hungry afterward, so we went to eat."

"Oh, I see," he said while moving closer to her.

He pulled her next to him by grabbing her by the waist.

"I need a shower and a nap. Don't get any closer unless you plan on holding your breath."

Jake inhaled deeply. "I love your special brand of stink," he breathed into her ear, making Akeema shiver. She moaned in dismay. No matter how weary she was, this man always made her body come to life.

"How 'bout you and I take that shower together so that I can give those tired muscles of yours a nice, wet, slippery massage." His teeth gently nibbled on her ear. She felt tingles all the way down to her toes. Her resistance against him was fading fast. "Jake, I need to go to bed…to sleep," she whispered weakly, "I need to recharge my batteries." He ran his tongue down her throat. He pulled her hard against him for full body contact.

"Let me charge up your battery first," he said huskily. He kissed her long and hard. They never made it to the shower.

An hour later, Akeema lay in Jake's arms, sexually sated and thirsty. Listening to his heartbeat, she marveled, once again, at her body's response to him. She couldn't understand why her heart wasn't in on it. Joseph entered her mind. What a time to think of another man! Even Jake didn't deserve that.

Akeema shoved Joseph out of her mind as quickly and thoroughly as she could.

"Are you hungry, baby?" he asked

"Uh-uh. The salad I had earlier was huge. I could use something cold to drink. How about you?"

Jake smiled. "I'm trying to imagine getting full on lettuce," he joked.

"For your information, mister, that salad had much more than lettuce in it. Now, this morning I made a huge pitcher of lemonade that should be ice cold by now. Would you like a glass?"

"Mmm, sounds good."

"Okay. Stay comfortable, I'll go get it."

"Thanks. If you see a steak to go with that drink, I'll be ever so grateful."

"You'd also be witnessing a miracle!"

By the time Akeema came back to the bedroom, Jake was sleeping soundly. He looked innocent and adorable. At that moment, she liked him a lot. Of course, she had to wonder why she liked him the most when he wasn't talking or interacting with her. Oh, well.

She sat the tray she was carrying down on her side of the bed. All it took to wake him was a light touch of her hand on his chiseled bicep. Slowly, Jake opened his eyes.

"Hey," he said drowsily.

"Hey, yourself. If I knew you were going to go to sleep on me, I wouldn't have made you a tray."

Yawning, he forced himself to focus. He was so hungry that the huge bowl of soup with melted cheese on top looked simply delicious. Along with the lemonade in a frosted glass, there was a cup with chunks of honey dew melon in it. Ambrosia! Leaning over, he kissed her thankfully before placing the tray on his lap to dig in. Akeema sat quietly, drinking and watching Jake chow down.

"What made you think to put melted cheese on top of the soup?" he garbled.

"Your love of cheese," she replied simply.

"Okay, smarty. I have to admit I've never had it like this before."

"Is it good?"

He looked down at the half-eaten bowl of goodness.

"Absolutely!"

"Good," she yawned.

Jake put the spoon down to pat her side of the bed.

"You look beautiful, but tired. Hop in and lay down.

When I'm done, I'll clean up these dishes. I know how neat you like things."

She smiled at his thoughtfulness. "Thanks, Jake, but don't worry about it. I want to see you out so that I can lock up," she replied, then yawned again. He frowned, confused. "You think I'm leaving?"

"Yes."

"Why?"

"Because you are. That is, after you finish eating."

He ate another spoonful. "I'm prepared to spend the night."

"I'm not asking you to."

"I don't mind. I can get up early to get home to change clothes for work."

Eyes closed, Akeema dropped her head, chin to chest. She tried to talk herself out of the talk she knew they needed to have. She was way too tired to offer up much compassion.

"I need alone time, Jake. Remember, this is a pop-up visit, I didn't invite you here."

He knew she was tired. While he quickly ate his soup, he thought he could have his way to spend the night. The melon was sweet and refreshing. His plan was to eat it all before he made love to her again. After blessing her with more orgasms, she wouldn't ask him to leave.

"I know sweetie. I came to take you out to eat, that's all. But you're so sexy my plan changed. I'd like to be with you as much as I can." He watched her reactions to what he'd said. Akeema didn't raise her head or open her eyes. However, he did hear her take a deep breath. Maybe she was giving it some serious consideration.

Slowly she stood up. Without saying a word, she went straight to the bathroom. Closing the door behind her, it was mere seconds before he heard the shower. "Yes!" he exclaimed.

Quickly, he finished his fruit. Then he bolted out of bed to wash the dishes. By the time Akeema came back to bed Jake had remade it. When he saw her, he turned down the top sheet to welcome her back. She gave him a tepid smile because that's all she thought she had the energy for. Neither spoke as Jake began to slowly and gently make love to her with his mouth and his hands. He instinctively knew that she wasn't receptive to being messed up after she'd just cleaned up. She screamed his name when her body convulsed with deep, deep pleasure. Afterward, she fell into a coma-like sleep. Jake looked at her lovingly. He had no intention of ever being without her.

CHAPTER 18

For Akeema, the next few weeks were extremely busy ones. For the children, the troop was dancing to 'Little Red Riding Hood,' of all things. The male dancer was going to perform in a wolf suit. Her costume was that of a sleek black panther. She had a twenty second solo that she was obsessing over. Akeema was almost always part of a trio or more. She got teased by the other dancers for being typecast.

School was over for the day, and she knew the last pupil to say goodbye would be Joey. Lately, the little rascal made sure he was alone with her every day. She loved that their time alone together was as special to him as it was to her. From the paperwork on her desk, she looked up to bid him farewell. What she saw made her smile. Joey was picking up the toys for her so that she wouldn't have to.

"Thank you, Joey. You're so nice to do that for me."

"You're welcome, teacher Akeema."

"Is your dad waiting for you? I don't want you to get in trouble with him."

Joey stopped working, a look of uncertainty on his face.

Akeema reassured him. "Come, Let's finish together before we both go meet your father, okay?" She was rewarded with his beautiful gap-toothed smile.

That's it, Joseph thought. School was over at least twenty minutes ago. He needed to go see what the problem was. He got out of his car, jogging to the giant double doors. He was about to grab the handle when the door opened, almost hitting him. Before him stood both Akeema and his son.

"Hey Daddy!" Joey said before jumping into Joseph's arms.

"How's my boy?"

"Fine! How you doin'?"

"Great now that I see you!"

Akeema listened to their exchange, loving every minute of it.

As soon as Joseph put Joey down, he extended his hand to shake hers.

"Hello, there. I'm glad to see you," he said warmly. Pleasantly, Akeema replied, "Likewise, I'm sure. I walked Joey out since he was kind enough to help me pick up after the other kids. He's my champion of the day!" She followed her announcement by playfully rubbing the top of his head.

"I wondered where he was. I was just on my way to find out."

"I'm sorry. He was late because of me."

"Nonsense, he did what I would have done."

"I appreciate you guys. Have a good one." She turned to go back to her classroom.

"Wait!" Joseph called out urgently.

Turning back around to face him, Akeema stood silently, waiting for him to speak.

"I saw in the paper that your ballet group was putting on a show next week."

She smiled and nodded.

"Will you be in it?"

"Yep," she said. Then, lowering her voice in a feline-like purr, she continued, "I play a black panther."

Joseph's heart skipped a beat. Or two.

"Daddy, what's a panther?"

Never taking his eyes off Akeema, he responded, "A big, black, cat-like animal that lives in the jungle."

Excited, Joey jumped up and down while clapping his hands. "Can we go see teacher Akeema dance like a cat?"

When Joseph didn't answer him quick enough, Joey persisted. "Daddy, please! Can we go?"

Snapping out of his daze, Joseph looked down at his anxious little one. "As long as it's not on a school night, son."

Promptly, Akeema chimed in. "There are two shows on Sunday. The first performance is a matinee."

"Perfect," Joseph said looking pointedly at her. Then, to Joey he smiled. "Well, partner, we're going to see your teacher, and our friend, dance."

"Yay!"

Akeema and Joseph laughed at Joey's exuberance. Inside themselves, they were as excited as he was. Even more so.

To Akeema, her drive time was her downtime. Therefore, she was surprised when her cell rang when she was on her way to rehearsal. It was Jake.

"Hello, beautiful. How's it going?"

"Alright, what's up?"

"I wanted you to see that I listened to you last night about popping up uninvited."

Oh-oh. Did he want to see her two days in a row? Emotionally, she wasn't interested. But, to her ever-present shame, her girlie parts twitched in anticipation.

"Good," she replied shortly.

"Do you and the other dancers have plans for dinner after rehearsal?"

"We rarely plan ahead, Jake. After we're done, we see how we feel and go from there."

"Well, since you hung out with them yesterday, I thought maybe I could be with you tonight."

Oops! She'd nearly forgot that she'd allowed him to assume she was with her peers instead of Joey and his dad.

"As it turned out, I was with everybody. Each of you got an exhausted part of me." She was in no mood to let him act like he'd been shortchanged in some way. She didn't feel like he was owed anything.

Jake knew immediately that the pity game wasn't going to work. There was a downside to having a girlfriend who was smart and quick on her feet – no pun intended.

"Aw now, baby," he cajoled, "I'm not trying to insinuate that you owe me anything special. I'm just greedy where you're concerned. The more of you that I have, is the more of you that I want." He said this in a voice that gave Akeema goosebumps. Her body was screaming at her to let him loose on her, to let him do whatever he wanted to do to her…for as long as he wanted to do it. She didn't trust herself to speak.

Jake asked, "You still there, sweetie?"

"Yes," she croaked, not sounding like herself at all.

He knew she was softening. Jake went for the jugular. "It gave me great pleasure to give you pleasure. Even though you were the only one climaxing, I totally understood, to a point. It pleased me to please you."

Memories from the night before came flooding back. Akeema had to stifle her moan of arousal. "I didn't ask for all that, homeboy," she said tartly. "I seem to remember inviting you out before anything was done."

He heard the edge in her tone. He didn't want to have an argument of any kind with her. As corny as it sounded, he wanted to make love not war. He didn't raise his voice one iota. He calmly pointed out the facts. "My love, I knew how wiped out you were. Did you sleep better after I finished touching you?" She couldn't deny it.

"Oh, yes!" she sighed.

"Good. That makes me happy. Now, not to be tacky in any way, I need you to please consider how hard it's going to be for us to physically be alone together." He paused to let that sink in before he continued. "We don't make love on Shabbats, and this Sunday will be your first performance of the new season."

Akeema's body yelled at her for satisfaction. If they didn't get together this week, she didn't know when they would.

"I'll see you tonight for dinner and sex," she said bluntly before disconnecting.

Akeema and Jake fell back on her bed, sweaty and sated. They were both in good shape, so it wasn't long before their breathing returned to normal. They lay next to each other without touching. Jake murmured, "I've never had this with anyone else."

"Me either," Akeema admitted.

"I used to think the term 'soulmate' was a corny expression. Now I think, if the shoe fits, wear 'em."

Akeema rolled her eyes. "I'm not gonna ask you to explain any of that."

"It's not a problem. Let's talk about it again in a decade or so."

In the darkened room, she squinted to see him. "You think we'll be together in ten years?"

"I do."

"Why?"

"Because of how we feel about each other, and the fact that we're so compatible," he responded.

"You can only say how 'you' feel about 'me.' Unless I tell you how I feel, you don't know."

Turning his head toward her voice, Jake said, "Of course I do."

"Why do you think you know?"

"Because of how you treat me and respond to me."

"In general, I'm nice to people who are nice to me. You are a satisfying lover, so my body responds to you. None of that means we're madly in love with each other."

"Speak for yourself."

"I thought I was."

"You spoke for me too. Thought you said we couldn't do that."

Akeema stretched, yawning long and loudly. "How about something cold and wet."

"I'm in on that. Let's go."

Naked, they strolled to the kitchen, still not touching. Pulling out the large pitcher full of lemonade, Akeema asked, "Ice with yours?"

"However you are having it, is good for me."

"Natural it is then," she announced.

Curiously, Jake asked, "Why don't you ever have cold beer around?"

Licking the sweetness from her lips, she replied, "I don't drink beer. During the off season I might have a wine spritzer every now and then, but that's it. I don't buy sodas because I like having a natural drink with sugar that I can control."

Jake nodded. Her answer was simple, logical, and wonderful. Like she was. On their wedding day he'd tell her that.

"Are you hungry?"

Wide-eyed, Jake said, "Don't tell me you are going to cook!"

"Okay."

Jake waited for more. He didn't get it.

"Um, I could snack on a little something," he finally said. "What 'cha got?"

"Popcorn hot off the presses."

"Will you put butter on it?" he asked hopefully.

"I'll put some on <u>yours</u>. I must abstain."

"How about I eat it with butter, then kiss you long, hard, and deeply," he whispered suggestively.

Akeema laughed, enjoying their banter. "You manage to make the simplest of things sound erotic."

Jake shrugged. "I'm just gifted, I guess."

They both knew he was only half kidding.

As they munched on popcorn at Akeema's kitchen island, her cell rang. Jake was surprised since that hadn't ever happened when he was there. He'd assumed she kept the phone muted.

She was as surprised as he was. It didn't ever occur to her to read the caller I.D.

"Hello?"

"Hey, baby girl! How ya doin'?"

Whoops, it was Aunt Jean. Akeema was so busy that she'd forgotten to call her – or go wash.

"Hey yourself!" she said without saying a name. She still wasn't comfortable letting Jake know that she had family in town.

Akeema left Jake in the kitchen by himself. She went to the bathroom, shut the door, then turned on the faucet at the sink.

Aunt Jean asked, "Are you cleaning up?"

"No, ma'am. Jake is here so I'm in the bathroom for privacy."

"Ugh. I wish you were through with that boy."

"I know, Auntie. Just give it time. For right now, we're getting along okay."

"Then, I won't hold you for long on this call. Have you bought a new wardrobe or are you using one of your rooms to put all your dirty clothes in?"

Akeema rolled her eyes. "I'm sorry. I've been crazy busy with work and rehearsals. I admit that I did go to the store to buy extra clothes to workout in."

"Your uncle and I will come over tomorrow, while you're at work, to get your dirties. Where are they?"

Akeema squealed, delighted. "In the mudroom, as usual. I have the white basket for the whites and the blue basket for the colors. The socks are already paired together."

"You might have a mess, but at least it's an organized one."

"I was taught well."

Feeling warmed by the sweet compliment, she quickly changed the subject. "Your uncle is here. Say hi before we hang up."

"Hey pretty one!" her uncle said. "How's my favorite girl?"

"Better since hearing your voice. How are you?"

"Better for the same reason."

Akeema jumped when Jake knocked on the door. She hoped she remembered to lock it. She didn't. He burst into the room so loudly that her aunt and uncle heard him with no problem. In her ear she heard her Uncle Rick ask if she needed him to come over. She quickly assured them that she could handle things before she hung up. She put on her best actress hat to show Jake a calm she didn't feel on the inside. He looked like he wanted to hit her – or worse.

"Since when do you come in on me when the door is shut? I don't do that to you."

With his hands in tight fists by his side, Jake said through clenched teeth, "I knocked."

"Yeah, but you didn't wait until I said you could come in."

"What are you trying to hide behind closed doors?"

Now, she could feel her temper rising. Now, she was clenching her teeth. "<u>Whatever</u> I want to." Akeema looked into his cold eyes. She made her eyes the same.

"Who were you talking to that you wanted to hide from me?"

"None of your business." She watched in morbid fascination as his white neck got pinker, then redder. The scarlet color traveled upward until his entire face and ears, matched his neck. She knew Jake was furious. Incredulous, he responded in a low, menacing voice. "What did you say to me?"

"None ya," she replied flippantly.

As he slowly walked toward her, Akeema realized she was facing the door so that she'd have to go past him or through him – to get out. She made herself not step backward.

"That's not funny," he said – still no voice raised.

"Listen, a friend called me. We talked then hung up. Over and out."

"Why won't you tell me who he was?"

Akeema's eyebrows lifted. "Why do you think it was a he?"

"Wasn't it?"

"Not entirely," she replied honestly.

"We agreed not to see other people."

"Romantically, I see only you. Sexually, there's only you."

Jake's head was about to explode. His world was almost all Akeema. He wanted to be that important to her. His anger was ebbing into major frustration.

Akeema saw his hands de-fist. She relaxed. A little.

"Let me just say outright, Akeema, that I want to know the people that are important to you."

She had nothing to lose by being truthful about this. "Listen to me, Jake. I'm not, nor have I ever been, the type of woman who parades her dates around to everyone I know. I'm basically a very private person."

"I get that. But it leaves me feeling like I'm on the outside of your life."

"In some ways you are. It's the same in reverse."

He shook his index finger at her as he pointed out, "Yeah, but the difference is that I've tried to introduce you to my friends, but <u>you</u> are the one who says NO! And please don't forget that you've met my parents already! I haven't met any of your relatives."

Jake was animated, not angry. Akeema could handle this.

"If you knew them, you'd be glad that they weren't in your life. They're sweet, old-fashioned, and nosy," she smiled.

"I think I'd like that," he replied shyly.

"You don't really know that until you have my loved ones butting into your business on my behalf."

"Akeema, I'd like to be the one to decide if I can put up with it or not."

She stared him down. "I have to be as sure as I can that you <u>will</u> stand it. I will not have my people hurt because you decide you want me, but not them."

He walked closer to her; their nude bodies were giving off heat that they both felt without touching. Akeema's pulse began to race.

"If getting you is a package deal, I'm all in."

She closed her eyes, hating her traitor of a body. "You make me feel all melty, even without touching me," she said in a low sultry voice.

He took one more step so that their naked chests grazed each other. "It's our chemistry, baby."

Moaning, she whined, "How can we argue one minute then make love the next?"

"Like this," he rasped. The bathroom floor welcomed their heated bodies.

"Can it be happening this quickly?" she gasped between breaths.

Jake shouted, "You tell me!"

In a matter of seconds, Akeema screamed, "Yes, yes!"

With him on top of her, she was suddenly aware of the hard floor on her back. "I don't think I ever came that fast before."

He lightly blew in her ear, making her shiver even more. "Come on, the next one will be slower."

Akeema's eyes flew open. "What next one? You can't be ready again so soon!"

"I didn't finish, you did."

When he moved inside her, she believed him. Alarmed, she said, "I'm wiped out. I don't think my poor back will make it."

He rained light little kisses from her ear and all along her jawline. When he reached her mouth, he kissed her long and thoroughly. Akeema forgot all about her aching back.

CHAPTER 19

The next day, Akeema found herself smiling all during the day for no reason. Who was she kidding? Between the erotic gymnastics last night and the great send-off this morning, she knew <u>exactly</u> why she was grinning like a fool. She stretched her long-muscled limbs to unkink them. After her workout during rehearsal later tonight, she might end up in traction! Between keeping her limbs limber and daydreaming about Jake, Akeema wrote each student a note inviting them to the ballet rendition of 'Little Red Riding Hood.' Since Joey and his father were coming to the performance, she was going to invite the entire class to join them. Akeema didn't want to give even a hint of favoritism to Joseph and Joey. A note would be pinned to each child with an invitation to the show. With each returned and signed note from a parent, Akeema offered a free ticket for each child – even if the student wasn't in her class. Only the adult parent would have to pay for a ticket. As long as the ticket request was returned to her tomorrow, she'd make sure the freebie would be sent home Friday after school.

While Akeema was taking care of business, her mind kept drifting to thoughts of Jake. How could someone satisfy her body so completely, but leave her cold emotionally? What if he wasn't the problem? Was there something inside of her that wouldn't let him into her heart? She was 28 years old and had never been in love. Not even close. Right after she had that thought, Joseph's face filtered through her mind. She knew there was 'potential' to love where he was concerned. After all, she had to admit, he had a leg up over every other man because she already loved his son.

Looking at the time, she realized she had wasted more of it than she planned. Quickly, she went from desk to desk to pin the note onto each student. Joey was last to leave again, but this time she helped him put away the toys so Joseph wouldn't have to fret over him. When they were done, she took his hand to walk with him to his dad. At the exit, she saw Joseph leaning casually against his van. Looking for his son, he saw them immediately. His handsome face crinkled with a wide smile. He had on his work clothes, black slacks, long sleeved white shirt, and black tie. As the shift manager at the small grocery store, he had the casual businessman look. She was fond of the dimpled chin that he'd passed on to Joey. To her surprise, she found herself wondering how he shaved that hole.

"Daddy!" Joey cried.

Jogging toward them, Joseph replied, "Hey! How's my boy?"

Joey giggled as his dad lifted him, threw him in the air, then caught him with no problem. Akeema's throat almost choked on the scream she swallowed. Putting Joey on his shoulders for a high ride, Joseph strolled over to his son's teacher.

"Hello, teacher Akeema," he said pleasantly.

"Hello, Mr. Smith. You seem to be doing well."

"I am. You're beautiful as always."

Akeema felt her chocolate skin flush with his compliment. She smiled bashfully before looking down at her shoes. "Thanks," she responded in a low voice.

"Daddy, can we all go eat now?" Joey asked.

"That's up to your teacher, son."

Akeema's head snapped up. "Thanks for the invite fellas, but I've still got work to do before I head off to rehearsal. Eat for me, okay?"

An enthusiastic Joey said, "We'll eat double so you will really feel it, okay?"

Smiling tenderly at her favorite, she nodded. Joseph paused a few moments just to enjoy looking at her. "Goodnight."

Giving each of them a brief look, she waved before turning to leave.

Joey and his father watched her walk away until she disappeared.

"Aw, come on, Akeema," Kristin protested, "I don't think you've had supper with us in weeks!"

"I <u>know</u> she hasn't," Sharon backed her up.

"I'm sorry ladies, I'm just beat."

"We're not asking you to go out and party," Kristin pointed out.

"I know, but I've got a room full of first graders to contend with tomorrow morning. All I've got the energy to do is wolf down a salad, take a shower, then crash. I'm sorry."

Sharon quipped, "That's all any of us want to do, girlfriend. We're just choosing not to eat alone. We like each other's company."

"And I do too. Please let me take a raincheck. We can maybe order in at my place and hang out."

"Okay," Sharon said grudgingly. "But on that day, it's you who will pay!"

Conceding the point, Akeema agreed to the terms. Since she was going straight home, she didn't stop by the restroom to freshen up. She slowly gathered her things with her weary body. It was times like this that she wished she had a massage therapist in her hip pocket.

Akeema walked slowly to her car. She was almost there when she heard, "Teacher Akeema, wait!"

She couldn't help but smile as she turned to face Joey and his father. She loved the little boy, but she desperately wanted to be on her way. She was too tired to meet them in the middle, so she stood still until they reached her.

Knowing that it was highly probable that Joey would jump into her arms expecting to be picked up, Akeema dropped her gear to the pavement while slowly bending to her knee. Her arms felt as heavy as lead, picking him up wasn't a great idea.

As expected, Joey ran right into her arms, giving her neck a hard squeeze with his sturdy little arms.

"Hey, buddy," she said affectionately. "You give such strong hugs, thank you."

"You welcome, we have food for you!"

"You do? How wonderful!" She gave each one of his dimpled cheeks a loud smooch.

Joseph noticed how gingerly she stood to her feet.

"You okay?" he asked, getting right to the point.

"Uh huh, just very tired. Thanks for asking. So, Joey said you guys have a surprise for me."

Smiling, Joseph replied, "That we do. How does a tub of chicken vegetable soup sound?"

"Like ambrosia! Where is it?"

"In the van. Wait here, I'll go get it."

As he sauntered off, Akeema and Joey walked to her car. She let him help her put away her gear. By the time Joseph came back with her food, the two partners were sitting on the car hood with Joey chatting away.

Joseph liked what he saw.

Akeema and Joey were connecting as only they could. Next to Joseph, Joey loved his teacher the most. He was comforted by the fact that Akeema loved him right back.

When they saw him coming, Josep loved the way their faces lit up at the sight of him. He hadn't felt such an outpouring of affection since his dear wife, Claire, was still alive. She was only 25 years old when she passed away from pneumonia. She was the only woman that he'd ever loved. Until now.

Without hesitation, Joseph gave Akeema the big, brown paper bag.

"Wow, this is heavy!" she cried. "Is there enough food for all of us?"

Hopping off the car to the ground, Joey gleefully jumped up and down. "It's all yours! The bread sticks too!"

Never taking his eyes off her, the senior Smith said, "You look like you're about to fall down. Joey and I will say goodnight so that you can get a move on. Enjoy your dinner!"

As he bent down to pick up his son, a car pulled up. Akeema recognized the gray BMW at once.

Jake saw Joseph and Joey with his lady before they saw him. His anger was tempered because he saw the child. He understood that chances were great that this was her student that she was so fond of. He wasted no time joining them.

With tunnel vision, he walked directly to Akeema, holding her gaze all the way. For her part, she couldn't breathe.

Kissing her on the lips for a deliberate five seconds, he said loudly enough to be heard, "Hey, baby."

He said those two words so intimately that anyone would think they'd just had sex. Joseph got the message.

Uncomfortable, Akeema tried her best to appear casual.

"Hey, Jake, I'd like you to meet Joey and his dad, Joseph. I'm not sure, but I think everyone has bumped into each other at one time or another."

Putting his arm around her waist, Jake pulled her closer to his side. She was his and he wasn't about to let little Joey's dad forget it. Jake replied, "Yeah, I think you're right." Turning to look at Joseph, he asked, "What brings you guys here tonight?"

"My little man here wanted to feed his teacher," he replied smoothly.

The tension between the men could be cut with a buzz saw.

Joseph put his son on his shoulders, preparing to leave.

Akeema walked to father and son to give them a personal goodbye with an extra thanks for the food and their thoughtfulness. Jake didn't get the cue – he went with her.

Sounding stilted to her own ears, she said, "I really appreciate your time and trouble. I'm going to enjoy the heck out of this soup."

To her mortification, Jake added, "Mmm, sounds good. I might get in on that."

Graciously, Joseph conceded, "There's plenty to share."

"We gave her a whole lot!" Josey said proudly.

Smiling up at the tot, Jake responded, "That's lucky for me, thanks guys!"

With a small smile and a nod, Joseph got Joey strapped into the car before settling in himself. He didn't give Jake or Akeema a second look. Only Joey returned Akeema's farewell wave.

Once the van was out of sight, Akeema turned to Jake, furious.

"That was despicable behavior!" she seethed.

"What?" he asked innocently.

"That 'this is my woman' performance act of yours was out of place!"

Calm for a change, Jake responded, "I'm having a hard time accepting your attitude. You are my woman and I'm your man. Why are you this angry, Akeema?"

She paused, when he put it that way, it forced her to look deeper at the situation. And at herself. Truthfully, she knew that Jake's declaration of ownership was upsetting because Joseph was there. Even though she'd always been honest with him about her having a boyfriend, Jake had put a spin on it that seemed close to marriage. Then, Akeema seemed to have an insight as to why he behaved the way he did. It was her fault. She hadn't been honest with <u>him</u>. Jake wasn't aware that as far as she was concerned, she was counting the days until she would part from him. He didn't know that none of her heart was his, only her body. Akeema resented the hold that he had on her. She was sure that her resentment blocked any heart-felt feelings she could've had for him. She couldn't help but wonder if his feelings for her would run so deep if he knew he was just being used for sexual release. Would he really want to spend his life with such a woman? She felt ashamed.

Jake watched the myriad of emotions flicker across her face, not understanding any of them.

It was getting late, so Jake decided to take charge of the evening in Akeema's silence. "Let's get you home so you can eat and get settled for the night," he directed.

Akeema looked at him steadily. It was time to end the charade.

In a level voice she asked, "Do you think you love me, Jake?"

She was standing in front of him, holding the brown paper bag with the soup in it. He walked closer to her before he replied, "I don't have to think how I feel, I know."

"What do you think you know?" she pressed.

"I know that I want to spend my life with you."

"As what? My friend?"

"Not just that," he hedged. This wasn't how he envisioned their declaration of love to each other. There was an edge in her voice that he didn't get.

Her eyes never left his. "As what else?" Jake felt nervous. Where women were concerned, he wasn't accustomed to feeling this way.

"Your husband," he said in a hushed voice.

Akeema knew this was it. It was time to remove herself from this man's life, once and for all. She cocked her head to the right. "Doesn't the Butler dynasty matter to you and your family? If you marry me, you won't have any biological children."

Jake shrugged. "That's no big deal. At least not to me. My mom might be a little disappointed, but it's not her life, it's ours."

Knowing their time together was nearing its end, Akeema decided to ask questions that she was curious about. "We've never talked about it, but I wonder if you'd like to be a parent one day."

"It's not a dream of mine," he said honestly. "I figured if you wanted us to have a couple of little rug rats, we would. Personally, I'm perfectly happy with just the two of us."

She noticed his stance was casual, relaxed. He was speaking his truth. He just didn't know it was a lie because he had her in it.

"Are you okay living in Condos and apartments, or would you like to buy a house?"

"Once we marry, our joint incomes would probably make it necessary to have a mortgage." He's thought about this, Akeema thought. His answers were coming quick and easy.

"Jake, do you work because you have to?"

"Excuse me?"

"I mean, is your family so wealthy that you don't have to work if you don't want to?"

Crossing his arms over his chest, he asked, "Why do you ask?"

"Just curious."

"I have had a trust fund since the day I was born. I've never touched it. I'm also an only child, as you know, so if my parents pass away before me, I assume I'll have part of their estate coming my way."

Jake was both wary and elated. He was always a little uncomfortable talking about the wealth in his family. But, Akeema was plainly not the gold-digger type. This was the first time they'd had a serious discussion like this. She could finally see them with a future together! He'd finally won her over! He closed the gap between them. He took the soup bag from her hands, placing it on the car hood. He wanted her hands and arms free to hold him when he gave her the lip lock of her life.

"Now," he said huskily, "may I ask you a question?" Akeema nodded.

"Do you love me even half as much as I love you?"

"No, Jake."

Her answer was immediate. She didn't have to think about it. Jake was confused. He didn't know how to respond. He heard Akeema take a long, deep breathe. He braced himself for bad news.

"When you asked me for a second chance, I felt spiritually obligated to give you one. What I didn't know then was that I can – and did – forgive you, but that doesn't mean that I would ever be able to trust you 100%. And, if I don't trust you all the way, it's impossible for me to fall in love with you."

"Are you trying to tell me you feel nothing?" Jake's voice was ominous.

The hair on Akeema's arms stood up. "Of course not. We've had an intimate relationship. And, I like you just fine." That sounded lame even to her.

"You like me 'just fine'? You think the kind of sex we have is common? You think everybody has what we have?"

Akeema shook her head vigorously. "No! Before you, I had never had the passion in my life that we share. I'm just doing a lousy job trying to say that mind-blowing sex doesn't equal love!"

Jake looked at her with a stunned, open-mouth expression. He was having a hard time accepting her words. He was surprised, sad, hurt, and angry. Very angry.

Akeema watched him warily. She knew the worst was yet to come. She didn't think for one second that their parting would be amicable.

For a while, Jake was speechless. To gain control over her, he'd deliberately used sex to ensnare her. He was sure that their intimate times with each other would gradually drift from flesh to heart. But, she was telling him that he was wrong in his assessment of their relationship. Tragically wrong.

"Don't you think that if we stay together, we'll get closer as we learn more about each other?" he asked in a controlled voice.

With her truth hat firmly in place, she replied, "I really doubt it. You see, I give you credit for not losing your temper – like you're doing – but, I've just been waiting for you to drop that ball so I can say goodbye forever."

Abruptly, Jake turned his back on her. Akeema took notice of the fists at his side. His shoulders were rising and falling as he took deep breaths.

Jake wanted to slap her.

"So, all this time you had no faith in me? You were just waiting for me to fail?"

Hearing it put that way, she felt like a monster.

"I'm sorry, Jake. I'm not proud of myself but, what you said about me is true."

"So, no matter how good I am to you, it won't ever make a difference?"

She felt like an ogre. "It makes a difference in how much I 'like' you, of course. My issue is that I love you as a child of the Most High, but I have serious doubts that I could ever love you as a woman should love her man. I don't want to waste anymore of your time."

Jake whirled around. His face was beet red. He roared, "Is this your way of punishing me all this time?"

Akeema jumped before taking two steps back. "No, no! The word 'punish' never entered my mind!"

Stomping toward her, he roared, "Why bother with me if our relationship was so hopeless?"

"You used the Word to point out forgiveness! I felt like I'd be a hypocrite if I didn't give you a second chance!"

"That's bull and you know it! You were just biding your time waiting for me to fail! Your heart was never in it!" he barked.

Akeema didn't deny it. She couldn't.

Frustrated by her silence, Jake began pacing from side to side while running his hands through his hair. When he stopped to stand in front of her again, Akeema prepared herself for more of his verbal onslaught.

With his eyes flashing and his teeth clenched, he said, "You got a good laugh when I told you that I loved you, right?"

Akeema shook her head vigorously. "Absolutely, not! At first, I thought it was just a line you were giving me so that you could have your own way. But, when I saw you were sincere, I knew I needed to be up front with you!"

"You're a liar!" he shot back.

Again, she tried to plead her case. "You're wrong, Jake! I never lied to you! I admit that I didn't tell you everything, but everything I told you was the truth!"

Moving closer to her, he spat, "You think I'm a fool? If you didn't lie outright, you lied to me by omission!"

Oops! She couldn't refute that statement either.

Once again, she was guilty as charged. He read it all over her face.

"Jake, please believe me when I say I'm s___"

She didn't get to finish the word 'sorry' because his open hand slapped her across the mouth. Before she could react, the back of his hand hit her cheek in the opposite direction. As he kept hitting her, Akeema went numb. She couldn't understand why she wasn't in pain. He was slapping her with enough force to snap her head left and right, right and left. She felt her knees buckle as she started to fall. He caught her, to punch her in the gut with his fist. She had no problem feeling THAT pain. Her brain yelled at him to stop, but she didn't have enough breath to say a single word. The air suddenly left her body after his stomach punch. Mercifully, she blacked out…

CHAPTER 20

Back in her aunt and uncle's guest room, Akeema felt unshed tears stinging her eyes. Memories of Jake's physical abuse continued to bring up raw emotions inside of her. For her family and the outside world to see, she handled it well. Only she and Yahuah, her heavenly Father, knew how terrified she was. Her strong exterior didn't match her gooey interior. Without His strength, Akeema never would have made it through the pain and shame of Jake Butler.

After he'd beaten her into a near coma, he was acutely remorseful. He'd taken her to the hospital, refusing to leave until he was sure she was alright. After hearing that she was battered and bruised, but okay, he went directly to the police to turn himself in.

While she was still in the hospital recuperating, police detectives paid her a visit to get her account of what had happened. They read Jake's statement to her, word for word. Akeema agreed with everything she'd heard. Jake had been 100% truthful. She realized that he was truly sorry for what he'd done to her. She refused to press charges, but she did get a restraining order…and some mace. Later, she found out that, in Texas, the state prosecuted the case on her behalf. She was determined to put the whole mess behind her. This also meant, to Akeema, that she would never lay eyes on Mr. Butler again.

Since Jake's record was squeaky clean, he was given probation and a fine. He was also warned to stay away from Akeema Dawn Sprite.

Through the court, he'd written her a letter of apology. The letter was forwarded to her, but she never opened it. Her aunt couldn't believe she didn't want to know what Jake had to say.

She assured Aunt Jean that she wasn't even remotely curious.

That weekend was the debut of her twenty second dance solo. She was sore all over, but only death would've been strong enough to keep her from performing. She wasn't strong enough to stand for the meet and greet, so she left instructions to tell anyone who asked about her that she had another engagement. She didn't want Joey and Joseph to worry about her.

Shortly after the Jake nonsense was over, Akeema let Joseph know that she was a free agent. She hadn't planned it, but, when the opportunity knocked – she answered.

One day after dance rehearsal, the floor manager yelled, "Akeema! There's a kid here to see you!"

"Coming!" she replied.

The erratic beat of her heart forced her to acknowledge her fear. If it was Jake she was walking to, what would she say and do?

As she neared the entrance, her eyes quickly roamed the area. Not seeing anyone, she was about to turn around when a sudden movement caught her attention. It was Joey!

"Teacher Akeema, here I am!"

Smiling broadly, she hugged him with a little distance between them, explaining, "Don't put your arms around me, Joey! I don't want you to get my sweat all over you."

"Aw, shucks, I don't mind. My daddy smells badder than you do after we play ball."

Akeema received that information with grace. She burst out laughing. Joey joined her contagious gaiety. That was the scene that Joseph walked in on. He stood in the doorway, enjoying their happiness. Joey noticed him first.

"Daddy, I found her. See?"

Smiling as he walked over to them, he extended his hand to shake hers. "Hi, Akeema," he said warmly.

"Hello, yourself. What are you guys up to?"

Holding her gaze, Joseph said, "Guess."

"We have food!" announced Joey.

"Ah, the food van blesses me again! I'm just getting ready to go. Let me get my things so we can head out, okay?"

"Okay!" shouted an excited Joey.

After a hasty spruce up in the restroom, Akeema joined Joseph and his son in their van. Once again, they brought her one of the super-sized salads that she liked. For dessert, Joey had decided cold pineapple chunks would please her. He was correct.

"Yum, this has got to be the sweetest fruit I've ever tasted. It's like candy!"

"I told you she'd like it, daddy!" said a proud little Joey.

Joseph nodded. "Yes, you sure did, son. Good boy!" Akeema turned toward the backseat so that she could see her favorite student.

"From now on, I want you to pick out all my fruit, okay?"

An excited Joey was thrilled. "Yes, ma'am!"

Joseph couldn't understand all the raving about fruit, so he stuck his fork into her fruit cup to taste it for himself.

"Mmm," he said, "I thought you guys were exaggerating, but this really is good."

When he went after more, Akeema made sure he didn't get it. "Oh no, homeboy! I didn't mind you getting a taste, but I'm not in on sharing my only sweet treat of the week!"

Joseph cajoled, "Aw, c'mon. Don't be like that. I promise we'll bring you double the amount next time, deal?"

She loved that he planned a 'next time.'

"Deal!" she agreed as she shifted her cup to her left hand so that Joseph could reach it.

From the rear, Joey chimed in. "You can have some of mine too!"

"Thanks, son."

They all ate happily and loudly.

Later, Akeema and Joseph talked while Joey played in the backseat, content with his Game Boy.

"What time is it? We don't want to keep Joey out too late. Tomorrow is a school day," Akeema pointed out.

Joseph reassured her. "Don't worry. I bathed him before we headed out this evening. All I have to do is put on his jammies, see that he brushes his teeth, and he'll be ready for bed."

"That's cool. You're such a good father."

"I try my best. He's such a good boy."

"I know. He has a huge part of my heart."

"I sense that. I'm thankful that he has you to love him almost as much as I do."

"I'm thankful to have him – and you – in my life."

"We feel the same, Akeema. But, I know you have a personal life all your own. I intend to always respect that."

"Thanks, but please know that I consider you and Joey part of my personal life."

"That's nice to hear, but your boyfriend doesn't seem to like that."

Akeema sat quietly. She was hesitant to bring him into the Jake mess. She sure wasn't eager to have Joey hear any of the sordid details either. It would surely give him nightmares.

"Well," Joseph said, "I guess I can assume by your silence that what I said was true."

"He's no longer my boyfriend. We broke up. For good."

He heard the finality in her tone of voice. Joseph wanted to know what happened, but not at the expense of her privacy. Besides, he had the feeling that the details of their parting wouldn't be good for tender ears.

Not knowing what to say, he muttered, "Sorry."

Surprised, Akeema asked, "Are you?"

"No." The word was said out loud before he could catch it.

When he dared to look at her, she was smiling at him. He grinned back at her, gratefully.

Gently, he asked, "Are you alright?"

"Getting there," she answered truthfully.

"Is there anything I can do to help?"

Shaking her head, Akeema said, "No, I'm okay. I have a court order that he's supposed to stay away from me."

Joseph felt his pulse accelerate. He had the sick feeling that she'd been physically hurt by her ex. He wanted to beat the mess out of him. He kept his voice calm when he said, "If you have any problems with him, please feel free to call me. I'll come to help you right away."

Akeema turned to look at him, awed by his statement. "Thanks, Joseph. I appreciate that."

"It's my pleasure. And can I say one more thing?"

"Of course."

"I know and understand that you need time to heal after going through this mess, right?"

"Yes," she breathed.

"When you are ready to resume dating, will you give me the heads up?"

Perplexed, Akeema replied, "There's no need to Joseph. No matter who I'm with in the future, I'll always have room for you and Joey."

He took a deep breath. Clarity was needed here.

"Thanks, I'm glad to hear that. But, what I want is the opportunity to date you myself."

Akeema was pleasantly surprised. But she had to be honest with herself. Right now, she was a mess.

"I like the sound of that, Joseph," she admitted. "I hope when I get myself together that you'll still be interested."

"Count on it," he replied.

"You never know. The love of your life could be right around the corner. Don't let her pass you by – whoever she may be."

"I won't. I promise you that."

Gazing at each other, they both felt a new connection. This was the beginning.

With his binoculars, Jake Butler barely breathed as he watched the occupants in the light blue van. They looked like a happy family of three.

His blood boiled.

CHAPTER 21

The next few weeks passed in a blissful haze for Akeema, Joseph, and Joey. Without any discussion about it, they were dating happily and exclusively.

Wise beyond his tender years, Joey never let on that his teacher loved him, and him her.

At least once a week, the guys would bring her a huge salad or a heaping bowl of delicious soup.

Since Joey loved to fetch her after rehearsal, Akeema let him keep doing it. Before long, the floor manager was calling him her 'little boy' instead of 'that kid.'

She never corrected him.

Also, during the week Joseph took them to the soul food restaurant that had the video game that Joey loved to play.

Akeema insisted on giving him the coins necessary to play it. When Joseph had balked at the idea, she had let him know that she wanted to do her part with the finances. After all, he'd paid for her food at the rehearsal hall and the diner. She let him know, firmly, that she would stop going out with them unless she could contribute in this small way. That was the end of that.

On one particular night, Joseph and Akeema saw a change in their relationship. Joey was in the game room while his dad and teacher were singing along with the juke box of oldies-but-goodies.

"I can turn the grayest sky blue," sang Joseph.

"I can make it rain, whenever I want it to," chimed Akeema. They were rocking their heads to the classic singing quintet. They were having a great time. As they looked around, they saw other patrons who were smiling and lip synching. When the song ended, Joseph and Akeema high-fived each other.

It's rare when I meet a musical kindred spirit. I like it so much," she said.

Joseph admitted, "I assumed you only liked the classical music you dance to. Imagine my surprise when I first heard you rockin' out to Marvin Gaye!"

"He's my all-time favorite!"

"We have that in common," he replied.

"Really? I didn't know that."

"That's why I'm telling you. It's nice to have a friend to share the big, and little, things with."

"You're so right. Between my two careers, I don't have time for really good friends. Till now, that is." She didn't know why she felt bashful when she said that. She looked down at her folded hands on the table. She wasn't sure she could look at him right then.

It was a good thing Akeema didn't look up. If she had, she would have met his intense gaze at her.

Joseph was glad that she felt so close to him and his little boy. But he had to admit that his own feelings for her were more than just an old-buddy, old-pal kinda thing. The last time he'd felt like this was for his deceased wife.

For Akeema's part, she wished she'd never had Jake Butler in her life. Their relationship had left her feeling sordid, dirty. Joseph was such a decent guy that he deserved to have someone better. Akeema knew that when he found his next lady love, she would be kicked to the curb.

Joseph and Joey would be part of someone else's life. Suddenly, she wanted to cry. Tuned into her, Joseph could tell that something was wrong. He had to make sure it didn't have anything to do with him.

"What is it, Akeema? What's on your mind?"

Half distracted, she answered truthfully.

"I'm missing you and Joey."

"What do you mean? We're both here with you."

"Yeah, you're here now, but you won't be."

Confused, Joseph replied, "If I'm supposed to know what you are talking about, then I'm dumber than I thought. What in the world are you trying to say?"

Akeema sighed. It was too late to lie her way out of this, even if she wanted to.

"I'm facing the fact that you're going to fall in love, and Joey will have a needed stepmom. There won't be a place for me in your lives. I totally get it, it just saddens me, that's all."

They sat in silence for a while. Joseph's vision of a romantic dinner with flowers and champagne was floating away in the distance. This wasn't as he imagined it would happen. Oh, well.

"You've got part of the picture right," he said.

Looking up at him, she asked, "What do you mean?"

"I mean that you have part of the future scenario right, but you're missing a very important part."

"What part is that?"

"You, Akeema."

She considered what he really meant by that.

"So, are you saying that I will be in you and Joey's life no matter who your love interest is?"

He placed his nice, masculine hands over her small feminine ones. "I'm saying that I want YOU to be my friend and love interest…when you feel like you're ready."

Akeema felt supreme joy, and a desperate fear. He was a kind, loving man who was raising a son all on his own. She liked and respected the man that he was. He was good looking, but that was just a bonus – it wasn't necessary. Though she wasn't a friend of his wife's, Akeema instinctively knew that he was a good husband to her.

However, she had to face her own lack of character. In a nutshell, she got beat up by her ex-boyfriend because she didn't love him, not even a little. She stayed with him for the pleasure he gave her body.

Jake had no right to lay unkind hands on her. She wasn't excusing him for that. But all the mess could've been avoided if she'd discussed her feelings openly with him. She'd selfishly let him hang around because her flesh, not her heart, craved him. The longer she stayed with him, made him more secure in their relationship. She knew he was a control freak, but he'd convinced her that his feelings for her ran deep.

To date, she hadn't shared any of the details about her break-up with Jake to Joseph. To his credit, he hadn't asked her why the relationship ended. Although she was undeniably attracted to him, she felt she'd be doing him a real favor by not getting involved with him romantically.

Joseph watched Akeema closely while she was lost in her thoughts. To him, she was the perfect example of a woman who was beautiful on the inside and the out. Until her, he couldn't imagine falling in love again after Claire died. He didn't know why, but he felt she would approve of Akeema loving him and Joey. It was such a blessing to meet a woman who loved his child before she loved him.

When Akeema finally spoke, it was with regret and sadness. "First of all, Joseph, please believe me when I say I'm thankful and humbled at your interest in me."

Joseph thought, uh-oh!

Akeema continued. "You and your son deserve a real decent woman in your lives. I'm afraid I'm a bit of a mess. I have issues in my life that have yet to be worked out."

Joseph shrugged. "Don't we all? I don't know 'bout you, but I don't know any perfect people down here except for young babies."

"Well, some are more imperfect than others."

"That's a given. But people who have a chance at a loving relationship get to learn about each other. We all have things we can live with, and things that are deal breakers, right?"

"Right. I'm giving you the heads up that you don't know me. I'm a deal breaker girl. Your best bet is to keep me for a friend and that's all."

Her distressed look concerned Joseph. He wanted to hold her in his arms to console her. "I'm sure there are things that you don't know about me. Some of those things we might decide to share with each other, but some of those things we'll take with us to the grave," he said softly, "And there's one thing, Akeema, that I want you to know about me."

"What's that?" she whispered.

"That I'm interested in the here and now. Unless something in your past must be dealt with now, I'm not remotely interested. Your past isn't a concern to me, and I hope you feel the same about me."

She gripped his hands tightly. Hope filled her heart for the first time. They had a chance!

"I do feel that way about you. When I'm sure the mess that I'm in is over, I'll come to you."

"I want to help you out of that mess. If our lives are destined to be joined, we have to help and trust each other, Akeema."

She thought about Jake and the restraining order she had against him. If he lost his temper again and came after her, she didn't want to put Joseph or Joey in danger. The trust would start now.

"I need to make sure that Jake will leave me alone."

Frowning, Joseph asked, "Aren't you two broken up?"

"Yes, and I have a restraining order to help protect me from him."

"Protect you?"

Silently, she nodded.

"Has he physically hurt you?"

Again, she slowly nodded.

Joseph felt his temper rising. "Did he lay a hand on you?"

A nod.

"Did he hurt you?"

After nodding, Akeema lowered her gaze.

Joseph knew that if he showed his righteous anger, she would be alarmed. He lifted his eyes heavenward as he prayed for strength and compassion from the Almighty.

Sitting quietly, the couple jumped when Joey re-entered the picture, noisily asking for money. Self-conscious, the pair separated their hands.

Following Joseph's old script, Akeema said, "It's your bedtime, mister."

"Aw, please! Can't we stay here a little longer?"

She hid her smile, "Well, I do have two more quarters for you, but only if you'll be ready to go home once they're gone. Okay?"

Joey nodded his head eagerly. When Akeema gave him the money, the little boy planted a loud, juicy smack on her cheek.

Joseph watched them with love and affection. He adored his family. He'd give his life to protect them. Jake Butler beware!

CHAPTER 22

Her boys – yep, <u>her</u> boys, would have none of that. At the meet and greet, they managed to be last in line so that nobody would rush them away from visiting with her. She pushed aside thoughts of Jake, who used to do the same thing.

When J & J (her pet moniker for Joey and Joseph) were with her, they had dinner, and played games together. Akeema dared to be happy.

The receiving line was pretty routine. A smile, handshake, and her signature next to her picture was all it took to keep the line moving.

Once she was in her car, she planned to call J & J to talk her home. Joey always talked to her first. When he was done, he left Joseph alone so they could have a nice, uninterrupted chat. Just thinking about them made her feel good.

When the door was locked after the last patron was gone, everybody went to the dressing room to take off makeup and put on street clothes. Kristen asked, "I probably already know the answer, but I'll ask anyway. Do you want to eat supper with us, Akeema?"

"Afraid not, girlfriend," she responded with a remorse she didn't feel, "my day starts early."

"Aren't you hungry? My stomach thinks my throat has been cut."

Akeema smiled. "I feel you on that one. I've got soup and salad waiting for me at the house."

"That aunt of yours must be nice to have around."

"No doubt about it. But, it's their house not mine. I'm the one who is around them!"

"True that!" Sharon chimed in. "Her aunt and uncle are the nicest people I've ever met."

Kristen turned to her, incredulous. "You've met them and I haven't?"

"Oops," Sharon said before she scurried off. Akeema braced herself for Kristen's wrath. "Since when does she rate an invitation before me?"

Akeema lifted both her hands in surrender.

"It's my aunt's house, and it was at HER invitation that Sharon accepted, not mine."

"Did your family come here to see you?"

"Nope. We ran into Sharon at the grocery store. It was a chance meeting, Kristen."

This seemed to relax her a bit. "Oh, I see. Well, I'd love to meet your family one of these days."

"Okay. I'll keep that in mind. When you're in the mood for fatty food, let me know. Aunt Jean thinks we're all too thin. She'd love to put some meat on our bones."

Now grinning, Kristen said, "You may count on me during the off season. What does she cook?"

Akeema shrugged. "She cooks any and everything. All you have to do is tell her what you want to eat, and she'll fix it."

"Great! When we're ready, we'll let you know, okay?"

"Okay."

Quickly, Akeema got her things together before she left the theater. She was past ready to talk to her boys.

Once settled in her car, she turned the air conditioning on low. Although the fall season kept the temperature moderate, her core was still a little warm. Just as she was putting in her earphones…

Tap! Tap! Tap!

Akeema squealed and jumped in response to the knocking on her window. She put her hand over her heart to slow down its rapid beat. Annoyed, she was prepared to give her cast mate a good tongue lashing.

Snapping her head to the left, her heartbeat seemed to pause. She forgot what she was about to say. Actually, she realized she couldn't speak at all. Akeema wasn't afraid, mad, sad, or glad. Shock has a way of numbing you. The handsome, clean-cut white guy with light brown hair and matching eye color, was staring at her. She counted slowly to five before halfway lowering the glass.

"Hello, Jake Butler," she said with a calm she didn't feel.

"Hello, Akeema Dawn Sprite," he whispered. She took note that he used her full name for the first time. She felt goose bumpy.

"Why are you here?" she asked bluntly.

"To see you and say hello," he answered promptly.

"Mission accomplished," she stated flatly.

"Yes, you are right."

"Then, I'll say goodnight."

His intense gaze held her for a few seconds.

"Goodnight, Akeema. Take care."

With that said, he took three steps back.

Akeema started her car, forcing herself not to rush. When she drove off, she saw him standing exactly where she'd left him.

"Did you call the police?" Joseph shouted.

"No. It wasn't necessary," she replied simply.

"Of course, it was! You have a court order that plainly states that he has to keep a distance between you!"

Akeema had never heard an excited Joseph before. She felt how much he cared about her.

"The restraining order has expired. He hasn't bothered me, so I didn't renew it."

"So, do you think it's a coincidence that he shows up after the order is no longer any good?"

"To be honest, Joseph, it didn't cross my mind."

She smiled as she imagined the shocked look on his face.

"Oh, my goodness," he said in a hushed voice. "Do me a favor. Look in your rearview mirror to see if you're being followed."

When she complied, she saw a sea of headlights behind her. "There's quite a bit of traffic behind me. I doubt if I'm being followed."

"Come over here. I'll follow you to your place." Akeema responded quickly. "Uh-uh. You're not bringing Joey out this time of night. I'm fine."

"I don't want you going home alone, Akeema."

"I'm living with my aunt and uncle, remember? I won't be alone at all. Stop worrying."

"I'll stop worrying when you're safe and sound in the house. Let's end this call so you can call your uncle to meet you outside to escort you inside."

"But we don't want to be paranoid over nothing."

But Joseph was steadfast. "You either do it, or Joey and I will be waiting in the driveway when you get home."

"Are you kidding?"

"Try me!"

Akeema called her uncle.

After she ate and helped Aunt Jean clean up the kitchen, Akeema retired to her bedroom to finish grading papers and plan tomorrow's activities for the kids.

After saying her nightly prayers, she fought the urge to call Joseph. They'd already talked that evening; she just wanted his voice to be the last one she heard before she went to sleep. She smiled at herself for being so sentimental. She'd just turned out the bedside lamp when her cell phone rang.

"Hi, Joseph." she said, confident that he was on the line without looking at the caller I.D…

"Good evening, precious. Are you okay?"

"Yes, even better now," she replied softly.

"Me too," he agreed, "I wanted us to end our day on an up note. I care what's on your mind when you're awake, and when you are sleeping."

"That's so sweet, Joseph. I'm so thankful for my J & J family. Do you know how much I think about you every day?"

"Tell me," he prompted.

"So many times, that I lose count."

"What kind of things come to mind?"

"Can I be honest?"

"Always."

"I think about when we're going to share our first lip lock."

Joseph smiled into his phone. "You are not alone on that one."

"Good. It's nice to know that we are like-minded."

Joseph said, "That we are. The timing of it is important since we always have Joey with us."

"We'll need to lull him to sleep, or something!" Akeema exclaimed.

"I'm all ears."

"My aunt has invited you guys to dinner this Sunday after I perform. She thinks it's about time for everyone to meet."

"Thank her for me and it's a date."

"Alright! She's pretty sure that once Joey is comfortable with her and my uncle, they can sit with him from time to time. Aunt Jean is anxious for us to have our first one-on-one date."

"I'd like that too."

"Well, since we all agree, I'm looking forward to that great day."

"Are you smiling, Akeema?"

"Yes, I am. Are you?"

"Absolutely!" he sighed.

"Well, as much as I hate to let you go, we all have to get up early in the morning. So, we'd better say goodnight."

"Okay. Sweet dreams."

"For me, that's a guarantee since I'm going to sleep with you on my mind."

Joseph couldn't see the air-kiss that Akeema blew in his direction.

CHAPTER 23

With each day that followed, Akeema's nerves got more and more jittery. J & J would be the first outsiders that she was going to introduce to Aunt Jean and Uncle Rick. It was important that they liked each other. She finally admitted to herself that J & J were so near and dear to her that she couldn't imagine them not in her life. She hoped and prayed that she was as important to them as they were to her. Akeema looked forward to the moment when she and Joseph would give Joey a little brother or sister through adoption. Like her, Joseph wanted as many children as their budget would allow. It was rewarding and strange to have intimate discussions with a man she'd never been intimate with. Was it really possible to fall in love with someone you'd never had sex with, or even kissed? She couldn't deny that her body longed to be closer to him. She knew that on a future date, they were destined to have the celibate talk. Although he'd been married, Akeema felt she'd been more sexually active than Joseph. She'd admitted it to herself, but she wasn't sure if she was going to tell him her secret. She felt like a wanton strumpet unworthy of his fidelity and trust. She couldn't help but wonder if he'd turn away from her if he knew of her sexual past.

Normally, it was the woman who excused the many lovers in a man's history. She was the exception to that rule.

Singing happily as she worked, Akeema's aunt was in her element. The house was fragrant from the delicious and kid friendly menu that she was preparing. Even the huge house salad was made with Joey in mind. It had small chunks of the sweetest apples and oranges that she could find. Inside the flaky crescent rolls were plump, juicy, beef franks. Instead of regular french fries, Jean chose tater tots that she sprinkled with a little garlic powder and pepper. Thirst quenchers were frosty root beer floats or chilled cranpineapple juice. Rick was allowed to help with the shopping; however, Jean wouldn't allow him or Akeema to help her with the cooking. They would have been in her way.

When Akeema came in, hurrying to her room, Jean called, "Where are the boys?"

Yelling as she kept walking, she replied, "They were dressed up for the show, so they went home to dress more comfortably!"

Just then, Rick walked in to kiss his wife gently on the side of her neck. "Hello, my lovely," he whispered into her ear before blowing in it. Giggling like a teenager, Jean said, "Can't you say hi to me without touching me?"

Swiftly, he corrected her, "My hands haven't touched you. But if that's what you want…"

Laughing now, Jean replied, "No, no, that's alright! I'll catch up with you later."

"Is that a promise?" he leered.

"Yeah, man. Now, get outta my kitchen! I've still gotta few things to finish up."

"Anything I can do?" Rick offered.

"Yes, sir. Get out!"

Surrendering, he pecked her on the cheek before backing out of the room.

After Akeema washed the makeup off her face, she changed into a long, loose, navy-blue skirt with a chiffon matching blouse. She was about to put on a pair of matching earrings when she heard the doorbell ring. She knew her uncle was the official door answerer, but she wanted to welcome J & J into the house personally. Running out of her room, she shouted, "I've got it, Unc!"

Rick stopped walking. "Okay!" he called before going to the kitchen to rejoin his wife.

As soon as Akeema opened the front door, Joey blessed her with a big smile. When she bent down to pick him up, he wrapped his arms tightly around her neck. Into her ear for only her to hear, he whispered, "You danced good today." Touched by his approval, Akeema whispered her thanks.

Watching them together, Joseph was satisfied – once again – that she was the right woman for him and his son.

Her eyes were closed as she shared that private moment with Joey.

When her eyes opened, they met Joseph's loving gaze. He marveled that they could share an intimate moment without words or touch.

"Can I have another hot dog biscuit?" Joey asked hopefully.

"Of course you can, dear," Jean replied.

She took two from the platter in the middle of the table to put on his plate. She was very pleased with his appetite.

"I'd like some more besh'et'ables too, ma'am."

"It's called salad, son," Joseph replied gently.

"Salad," Joey repeated correctly.

"Very good. Would you like for us to have this at our house sometimes?" Joseph asked.

With his mouth half full, Joey said, "Yes, sir! Can we have it in the morning for breakfast?"

The grownups all got a chuckle out of that. It was Jean who rescued Joseph.

"This kind of food is for lunch or dinner, sweetie. If you want, I can make doggie bags for you and your dad to take home with you."

"I want, I want!" he squealed.

To show they were in sync, Joseph said, "We want, we want! Thank you, Mrs. Jean."

"It's my pleasure, son. I always make more than enough. I'm sure my husband and niece are glad they won't have to be eating the same thing for a week."

Rick leaned over to kiss his wife softly on the lips. "Don't let her kid you, man," he smiled. "We love her cooking AND her leftovers. No food is wasted in this house."

Akeema and Joseph watched the senior couple affectionately. They would've been surprised to know that each was thinking the same thing; what a blessing it was to find a love that lasted a lifetime.

While the ladies were cleaning up the kitchen, the men were playing a raucous game of dominoes. Jean was surprised that eight-year-old Joey knew how to play, and play well.

For her ears only, Jean asked Akeema if Joseph knew about Jake.

"He met him when we were still dating."

"Does he know that Jake hit you?"

"Yes."

"Did he go after him?"

"I stopped him."

Frustrated, Jean threw down her dish towel.

"Why, for goodness sake? He needed a good butt kicking."

"I didn't want him going after Jake because he could have been arrested for assault. Joey already lost his mother to death; I didn't want his father in prison."

Jean nodded. It was a blessing that Akeema had a cool head when it was called for.

Jean admitted, "You're right of course. But I don't like it."

"To tell the truth, auntie, I don't either." Falling silent, they listened to the fellas having fun in the next room, bringing smiles to their faces.

"I very much like your J & J, Akeema."

Relieved, she turned to her aunt. "I'm so glad! From the sound of things, Uncle Rick is enjoying them too."

"My man is easy pick'ins, you know that. He likes almost everybody on the planet. Jake is one of the few exceptions in his life."

Regretfully, Akeema knew that what she said was true, and that she was responsible for bringing him into their lives. Her secret lustful nature didn't just hurt her. She was determined not to wound J & J with her desires of the flesh. She needed to start being open with the people she loved. Her lying by omission had to stop.

"I saw Jake the other day," she confessed.

Jean's imposing back stiffened. "From a distance?" she asked in a frosty voice.

"No. He knocked on my car window after I'd left the rehearsal hall."

"Did he lay hands on you?"

"No, ma'am. I was in the car with the doors locked."

"What did he want?"

"Nothing. He said 'Hi' and when I said goodbye, he didn't try to detain me in any way."

"Is your restraining order still active?"

"No, ma'am."

"Are you going to get a new one?"

"I don't think so," she answered slowly.

Jean gave her a stern look. "I'm listening," she said. Akeema heard the edge in her voice.

"He hasn't done anything to hurt or scare me, Aunt Jean."

Jean folded her arms across her large bosom. "So, popping up on you unannounced or invited didn't concern you?"

"Not too much," she shrugged. "I was safely locked in my car, and I have mace if needed."

"Where was the mace when Jake showed up?"

"In my purse."

"And how quickly would you have been able to put your hands on it, if you'd needed it?"

Akeema hung her head. "Not quickly," she admitted.

Jean took several deep, controlling breaths. She knew how her loud voice could be heard in every room in the house. They had company, and she certainly didn't want to upset the child. In a low, ominous voice she ground out, "May I suggest you get an extra mace for your glove box? If it's overcrowded, clean it out so that you can reach your weapon of choice in a matter of seconds."

"Yes, ma'am, I'll do that." Akeema responded.

Jean nodded. "Good. And, just as an FYI, your uncle and I will go with you to get a gun, if or when you want one."

Surprised, Akeema didn't verbally say anything, she just gave a short nod.

Just then, Joey bounced in because he missed his Akeema. As they often did now, Akeema bent down to scoop him into her arms for a big hug. She was going to hate when he got too big to do this. Her dream was that she and Joseph would have a new little one to do all the hugging and loving with.

Observing them together, Jean felt all the Jake angst ebb away from her. Her niece was created to love children. She hoped and prayed that she and Joseph would get married and extend their family. Soon.

A lively game of Pictionary showcased Joey's above average artistry. His drawings were so good it seemed a shame to erase them!

Promptly at 8 PM, Joseph said it was time to go. Joey complained, "Aw, daddy, can't we stay a little longer? Please?"

All heads turned to Joseph. Everybody else in the room agreed with Joey.

Keeping his focus on his son, Joseph was gentle, but firm. "If it was Friday night, we could stay longer if Jean and Rick said it was okay."Rick interrupted with a booming, "It would be okay then as it is now!"

Smiling at him, Joseph gave him a short nod before turning back to Joey. "But, since it's Sunday, you and I have work and school to get to early in the morning. We have to have time to get home, then get you bathed and ready for bed." Faced with the facts, a defeated Joey looked down at his shoes. The room was completely silent. All at once, Rick reached down from his great height to lift Joey, putting him squarely on his shoulders. A wide grin crossed Joey's face, causing everyone else's face to light up.

"Okay, big guy, how 'bout going to the kitchen to get that yummy food you and your dad are going to eat tomorrow for dinner!"

"Yay!" Joey exclaimed as he held on to the top of Rick's head.

As they all walked away, Akeema and Joseph were left alone.

Joseph walked toward her, looking happy. When he stood directly in front of her, he said, "I'd like to kiss you goodnight."

"And I'd love to be kissed goodnight!"

"Promise me we will get there."

"I promise."

When the chatty trio re-entered, Joey was still on Rick's shoulders, eating a cookie. Jean said, "Gimme your keys, Joseph. We're going to load up the car while you two say your goodnights."

Before either Akeema or Joseph could utter a word, the house was empty. Joseph wasted no time as he grabbed his lady love, holding her against him. Both of their hearts began to beat faster at their nearness.

He whispered, "There are times when our prayers are truly answered."

Their lips came together gently, gingerly. The kiss deepened as they explored each other's mouths for the first time. They liked what they felt and what they tasted. From now on, they both knew they would be doing more of this.

When the kiss ended, they continued holding each other. There was no bumping or grinding. He wasn't pressing his hardness against her softness. They were comforted by their closeness.

With her cheek resting on his shoulder, Akeema murmured, "Everyone is waiting for us. I guess we need to go."

"You feel and smell so good, baby."

It was rare that he called her by anything but her name. She felt tingly without arousal.

"Back at cha," she managed to say before separating from him.

For a few seconds, they just looked at each other. No words were spoken; none were needed.

Finally, he held his hand out to her. She put her hand on his palm. Joseph led her outside to the waiting party. Joey gave Akeema, and her aunt and uncle lots of hugs and kisses. When Joseph drove off, he could see the trio waving to them in his rearview mirror. His heart swelled with happiness.

Akeema and her family didn't go in the house until the car disappeared. Rick grabbed the hands of the women in his life and escorted them back inside. The evening was a success. They had two more people to love.

From the black rental car parked across the street, Jake Butler watched Akeema as she walked inside the home of her aunt and uncle. He loved her. He missed her. He wanted to destroy her.

CHAPTER 24

After Akeema and Joseph agreed to date each other exclusively, it was only a matter of time and opportunity before they got around to discussing pre-marital sex. To have some privacy without disturbing her aunt and uncle, Akeema visited J & J at their place once a week. On that night, the trio prepared a meal together and helped Joey with his homework. When they had time, they played a game or watched television. Once the littlest J was bathed and kissed goodnight, the adults had their alone time.

Akeema sat on Joseph's couch with her feet on the mahogany coffee table. Everything in the room was in varying shades of brown. If they ever married, this room would be the first to get her attention.

"Here you go, dear," Joseph said as he passed her an eight-ounce bottle of cranpineapple juice. Like milk and water, he kept this juice in the refrigerator for her – even though he and Joey discovered they liked it too.

When he sat down heavily beside her, the leather seat cushion made a "whoosh" sound. Akeema hid her smile.

They each drank thirstily to wet their whistles. Joseph downed his juice in a few seconds. Akeema still had half of hers left. Since her thirst was quenched, she offered it to him. He smiled before taking it to polish off. He burped out loud once he was done. Akeema didn't hide her grin this time.

Putting his arms around her shoulders, Joseph asked what she wanted to do.

"I'd like to talk if that's okay with you," she said.

"Always. What's on your mind?"

"Your marriage, unless it bothers you to talk about her."

"No, not anymore. What would you like to know?"

"Was she a virgin on your wedding night?"

Caught off guard, she heard his surprised gasp.

"Why does that concern you? I don't want to divulge Claire's intimate life without a darn good reason."

She stood corrected, and ashamed. "I'm sorry, Joseph. I didn't mean to insult or disrespect you or Claire in any way."

Easily, he responded, "Apology accepted. Now, tell me what's really going on?"

By this time, she wanted to forget the whole thing. "I've gone about this so clumsily. I feel like I'm trying to run a marathon with two left feet. Just do me a favor and forget about it."

He gave her shoulders a reassuring hug. "Let's understand each other, we won't avoid sensitive issues that need discussion, especially Biblical things."

There he had her. She just needed to be more tactful in the way she came at him. She nodded her agreement.

"Okay, am I right in assuming you want to talk about sex between you and me?"

Akeema sagged with relief. She nodded again.

"Alright. Do you want to do what Yahuah, our Father, tells us to do?"

Honestly, she replied, "Kinda."

Joseph smiled. She'd answered him in a little girl voice.

"Are you sexually attracted to me, as I am to you?" he asked softly.

She nodded with a smile on her face. She was glad he wanted her heart and her body.

"Have you been sexually active recently?"

"Yes," she whispered.

"Did you feel guilty about having sex outside of marriage?"

"Not guilty enough," she admitted dryly.

"Most of us guys are pre-programmed to enjoy sex. It's a problem for women sometimes who feel like they must fake enjoyment to please their man. Do you enjoy sexual pleasure, Akeema?"

"Oh, yes," she breathed.

With a wide grin on his face, Joseph turned her face to him with his index finger. Looking deep into her eyes, he said, "I'm so glad, baby."

For the first time in their romance, Joseph didn't restrain the passion in his kiss. He let her feel his longing for her. Her response to him was quick and sure. She melted in his arms as she moaned into his mouth.

Coming up for air, he broke the kiss. He rasped, "Can you feel how much I want you? Can you?"

"Oh, yes, Joseph, yes!"

They resumed kissing passionately. Joseph savored her mouth, ears, and neck. He licked and suckled every part of her that wasn't clothed. She was on fire!

In a harsh, throaty voice, Akeema said, "I want to feel you inside me, gliding me to a climax. Take me now, Joseph! Now!"

He laid her down on the couch to cover her with his body. They still had their clothes on, but they were experiencing one of the most erotic moments that either of them had ever had. They felt the heat coming from each other in places they were on the brink of exploring for the first time.

Joseph spread Akeema's legs apart so that she could feel his hardness. She lifted her pelvis to rub against him seductively.

"Touch me, Akeema. Please let me feel your hands on me!" he beseeched. She grabbed each butt cheek to squeeze before pressing him down upon her. He was close to letting go.

Suddenly, he tore himself away from her. When he stood up, she could see his readiness for her. Akeema started to slide off her skirt and panties. To her surprise, and dismay, Joseph stopped her.

"Sweetheart, what is it?" she panted,

Painfully, Joseph walked away from the couch. He needed some distance between them. Akeema felt that space. Without his body covering her, she was cold.

With his back to her, Joseph wailed, "For goodness sake, Akeema! I'm a man, not a monk!"

She agreed with him. "I'm well aware of that, my love. Lucky for us, it's the man that I want. Come here." Her deep alto voice was sex personified. Joseph had to fight his urge to ravage her. Now. "We need to discuss this while we still can. Please sit back up. It's hard to focus with you lying there."

With a glazed look in her eyes, Akeema declared,

"The only thing I want to focus on is you pleasing me, and me pleasing you. Everything else can be discussed later. I'm ready for you now. Come to me. Come to me!"

Joseph felt the bulge in his pants growing again. Without actual intercourse, he'd never been this aroused in his life. If she could do this to him fully clothed, what would hot, naked sex do to him? He felt weak in the knees, literally. As her long skirt billowed around her, Akeema began slowly rubbing her thighs up and down. She opened her mouth so that Joseph could see her slowly licking her lips. He thought he might explode. He closed his eyes against the sight of Akeema readying herself for him.

"I don't want us to have sex and then regret it!" he blurted.

"As long as we please one another, what is it to regret?"

"We are about to go against His Holy rule! Don't you care about that at all?" It felt like Joseph had just dumped a bucket of ice-cold water on her. The heat that had almost consumed her was gone.

Gradually, she sat up. Then, she stood up to go to the guest bathroom. Separated, they repaired their clothes to a neat look, instead of an I'm-about-to get-naked one. Akeema didn't know that just as she was splashing water on her face and neck, Joseph was in the master bath doing the same thing.

Joseph wasn't back yet when Akeema made it to the couch that she chose not to sit on. Instead, she went to the matching easy chair to have a seat. When Joseph entered the room, she noticed that he also avoided the couch. He sat alone on the loveseat directly across from her.

Leaning forward he asked, "Are you okay?"

"I'm better. How about you?"

"I'm thinking clearly. Shall we talk now?"

Akeema nodded.

"Claire wasn't a virgin on our wedding night, but it was the first time that she and I made love to each other."

"I see," she replied.

"Do you?"

"Yes. During your courtship and engagement the two of you abstained from havIng sex."

"True that."

Shaking her head, she said, "I'm amazed. You guys must have had a short engagement."

"We were together a year before we married."

Akeema sputtered, "A – a year? You went through, uh, what we, uh, <u>almost</u> did for that long?"

"No, sweetheart. I can assure you that what we just did was a first for me…with no entry."

Akeema ducked her head in shame. "If you hadn't stopped us, I wouldn't have cared. I wanted you."

"I wanted you, too. I still do."

"I'm glad we felt the same way. I was beginning to feel that I had corrupted you."

He smiled gently. "No, my darling. My lust was all my own. Just like the dreams I'll probably have tonight."

"I've heard countless times that there are millions of screwing Christians."

Joseph looked at her steadily. "Is it your opinion that the sin doesn't count as long as millions of people do it?"

She always knew that saying was ridiculous. Now she felt ridiculous for saying it. "No, of course not," she responded.

"Okay then. Now, one thing is certain – whatever we decide to do, we'll both have to commit to it."

"Agreed."

"So, are we putting our will over our Father's?"

Akeema cringed. She wished he hadn't put that question to her that way.

Undecided, she shrugged. "I obviously feel two ways about it. How about you?"

"My spirit is willing, but I just got an example of how weak my flesh is."

"Only when you are with me," she said sadly.

He leaned forward to reach for her hands, kissing them tenderly. "I don't want to hear you being down on yourself because you are a sensual being. Akeema, don't you know that most men love that in their women? I sure do."

"Really" she asked hopefully.

"Really," he echoed.

To him, she still looked uneasy about something. Since they'd decided to have this heart-to-heart, he made the decision to go all the way. If there was a problem, he'd rather know it sooner than later.

"Even before we had our private time together, I prayed to our Father that He approve of you being a wife to me, and a mother to our Joey. Is that something that pleases or concerns you?"

With a huge smile on her face and eyes shiny with tears of joy, she jumped out of her chair to join Joseph for a tight embrace. They were both laughing as he lifted her off the floor to twirl her around and around.

Slightly dizzy and breathless, he put her feet firmly back on the floor. They shared a lingering kiss that was full of love, not lust.

As he looked into her eyes, Akeema saw he had his own share of happy tears.

"So, I take it that you are pleased?"

Throwing her head back, she laughed. "Yes, yes, yes!" she exclaimed.

By the time Akeema drove home that night, she and Joseph agreed that they were engaged to be engaged.

CHAPTER 25

When Akeema got home, her aunt and uncle had retired for the evening. She was glad because she wanted to call Joseph.

Ready for bed, she propped up her pillows to get good and comfortable. They didn't have long to talk, but she wanted to be prepared in case they did. He answered on half a ring.

"Are you ready for bed?" he asked softly.

"I'm ready for bed and a chat. What are you up for?"

"Uh, could you put that another way?"

They both shared a chuckle.

"Akeema, we got a little side-tracked with our pre-engagement that we didn't answer the hard question between us."

She didn't fake ignorance. She knew exactly what he was referring to.

"Are we going to abstain?"

"That's the question. I'll come right out and admit that I want to, but I know it won't happen if you don't want it. Now, share your truth with me, sweetheart."

Since he couldn't see her, Akeema did nothing to stop the tears from falling down her face. She'd kept her shameful secret to herself for so long that she was experiencing relief at finally sharing it with someone who wouldn't judge her, finding her lacking.

"My truth, Joseph, is that I'm a sex addict."

Did he hear her correctly?

"Excuse me?" he asked.

He heard her slowly breathe in and out.

"I love having good sex," she clarified.

"You said that like it's a bad thing."

"Isn't it?"

"Are you unable to hold a job because you're too busy having sex?"

"No. I actually have two jobs as you know."

"Yes, I know. I'm just reminding you."

"Oh."

"Do you work as a prostitute to have sex with all kinds of men…or women?"

"No, of course not!" she said hotly.

"Are you consumed with pornographic movies, books, or magazines?"

"No!"

"Are you unable to function because you're busy masturbating when you don't have a partner?"

"Are you nuts? I have all kinds of things that I get done every day!"

"You're right. Now, I have only one last question for you,"

Exasperated, she replied, "That's a relief. What is it?"

"When do you have time to be a sex addict?"

Akeema stammered, "Joseph, I don't have enough words to explain how much I love – not like – good sex! I mean I don't always wait for…look, I'm often the instigator – me! I'm the one saying, 'let's get it on!' I'm the one that has the 12–15-hour workdays, but still wants – no, <u>crave</u> orgasms! Do you understand?" she wailed.

Calmly, Joseph replied, "Sounds like we're going to have a short engagement."

"Huh?"

"My sweet baby, listen to me. You are not a sex addict, you are highly sexed – like me. You are an answer to a prayer that I made years ago."

"I am?"

"Yes. You see, even before Claire got sick, she had sex to please me. She confessed that she 'liked' sex, but it wouldn't seriously bother her not to have it."

He heard Akeema's quick intake of breath. "And you married her anyway?"

"Yes, I loved her more than myself. Knowing how she felt, we made love two or three times a week, if I was blessed."

"My ex and I had sex that often just going together. I can't imagine being married to you and sleeping next to you without wanting you, Joseph."

Listening to her, he closed his eyes while he thanked his heavenly Father for this precious gift.

"Ah, baby, that's music to my ears."

"As long as we're not sick, can we do it every night?"

Joseph closed his eyes again. This time he was fighting arousal. "Yes, yes," his voice was husky, "If you'd like it, we can wake up in the morning with me inside you, and again before we go to sleep at night."

Akeema moaned. "Really?"

"Oh, yes. I suggest we learn to sleep with the TV on so that whenever we got started, Joey will think the sounds coming from our bedroom will be some movie or another."

"What a good idea! Is that what you and Claire did?"

"No, it wasn't necessary. She was a quiet lover."

"If you do me right, you'll hear me appreciating it, believe me!"

"I do," he sighed. <

"We almost had sex on the couch! Joey could've caught us going at it!" she said, horrified.

"I know. That was one of the reasons that I had the strength to stop."

"What kind of mother will I make?!" she wailed. "I didn't think of him at all in the heat of the moment."

"You're great with kids. You'll be a great mom for our Joey, who already loves you dearly."

"I couldn't love him anymore than I do. It's as if he came out of me, Joseph. I think it's a spiritual thing between us."

"Agreed. That's why I strongly suggest we abstain until we marry, Akeema. I don't want to willfully disobey His holy rule when He is blessing us."

"Our blessing is also a curse," she said in a hard voice.
"What do you mean?"

"He blesses us as compatible mates in every way, including sexual, but tells us we can't have sex and please Him too. It kind of sucks, doesn't it?"

Her words hurt. He asked her for her truth, and she was giving it to him. He hoped they'd have a long and happy life together. She had to feel comfortable talking to him about any and everything. He closed his eyes, bowed his head, and prayed.

Holding the receiver on the other end, Akeema was unnerved by Joseph's silence. Did she share too much? Did she owe him an apology? Before she dissolved in a hysterical panic, he spoke.

"The first thing I want to say outright, Akeema, is that I'm in love with you. I'm pretty sure that our pre-engagement verifies that, but it's important to me that I know you know exactly how I feel."

More silent tears dampened her cheeks. "I love you too, Joseph," she said sweetly.

"I never thought I'd hear those words again from a romantic relationship."

"I never thought a man would consider me as a wife since I can't bear children."

"Again, sweetie, aren't we blessed?"

"Yes, we are. We should be as obedient as we can, shouldn't we?"

"Absolutely. We know there aren't any perfect people on earth. After all, if we could achieve perfection on our own, our Lord and Savior, Yahusha, wouldn't have had to be crucified for us."

"That's true. But, are we going to be able to wait for something we enjoy so much?"

"Not if we try to do it on our own strength."

Perplexed, Akeema said, "That confuses me. Our personal life is just between you and me. Nobody else can help us."

"You are wrong, sweetheart," he said gently.

"I am? Who can help us, other than us?"

"The Most High."

Akeema was shocked. She was so busy being ashamed of her lust, she hadn't prayed about it. Not once.

Joseph continued. "We have to call on HIS strength to help us. That doesn't mean that our flesh won't protest, but if we have Yahuah's armor, we'll be able to pass any and every test."

Uneasily, Akeema admitted, "I can't promise that I'll stop when the petting gets heavy."

"I'm not asking that of you," he replied.

Her shoulders slumped with relief.

"What I want," he said, "is for us to not let the petting get out of hand."

"But, Joseph," she protested, "we were fully clothed, and we got boiling hot!"

"I know, that's why we control our make-out sessions. We've prayed about it, so now, all we must take care of is what we do in the natural. Then, our Father will handle the supernatural."

Akeema asked, "What did the supernatural have to do with this?"

"The adversary works through our flesh. Through our free will, you and I will strive to be obedient. Yahuah will help us because we've asked for His help. He will fight the demons we can't see. I'm confident about that."

She admitted, "I'm really going to need your help, Joseph."

"You will have it."

"I'll try not to make it too hard for you. Oops! I could have put that a better way."

He laughed. "You put it just fine. I love your sense of humor, along with everything else."

"I'm glad," she said, stifling a yawn.

"We're going to be in a near coma in a few hours. We need to get some sleep, honey."

"I know, I just hate to hang up."

"I'll call you in the morning to start our day," he promised.

"Oh, don't worry about doing that. You've got to get Joey and yourself up and running."

"That's true. But I don't want to go all day without hearing your lovely voice."

"My, my. Since you put it that way, if you don't call me, I'll probably call you."

"Now go to sleep knowing how much I love you."

"Right back at 'cha, homeboy."

"Well, goodnight to the future Mrs. Akeema Dawn Smith."

"Joseph, Joey, and Akeema Smith." she replied.

"I love the sound of our family."

"Hearing you say that is the biggest turn-on I've had tonight."

Akeema agreed.

CHAPTER 26

There it was. Her voice. The deep, rich alto with the slight British accent was heard as she read her students the story. Every school day, Principal Derek Wilson walked the hallways to see what was going on in his school firsthand. He altered the times of day that he checked everything to keep the teachers and cleaning crew on their toes.

As he listened to Akeema's calm, cultured voice, a small smile lit up his handsome face. He wasn't looking at her since he was standing out of sight, but he had a vision of her loveliness in his head. Her long, lithe body was made for dancing. Her understated look in clothing enhanced her natural beauty. Her unblemished, dark chocolate skin, big, beautiful eyes with the barely there slant, and her large, full lips that were usually smiling, was a permanent picture in his head. From a distance, anyone that didn't know her might describe her as lovely, cool, and aloof. But Derek had seen her down on the floor with children climbing all over her. Only with her, did he regret his personal rule of not dating anyone that worked for him. He captained an orderly ship, and he was determined to keep it that way. Resuming his stroll, he deliberately stood in front of Akeema's classroom door. Feeling his presence, she looked away from her book for a few seconds to favor him with a small smile. Derek smiled back with his eyes before moving on. That felt good.

Joey efficiently cleaned up the classroom while Akeema sat at her desk, grading papers at the speed of sound. It was Monday and she still had a lot to do. Her dance performances were Sunday, Tuesday, Thursday, and Friday. This morning she invaded Joseph's kitchen to get dinner started. She was treating her boys to a pot of chili beans with smoked turkey and ground beef. She placed all the ingredients into a slow cooker. Akeema's dinner would be almost complete by the time they all got back to the house. On his lunch break, Joseph went home to make sure the house wasn't on fire.

Akeema still needed to get a pan of sweet corn-bread in the oven. She was surprised and pleased when Joseph volunteered to prepare the bread. And, for the first time, Joey was riding in with her.

Feeling cramped, Derek stood up from his desk, stretching his bulky muscles. He took off his tie and suit jacket. Everyone in the outer office had already left, leaving him completely alone. He reveled in the quiet.

He walked to the big picture window that over-looked the parking lot. This time of day, the only cars left were his and the cleaning crew's.

When he saw the 2018 Ford Tempo, he knew Akeema Sprite was still in the building. He contemplated a second visit to her classroom but thought better of it. He didn't need to play with fire.

He was about to sit back down when Akeema came into view, but she wasn't alone. She had a purse on her shoulder, a briefcase in one hand, and a little boy's fingers in her other hand. He enjoyed her toned backside as she slowly walked so the child could keep up with her.

When they reached her car, she put her belongings in the front passenger seat, so she was free to assist Joey into the backseat. Once he was in, she made sure his seatbelt was securely fastened before she locked him in. He watched the car as it pulled away. He guessed that Akeema was taking the child home because the parents probably had car trouble. It was just like her to do such a thoughtful thing. She was known for loving her students, as they loved her. Derek couldn't imagine why some man hadn't made her his own.

"Daddy, do we have dessert?"

"You could eat that cornbread," Akeema teased.

Sheepishly, Joseph said, "I think I put a little too much sugar in it."

She replied, "If you had some frosting to put on top of it, you'd swear it was cake!"

"Sorry folks," he said, hanging his head.

Joey felt ignored. Nobody had answered his question. "I ate all my food. Can I have dessert now?" he asked.

Akeema looked at Joseph. "It's almost his bedtime. It might be hard for him to settle down with all that sugar in him." Joey wasn't a dumb kid. He knew this wasn't going to get him his coveted cookies or ice cream. Besides, he wouldn't say it out loud, but he agreed with Akeema; that was the best cornbread he'd ever had!

Emerging from Joey's bedroom, Akeema looked beat. Wearily, she dropped to the couch, sitting next to Joseph. She smiled at the 'whoosh' of the couch as it greeted her. Joseph gave her a welcoming bottle of cran-pineapple juice. After a deep swig, she said, "Mmm, that hit the spot. Thank you."

Joseph pulled her closer to him, kissing her cheek with a loud, playful smack. "You're more than welcome, sweetheart."

When she emptied the bottle, Akeema was about to take the trash to the kitchen when Joseph stopped her. He took the bottle from her, sitting it on the coffee table. "I'll take that to the kitchen later," he said. "You look worn out. Rest a while before you go home."

Akeema let her head fall back against Joseph's arm. "I might just sleep in the car, I'm so tired. But it's a wonderful weariness."

"You can sleep in the guest room if you don't want to drive home. You might want to call your aunt and uncle, so they won't worry about you."

Akeema yawned. "That sounds like a plan. Thanks for the invite, my love."

"Always. Remember, this is your house too – you just don't live here yet."

She smiled dreamily. "I can hardly wait. I'm glad we're getting closer to that time. Aunt Jean said we should let Joey spend the night with them so that he'll be comfortable with them while we are honeymooning."

"She's right. That's a good idea. I'll get together with them to work it all out."

"Good, they'll be thrilled. They're chomping at the bit to get their hands on him."

Joseph chuckled. "They don't know what it's like to have all that energy with them around the clock. By the time we pick him up, I'm afraid they're going to be exhausted."

"We'll be exhausted too…but for a different reason," she purred.

He nuzzled her short hair.

"That's right, baby. I intend to wear you out with my love."

"Back at'cha, homeboy."

They cuddled for a while before Joseph asked, "Do you have any homework left to do? I'll be glad to help."

"Nope. Since you helped with dinner, I got it all done while Joey helped me straighten up. My boys got me through this day."

"Your boys love you very much," he said huskily.

Akeema turned her face to him to meet the kiss she knew was coming. It was a deep, thorough lip lock that left them both breathless. They kept holding each other when the kiss was over. She kissed the side of his neck a few times before saying, "I'm not sleepy anymore. I'm not tired either. I don't know what you do to me, but all of my inside lights shine for you."

Joseph 's guest room remained guest-less. Akeema decided not to stay the night.

After a quick shower, Akeema was restless and unsettled. Usually, she was a morning shower person. Tonight, she thought a lukewarm cleansing would relax her. Instead, it seemed to have invigorated her. She wanted to call Joseph, but she didn't want to disturb him in case he was able to do what she could not do, sleep.

When her phone pinged with an incoming message, she smiled. It must be Joseph calling because he was having a sleepless night too. Quickly, she read the missive: Hello doll! I'm laying here with you on my mind. Wish you were here, or I was there. Call me. Jake B.

JAKE? Why in the world was he texting her like they were active in each other's life?

Should she text him back to let him know she was engaged now? Would he leave her alone if he knew she was going on with a life that didn't include him?

She didn't want to worry her aunt and uncle over a simple message. And, she didn't want to rile Joseph who would pressure her into getting another restraining order, or beat the crap out of him.

One thing was for sure, she couldn't keep thinking about Jake this time of night. She had a performance coming up, and she didn't want to start the day off sleep deprived. She knelt by her bedside to say her nightly prayers. When she got into bed, she was relaxed and drowsy. Akeema lifted up a quick prayer of thanks. She turned out the light, assumed her sleep position, then entered her dream world.

Sitting in his car, Jake saw Akeema's room darken. He thought the text that he sent her would keep her awake for a while. To his surprise and dismay, she was going to bed in less than five minutes after hearing from him. Did he mean so little to her?

CHAPTER 27

Akeema stood transfixed by the standing ovation that she and the other four dancers were getting. This kind of adoration was usually saved for the dance leads. This was a rare audience. This was a special time.

All five dancers looked straight ahead, not at each other. If they made eye contact with one another, they feared they just might pass out in a puddle on stage.

Being the tallest, Akeema stood in the middle of the line, holding hands on her left and right. She felt like the anchor, keeping them steady.

When the applause began to ebb, Akeema leaned forward for a bow that everyone else on stage followed. When the curtains closed, the stage manager hurried them out of the way so the next scenery could be brought out.

Once backstage, the quintet held each other for a group hug and cry. Part of Akeema's tears were because none of her loved ones were there to share this with her.

Later, at the Meet and Greet, fans were pass- ing up the chance to meet the leads. On this special night, the co-stars had their attention because of the popular quintet.

By the end of the evening, Akeema's hand was tender from shaking hands and autographing programs. A couple of guys slipped her their phone numbers – a first!

This time when the cast suggested they go out for a celebratory dinner, Akeema was in on it! Having learned her lesson with the Jake drama, she called Joseph immediately.

"Oh, honey, I wish Joey and I could have been there to stomp and clap the loudest."

"Thank you, I wish that too. So, I'm calling now so you won't worry or wait up for me. I'll call you in the morning, okay?"

"Actually, no. I'd rather you call me tonight, no matter how late."

"I want you to get some much-needed sleep, Joseph. Be reasonable."

"I'm a poor guy in love who is a little overprotective. Promise you'll call me." He heard her sigh of resignation.

"Fine, I'll call."

"Promise?"

"Yes, Joseph, I promise."

"Thanks, baby. Now, I know I don't have to be concerned that you'll eat too much, so have a good time while you're missing me."

"Yes, sir. Kiss Joey goodnight for me."
"Will do. I'll talk to you later. Love you."
"Back at 'cha, homeboy."
When they hung up, they were both smiling.

Strange. She wasn't prone to breaking her promises to him. Joseph glanced at his cell. It was a little after 1:00 a.m. Could she be home sleeping before calling him? It was certainly possible. He'd feel like an idiot if it was just that simple and he made a big deal out of nothing. He decided he'd been patient enough. He called her. He was greeted by her voice mail. Crap. Now what? Without giving it much thought, he called her aunt. She picked up on a third of a ring.

"You guys having car trouble?" she asked without saying hello.

"No. I'm sorry for calling so late, but Akeema promised to call me when she got home. It's after 1:00 in the morning and I haven't heard from her. Would you mind checking on her for me?" Joseph heard the desperation in his own voice.

"Of course I don't mind. Hang on a minute."

"Thanks, Jean."

He heard her put the phone down, then silence. The longer she took, the more he fretted. At last he heard her pick up the phone.

"Joseph?"

"Yes, ma'am!"

"She's not here! I checked her room and bathroom, the living room, and the driveway. I'm going to wake

Rick so we can go to that all-night pancake house to see if she's there."

"Oh, Jean, I'm sorry to get you up like this, but I'm so thankful you are there."

Kindly, she reminded him, "She's our family and we love her too."

"I know. I'll be up whenever you call."

"I get that. I won't make you wait longer than necessary, I promise."

"Thank you. Talk to you soon."

When Jean walked into their bedroom, Rick was already up and dressed.

"Heavenly Father, please let them find Akeema safe and sound. We are all counting on Your strength to get us through whatever is to come. We love You and we thank You in Your beloved Son's precious name. Amen!"

His phone rang a second after he finished his prayer. "Is she there?" he asked anxiously,

"Her car is here," Rick said, "and the glass on the driver's door has been shattered."

Joseph felt cold. It was like having blood in your veins that felt like ice water. He gulped back the bile that entered his throat. "Call the police!" he ordered in a ragged voice.

"We have. We're waiting for them now."

"I'll be right there!" he practically shouted.

Rick tried to placate him. "Nonsense. It's silly to disturb Joey when you weren't a witness to anything.

He's going to be upset enough when he's told what's going on. Let him get some good sleep now while he can. It might be the last peaceful slumber he has for a while."

An agitated Joseph was a parent first. "Yes, you're right. Please call me after you talk to the police."

"Will do. Talk to you soon." Click.

Joseph sat on the couch, phone in hand. The realization that Akeema was hurt or worse, filled him with dread. Overwhelmed, he began to cry.

With the TV on for noise, Joseph sat on the couch as he prayed and cried repeatedly.

There wasn't any booze in the house, and this was only the second time that it mattered. When his wife passed away, he wanted to drink himself into oblivion. He couldn't, however, because he had to be there for Joey. He'd lost his mother, and he was too young to even remember his paternal grandparents. Joseph and Claire had taken him to Atlanta, Georgia to meet his papa and meemaw. At that time, Joseph's father had shared his concern about Joseph's mother, Mary. The dementia that eventually required her admittance to a senior living facility, was evident but manageable. Her only grandchild, Joey, had stolen her heart. She fed him, bathed him, and played with him around the clock. When anyone tried to take care of him to give her a break, they got cussed out - something the disease prompted her to do. When, for her own safety, she was committed to controlled living, Bill, Joseph's dad, had sold their home to follow her there. Claire was always diligent about sending pictures of Joey to Atlanta. Since her passing, Joseph hadn't bothered. At least twice a month, he and Joey sat down in front of the laptop to visit with Bill. Mary made fewer and fewer appearances as the dementia took more control. Currently, Joey knew 'about' his grandparents without actually knowing them. His heart was attached to Akeema.

Poor Claire had been a 'Fire Station baby' – her words. When the firemen heard her yelling her little lungs out, they saw a note pinned to her blanket that said her parents were drug addicts who couldn't take care of her. She was taken to the hospital to be detoxed. Then, came the multitude of foster homes that she visited but never felt a part of.

Joseph considered Claire a miracle from the Almighty. She rose from the many challenges in her life to become a social worker herself, that helped kids who were alone in the world.

Even after a year had passed, Joseph still felt her loss. He was blessed that Akeema understood this. If he lost her too, Joseph didn't know how he would survive.

When his phone rang, he was afraid and desperate to pick it up.

"Yes?" he croaked.

Rick didn't mince words. "Inside her car they found her briefcase and purse. Her wallet had her cash and credit cards in it. They consider this a possible abduction."

Joseph suppressed a scream.

"What's being done?"

"The search has already started. They will keep us informed."

"Us?"

"Of course. You're her fiancé. We consider you and Joey part of our family."

"Thank you, sir. After I take Joey to school, I'll head to your house."

"You're more than welcome, son. But, to tell you the truth, if I had a job to go to, that's where I'd be. Just sitting around here could make you lose your mind. If Jean and I weren't retired, you'd be here by yourself."

"You've got a point," Joseph admitted. "but I don't know how patient with people I can be today. I have staff that answers to me, and I deal with the public. I don't know if I can deal with petty problems right now."

Rick heard the edge in Joseph's voice. He was not just afraid; he was mad as hell.

Holding his wife in his arms as she sobbed, was devastating to Rick. He loved her more than anyone else on the planet. Jean and Akeema were the near and dears in his heart. He would gladly give his life to save either of them. He'd also kill anyone who dared to hurt them.

"There, there, honey. They're going to find her. She'll be alright. Trust in the Most High."

Sniffling, Jean replied, "What if His will is to take her from us?"

Rick wanted to cry along with his wife. "Then we know He will get us through it. We need to depend on His strength, not ours."

She blew her nose before she said, "I know that in my soul. But my flesh is telling me that if she's dead, I won't make it!" Jean wailed.

Rick held her tightly while rocking her back and forth. He didn't trust himself to speak.

Mrs. Endicott didn't quite know what to do. She didn't know the teacher she was filling in for, but she'd heard all kinds of good things about Akeema Sprite. It was odd to see a room full of subdued seven and eight-year olds. One little boy, in particular, looked devastated. She'd tried any number of games but was met with a tepid response. Mrs. Endicott felt like a failure.

Unknown to her, Derek Wilson was observing her class. The chubby, gray-haired woman was middle-aged, but looked like a grandmother compared to Akeema. Derek remembered the younger woman on the floor with the children climbing all over her. If this poor woman got down on the mat, she'd probably need help getting up!

One thing was for sure; If he ever saw Akeema Dawn Sprite alive, he was going to ask her out on a date.

"Mr. Smith," the clerk spoke quickly, "there's a lady at the complaint booth who's hoppin' mad – and loud. Becky sent me to get you."

Joseph held his head with both hands. He wanted to disappear. "Jeff, how long have you worked here? A couple of years?"

"Two years full time, sir. Before that I worked part time after school. All together, I've been here for over four years."

Joseph tried to act like the professional he wasn't feeling. "I hear you're wanting to get into management, is that right?"

The gangly, freckle-faced young man nodded eagerly.

"Do you think you can handle Mrs. Loud and disruptive?"

Jeff's face and hair color were both red. He stared at his boss like he'd lost his mind. Joseph was hiding his irritation…or at least he was trying to. "Does your silence mean I need to get someone else who's equal to the challenge?"

"No!" Jeff practically shouted. "I believe I can handle this, sir."

Joseph was surprised he wasn't saluted.

"Good. Take her to the conference room where you'll be videotaped. Be sure to let the customer know that the session with her is being recorded."

"Yes, sir!" Jeff turned away from Joseph, almost running out of the office.

Joseph felt like he'd just dodged a bullet.

Mrs. Endicott sat behind the desk watching the somber little boy picking up floor mats and toys. She hadn't asked him to do that, yet she felt compelled to let him. When he was done, he walked directly to her without hesitation. She sat up straighter, preparing herself for…what?

Gravely, he asked, "How long will you be here?"

"I'm not sure, uh, what was your name?"

"Joey."

"Okay, Joey. I just fill in when the regular teacher can't make it. I haven't been told if I need to come back tomorrow yet."

"Is teacher Akeema real sick?"

"I'm afraid I don't know, dear. But, if I hear anything about her, I'll be glad to tell you." Mrs. Endicott saw a hint of a smile on the child's lips. She decided she was going to Principal Wilson for an update on this beloved teacher.

"Daddy, are we going to teacher Akeema's house to see how she is?"

"Yes, son, we're going to her house."

Joseph didn't want to tell Joey that Akeema was missing while he was driving. He also didn't want to tell him about her by himself. Rick and Jean would be invaluable in helping him explain the situation to Joey. Just thinking about it made him sick.

"How's my favorite boy?" Rick bellowed as he lifted Joey into the air.

His squeal and giggles were music to Joseph's ears. He knew what a blessing it was to have Jean and Rick in their lives. The house was fragrant with their dinner.

When Jean walked into the living room, it warmed her heart to see her husband's first genuine smile in the last 24 hours. When Joseph saw her, he went to give her a bear hug with a kiss on each cheek.

"You guys hungry?" she asked pleasantly.

"You bet," replied Joseph. "What smells so good?"

"Creamy chicken noodle soup with potatoes and carrots. I also prepared a salad for anyone wanting to chow down on some roughage."

"Sounds good. When do we eat?" Joseph faked an appetite. As black as he was, the thought of eating made him feel green.

Surprisingly, Joseph was able to eat a healthy serving of soup and salad. Even Joey ate enough to satisfy Jean. The delight on Joey's face, when she put fudge brownies on the table, gave Jean her first smile that day. Joey's effect on the grown-ups was just what they all needed.

Finally, the time they'd all feared was upon them.

"Is she STILL sleeping? Did we save her some food?" Joey asked.

A short shake of Joseph's head let Rick and Jean know that this was on them.

"No, sweet boy, Akeema isn't sleeping," replied Jean.

Joey's face brightened. "Is she in her room? Can I go get her? Is she feeling good again?"

Joseph couldn't stand it. Abruptly, he left the dining room table.

Rick sat Joey on his lap. A quick nod to Jean let her know he was giving her the ball to run with.

"Our Akeema isn't here Joey. She had an accident."

Joey frowned. "Is she in the hospital?"

"Right now, we're not sure where she is. The police are looking for her," Jean replied gently.

Joey had his thinking cap on. "Did she hit her head? Can she remember us?"

What he said was plausible, Jean decided to use that. "That's exactly what we think might've happened. You're such a smart boy," she praised.

Joey grinned at her compliment. "So, the police are going to find her and help her?"

"Yep, we sure hope so."

He nodded. "I know what we can do for her, auntie."

"You do? Tell us."

"We need to pray."

Tears stung Jean's eyes. Rick swallowed the rock in his throat. Joseph, who had been listening, bowed his head.

Out of the mouths of babes.

CHAPTER 28

L ater that evening, Rick, Jean, and Joseph sat in the comfortable living room watching the Disney Channel with Joey. Every pair of adult eyes were covertly watching the child that was loved so much.

Joseph could tell his son's energy was ebbing. Any other time, he would have picked him up to take him home. Tonight, however, he didn't want to leave. He wanted to be near Akeema's loved ones, because they were now also his and Joey's.

Jean saved the day. "Joseph, you know we have a guest room in this house. You'd be doing me and my old man a favor if you guys spent the night, or nights, here with us. It's lonely with Akeema gone. Not only that, but we'll also be together when we get updates from the police."

He shot a look at Rick who was holding a half-asleep child to his side.

Rick exclaimed, "Yeah, man, we'd love to have you guys here. Why don't you go pick up some clothes, personal things and toys while we put this little one to bed."

"Thanks, we'd love to stay. We love you guys," Joseph said emotionally.

Jean chimed in, "And, we love y'all too! We're family."

With that said, Jean walked over to Joey, taking him from Rick's side. Holding him close with his head resting on her shoulder, Jean closed her eyes as she enjoyed the warmth of him next to her.

Watching them together, touched a tender part in Joseph's heart. Before he began weeping, he quickly got moving. He needed to go home to pack.

He hurried out to the car, drove about a block, parked on the side of the road, then wept loudly and bitterly.

Back at his house, Joseph checked the mail for any bill that he needed to pay. He and Joey were going to be gone for at least a week, so he wanted everything up to date.

Sorting through the mail, he came across an envelope addressed to him in a scrawl he didn't recognize. There wasn't a return address, so he didn't have a clue who was writing him. Since chain letters were no longer in style, he tore into the envelope out of curiosity. What he read made his blood run cold:

Joseph, Akeema is mine now. You and your son can find someone else to love. We couldn't be together in life – but we now have each other forever. J.B.

When he screamed, Joseph didn't recognize his own voice.

By the time Joseph got back to Jean and Rick's place, he was a basket case. He could barely breathe through his panic and shock. Blessedly, Joey was sound asleep, so they took time to fall apart together.

Jean was the first to regain her sanity. She called the police to report the letter that she saw as evidence. Two detectives were knocking on her door within fifteen minutes.

They were asked questions that they had no answers to. They only had the letter that verified deliberate misconduct by Jake. Joseph did mention the restraining order that Akeema let lapse. Since he wasn't bothering her, she hadn't seen the point in refiling against him. By the time the detectives left, it was almost midnight. Nobody was sleepy. They were all restless and mad at Jake.

Trying to settle down and get some inner peace, Jean suggested they hold hands to form a prayer circle. They all prayed, cried, and praised Yahuah, the heav- enly Father. When they finished, they were exhausted and ready for bed.

At about 4:00 A.M. Joseph dreamed a phone was ringing at a distance. By reflex, he laid his arm across Joey's little back. They were both sleeping in Akeema's bed at Joey's insistence. Her fresh scent welcomed them every time they moved. The ringing stopped, allowing Joseph to drift back into a deeper slumber.

"No! No! Dear God, No!"

Joseph sat up in bed. This wasn't a dream! He looked down at his son who was sleeping soundly.

Carefully, he got out of the room without disturbing Joey. In his bare feet, he hurried down the hallway to the master bedroom where he heard Jean sobbing.

With no thought of knocking, Joseph burst into the room, prepared for the worst. The scene that he walked in on broke his heart. Rick and Jean were standing in the middle of the room, clinging to each other. Jean was crying against her husband's chest.

Joseph couldn't speak.

Rick finally noticed he and Jean were not alone. Joseph was standing in the doorway, so still that he looked like a bronze statue. Looking at Joseph with little emotion on his face or in his voice, Rick said, "They found them." That should have been good news. However, Akeema's aunt and uncle were not celebrating.

"Tell me," Joseph demanded hoarsely.

"Next to the lake, a guy who was fishing saw a sleeping bag," Rick replied. "He was curious to see what was in it, but as he got closer, he smelled something unpleasant."

Joseph felt like passing out and vomiting at the same time.

Rick continued. "The guy called the police.

Both Jake and Akeema were inside. A note was pinned to the inside of the bag."

"What did it say, man?" Joseph cried.

"We're together now. Please bury us together at the same time, same place. That was it."

Joseph's knees buckled. He hit the floor hard, his head bowed.

"Tell him the rest, honey!" Jean was concerned for Joseph.

Hearing Jean say there was more to be told kept Joseph from passing out.

"He shot Akeema, then himself. He died. Akeema didn't."

The room was quiet except for Jean's sniffles. Hotly, Joseph shouted, "You couldn't lead with that? Why did you do that to me?"

Jean replied, "There's more."

"She's alive! Isn't that the most important thing?" cried Joseph.

"He shot her in the head. Our girl is in a coma."

"Do the doctors think she'll wake up?"

"They don't know," Jean responded.

"I'll get dressed and go to her," Joseph said as he turned to leave the room.

Rick stopped him. "Only family can visit."

Joseph turned back around to face them. "Are you kidding me? Get me in there!" he screamed.

Wiping her nose with a tissue, Jean replied,

"That's just what we plan to do. You and Rick can go to the hospital, and I'll get Joey to school. After he's situated, I'll meet you guys in her room."

Joseph felt terrible. Joey hadn't even entered his mind. He felt like a terrible father.

He stammered, "Uh, listen folks, don't, uh, why don't I worry about Joey. I'll take care of him so that you two can go to Akeema. I'll meet you guys after I get Joey to school, okay?"

Suddenly, Jean was all business. "No, that's not okay. Akeema is the woman you've chosen as part of you and Joey's family. You need and want to get to her asap. Rick and I are your support system. Now, stop wasting time and go get dressed. Both of you."

She wasn't in the mood to play around. Rick and Joseph got busy doing what she said.

At the hospital, Rick and Joseph were the only ones sitting in the waiting room. Neither man spoke as they struggled not to be overly emotional. If they could help it, they were unwilling to be in public crying like blubbering idiots. When they saw the gently chubby nurse coming toward them, they jumped to their feet. She spoke in a voice just above a whisper, but she was clearly heard. "Please follow me to Miss Sprite's room."

Apparently, she knew who they were so no further words or verification was necessary. It felt like they were walking a mile. Both men were filled with dread and anticipation. When they reached Akeema's room, the nurse stepped aside to let them in.

There she was.

If it wasn't for the tubes going in and coming out of her, along with the beeps, bells, and hissing noises, Akeema appeared to be sleeping peacefully.

The two men in her life carefully walked around the medical equipment to reach the side of her bed. It was then that they saw a huge bandage that covered the left half of her head. Her face, however, was relaxed and beautiful.

The nurse was standing just inside the doorway, silently observing the visitors. When they looked her way, she was prepared for their questions.

"What's under the bandage?" Rick asked solemnly.

"Basically, her wound. Miss Sprite was shot."

At her words, both men looked stricken. No one said a word because they couldn't. The understanding nurse walked closer to Rick and Joseph. "The bullet was removed, and she's in no pain," she comforted.

Under her keen gaze, she could see the effect of her words on the men. She'd helped them a little. Before she left them to have their private moment with the patient, she said, "You will have an opportunity to speak with her doctor after 9:00 a.m. when he starts working the floor."

"Thank you," the men said in unison.

Left alone with Akeema, the men stood next to her bed, one on each side. They began to lightly move their hands up and down her arms, carefully avoiding the IV's. Her skin was warm and soft, full of life. They were relieved by this small contact with her. It gave them a renewed sense of hope.

As the hours slowly passed, neither Rick nor Joseph left Akeema's side. With the dawning of the new day, they saw the morning light filtering through the blinds on the hospital windows. The next time they saw the nurse, she had news for them. "A lady named, Jean, is here to visit this patient. Only two at a time can visit in the ICU, so please decide who is going to swap out, so that she can come in."

When she left the room, Joseph faced Rick – ready to fight for his position. Thankfully, he didn't have to.

"I need to see my little woman," Rick said of his 6-foot-tall wife. "I'll see you later, alright?"

Joseph smiled and nodded gratefully.

Jean recognized her husband lumbering toward her from a distance. After almost forty years of marriage, her heart still skipped a beat at the sight of him. As he neared her, she could see the wide grin on his face, his special gift just for her. She sprang to her feet, anxious to feel his strong arms around her. They crashed into each other as Rick gave her a back-crunching hug.

"Hey, sweetheart," he said gruffly.

"Hi, honey. How's my mister?"

"Better, now that you're here."

"Oh, you sweet talker. That's music to my ears."

"Your voice is my music." Jean laughed. "We sound like young honeymooners." "Forever," he whispered.

They held each other a while longer before Jean asked, "How's our girl?"

"Resting quietly."

"Has she awakened yet?"

"No, not yet."

"It's in our Father's hands, He'll take care of her."

"Yes, He will."

"Are you hungry?" Jean asked her hubby. Caught off guard, Rick said, "I haven't thought about it. But, now that you asked, yeah, I am."

Jean walked back to where she'd been sitting. She had a shopping bag full of goodies.

"How does a breakfast sandwich, with scrambled eggs and melted cheese on toast sound?"

"Delicious," he said as he licked his lips.

Smiling, she handed the wrapped-in-foil goodie to him.

As he ate, she pulled out an ice-cold bottle of water. In four healthy bites, the sandwich was history. Jean gave Rick a napkin that he really didn't need. There wasn't a trace of food left.

Sheepishly, he said, "I guess I was hungrier than I thought. As a matter of fact, I'm still a little hungry."

Out of her bag of tricks, Jean produced another sandwich. She loved the shine in his eyes as he took the foiled sandwich.

He was about to open it when he hesitated. Seeing him pause, Jean asked what was wrong.

"Am I eating Joseph's breakfast?"

"Nope. I still have his food and water."

"Is this your sandwich, honey?"

Shaking her head, she remarked, "I know my man. I knew you'd eat more than one."

As he unwrapped the savory goodie, he groused, "You know your FAT man."

"There's not an inch or a pound that I don't love."

Rick gave her a sexy wink before chowing down on his food.

Meanwhile, Joseph was having a chat with his sleeping lady love. Since her hand had an IV in it, he gently placed her pedal soft hand on top his.

"Akeema, I'm so glad you're here. I hope and pray that my voice reaches you so that you know your loved ones are with you, and that you're safe."

His eye leakage forced him to stop long enough to control himself. He didn't think anything would be accomplished by sobbing out his woes. Once he'd gathered himself, he continued.

"Your aunt and uncle are here; you'll see or hear them soon. Joey is too young to visit, but he sends his love. He also starts and stops each day with prayers for you. As soon as I can, I'll contact our Bible fellowship group, so that a prayer chain will get started."

Just then, Jean and her huge shopping bag walked in. She was all business.

"How is she?"

"Resting comfortably."

"Have you called into work this morning?"

Joseph looked startled.

"It hasn't even crossed my mind."

"Do you have your cell with you?"

"No," he said regretfully.

"That's okay, son. Rick is in the waiting room; use his. Are you hungry?"

"Now that you mention it, yes."

Jean reached into her shopping bag for his water and sandwich. Handing them to Joseph, she demanded, "Go eat and take care of your personal things. Send Rick to me."

Joseph felt the urge to salute her but kept himself in check. All he said was, "Yes, ma'am." Walking past her to leave the room, he gave her a quick peck on the cheek on his way out. He felt better.

Looking down at her niece, Jean loved her as if she was a child she gave birth to. Just as she and Rick were about to enter the adoption process, Akeema had been orphaned. Next to Rick, her sister's daughter was the love of her life. If Jake hadn't blown out his own brains, Jean had to admit to herself that she could have ended that white boy's life.

Jean gently kissed Akeema's forehead. Her skin felt soft and warm. She looked more like a model than a dancer or teacher. Her features weren't stressed at all. Her large, slightly slanted eyes gave her an exotic look. The thick, manicured brows that framed her eyes were perfectly shaped. With no blush or contour, Akeema's high cheek bones were very prominent. Her full, shapely lips looked a little chapped. When Rick walked in, Jean was hovering over their niece as she was smoothing on some lip balm.

Rick watched the women in his life with love and pride. His heart was so full of love for them; it was close to bursting. He walked to Jean's side, hugging her at the waist.

"Do you think she is going to wake up, honey" she asked.

"Lord willing."

Principal Derek Wilson read, then re-read, the newspaper headlines. He had a hard time accept- ing that one of his favorite teachers was involved in an attempted murder and suicide. Akeema Sprite was respected by her colleagues and beloved by her pupils. As far as he knew, she didn't have friends at school, but that seemed to be her choice. She'd let everyone know that since she danced and taught school, she didn't have a lot of time to forge deep connections with people. She didn't apologize for it, she simply stated the fact. Her directness was one of the many things he liked about Akeema. This woman had no coy batting of fake eyelashes, giggles, or hair weaves down her back. She was naturally beautiful with little need for excessive makeup. When she wasn't on stage, the only enhancement that Derek had seen was a little color on her lips and cheeks. She carried herself regally and gracefully. Her clothing was simple, he'd never seen her in shocking pink or bold flowers. When dealing with the seven-and eight-year-olds in her class, she smiled wide and often. With adults, she was always cordial, but cool. Derek learned to look into her eyes which were warm and welcoming. During his tenure, Derek had met many young, attractive women. However, he made the decision not to court any of them. He was determined to keep gossip and messiness out of his administration. Then Akeema arrived, and his world tilted. He'd just decided that she was the exception to the rule when she disappeared. Now, she was back, but in a coma. There was nothing to do but put her in the heavenly Father's hands.

CHAPTER 29

As they prayed and waited for Akeema to wake up, those that loved her settled into a daily routine. Each weekday morning, Joseph would ready Joey for school. They were back home now, so they would breakfast together. When it was time to go, Jean and Rick took Joey to school while Joseph went to the hospital. At noon, when Joseph went to work, Rick spent time with Akeema while Jean prepared dinner for everyone. When it was time to pick Joey up from school, Rick performed that duty. Rick took Joey to his and Jean's house to do homework and eat dinner. Then, the boys would play games or watch TV until Jean joined them. After work, Joseph went directly to the hospital, often passing Jean on her way out. He had roughly thirty minutes alone with Akeema before visiting hours ended. Then, Joseph went to pick up Joey at Jean and Rick's. Before they left there, Jean fed him, and they all prayed together. Joey was included in this ritual, and it was usually his talks with the Most High that brought the adults to tears.

Joseph and Rick took pictures, using their cell phones, of Akeema sleeping peacefully. They made sure that Joey saw them, which always gave the little boy joy. Jean made sure that a colorful patchwork blanket covered the sterile white gown, sheets, and pillowcases. Little Joey could see her, and he understood that Akeema was in a deep sleep because she was so sick. They told him, honestly, that they were waiting to see the holy Father's will to be shown, life or a trip to heaven. Since he'd witnessed his mother's passing, he understood who was in charge.

On one quiet evening, Jean sat next to Akeema's bedside, knitting a new periwinkle blanket. She knew the vibrant purple-blue color was one of her and Joey's favorites.

The classical music that was playing was what Akeema enjoyed both listening and dancing to. It almost put Jean to sleep.

"Hello," a deep baritone said, making her jump.

"Oh!" Jean said as she gave her chest a pat.

"You startled me! Are you in the right room?"

He glanced at the patient, then nodded.

Jean stood up, walking to him. She extended her hand to shake his. "I'm Akeema's aunt. Jean is my name." She looked him up and down, liking what she was looking at. A black man, well-built, clean shaven with short hair, great smile, and beautiful dark brown eyes.

"I'm Derek Wilson, ma'am. I'm the principal at Roosevelt Elementary where Miss Sprite is a teacher. Well, I guess I didn't have to say that last part, did I?"

Good looking and educated. Jean was impressed. If Akeema didn't already love Joey and Joseph, this man would've been a good suitor for her niece. Oh well.

"I'm pleased to meet you, Mr. Wilson. Thank you for personally coming to check on my niece. I'm sure she'd appreciate it if she knew."

Not knowing how to respond, Derek nodded again before going to Akeema's bedside. Even in a coma, he thought she looked beautiful. Without thinking, he gently rubbed her velvety-textured forehead. He regretted the many times he talked himself out of asking her out to dinner or a movie.

Well, well, thought Jean. This handsome young man had a crush on her niece. She'd grown to love Joseph, but she couldn't imagine turning this guy down for anything!

"So, Mr. Wilson," she pried, "is it your policy to visit all of your sick teachers?"

Never taking his eyes off Akeema, he replied honestly. "No, ma'am."

"No? Then why are you here?"

"I care," he answered simply.

"I can see that. Do you know she's engaged?" He met her watchful eyes then. "No, I didn't know that. She doesn't talk about her personal life to anyone."

"Yes, she's very private."

"I hope he's a good guy that's good to her."

"He is. Otherwise, he'd have to deal with me and my husband."

Derek smiled a little. "I can believe that."

"Is my niece friends in any way with you?"

Sadly, Derek shook his head. Then, Jean watched him go into business mode. "Do the doctors say she'll wake up?"

"They hope she will. Her other body functions are doing well, so that's a good sign."

Derek nodded. "I'll keep her in my prayers. Please keep me up to date on her progress."

"I will. Since I bring Joey to school these days, I'll stop in to visit you when I have an update."

"That would be great. I'll say goodbye now. It was a pleasure meeting you."

He turned and left without waiting for a response. What Jean didn't know was that Derek was through talking to her because he was busy berating himself for not making a play for Akeema when he first saw her. He'd only seen her surrounded by children, and once as she danced. Because of his self-imposed detachment, he couldn't even imagine her with another man. To his surprise, he had TWO rivals. One of them had been so obsessed with her that he couldn't see his life without her in it, and he was unwilling to let her have a life without him. If Derek hadn't delayed having Akeema as his girlfriend, she might never have met that killer guy at all!

Here he was, a 35-year-old man with a great career and no romance in his life. And, to top it off, the woman he wanted was engaged and in a coma!

Driving home from the hospital, Derek was totally disgusted with himself.

Weary and disheartened, Joseph walked into Akeema's hospital room. Tears were already filling his eyes by the time he reached her bedside. Looking down at her, he took his daily assessment of his beloved fiancé. She lay there so peaceful, so beautiful, so still. Her loved ones were in the fourth week of their faithful vigil. Joseph now had a secret that nobody but him and the Most High knew; he was losing hope.

Being a widower, he was all too familiar with watching a loved one slowly leave this world. His eating and sleeping habits were suffering big time. Tall and well-built, he'd lost fifteen pounds. Jean and all his coworkers noticed. Everyone was blessing him with food offerings that largely remained un-eaten. He got snatches of sleep, but dreams of death and funerals kept waking him. Oddly enough, the only time he got any quality sleep was in the big chair next to Akeema. He had almost four hours of alone time with her that he cherished.

Talking to her, he always gave her reports on his workday and on Joey. Being able to reach out to her comforted him as nothing else did. He truly loved this woman, but he was afraid. The pain of possibly losing two women to death was more than he could bear. He had to fight the urge to disappear. Indeed, if Joey didn't love her so much, he would have been more inclined to pack up and leave. The thought of it didn't comfort him. He felt like a coward.

Touching her arm lightly, Joseph said a quick prayer with his head bowed and eyes closed. Looking at her face again, he gasped. Her eyes were open! She was looking at him intently. The tube down her throat prohibited her from speaking. Quickly, Joseph pushed the call button. Almost immediately, he heard movements and voices coming his way. When two nurses hurried in, Joseph didn't have to be told to get out of the way.

Suddenly, the room was filled with hospital staff. He couldn't see Akeema at all, but he heard her gagging and coughing. Nurses with soothing voices were talking to her to keep their patient calm.

Joseph watched the faces of the caregivers closely. When he saw their worried features relax, then turn to smiles, he had to restrain himself from hopping up and down while shouting hallelujah!

He was so caught up with the action, he forgot to call Jean and Rick! In seconds, he dashed off a text to each of them with the blessed news. When he felt the vibration of his phone, he stepped out of the room to answer the call.

It was Jean. "She's awake? Is she talking? What did she say?"

Joseph patiently waited for a chance to speak.

"Joseph, are you there?"

"Yes, ma'am, I'm here. The doctors are with her right now. She's awake, and I'm pretty sure the tube is out of her mouth."

"Oh, how wonderful! Praise our heavenly Father!"

"Amen!"

"Well, I have my purse on my arm to walk out the door. I'm on my way to you guys."

Before Joseph said okay, she'd hung up.

When Jean got to the hospital, she met Joseph as he stood in the corridor outside of Akeema's room.

"The doctor is still in there? Is she alright?" Jean asked as she looked inside to see what was going on.

"Yes, as you can see, they're still in there. I don't know how she is yet."

Joseph watched as Jean squared off her shoulders before she walked into Akeema's room. He stood just outside the doorway to see what was about to happen.

Jean stood behind everybody in the room. She didn't shout, but she spoke loud enough for them all to hear her.

"I'm Akeema's aunt. Please tell me what's going on. Now." she said with authority.

A short, portly man separated himself from the group. He had a receding hairline and eyes that were so unwavering they held your attention – even behind the black framed glasses. His English was heavily accented, yet understandable.

"Your relative is awake," he said simply. "You may come to my office at the end of the hall if you have questions for me after your visit. I'm Dr. Geiger."

He then bowed at the waist before leaving the room. Joseph stepped aside to let him pass. Following his lead, the others left too, with pleased looks on their faces. Together, Jean and Joseph walked hand-in-hand to Akeema's bed. Her eyes were closed.

In a low voice, Joseph remarked, "I know it's tacky, but I'd love to shake her awake."

At the sound of his voice, Akeema's eyes popped open.

Jean exclaimed, "Oh, baby girl! You're awake!"

Akeema stared at her aunt emotionless.

"Tell me how you are doing," Jean prompted her.

"Who are you?" Akeema asked in a rusty voice.

Taken aback, Jean asked, "What do you mean, who am I?"

Joseph could tell Jean was losing it.

"Careful, careful," he said gently.

Akeema switched her gaze to him. He could tell she didn't recognize him either.

"Hello, sweetheart. It's me, Joseph," he said softly.

She frowned. He could tell she was trying to conjure up a memory of him. Then, pulling out his cell phone from his shirt pocket, he had an idea.

Disapprovingly, Jean asked, "Who are you calling at a time like this?"

"Nobody. Wait just a minute."

Crossing her arms over her ample bosom, she did as requested.

Finally, he found what he was looking for.

"Look, Akeema. Look at this."

Joseph and Jean saw her beautiful face light up.

"Is he mine?" Akeema whispered in awe.

"He's ours, honey. His name is Joey."

"Joey," she repeated, totally enthralled.

When she looked up at Joseph, she asked what was expected of her. "Are you my husband?"

Joseph sat on the bed next to her, taking the hand that didn't have the IV in it. "Not yet. You and I are engaged."

Again, Akeema frowned. "We had a baby BEFORE we got married?"

Oh, dear. He started this mess. What was he supposed to say now? Joseph threw a desperate look at Jean.

She didn't help. "You wanted to run this, homeboy, so run it!"

Embarrassed, but stuck in the muck, he took a deep breath. Nothing worked better than truth.

"Joey is my son with my first wife, Claire. I'm a widower. Once you and I are married, you'll be his stepmother, or his adoptive mother if you'd like. He already loves you so much."

"I love him too…I think."

"You've had a head trauma. You just need a little more time to de-fog. We're here to help you remember who, and what, is important to you."

Akeema cast a doubtful look at Jean, who had a perturbed look on her face. She was still a little miffed that Joseph had taken over. She was the only one in the hospital with a bio link to Akeema. Plus, although they weren't married yet, Joseph was behaving as if they were.

"Is my mother out of town, or something? Why isn't she here?"

Caught off guard, Jean blurted out, "My husband and I raised you!"

An excited Joseph asked, "Do you remember your mom?"

Akeema asked, "Was I in a car wreck?"

The room went silent. Akeema watched them expectantly. Jean and Joseph didn't know what to tell her or how. They weren't sure how much shock she could, or should, take.

"Was I in some kind of fight? I obviously lost." She said seriously.

To Joseph, Jean announced, "I'm going to see Dr. Geiger for a moment. Keep our girl company." She then hot-footed out of there before anyone could say or ask anything.

Akeema was stunned. Not by Jean's sudden departure, but because she wanted to say something, and she couldn't seem to find the words to say it. What in the world was happening? As Jean left, Joseph realized he was uncomfortable being left alone with his fiancée. He got a flashback from the last weeks of his wife's passing.

He pasted a fake smile on his face before turning to look at Akeema. What he saw, terrified him.

Her mouth was moving as though she was trying to say something. However, she wasn't making a sound. She looked shell-shocked, her eyes were wide with fear and confusion.

"Akeema, are you trying to speak?"

Her wordless mouth kept moving.

"Do you understand me? Nod your head if the answer is yes."

She nodded.

"Can you make a sound with your voice? Let me hear you try."

Akeema hummed successfully.

An excited Joseph exclaimed, "That's very good, sweetheart! So, the issue is finding what words to say. Is that what you mean?"

With a small smile of relief, she nodded.

Joseph lifted her hand to his lips, kissing it softly. "You're going to be fine. I'm willing to bet this is just part of your head trying to heal. I'll be sure to tell Dr. Geiger about it, okay?"

Akeema nodded. She looked calmer. Joseph felt his own panic subside. He was relieved that Akeema looked relaxed because he'd run out of words to reassure her.

When Jean and Dr. Geiger made it back to Akeema, she was sleeping while Joseph continued to sit on her bed, still holding her hand.

Seeing them walk in, Joseph met them in the middle of the room. He didn't know if it was proper to shake the good doctor's hand, so he chose to let him make the first move. He didn't. Curtly, Dr. Geiger asked, "How did she respond to the answers to her questions?"

Helplessly, Joseph admitted, "While I was trying to figure out what I should say, I noticed she was having a problem."

"What?"

"She couldn't talk."

"What?" Jean erupted loudly.

The doctor turned to her with a stern look. Jean shut up.

"I noticed her lips were moving, but she wasn't saying anything."

"Could you tell if she understood you?" Dr. Geiger asked.

"Yes, I had her nod or shake her head to yes or no questions, and she was dead on."

A quick nod, and to Akeema's bed the doctor went. Gently, he roused her by shaking her arm.

Opening her eyes slowly, she focused on the doctor. He liked that.

"Hello, Miss Sprite," he said kindly. "I'm Dr. Geiger. Do you remember me?"

Akeema nodded.

"I understand you are having a little problem finding words, is that correct?"

Another nod.

He gave her hand a pat. "Don't worry. Head injuries like yours can result in this problem sometimes.

We're going to start testing you tomorrow so we'll know exactly what's going on, okay?"

"Uh-huh," she said.

"Very good, my dear. We're going to have you talking in no time."

Dr. Geiger gave her hand another pat, along with a reassuring smile. He left the room without saying anything else to Jean or Joseph.

Akeema watched the doctor until he was out of sight. Then, she looked at the visiting parties to hear what they had to say. Jean looked a little nervous, but she was making an effort.

"Have you eaten anything yet?" The doctor said you can eat, as long as the food isn't heavy – whatever that means."

Akeema smiled, shaking her head.

"I have some chicken vegetable soup in my thermos. Would you like some?"

Akeema looked doubtful. She believed these people were her people. Otherwise, they didn't have a reason for hanging out with her. But, she didn't remember them. When her so-called fiancée had showed her a picture of his son, she'd felt a real tenderness toward him. Right now, that little boy was the only one she was interested in seeing.

"Can you shake or nod your head, honey?" Jean was talking to Akeema, unaware that her niece was thinking about Joey instead of her. A worried Jean got even more concerned when Akeema kept looking at the ceiling. Turning to Joseph, she asked, "She's not responding to my question. Do you think her hearing is going out like her speech?"

Joseph rushed to Akeema's bedside, panic tying his stomach in knots.

"Akeema, do you hear me?" he shouted.

She flinched as his voice yanked her attention from herself to him. She nodded.

His shoulders sagged with relief. He smiled at her warmly. She stared at him.

Without asking Akeema again, Jean poured a cup of soup for her niece. Inhaling the homemade goodness, the patients mouth watered. Jean busily adjusted the bed to a sit-up position. On a spoon half-filled with soup, Jean chimed, "Open up, sweetie!"

Akeema did as she was told. She closed her eyes, enjoying the savory concoction. She ate in no time, eagerly nodding her head yes when Jean asked if she wanted more. Standing out of the way, Joseph watched as Jean fed Akeema. He remembered when Joey had to be fed. He was glad that his now-deceased wife had taken over the chore. He knew he didn't have the patience for it. He wondered how long it would be before his fiancée regained use of her limbs. Facing his own faults, Joseph knew he wouldn't enjoy treating Akeema like a child.

CHAPTER 30

Naturally right-handed, Akeema found it to be quite a challenge eating the sandwich with her left. The innards kept falling out on the plate because of her weak grasp. Jean was her loving cheerleader. "That's it, honey! You've eaten almost all of it! Keep going. You're almost there!"

Her enthusiasm made Akeema smile. She was glad they were alone. She wasn't comfortable trying to eat with Joseph in the room. She kept trying to conjure up warm feelings for him since they were engaged. But so far, she was simply thankful that he was the faithful sort. Each morning, he was there until time for him to go to work. For the most part, they watched TV together. She could make simple sentences now, but the meaning wasn't always what she intended.

As far as she was concerned, her aunt and uncle were dream people. She felt completely at home with them, even though she was in the hospital.

Together, they laughed at her gaffes while she struggled to get better. Her right arm and leg were her biggest challenges. It was hard to believe that she was ever a graceful ballet dancer. In addition to her good southern cooking, Jean had a surprise for Akeema; a picture book.

"Through the years, Rick and I have kept many photo albums. What we've done for you, is put together a personal album for you with friends and family. We've put their names and relationship to you. For those who've passed away, we wrote that down too."

"Are Joey's face here?" Akeema asked in her broken English.

"Absolutely. Your dancer friends are also in here, sweetie."

Frowning, Akeema asked, "Dancer friends…too?"

It took Jean a few seconds to figure out what Akeema wanted to know.

"Do you want to know if you had friends among the people you danced with?"

Her niece nodded vigorously.

"Sure! Pictures of Suzy, Kristin, Sharon, and Chelsea are marked for you."

Confused, Akeema replied, "They no here."

"No, they haven't visited you here, but they call to check up on you. When you tell us you want them to come here, I'll call them for you. They all gave me their cell numbers."

Akeema smiled. She didn't remember them, but it sure was nice to know they were there for her. She knew she was a blessed woman.

Jean placed the album down on the swivel tray table for easy access to Akeema. With her left hand, she slowly began leafing through the many pictures with notations. Jean turned on the TV, listening to it as she knitted. In the midst of reviewing her life in photos, Akeema had a visitor.

At first, she thought it was her uncle who was coming to see her. She looked up from the album with a welcoming smile on her face. In awe, she continued to grin at the handsome man standing in her doorway. She sincerely hoped he had the right room. To her, he was gorgeous.

The man was black, tall, muscular, and handsome! He looked marvelous in his dark suit, with the bright red tie. The cleft in his chin and light brown eyes completed his look of near perfection. She couldn't help but wonder if his picture was going to be somewhere in the photo album.

Slowly, he came toward her, a gentle smile on his shapely lips. His kissable lips. Oops! Where did that come from? Had she kissed him at some time in her life? This she really wished she could remember. She found it strange that she'd never had thoughts of Joseph like this. Now, next to her bed, she could smell him. Even his smell was gorgeous. Akeema felt her pulse accelerate out of nowhere. What was happening?

"Hello, Miss Sprite," he said cordially in a deep baritone.

"Hi," she said simply. This word she knew how to say when she wanted to.

"How are you today?"

"Okay."

"I'm glad to hear it. You certainly LOOK well. I'm hopeful that this means you're doing well."

"Better," she replied.

"What a blessing."

"Yes."

Jean put her knitting down to join Akeema and the school principal. "Good afternoon, Mr. Wilson." She could tell that she surprised him. His focus had been 100% on Akeema. Derek had seen only her.

"Hello, ma'am. I'm sorry I didn't see you when I came in."

"I noticed, but that's alright. Thanks for coming to check up on my niece."

"No problem. Her class and the other teachers miss her so much."

Jean had made an attempt at giving Akeema a hint about this portion of her life. "I'm not surprised. We all know how much Akeema loved teaching those little ones. Since you are the school principal, it's very nice of you to follow up with things yourself instead of assigning them to someone else."

"I care about all my teachers, of course. But Miss Sprite is exceptional. Both the students and their parents really like her. It's very rare," he said as he looked into her eyes.

Akeema smiled with pride. This handsome thing was her boss, and he liked her.

"Thanks," she said clearly.

"Thank YOU, Miss Sprite. I look forward to the day you're back in your classroom."

She nodded happily.

Looking at his watch, he knew he needed to get a move on…regrettably.

"Well," he sighed, "I need to get back to the school. You'd be surprised at what can happen out of the blue. See you next time."

Her heart leapt. He was coming back to see her!

"Okay," she said, letting him see her joy.

Derek was pleased that she was glad to hear he was coming back. Usually, she was such a cool customer, he couldn't tell what she was feeling.

He shook Jean's hand before briskly leaving the room. Akeema was jealous. She wanted to feel his touch like Jean had.

By the time Joseph made his evening visitation, Akeema had completed the review of the picture album.

The one thing that caught her attention was the absence of her romantic interests. The only boyfriend in the whole book was Joseph. Was it possible that she'd been so busy with her careers that she'd only had time for one boyfriend? Was Joseph really the one and only of her life? After meeting Derek, it didn't seem very likely.

Joseph had a beautiful bouquet of flowers in a frosted crystal vase for her. Kissing her cheek, he put them on the tray table in case her arm was too weak to hold them.

"Good evening, sweetheart. How ya doin' today?"

"Okay. Thanks flowers," she said warmly.

He hid his discomfort at her broken speech. One of the many things that he'd enjoyed about Akeema was her cultured way of speaking with that soft British accent. This new way of communicating took some getting used to.

"You're more than welcome. I wish I could do more to make you happy."

Akeema frowned at that. Was she looking depressed or something? She knew she was where she needed to be in order to get better. She didn't think of herself as a sad sack, did he?

Akeema was desperate. She wanted to talk to him about this, but the words failed her. Joseph watched her closely. Something was wrong. He felt helpless… again. This was beginning to be a habit. A habit that he didn't like.

"What is it, dear? Can you tell me?"

She tried. "I happy."

"You're happy? Is that it?"

She nodded.

He kissed her hand, not letting it go. "I'm thrilled. Our heavenly Father has been good, hasn't He?"

She gave him a nod and a smile, but he could tell that something was still amiss.

Joseph didn't know what to do. He was irritated, not with her, but with the situation.

"It's too bad I can't read your mind," he said under his breath.

Akeema suddenly snatched her hand from his. Her beautiful face wasn't tearful, it was angry. Without meaning to, he'd offended her. "Akeema, what did I do? I've upset you and I'm sorry!"

With her weak left hand, she began to write furiously in the air.

"Wh-what? Do you think you can write?"

Akeema nodded, hoping that she could.

Joseph went to the desk that they never used. He found a pen and some hospital stationery. He hurried back to the bed, removing the vase from the tray table. He wanted her to have plenty of room for her to write. Carefully, he put the paper down in front of her before placing the pen between her thumb and index fingers.

What Akeema wrote with her left hand was messy, but legible.

Joseph read her scribbling out loud in an effort to understand and let her know what he thought she wrote.

"I'm here, I like. Okay, you like it here?"

A definite bob of her head verified that he was on the right track.

"Better doctor? You need a better doctor?"

A vigorous head shake on that guess. Joseph tried again. "The doctors are better here?"

Frustrated, she wrote a huge 'I' on the paper.

"I...meaning you?"

A nod.

Joseph felt like he should have a dunce cap on his head. He wasn't a fan of this game.

"Well...I know you're not saying that you're a better doctor. Let's see..." he frowned as he tried to make sense of things. "Wait! Do you mean that the doctors here will make you better?"

"Yes!" Akeema shouted.

They both clapped their hands. Joseph made himself not moan when he saw her writing again. "Need here? I don't…oh! Are you telling me that you need to be here so you can get better?"

"Yes, yes," she exulted.

He gave her a hug, ever mindful of her IV. It was the first time he'd touched her, except for her arm and hand. It was the first time in weeks that he was close enough to enjoy her unique smell. He inhaled deeply. Akeema noticed what he was doing, but couldn't begin to imagine why he was doing it.

Later that evening over a bowl of delicious chicken and dumplings, Joseph brought Jean and Rick up to date on his most recent visit with Akeema. Joey was napping on the couch after Jean had stuffed and bathed him. All Joseph would have to do when he got home was to put him in bed. Jean hit her forehead several times with the palm of her hand. "Now I understand that look of panic on her face whenever I assured her that I'd stay on the doctors to let her come home!"

Rick agreed. "Yeah, and she was getting it times two because I literally repeated everything that you said. I thought I was giving her some kind of get-well quick hope!"

"I'm just thankful that I figured out what she wanted us to know!" admitted Joseph. "I felt sorry for her being in the hospital. Poor Akeema doesn't want all that pity we keep throwing at her. She's got the right attitude."

"Yep," Rick agreed, "We kept trying to put our feelings about hospitals onto her. Live and learn."

Jean asked Joseph, "Did she show you the photo album that we made for her?"

"She sure did. She seemed excited about seeing Joey."

Jean sighed. Sadly, she said, "I'm jealous of a little boy."

This caught Joseph's attention. "Our Joey?" he asked – even though he knew the answer.

Rick chimed in. "So am I," he admitted.

"Why?"

Jean responded, "Because he's the only one that excited Akeema. Part of the reason she works so hard at getting well is so she can get her hands on him."

Joseph nodded in agreement. "I'm engaged to her, but it's my son that she wants to know. Me, she simply endures. Can you imagine how that makes me feel?"

Rick made a face. "Ouch."

"Yeah, man, it's rough."

"During our girl chat today, she let me know how anxious she was to talk to Joey. But she wants to be able to communicate better with him. When she's ready, I'm to bring my laptop to the hospital so that they can see each other."

"At least we know that she has somebody that gives her the incentive to do the best she can to get well," Joseph said hopefully.

Jean and Rick nodded their agreement. The room was quiet as each member of the trio were lost in private thoughts. Suddenly, Jean sprang to her feet. With hands on her hips, she snapped, "Wah, wah, wah! Aren't we a pitiful sight? Our girl would be dead if it wasn't for our heavenly Father's mercy! Instead of being thankful to Him as we praise Him, we're sitting here feeling sorry for ourselves! I'm ashamed to call myself His child."

Rick and Joseph lowered their heads in shame. Continuing, Jean said, "Gentlemen, the bottom line is that we're blessed to still have her. If it takes a while for her to remember us, so be it! We keep right on loving her as we SHOW her love. And, heaven forbid, if she never remembers us, she'll respond to our affection. Got it?"

The men nodded.

"Let me hear you!" she demanded.

"Yes!" they yelled together.

"Daddy?"

Oops.

CHAPTER 31

T he days turned into weeks with Akeema steadily improving. Now, she was in a rehab facility where she was learning to walk and talk. The only thing that wasn't getting much better was her memory.

For those who knew her before the shooting, she was noticeably different. Previously, she'd preferred short hair that required little more than a razor to maintain. Now, her natural textured hair was chin-length and growing because she didn't want to look like a tall gangly boy – her words.

At Jean's house, she had a closet full of clothes in black, navy, brown, and denim. With shoes to match. She told her aunt that she looked like she was always dressing for a rainy day. Jean got it since she'd given up years ago trying to liven up her wardrobe. Now, they enjoyed shopping together. They purchased clothes online and from TV shopping channels. They bought bright, festive tops to go with her dark pants and skirts. Conversely, they got colorful, patterned bottoms that complimented her dark tops. Before this, Jean had never, ever, been consulted on what her niece should or shouldn't wear. Akeema had always loved and respected her aunt and uncle as surrogate parents. Now, she and Jean were more like best friends. Jean loved being her confidant; she loved their new relationship. Joseph, however, was struggling with the 'new' Akeema. She was treating him like an old-buddy, old-pal friend, instead of a romantic interest. Although he believed marrying a friend would help a marriage to succeed, he also believed if you weren't sexually attracted to each other, your union could be doomed. Joseph was also adjusting to her new, outgoing personality. The 'old' Akeema was cool, calm, and for the most part, collected. Then, you'd see more of her easy-going winning smile. Now, she was happy and…giggly. With her deep, rich alto, it was disconcerting to hear her let loose in a high-pitched squeal. Joseph had certainly heard Akeema laugh before, but not from the belly – with a snort! He realized he'd never heard his betrothed laugh heartily before. As the kids would say, she was always too cool for school. Not anymore.

When he watched her walk with the help of a cane, his heart ached for her. Although she could stand for hours on her own two feet, she was wobbly and unsteady when she walked. Accustomed to seeing her glide around gracefully, Joseph felt pity for the now ex-dancer. He lamented the loss of her ballerina gift to the world. Akeema, on the other hand, thought of dancing in the future differently. She considered opening a child's dance studio! That way, she'd have double the pleasure of working with children. This love of young ones seemed to be innate in her spirit. Joseph sure wished she showed some of that excitement for him.

On this day, Akeema was jumpy and almost excessively giddy. Her aunt brought her laptop so she and Joey could visit! Her speech wasn't perfect yet, but it was good enough to converse with an eight-year-old.

"Are you ready, honey?" Jean asked Akeema.

"Past!" she replied.

It was Sunday afternoon, and Joseph and his son were home from church in comfortable clothes. Joey was too excited to eat his lunch. Therefore, Joseph decided to leave it alone for now. When Jean received Joseph's call that they were ready to talk to her niece, she was surprised by the reserve in Joseph's voice. She was determined to get some private time with him later to see what was wrong. Meanwhile, she had her hands full keeping Akeema calmed down. She acted like she was about to talk to Bette Davis – her new favorite actress.

Knowing that the little boy would see her from the waist up, Akeema was dressed in a festive pink peasant blouse. Her dangle, gold-colored earrings completed the pretty picture.

When Joey's face appeared on the screen, he and Akeema started clapping their hands and blowing air kisses. At that moment, they were the two happiest people on the planet! Akeema was the first to speak. "Joey! How's my favorite guy?"

"I'm good now!" he exclaimed, "I miss you sooo much! When are you comin' back to school?"

"I miss you too, pumpkin. As soon as the doctors are done fixing me, I'll be back." Jean was surprised and pleased to hear Akeema speaking so well. She imagined her practicing like crazy to be ready for this day.

"Did you get the pictures I made for you?"

"Yes!" she said happily. "Auntie and I put them on the wall by my bed. Thank you!"

"You welcome, Akeema. Do you want some more of them?"

With a nod and a huge grin, Akeema said, "I want anything from you!"

Joey smiled broadly, happily.

They chatted for about fifteen minutes about his school work and her physical therapy. When it was time to sign off, they blew more kisses at each other before a final wave good-bye. When the screen went black, both Akeema and Joey burst into tears.

He couldn't get Akeema out of his mind. He was busier than busy, but thoughts of her kept invading his senses. Finally, he gave in. It was Sunday so he decided not to go to her, he called instead.

"Hello," she said happily. She didn't know who was calling, Akeema was just glad that someone thought enough of her to talk to her.

"Hello there, young lady. This is Derek Wilson. Are you doing alright today?"

Her heart literally skipped a beat...or two.

"Yes, Derek, I'm okay. You?"

"I'm good. I was thinking of you, so I decided to call. I hope this is okay."

"Yes, it's okay. Have you had Sunday food?"

"Yeah, I got a big Italian meatball sandwich after church, so I'm stuffed. What have you eaten today?"

"Aunt Jean will bring food later. She cooks real good."

"I'm sure she does. Since you're a woman of leisure, be careful not to eat too much of that good food. You'll end up fat instead of fine," he teased.

Akeema laughed. "Auntie calls me skinny!"

Sincerely, Derek said. "To me, you're like the baby bear. You're just right."

"Baby bear?" Akeema asked, confused.

Derek mentally kicked himself. A person suffering from memory loss probably wouldn't remember childhood nursery rhymes. Instead of panicking, he decided to tell her the story. To his pleasure – and relief, she got a kick out of it, laughing gleefully. Before long, at her request, Derek was telling her about Humpty-dumpty, the big bad wolf and the three pigs. To his delight, she enjoyed them all.

Out of the blue she asked him, "Do you come to me cause you're my su…uh-supe, oh darn it!" she exclaimed.

"Your supervisor?"

"Yes, that's it! Say it again, please."

"Super-vi-sor," he said patiently.

"Supervisor," she repeated slowly.

"Very good. You're a quick learner."

"Not always."

"Nothing on earth is 'always' if people are doing it. We people mess up sometimes."

"Nice to know I'm not the only idiot," she said.

"Not by a long shot, my dear."

She smiled at him with a wide grin. He wanted to kiss her. The thought startled him. Belatedly, she felt stupid, once more, for forgetting that he couldn't see her smile at him on the hospital phone. The silence grew between them while each was distracted by their own personal thoughts.

"Oh!" Derek said to save the day. "You asked me a question that I forgot to answer." Akeema had to think about it for a while before it came back to her. "That's right!" she said.

"Since I'm the boss, that's another word for supervisor, I could have sent someone to visit you, or do like I'm doing now – calling you."

"So…why have you been here?"

"I wanted to see you for myself. To know that you were being cared for."

"Thanks, that's nice. Will you come again?"

His breath caught in his throat. "Do you want me to, Akeema?"

"Yes, Derek."

Derek grinned from ear to ear. She wasn't coy or using womanly wiles on him. She was just honest and to the point. He really liked this woman.

"Then, I'd love to come. What time is good for you?"

"Lunchtime is good. My aunt is here then. She cooks for me, even though I told her she doesn't need to."

"I had the pleasure of meeting her. She's great."

"She is. Hey! Would you like her food too?"

"Oh, don't worry about me. I can bring my own."

"Auntie loves to feed people! Let me know when you're coming so I'll have her feed us all!" She sounded so excited. He wanted to keep her happy.

"I'll be there tomorrow at noon."

"Auntie, he's so cute, isn't he?"

Jean was disturbed. Her niece was gushing about a man that wasn't who she was engaged to! Not once had Akeema commented on Joseph's attractive looks. She was only in love with his son, Joey.

"Yes, Akeema, he is quite good-looking. But, so is Joseph, don't you think?"

"Joseph is such a good father, right? I could just eat that little boy up! I hope we'll always be the best of friends."

Oh, dear.

While talking to Akeema on the phone, she and Rick were sitting on the couch in their living room, enjoying each other's company. To share what was being said with her husband, she put the phone on speaker.

"Well, dear," Jean said cautiously, "I can bless-edly say that Rick and I are the best of friends. Since

Joseph is your fiancé, I think you can feel confident that you and he WILL always be the best of friends. Do you understand?"

Absolute silence.

"Akeema? You still there, honey?"

"Yes, ma'am," she replied in a little girl voice. "I…I really like Derek, I do."

Jean and Rick exchanged a quick glance. Forcing a lightness into her voice, Jean said, "That's great! It's good to get along with your boss."

Slowly, Akeema admitted, "I haven't worked with him yet. I don't know him that way." This wasn't getting any easier.

"What do you mean, Akeema?"

"I like him as a man," she answered simply.

Oh, boy.

"Well, uh, that's natural, dear. He is a man, so it's okay to like him as one."

"Auntie, I feel more…different for Derek that I don't feel for Joseph. Why is that?"

Yikes!

"Derek is a new friend; Joseph has been in your life longer in your memory."

"True. So, why do I feel a, a…deeper way for the man I'm NOT supposed to marry?"

Jean looked at her husband helplessly. Sadly, he returned that exact look back to her.

"Because of your memory loss, you're experiencing a lot of things for the first time. It's possible that you felt an attraction to this Derek before the assault."

Akeema was quiet as she considered what her aunt said to her. "Then, Auntie, should I marry one guy when I want to get to know another guy?"

One thing was for certain: Jean would not lie to Akeema.

"In my opinion, honey, no – you should not."

CHAPTER 32

Joseph felt like a heel. He loved Akeema as a person. He adored the love that she and his son shared. He was thankful for the family of hers that she shared with him. He felt like Rick and Jean were his and Joey's bio aunt and uncle; he couldn't imagine being without them. He felt that close to Akeema too – just not as his wife. There. He finally faced the truth. But she was in the middle of her rehab stay. He didn't want to hurt her by breaking off their engagement. He seriously thought about that. He wasn't sure that ending their romance would hurt her. The truth was that she treated him mo333re like a brother than a fiancé. The loss of Joey would hurt her. Big time. The irony of this didn't escape
him. His son was his love nemesis. Who'd a thunk it?

Early the next morning, Joseph lay in his bed, wide awake. He decided to let himself have a personal pity party. Claire had been the love of his life, and mother of his child. When she'd passed away, Joseph feared he'd never love again. Joey's teacher, Akeema, had come as an unexpected surprise. After his son lost his mother, he lost all interest in school as he clung to Joseph for dear life. Joey was so afraid of losing another parent to death, that he found it almost impossible to concentrate on his studies. In desperation, he'd asked Akeema for extra tutoring. She happily agreed, and Joseph saw Joey blossom under her care. Before long, his son wasn't the only one Joseph was watching. He watched the beautiful teacher with his son and the rest of her classroom. Each child responded to their teacher without reservation. Joseph watched her sit down on the floor with her students without hesitation. He observed her graceful dancing on stage where he saw a talent that seemed greater than the leads. When she wasn't dealing with the kids, she was the epitome of being cool, calm, and collected. Her deep voice was cultured and sexy. SHE was cultured and sexy. Was.

The new Akeema was a joyous soul. She laughed easily and loudly. She watched game shows instead of PBS. Although he certainly understood her loss of graceful movement, it didn't stop him from missing it.

The insistent sound of his cell phone snapped him out of his self-analysis. He didn't look at the display, assuming it was Jean or someone calling in sick from work.

"Joseph Smith here."

"Akeema Sprite here," she said amused.

"Akeema! Hey, honey, anything wrong?" He asked the question not believing anything was seriously amiss. She sounded too cheerful.

"Nope. But the phone rang so many times I thought you were still sleeping."

"Uh, no, I'm awake. I'll be on my way to you soon. What's up?"

"Do you love me, Joseph?"

Surprised by her question, Joseph teased, "How could I possibly love someone that I see twice a day during the week, plus half a day on weekends?"

Akeema's sense of humor went from I Love Lucy to the Three Stooges these days. She thought Joseph was answering her seriously.

"So, you don't love me because you come to see much more of me than you want to?"

Uh-oh. She wasn't kidding. Joseph hurried to reassure her of his devotion.

"Akeema, I was just being funny! Or…trying to be. I wouldn't see you so much if I didn't care."

He was still in the gray area as far as she was concerned.

"I know you CARE," she emphasized, "I want to know if you LOVE."

"Of course," he said softly.

He wasn't about to tackle the difference between loving or being IN love. They'd both end up with headaches. Him from trying to explain, her from trying to understand.

"Do you like any other women besides me?"

What an odd question, he thought. "I'm crazy about your aunt. Joey is too."

Chewing her bottom lip nervously, Akeema tried again.

"I mean other YOUNG women, Joseph. About my age."

Oh, now he understood. Kinda.

"You're the only one I'm seeing since we are engaged to be married. I don't date anyone else but you."

He was telling her the truth…just not the 100% WHOLE truth.

Akeema still wasn't sure that her question had been answered. "Do engaged people date other people?"

"Not that I know of," Joseph answered.

"Is that something you would do?"

"No. I was completely faithful to my wife when we were engaged and married to each other. Why?"

"I'd like to see another man," she replied truthfully.

"A friend? That's fine, Akeema."

Biting her lip again, she admitted, "Right now, he is a friend and co-worker. I like him a lot."

It was the way her voice softened at the end that gave him pause. He realized there were times when he was slow, but he was a long way from being stupid.

"Is this man someone you'd like to see a lot?"

"Yes, Joseph."

"More than me?" he asked quietly, holding his breath as he waited for her to answer. She had no desire, whatsoever, to hurt him. She just wanted to see more of Derek.

"Not more exactly, but at least as much."

Ouch.

"I see," he replied slowly. "Would you prefer that you and I cancel our engagement?"

She bit her lip again. It bled.

"Could I continue to see Joey and keep you as my good friend?"

Her thoughts were of Joey first, then him. Double ouch.

Joseph pushed his hurt feelings aside. He realized his emotions were rooted in pride.

"Of course," Joseph responded.

What she said next stung a little, yet also made him smile.

"That's fantastic, really fantastic! I'll get to have all of you in my life! Nobody else on earth is more blessed than I…or is it ME?"

"I'm not sure, you're the teacher. I'm sure either one will do."

"You're probably right. Hey! I'm taking up your morning time, right? You need to get dressed. Are you coming to see me this morning?"

"Yes, I need to tend to Joey. I was coming to see you as usual, now I don't know."

"What don't you know?"

"If I should visit you."

"Why not?" she asked innocently.

He realized yet another fault in himself: he was being petty. He wasn't being the 'good friend' that he assured her he would be.

"You're right. There's no reason I shouldn't come to see you as usual. I'll see you later."

"Good, hurry up!" Then, she was gone.

He phoned Jean and Rick to let them know that he was no longer engaged to their niece. Joseph found that he was sad, and glad.

"I'm getting better at this game than you are!" Akeema boasted.

Since Joseph had lost three games in a row, he wasn't about to argue with her. He'd rather have his tongue removed than take this joy from her.

"Do you have enough time to take me for a walk, Joseph?"

"I sure do. Let me get your cane for you."

Together, they walked slowly down the rehab corridor. The shot in the left side of her head had affected the right side of her body. Her lips drooped slightly, but her arm and leg had to have long, intensive workouts every day. She didn't know if her speech was actually getting better, or if people in her world had gotten used to hearing how she said things.

As they walked, Joseph didn't touch her, but he walked on her right side, close enough to catch her if that side weakened and failed. So far, her stride was slow and sure. Joseph was struck by the number of people that spoke to Akeema by name. Employees and patients alike all seemed to know her. The 'old' Akeema was pleasant and cordial, but this 'new' version was happy and welcoming. Her deep, sultry voice seemed to wrap itself around your heart. And she used to be his girl. He was determined not to show her the sadness that almost overwhelmed him.

"What did I do to make you stop loving me?" she asked out of the blue.

"I haven't stopped loving you, Akeema."

"My memories of you are lost, I get that. We had to get to know each other all over again, right?"

Joseph nodded, not sure where this was going.

"Why did you stop wanting to get to know me again?"

Wow. This was a fair question. Too bad he was at a loss for an answer.

"What have I done to make you feel like that?"

She stopped her slow gait to look at him.

"When you don't know I'm watching you, you're sad, closed off. You make me feel…what's that word?" she frowned while concentrating.

"Like I'm trying to protect you from what I'm thinking?"

"Yes! Isn't there a word for that?"

"Probably. We'll probably remember it when we're not trying to remember it."

Akeema looked downcast. "I'm sure you're di… disconnected! That's it, Joseph! There are times I feel DISCONNECTED from you."

Oh, man! In an effort to protect her, he'd only succeeded in making her feel shut out!

No wonder she was getting interested in other men!

The stricken look on Joseph's face didn't escape Akeema's attention. He was upset, and it was all her fault.

"I'm sorry, Joseph. I didn't mean to make you feel bad."

He heard the slight tremor in her voice. Was she about to cry?

The old Akeema…there it was again. His almost constant comparison from the 'old' Akeema to the new one. That's it. Dang it!

"Oh, Akeema, you're not at fault," he said gently. "This is my crappy way of trying to not upset you about anything. The end result has been more bad than good for you. I'm the one who's sorry."

He moved closer to kiss her forehead, making her smile.

"That kiss felt familiar," she whispered.

Returning her grin, he said, "It should. Me, your aunt, and your uncle kissed you in just that way while you were unconscious. I still do it to show affection without being too invasive."

Akeema shifted her stance, wincing.

"Do you need to sit down?" Joseph asked anxiously.

She shook her head. "Nope. Moving is better. Standing still for too long can be a challenge. Challenge – is that the right word?"

"Yes, it is. You're doing so well with your vocabulary, Akeema. I'm proud of you. We all are."

"Thank you, Joseph. I don't know what I would have done without you guys."

"Speaking for us all, we feel the same. I think that's part of the reason I've been so shut off at times. I didn't want to do anything that would cause you to have a setback."

"What's the other part?" she asked promptly.

"The other part was hiding from you how hard it's been to accepting the 'new' you! I fell in love with one woman, and now you're someone else."

"Worse?" she asked timidly.

Quickly, he assured her, "Absolutely not! You are still a very beautiful woman – inside and out. You're just different, that's all. It's taking a minute to get used to. I'm getting there."

"Since our last talk, I've really been thinking about us. I've been replaying our talk over and over. I think I may have figured it out."

"Okay, I'd love to hear it"

"I think you've been telling me that you still love me as a person and a friend. However, you haven't fallen in love with the new me yet."

Joseph lifted up a silent prayer. She understood. He was gratified that she'd said the word 'yet.' Even though she was interested in another man, she hadn't written him off all the way. The possibility of them marrying and parenting Joey was still alive. He was glad about that.

"I don't know why I couldn't say it as clearly as you just did, Akeema. Thank you."

Breathing a little heavily, she steered them to the waiting area so she could sit down. She needed a little rest before they walked back to her room.

They sat quietly next to each other, holding hands.

After catching her breath, Akeema asked, "Can you and I agree on something?"

"Sure, what's up?"

"First, that we will always be friends."

"Check," Joseph said.

"Second, that Joey and I will always be in each other's lives and hearts."

"Check."

"And, as I date whoever I'm interested in, that you will do the same if you meet someone that catches your eye."

He paused a little before saying the last "check."

Once they were alone in her room, with Akeema settled in her bed, she had one last point to cover with her ex-fiancé.

"You and Joey are like family to me, Joseph. I can't imagine my life without you guys. It's been strange being treated like your kid sister when I was really the woman you were about to marry."

Joseph wondered where she was going with this.

"All of your kisses were on my hand or forehead; do you know that?"

He nodded. "Yes, we've discussed that. I felt that since you didn't remember me, it might scare you if I handled you too personally."

"So, the man I'd pledged to share my life with, acted like my brother."

Joseph looked down at the floor, shuffling his feet. He was embarrassed. In trying to do the best for her, he may have done the worst.

"Before this awfulness happened, did we have a good sex life?"

Joseph's head snapped up. Did he hear her say what he thought she said? "Excuse me?"

"I asked you if our sex life was good."

"Uh, we never had it."

Akeema's eyes bulged. "We were engaged to be married, but didn't make love?"

Shaking his head, he replied, "We decided to abstain, Akeema. To please our Heavenly Father."

"Really? I've had some pretty racy dreams. I'm almost positive some of them had you in them."

"You're not a virgin. But, you and I had some very intense make out sessions."

"Kiss me, Joseph. Plant a good one on me, please." His pulse raced. He didn't want to mess this up. Very much on purpose, he let himself think of a heated session they'd shared in the past. By the time their lips touched, he was more than ready. Joseph held nothing back. He kissed her as if he wouldn't ever get to do it again. When he was done, Akeeema was breathless again, for a different reason this time.

She only had one word to say; "Wow!"

Joseph chuckled. "I've missed that."

"Me too. You WERE part of my dream, by the way."

He kissed her nose playfully. "Was that a brotherly kiss?"

"No way! Boy, that was hot!"

He loved her enthusiasm. "Do you want to get re-engaged?" he asked, only half-kidding.

"Not today," she said seriously, "I have Derek coming for lunch. But, to get me out of feeling like I'm your sister, we should do more of that!"

CHAPTER 33

A unt Jean baked a quiche for Akeema and Derek to feast on. She also had a thermos of pink lemonade to quench their thirst. Akeema was jumpy with excitement. So far, she was having a great day. After the tray table was set up with her aunt's good dishes with the rose pattern, Akeema had news for Jean. "I love kissing men!" she declared happily.

Jean sputtered the lemonade she'd been drinking. Laughing, she said, "When did you discover that?"

"Today! Joseph finally let loose and kissed the heck outta me!"

Jean threw her head back and roared! She loved how candid Akeema was these days. Akeema of old was controlled and very private. This emotional young woman loved to share. Rick said that Akeema's personality was close to Jean's now and he loved that. So did Jean.

"Auntie, if Derek acts like he wants to kiss me today, is it okay since I already did it with Joseph?"

"Sure, if you want to. Since you're not engaged anymore, you are a free agent." Palms in the air, they high fived.

AKEEMA'S SECRET

Derek stood out of sight, watching Akeema. As always, he was stunned by her beauty. To him, she was a rare bird. It didn't surprise him that she was always with one guy or another. She was having a lively chat with a female staffer. She was animated, her large, gently slanted eyes were shining. Her high cheekbones and full lips didn't seem to have makeup on them from this distance, but that didn't really matter. The only place she ever wore heavy face paint (as he called it) was on stage. He used to see her at school where he'd seen a light glow added to her cheeks, and color on her lips that closely matched her dark skin tone. Something said, made her laugh now. The dark richness of her voice would turn on any hetero guy with even an ounce of libido.

Critically, Derek looked down at his attire. For once, he tried to dress like a guy going to the movies with his favorite date. Akeema hadn't ever seen him dress casually. He wanted her to see him as just a man, not a principal. He had on a pair of starched and ironed jeans that were a little too tight. His short-sleeved t-shirt was tucked neatly into his pants, displaying his toned pecs. His black jean jacket matched his pants exactly, even though he'd purchased them separately. His clean, black-leathered briefcase went well with the black suit and tie that he would change back into when he went back to work. With almost perfect timing, the staffer left the room just as Derek was ready to walk in. Once he saw her back, he made his move.

Akeema had just checked the time by the little clock that Aunt Jean had put on the utility table next to her bed. When Derek suddenly appeared, Akeema whistled when she saw him. He was surprised because a woman had never done that at just the sight of him. She surprised herself because she didn't know she could do that! Excited, she exclaimed, "You look better in your casual clothes than you do in a suit and tie! Woo-woo!"

He adored her. This tall, classy woman just whistled and said 'woo-woo!' Sitting on the side of the bed, he could see that she wore a cute pink and blue lounge set that fit her loosely. Akeema looked wonderful!

Grinning broadly, he replied, "Thanks, kind lady! And may I add that you are looking causally fine as well."

She released a girlish giggle before bowing her head in appreciation.

Akeema clapped her hands. "This date is starting off great, isn't it? Shall we dive into whatever Aunt Jean cooked? I'm hungry!"

"Me too. Everything looks so nice."

"She did a good job for us," she said as she was unwrapping the foil covered food.

Derek watched her smile melt into a frown of confusion. Looking down at the meal, he grew even hungrier.

"Now it's my turn to say wow! This looks and smells wonderful, right?"

"Yeah, it smells good, but…"

"But what, Akeema? What is it?"

Silence.

Derek was a little slow for the smart man that he was. He knew that she'd suffered a memory loss. Language was making a comeback for her, but plenty of things had gotten lost. This was apparently one of them.

"It's a French egg dish that we call a quiche."

"Keesh?"

"Yes. It's pretty good if it'done right."

Her chin snapped up in her aunt's defense. "If Aunt Jean cooked it, you can bet it's done good!"

Derek nodded. "Shall I slice it for us?"

"Slice?"

"Yeah, you slice it like a pie."

"Okay, please slice our keesh."

Jean also included a salad to go with the dish.

Once plated, Akeema agreed that it looked good enough to eat. After she said grace over the delicacy, she followed Derek's lead on how to eat it.

"Ah, it's broccoli and cheese, one of my faves," he exclaimed.

After the first bite, he closed his eyes in bliss. Akeema put a little sample on her fork. She had to admit, it was delicious.

When they were done, Derek quickly packed everything up before he had to go.

"Hey, you wanna watch a little TV? There are some fun game shows on."

"Naw, I've gotta get a move on. I'm having so much fun that I lost track of time. I really need to get to work."

"Oh, crap! I forgot all about that! I'm sorry for making you late."

"Nonsense! I saw what time it was. I could've left on time. I'm just having a hard time leaving you," he admitted.

When he saw Akeema slowly getting to her feet, he helped her stand. He contemplated calling in sick.

"Derek, I'd like it very much if you kissed me."

"Really?" he felt like he might faint.

"Yes. Invasively, please."

He took more steps toward her. "Your wish is my command," he murmured.

With both hands, he grabbed her by the waist to gently pull her toward him. Before their lips touched, they had breast to pec contact that was thrilling. Although they were each fully clothed, they shared a sensuous experience. As their lips came together, the electricity between them was undeniable. They explored each other slowly, thoroughly. Aunt Jean's quiche tasted even better the second time around.

"Is it possible to like more than one guy at the same time?"

Jean sighed. Her niece didn't know a thing about playing the field. She had two handsome suitors vying for her attention, and one of them had a son that she adored. She wanted to remain – or at least appear – to be impartial. Joseph and Joey were like part of the family now, but who Akeema chose as her mate had to be on her.

"Sure it is," Jean responded.

"Good, because I want to keep seeing them both."

Jean pointed out, "That's already a done deal. When you start working again, you'll see Derek at school because he's your boss. You will see Joey as you teach him, so that will keep you in touch with Joseph."

"You're right! It's nice to know that I won't have to do without either one of them."

She was a grown woman with a teenager mentality. Jean knew she needed a reality check. She didn't want to tell her, but she knew she had to.

"Uh, listen Akeema. The three of you are getting to know each other now. Nobody has a hold on the other so things can stay the way they are for now."

"For now?"

"Yes, dear. Put your thinking hat on. Your uncle and I started out as friends, and we dated others. As we got to know each other, we fell in love. We were only intimate with each other after that. And we only dated each other."

Akeema nodded. "Auntie, do you think I'll fall in love with Derek or Joseph?"

Jean reminded her, "Don't forget that before the memory loss, you loved Joseph enough to marry him. That meant being Joey's stepmother."

"Ah, yes, Joey." Akeema sighed. "For all the things I forget, my heart has never stopped loving that little boy. Isn't it a shame that I don't remember the love I had for Joseph?"

"It is indeed." Jean said regretfully.

Quickly, Akeema added, "But, I'll tell you what I DIDN'T forget!"

"What's that?"

"His kiss! I remembered what it was like to be kissed by him. Homeboy can throw down!"

"I'm glad for you. Do you remember anything else about him?"

"I've been having sex dreams that include him. But, when I talked to him about it, he said we chose to ab…uh, ab…"

"Abstain?"

"Yes, that's it! Abstain. So, I don't know if I'm having flashbacks or wishful thinking. Did I have a lot of boyfriends?"

"Not that I know of, dear. You were very private about your personal life."

"Really? That's funny because I can't imagine anything going on in my life that I'd hesitate to share with you and unc."

"I'm glad you feel that way now. I hope as your memories return, that you will still feel that way."

Akeema sighed. "You can bet on it," she said confidently.

With everything packed up, and their hugs and kisses out of the way, Jean was ready to go home to her husband and Joey. She was almost at the doorway when her niece called to her. Turning to face her, Jean asked, "What is it, Akeema?"

"Do you and Uncle Rick still have sex?"

Jean stared at her open-mouthed, stunned. Seeing her reaction, Akeema was alarmed.

"Did I ask a bad question? Are you mad at me?"

Re-grouping from her shock, Jean took a deep breath, holding it a while before speaking. "No, your question wasn't bad, and no – I'm not mad at you, not even a little." She watched Akeema's face relax as she unclenched her jaw. This new openness between them had its pros and cons.

"The answer is yes; your uncle and I still make love."

"Is it still good for you, or are you doing it as a wifely obligation?"

"What an odd question, Akeema. Why do you ask?"

"I was watching a movie, someone was called 'frigid.' I didn't understand that word, so I looked it up in the dictionary."

"Did you understand the meaning?"

She nodded.

"Why did you think it might apply to me?"

She shrugged. "I don't know. From my dreams, movies, and books, sex seems to be an aerobic thing. I wondered if people past child-bearing years kept doing it."

Hiding her amusement, Jean answered, "Yes, we still enjoy it. As we've gotten old, we don't do it almost every day anymore, but unless one of us is sick, we indulge at least twice a week."

Akeema smiled while clapping her hands. "How wonderful! I can hardly wait 'til I'm outta here, so I can have orgasms again!"

Jean smiled before getting the heck away from there! An aunt can take just so much.

CHAPTER 34

The day finally came when Akeema graduated from rehab. Four months was a long time to be away from home, but it proved to be worth it. Her right dominant side was functional, but weak. The left side was stronger and clumsy. Through diligent study, her vocabulary was practically back to her normal. With each passing week, more of her memory was restored. She was relieved to know that it was possible that her lost memories might come back to her. Except for the shooting, she wanted to remember everything. It was estimated that she'd regained about sixty percent of her day, her aunt and uncle, Joseph, and Kristin from the ballet company came to help her pack. Derek apologized profusely for not being there, but he promised to help with the unpacking once he was off work.

Akeema scanned her room and bathroom one last time. Nothing of hers was left in sight. She was both elated and deflated. She'd survived a near death experience. It was good to be alive. She knew the Man upstairs must still have work for her to do.

They made her sit in the wheelchair to leave the rehab center. She could walk without a cane now, although she depended on it by days end. When Akeema was wheeled out of her room, the staff were all waiting to applaud her. She was given flowers and a huge good-bye card with a private sentiment and signature from everyone. She fought back the tears. These people had been good and patient with her. She would miss them. And they would miss her.

Aunt Jean's welcome home dinner was out of this world! There was something for everyone. Akeema's ballet posse were there, so she'd put together the biggest non-meat salad known to man, or woman. Suzy, Kristin, Sharon, and Chelsea wouldn't have a problem putting on their tutu's the following evening. Even Barney, the dancing taskmaster to them all, made an appearance with his pink hair and ruby red lips. Uncle Rick's reaction to him was priceless! Joey was stuck to her side like glue. When you saw Akeema, you saw him. Uncle Rick had an earlier chat with Derek and Joseph regarding his niece. Since they were both dating her, he let the men know that he wouldn't tolerate any jealousy nonsense around her. Until she made a choice, or one of them stepped aside, they would be respectful to her and to each other. Period.

In addition to the massive house salad, Jean prepared turkey and dumplings, sweet cornbread, spaghetti with meat balls, fried chicken, and a broc- coli, carrot, cauliflower mix with a secret sauce from

Jean's head. At Akeema's request, the only dessert was a dreamsicle float. The four female dancers had one drink with four straws that they all drank from at the same time. They swooned happily-even at the brain freezes that followed.

After all the eating, Jean and Rick ushered their happy and bloated guests to the living room. It was time to work off some of those recently consumed calories with a lively game of charades. Nobody could believe it when two huge bowls of popcorn were put out on the coffee table for consumption. To a person, they all scoffed at the possibility that anybody would touch that corn. Jean smiled demurely as she put out the two bowls: one with butter and the other with a little salt and pepper. She then went back to the kitchen where she prepared many doggie bags that she and Rick would hand out at the door as people were leaving.

Everyone was so involved in the game that Akeema left the room without catching anyone's attention. She went to the kitchen with Aunt Jean, closing the swinging door behind her. Jean was surprised to see her.

"Hey, baby girl. What 'cha need?"

"Just a few minutes alone with you."

With her hands constantly moving, Jean said, "Have you forgotten that you live here? When everybody leaves, you'll have me all to yourself. So, feel free to re-join your friends."

"Okay, but I have two issues that I want to discuss now, not later. Is that alright?"

"Sure, honey. Come on with it."

"First, I'm not going to have you slaving in here doing this clean up alone. Put me to work."

"I'm alone for just a little while. Your uncle will come to help when your guests are gone."

"Well, tonight he'll have less to help you with." Akeema said stubbornly.

Smiling at her niece tenderly, Jean gave in.

"Fine. Now, what's the second thing you want to cover?"

"Which guy should I kiss tonight? Is it okay to lay a good one on them both?"

Jean didn't see this coming. Akeema hadn't EVER asked her about romantic, or intimate issues – not even when she was a teenager!

Oh, dear. "It's okay to kiss them both, I just think it's a little on the tacky side. But I have to admit that I'm old-fashioned by today's standards."

"By YOUR standard, what do you suggest?"

"I think you offer them your cheek or a hug. No lips when they're with you at the same time."

Akeema's expression brightened. "I'm feeling that! That's just what I'm gonna do, auntie. I'll give one a hug and the other a casual kiss."

Jean nodded her approval.

Working as a team, the 'to go bags' were done and the kitchen was spic and span by the time Rick peeped in.

"How are my ladies doing?" he called. "Fine, Unc!"

"Okay, baby. How's it goin' out there?"

"The natives are getting restless for the lady of honor," he replied. His gaze rested on Akeema.

"Okay, okay. I've been missing in action long enough. Who's been winning the most?"

"Barney."

Akeema whooped, "You've gotta be kidding!"

Rick smiled. "It's driving the macho men out of their minds."

Jean teased, "Does that include you?"

He shook his head. "I was the referee – not the competitor."

"I've gotta check this out," Akeema said as she was leaving.

Rick went to his wife, grabbing her around the waist. When he turned her to face him, he kissed her long and deeply.

Sagging in his arms, Jean moaned, "You still make me weak in the knees…and everywhere else."

"You always have a way of making me feel ten feet tall."

Jean inhaled his sexy man scent. "Mmm, baby. I look forward to being alone with you tonight."

Rick rained light kisses on the side of her neck. "I look forward to being alone with you EVERY night!" Jean pressed against her husband, excited at the feel of his excitement for her. Neither said another word as they each thought the same thing; How could they escape to their bedroom without being noticed?

Derek was getting tired, but he didn't want to be the first to leave – or to be precise, he didn't want to go before Joseph did. Akeema was playing hostess, refilling drinks and replacing snacks for a group of stuffed guests with the munchies. Two game tables were set up in Jean and Rick's expansive country-decorated living room. One table for cards, the other for dominoes. Akeema didn't play any of the games, but she managed to keep the scores for both tables. Her aunt and uncle hadn't been seen for a while, but it didn't seem to matter. Everyone was having a good time.

The next time Akeema went to the kitchen, Derek followed her. Joseph noticed but stayed put.

Closing the door behind them, Derek made a beeline to Akeema, holding her in his arms.

"I've longed to hold you all day," he whispered in her ear, smelling her clean freshness.

"And, I've longed to be held," she admitted. He positioned her for a kiss, but she pushed him back. Confused, he asked, "What's wrong?"

Akeema responded, "Auntie said I should be a lady tonight with you and Joseph by not kissing you guys."

Her newly acquired child-like innocence was endearing to him. But he sure wished 'auntie' would mind her own business.

"I understand, but I don't like it."

Akeema made a 'yuck' face. "Me neither."

Derek smiled, rewarded by her honesty. "I'm glad you at least WANT to kiss me."

Without hesitation, Akeema answered, "Oh, I do! I'm thinking about sneaking a little one, as a matter of fact. How do you feel about that?"

Taking a step closer to her, Derek replied, "Great!"

Before she could change her mind, he kissed her. Softly at first, then deeper, and longer.

That little smooch turned into a main event that left them both breathless and clinging to each other. "Oh, baby, where've you been all my life?"

Promptly, she replied, "Down the hall from your office."

Their mutual chuckle helped ease the carnal fire between them.

Just as they parted, pink-haired Barney crashed the party.

"There you are, darling!" he exclaimed.

"I need to run, but I wanted to say goodnight. I'm glad you're home. Get better so you can come back to us."

Akeema smiled bravely. She knew, and accepted, that her dancing days were behind her.

Barney blew her a kiss before leaving as quickly as he had come.

Alone once more, Derek was okay with leaving since the taste of Akeema was in his mouth.

"Well, cuteness, I guess I'd better head out too. School starts early in the morning for me."

"I know. I can't wait to get back there myself."

"Do you have a timeline on that yet?"

"I'm an outpatient for the next two weeks. At that time, I'll be re-evaluated. If all is good, they'll give me a written release to come back to work."

"I can hardly wait. Goodnight, chocolate drop."

Then Derek kissed his index finger before pressing it to Akeema's lips. Before he was too tempted to grab her again, he walked out. After that, everyone came to say their goodbyes. Akeema knew she'd have no problem sleeping tonight.

Joseph made sure he was the last to leave. Jean and Rick hadn't been seen for over an hour, so it was safe to say that they were already in bed.

He sat in the living room alone after folding up the table and chairs, putting them away, and clearing out everything in the great room that belonged in the kitchen.

Akeema plopped down on the couch next to Joseph, enjoying the 'whoosh' that the cushions made under her weight. She giggled.

Joseph smiled at her warmly. He was still getting to know the new girlie Akeema. His ex-fiancé had been all woman behind a calm, cool exterior. He realized that he'd never heard her belly-laugh until after the shooting. He no longer hoped for her to go back to her old self. He was beginning to prefer this new one.

"Whew! That was fun, but I'm exhausted! How you doin'?"

Putting his arms around her shoulders, he replied, "I'm okay now."

He gave her a peck on the cheek. She snuggled against him, wiggling until she found the most comfortable position.

"I hate to wake Joey up just to take him back to bed," he lamented.

"Then don't!" She insisted. "If Aunt Jean was here, she'd suggest that you both spend the night. It's silly to go home this late when you don't have to!"

He didn't put up much resistance.

Symphony music was playing softly in the room. It was very relaxing after all the noise and activity that was going on just minutes ago. Akeema felt droopy, Joseph felt amorous.

As he lifted her face to meet his kiss, she pulled back, surprising him.

"What's up?" he asked.

"Nothing. I already kissed Derek tonight and I have the feeling it will be tacky to start kissing on you. Am I wrong?"

Given a choice, Joseph would rather be kisser number one – but he didn't have a choice. The option of not kissing her at all didn't appeal to him. Why did he think it was a good idea to break off their engagement?

"Well, let's see…you don't have a boyfriend, fiancé, or husband. You're as free as you can be. You get to choose who you want to kiss and when. I'll respect your decision."

"I certainly WANT to kiss you, that's for sure," she mused out loud.

Joseph smiled. "If we were voting, you know which side I'm on."

Akeema returned his smile. "Do you mind kissing me after another man?"

"Somewhat."

Perplexed, she asked, "What does that mean?"

Patiently, Joseph said, "Take a minute to think about it. What does it sound like?"

Akeema concentrated out loud. "Somewhat, somewhat…it kinda sounds like you're in the middle… maybe like…kinda sorta?"

Now he laughed. "I couldn't describe it better myself. Very good."

Akeema basked in his praise. It mattered to her what he thought of her.

"So, you wish I hadn't kissed Derek, but you'd still like to kiss me if I say okay, right?"

Looking at her tenderly, Joseph nodded. Something in his gaze touched her heart. She wanted to kiss him too. "You know what? I'm glad I told you that Derek and I kissed tonight. It feels like I didn't do it behind your back. It doesn't seem so…tacky now."

"Good."

It took all his strength to sit still. He wanted HER to make the move toward him. For a few seconds, Akeema thought of Derek. Strange. She realized that the reverse was not true; she didn't have thoughts of Joseph right before she kissed Derek. She made a mental note to visit this again – later. Now, she wanted nothing more than to lock lips with Joseph. Right here, right now.

Later, alone in her bedroom, Akeema replayed her first day back home. Aunt Jean told her that she had home movies of her life to show her. She would see herself dance. She'd see herself doing something she could no longer do. The thought of that made her sad. She deliberately pushed those thoughts aside to focus on the men in her life. Her body felt all tingly after her make out session with Joseph. She had a feeling of wanting more. From watching movies with romantic scenes in them, she knew her body was yearning for sexual release. Derek and Joseph had never had intercourse with her, but her many hot dreams assured her that she wasn't a virgin. She couldn't fathom why her nim-nut memory remembered orgasms – but not who she had them with. There were late nights when she woke up panting and convulsing in her private parts. Sometimes she had to cover her mouth to smother a scream. She wanted that. But she didn't want multiple partners. Something deep inside her didn't want to sleep around. And yet, she sure didn't mind kissing around. She was so attracted to Derek and Joseph that it confused her. Initially, she'd had a brotherly affection for Joseph, until he kissed her like a man to his woman. She knew she had been in love at least once since she'd been engaged. But she couldn't love Joseph now because she wanted to be close to Derek at every opportunity. He told her she was the first teacher he'd allowed himself to date while he was a principal. Telling her that made Akeema want him even more. She wasn't confused about what being 'in love' was. She had a shining example right under her nose. Aunt Jean and Uncle Rick were the very picture of it. Ultimately, she wanted what they had. She had no doubt that they were attracted only to each other. At this time in her life, Akeema couldn't imagine giving up either man, especially Joseph; Joey came with him. She'd love to give that sweet child some siblings to play with. Even more, she'd love to be his mother. She wasn't sure if Joey would still be a part of her life if she chose Derek to couple with. She taught first and second graders. Even when she was done with personally teaching him, she'd have access to him through six grades of elementary school. Aunt Jean told her that the child considered her and Rick family now. Would Joseph hurt his son by separating him away from people who loved him, and who he loved in return? She hoped not. Wearily, she snuggled into bed, trying to quiet her brain. She had much too much on her mind for a peaceful slumber.

CHAPTER 35

Half asleep, Akeema smiled drowsily as she felt little Joey quietly sneak into her bed to cuddle with her. He pressed his little body against her back as he hugged the side of her waist. Life didn't get much better than this. She whispered,"Good morning, sweet boy."

"Mornin,' sweet Akeema." "Are you okay?"

"Right now, I am," he replied quickly.

"Me too. Where's your dad?"

"Sleeping."

"He'll wake up looking for you."

"I'm here."

Akeema suppressed a giggle. "I know and you know that, but Joseph won't. So, it's probably a good idea for you to go back to him. Right?"

She heard him sigh his agreement. Slowly, she flipped on her other side to face him, holding the warm tiny body as closely as she could without smothering him. Joseph found them in that position. He felt an incredible urge to join them. Being held in the cocoon of Akeema's embrace, Joey had his eyes closed in heavenly bliss.

When her hold lessened, he opened his eyes to see his father looking at him from the doorway. Excited he yelled, "Daddy!"

At his shout, Akeema was startled. She looked over her shoulder, seeing Joseph. As their eyes met, he gently said, "How are my two favorite people doing this morning?"

Together, Joey and Akeema chorused, "Good!"

With energy that only an eight-year-old has first thing in the morning, Joey began jumping up and down on the bed. Laughing, Akeema sat up to bounce her bottom on the bed. Joseph was not about to be left out on the family fun. He ran to the bed where he joyfully began tickling his son and his former fiancé. They were having so much noisy fun that nobody noticed Rick and Jean watching them.

Amused, Jean said to her husband, "Will you look at this mess? They look as happy as a family can be. I kinda hate to break this up."

"They should have a good marriage."

Jean scoffed. "Except for the fact that Akeema has a crush on her boss."

"What?" Rick bellowed.

The frolicking trio heard him, stopping their play.

"Good mornin'!" Joey said happily.

Jean gave Rick a quick warning look that said 'shut up.' He did.

"Mornin' everybody. Don't let us interrupt your fun for now, but don't forget that Joey has to get to school. I'm on my way to fix breakfast. Any special requests?"

Joey didn't hesitate. "Pancakes!"

"Yum, that's a good idea, Joey. Count me in!" Akeema exclaimed.

Joseph made it unanimous.

"Okay, I'll see you guys in the kitchen in fifteen minutes," Jean ordered.

Akeema was astonished. "You can whip up all those pancakes in just fifteen minutes?"

"Watch me!"

Rick gave the group a sly wink before chasing after his wife.

"Can I have just one more, Mama Jean? Please."

"You're such a little thang, Joey! This will make SIX pancakes for you. Do you really have room for more?"

"Yes, ma'am! Your pancakes are better than everybody else's pancakes!" Joey declared.

Blushing prettily, Jean said, "Such praise for a little flour and baking powder. Here ya go, partner!" Jean placed the smallest cake on the little boy's plate, with a barely there drop of butter.

To the grownups, Jean pointed out, "Pound for pound, Joey is eating you guys under the table. It's a shame," she said.

At that challenge, Rick pounced on the pancake platter sitting in the middle of the table. Since they had guests, he'd controlled his appetite so that everyone would have all that they wanted. Now, all bets were off!

Good naturedly, Joseph also took up the challenge. Swiftly, he stacked six pancakes on his plate, bringing his grand total to ten! Never a butter addict, he was satisfied with a healthy amount of syrup. With grins on their faces, the men pounced on the cakes with gusto! Jean, Akeema, and Joey watched in amazement as Rick and Joseph did some serious damage to the pancake platter. When all was said and done, the score was Joseph twelve, Rick 15, Joey 6, and Jean and Akeema wimped out at three each. When Jean asked if anyone wanted more food, the kitchen rocked with the stuffed moans and groans of its occupants.

Later, Akeema and Jean were left alone in the house. On video, they were watching several of Akeema's ballet performances.

"Look how beautiful you are," Jean said with a sigh.

Akeema watched in awe. She couldn't believe she'd ever been that graceful. To herself, she had to admit that she was once a good dancer. But now, she was a has been. Something inside her began to ache. She felt her eyes fill with tears before falling down her cheeks.

Akeema did nothing to stop or hide them. Jean was so enthralled by the images before her, that she didn't notice her niece was getting emotional. When she heard her sniff, she turned to look at her. Tears were cascading down Akeema's face. Without a second thought, Jean grabbed her to pull her close. That's when Akeema completely broke down. She openly sobbed on her aunt's shoulder, drenching it. For a long while, nobody said a word. Nobody had to.

Once Akeema quieted down, Jean spoke to her.

"You've been through a lot, and you've lost a lot. But the most important thing to remember, and be thankful for, is that you've survived. The Most High has seen to that."

Akeema looked at her aunt through watery eyes. The post-nasal drip was causing her sniffles, but the gut-wrenching sobs had ended.

"Did my parents live long enough to see me on stage, auntie?"

Jean shook her head. "No, honey, I'm sorry. They loved your voice though. They thought you'd grow up to be a singer."

"I sing with the commercials. Right now, I can't remember any songs."

"Don't worry about it, baby girl. As more of your memory comes back, your music will too."

Akeema smiled, wetly. "Joey has been teaching me to sing with him."

"That's cool. It wouldn't surprise me to know that he's teaching you songs that he learned from you."

"I never thought about that," Akeema replied.

Jean smiled, glad that the crying and sniffling were ending. She wanted to turn the TV off, but she didn't want to bring attention back to it.

"Auntie, can the person that shot me get to anybody else?"

Oh, dear.

"No," she said firmly.

"Did they catch the one that did this to me? Is he in prison? Did he say why he chose me to do this to?"

She wished Rick was with her. She really didn't want to tell Akeema about this by herself.

Resigned to her fate, Jean said tersely, "Wait a minute."

As Akeema did as she was told, Jean turned the TV off, then hurried away to get a box of tissues. She wanted to be prepared for any hysterical outburst this time…by either of them. It was time. Jean held Akeema's hands as she told her about Jake. This time, there were no tears. Akeema stared at Jean with wide, staring eyes. She was numb with shock. The man she'd chosen as her only boyfriend was so distraught after their break-up that he couldn't live without her, and he refused to let her live without him. He was dead, and by Yahuah's Grace – she wasn't. How in the world could she have ever loved a controlling, obsessive maniac like that? Was her choice in men so lousy that people were hurt or killed because of it?

Derek and Joseph came to mind. She wanted them. Both of them. She ached with longing for them. Jean sat very still while Akeema processed all the details of her personal life. She could only imagine how difficult this was for her niece. Suddenly, Jean saw alarm cross Akeema's pretty features. She held her tongue. Jean knew that she shouldn't force Akeema to share any-thing with her that she wasn't ready to.

In a voice that was barely audible, Akeema said, "The dreams. He's the man in my dreams." Jean couldn't force Akeema to share with her, but maybe she could guide her a little. "What dreams are those, sweetie?"

"Orgasm dreams, auntie. I wake up panting and sweating while breathing fast. I asked Joseph and Derek if we had sex and they both said no. I've seen a few hot movies, so I thought maybe that's why I was having hot dreams."

"You never saw your dream lover's face?"

"I saw more of his fit body than anything else. I remember he had thick brown hair; I think."

Jean nodded. "Yep, Jake had that. On one of the tapes, I filmed a meet and greet at the theater. I have a little footage on Jake, if you want to see him."

Akeema shivered. "I don't know if I'm ready to see the man who tried to kill me in my dreams every night. Not now…maybe never."

"I understand, it's totally up to you. If, or when, you change your mind, just let me know."

Akeema nodded. The silence between them lingered. Jean was speechless because she didn't want to say anything that would upset her niece any more than what she already was. Akeema was mute because she was grappling with the truth about herself: she was a poor judge of character. She had great men around her like Derek and Joseph, but she'd chosen Jake as the main man in her life. She tried to give herself a break. He must have duped her into believing he was a stand-up guy. He had to be a big-time, first-class liar. The one thing she was sure of about him was that he was an outstanding lover. Even now, her body tingled at the erotic dreams she'd had about him. Almost immediately, she felt ashamed. She couldn't understand herself; then or now.

Jean was still holding her niece's hands silently. She was waiting for Akeema's volcano to blow. In the meantime, she lifted up a fervent prayer for wisdom and His will to be done. Jean asked that her body be used as Yahuah's vessel to help guide Akeema through her difficult times.

"Auntie, how many men have you had sex with?" Caught off guard, Jean sputtered, "Excuse me?"

Seeing her aunt's reaction, Akeema backed up. "I'm sorry, never mind." She took her hands out of Jean's. Nervously, she feared that she had unintentionally insulted the woman she loved so much.

Seeing Akeema on the brink of tears again, Jean hurried to release the tension between them. "You have nothing to be sorry for, my dear," she said quietly. "You just surprised me, that's all."

"Was the question too private?" Akeema asked timidly.

"For most people, yes. But, when you and I are alone together, we can discuss anything, okay?"

Jean saw Akeema relax. Whew, dodged that bullet.

"I'm kissing two men these days and I'm so enjoying it."

Jean smiled. "Good. I'm sure Joseph and Derek are enjoying themselves too."

"So, is it okay if I have sex with both of them?"

Jean forced herself not to squirm…outwardly.

"Uh, well, uh…listen. I'm from another generation. You'll probably get better answers or up-to-date opinions from your peers."

"Peers?"

"Yes, dear. Someone in your age range."

Akeema seemed to consider this. Jean felt a little guilty for pawning her niece off on others.

Looking confident, Akeema replied, "I prefer wisdom. You have plenty of that, so I wanna know what you think, please."

Resigned to her fate, Jean answered honestly.

"As long as everyone involved consents, it's alright to have multiple sex partners – as far as the law of man is concerned. You also need to buy condoms so that sexual diseases won't get passed around."

A horrified Akeema sputtered, "Disease? Did you just say that sex causes disease? How?"

Jean sighed. What a ridiculous position to be in.

"Calm down, dear. It's not as bad as it sounds."

Akeema placed her right hand over her heart, briefly closing her eyes. "Auntie, you almost gave me a heart attack! Please explain."

Jean took a deep breath before continuing. She was determined to undo the mess that she'd created.

"First of all, let me say clearly that I don't believe that Joseph or Derek are sick with any sexual diseases."

"Thank goodness," Akeema said under her breath.

"However, when you have multiple sex partners, it's better to be safe than sorry."

Akeema nodded her agreement.

"Also, there are times when our female parts can get infected, causing unprotected sex to infect the man."

At Akeema's stricken look, Jean rushed to reassure her. "Of course, during your long stay in the hospital you were checked out from head to toe and everything in between! You don't have anything to worry about in that area."

"Do you and unc use condoms?"

Jean couldn't help but chuckle at that.

"Nope, most married couples don't, unless they are using them for birth control."

That made perfect sense to Akeema.

"If you're a child of the Most High, sex is only for married couples."

Sadly, Akeema said, "Aw, shoot! I was hoping that wasn't true."

"I'm afraid it is."

Again, they fell into silence. Akeema's next question surprised Jean again. "Am I a good Christian, auntie?"

"I'm not your judge, Akeema. Remember that our Savior shed His precious blood to cover our sins. I doubt that we have any perfect people walking around down here."

"Joseph told me that spiritually, I'm part of an online fellowship. Do you and unc praise and worship with me on Sabbaths?"

"We visited from time to time. Now, I join even more because they asked me to keep them up to date on your recovery and rehab. I've been enjoying the services and the fellowship."

Akeema smiled at her aunt, glad to hear that she enjoyed the holy day with her spiritual friends. Too bad Akeema didn't quite remember them.

Last night, Akeema had gone to bed late. She was now tired, and Jean could see it.

"Well, honey, it's time for me to fix lunch before I prepare dinner. Why don't you take a little nap to re-charge your batteries."

Akeema wanted to be useful. "Let me help you do all that. You taught me well, you know."

"You listen to your busy-body aunt. Go get a few z's while you still can. When your people get off work and out of school, you're going to need all the energy you have in reserve. Now, scoot!"

Truer words were never spoken. Obediently, Akeema stood up, kissed her aunt on the cheek, then retired to her room.

As Jean watched her walk away, she sagged against the back of her couch. The new Akeema was wonderful, but exhausting.

CHAPTER 36

Coming up behind his wife's back, Rick grabbed her around her soft, ample waist. He kissed the side of her neck serval times, making her giggle. "Stop that, you crazy man! I'm fixin' your lunch. Don't make me burn it." Inhaling deeply, he replied, "Mmm, it and you sure do smell good. What are we having?"

"Grilled turkey and cheese sandwiches with a salad."

Rick made a face behind Jean that she couldn't see. "Why the salad? I'll just have a couple of sandwiches, thank you."

Jean turned in his arms to face him. "I figured that, my love. The salad is for Akeema." With that said, she wrapped her arms around his neck to kiss him long and hard. She pressed herself suggestively against him, feeling his readiness for her. Before she could stop him, he picked up his lady love to plant her butt firmly on the kitchen counter. His lips never left hers.

For a few moments, she reveled in the passion between them. Forty years of marriage and his love-making still made her lose her mind.

Rick was very adept at pleasing her. Quickly, he wrapped her legs around him as he pushed her panties to the side, sliding his fingers inside her. Jean moaned into his mouth, on the verge of exploding. Gasping, she broke the kiss to suck in some air. Next to her ear, Rick was murmuring, "Baby, oh my baby." While he increased the pace of his strokes. She cried out his name as the wetness from her orgasm drenched his hand. Jean was still convulsing when Rick swiftly unzipped his pants to enter her. Together, they climaxed powerfully and loudly.

Clinging to each other, their breathing slowly returned to normal. Jean teased, "For an old codger, you're still pretty good."

"I was just thanking you for the gift you gave me this morning. All I had to do was lay there as you did wonderful things to-and-for-me. I love you so much."

"And I you."

This time, the kiss they shared was tender and heart felt.

"Auntie, you alright?" Akeema yelled. "What's burning?"

"Oh, no!" "Crap!" They said together.

They hurriedly put their clothing back together.

Jean needed to wipe up and change her underwear. When she got to the kitchen door, she responded to Akeema. "I'm fine, dear. I'll call you for lunch in a few!"

"Okay!"

To her husband, she hissed, "Take that skillet off the fire before we burn the house down!" On her way to their bedroom, Jean thought, "I'm getting too old for this!"

Akeema was antsy. She was sitting with Jean in the school parking lot, waiting for Joey to get out of school. Jean had tried, unsuccessfully, to get her niece to stay home. Akeema would have none of that.

Now, they were eagerly anticipating the last bell to ring so they could see their favorite little boy. They hadn't seen him in seven whole hours, which seemed like a lifetime ago. Akeema wanted to go inside. She kept tapping her fingers on the dashboard, patting her foot on the floorboard, and adjusting her outdoor side mirror – over and over. Finally, Jean couldn't stand it anymore.

"Look, Akeema, we're kinda early. Why don't you go inside to say hi to Derek? I'll stay with the car since Joey is accustomed to finding me right here."

Akeema's beautiful face lit up. "Auntie, that's a great idea! Where's the principal's office?"

"Straight down the hall. You don't have to turn left or right to run into it."

She frowned. "Do I have to run into his office? I can walk okay, but I'll probably fall flat on my face if I try to do anything else."

Jean suppressed her chuckle.

Akeema walked slowly down the corridor, savoring every sound and smell. All of this was very familiar. Now, more than ever, she wanted her doctors to release her so she could get back to work. Preparing for the final bell to ring, the hallway was pretty empty because everyone seemed to be in an office or a classroom. Akeema found herself drifting toward the sound of laughing children. Observing them from the doorway, she knew without a doubt that this was HER room! She stepped inside, unable to stop herself. When the kids saw her, the room erupted with excitement as her students all ran to greet her. Losing her balance, she tumbled gleefully to the floor. Even this felt nor- mal to her. She was showered with hugs, wet kisses, and Joey.

Mrs. Endicott, the substitute teacher, observed the chaos with envy. This beautiful young woman was very loved by these children; some of them were crying with happiness! Unobserved, she quietly sat at her desk, staying out of the way.

"Teacher Akeema, are you feeling good?"

"When are you coming back?"

"Did you see your face on TV?"

"Can we play some games before we go home?"

Before she could even begin to answer their barrage of questions, the bell rang. She gave them all a smile, hug, tickle, or kiss. Then she gingerly stood up so the kids would begin to go to their waiting parents.

Clapping her hands together, Mrs. Endicott was stunned to see how quickly the class quieted down for Akeema. She envied her unobtrusive control over them. Although she was old enough to be her mother, this young woman had a majority and grace far above her years. When Akeema spoke, her smoky alto voice was never raised, but clearly heard.

"It's been so good seeing you all because I've missed you so much! As soon as the doctor says I can work again, I'll be back with you, okay?" Most of the children nodded their little heads, but Joey asked, "You're so pretty, Teacher Akeema, are you still hurt?"

Akeema looked at him with adoring eyes. With her left hand, she touched the left side of her head. "When this part of me was hurt, it made my other side," she said while holding up her right hand, "stop working so well." A cute little blonde girl with pigtails observed, "You look so pretty and you're walking. Why can't you come back now, teacher?"

Patiently, she responded, "I'm better, but I get tired very easily. I have to build up my strength so that I can keep up with you sweet little munchkins all day, five days a week." Behind her, Akeema heard muffled voices and footsteps. Turning away from the children, she faced a variety of parents, teachers, and cleaning crew waiting their turn to welcome her back. For a few minutes, she was the most popular girl in school. It was a heartwarming reunion.

Aunt Jean, Joey, and Akeema were halfway home before Akeema realized she hadn't visited with Derek. She hadn't even thought of him. Interesting.

Keeping Joey in mind, Jean had macaroni and cheese with crescent dogs for dinner. A nice salad for Akeema completed her culinary duties for the evening. The table talk was animated with Joey holding court. Jean and Rick ate their full meal, but Akeema snacked slowly on a crescent dog, preferring to eat most of her meal with Joseph when he got off work. Rick sat back from the kitchen island, patting his over-full stomach. He belched loudly, making everyone laugh. Grinning, he asked, "Who'd like to play me a few games of Go Fish?"

Joey threw his hand in the air, waving it.

"Me, me! I bet I can beat cha!"

Chuckling, Rick replied, "We'll see about that, young man! Anyone else up to the challenge?"

"I'll be in after I spruce up a bit."

Akeema went to her aunt's side, taking the dish towel from her hands. "Aunt Jean, I'll do the sprucing. Go ahead with the fellas while I clean and wait for Joseph." For once, Jean didn't argue with her. She knew Akeema was anxious for a little time alone with Joseph, and she wanted to spend time with Joey and her husband.

"Thank you, dear. I'm gonna show these men who wears the pants in this house." With that said, the trio left Akeema alone in the kitchen.

Whistling a happy tune, she cleaned up the kitchen so well, that she knew her effort was good enough to impress her hard-to-please favorite aunt.

When Joseph finally arrived, he was disappointed when Rick answered the door instead of Akeema. He followed the man of the house to the living room to kiss Jean on the cheek and throw his son gleefully in the air a few times. He was blending in well with the family while his thoughts were on Akeema. Where was she?

As if reading his mind, Jean quipped, "If you're hungry, Akeema is keeping your dinner warm in the kitchen."

"Daddy, we had good ole hot dog biscuits! Go get 'em!"

Joseph smiled. "Will do partner," he said to his son. Catching Jeans eye, Joseph wanted clarification.

"Dog biscuits? Really?"

Jean understood his concern. "I made one of Joey's faves and it turned out that the grown-ups like 'em too! You have crescent rolls with beef franks inside them. There's also enough salad for you and Akeema to share, if you'd like."

"Thanks, Jean. That sounds great. I'm all kinds of hungry. I'll be back after I chow down." He gave Joey a final tickle before going to his lady love.

Akeema was waiting in the kitchen, patiently. She understood his need to see Joey first. When Joseph walked through the swinging door, Akeema was standing on the other side with her arms reaching out to him. Smiling, he scooped her into his arms, kissing her deeply. When the kiss ended, they were breathless and leaning against each other.

Joseph whispered, "That was a very special hello."

Akeema smiled, happy that she'd pleased him.

"Are you hungry?" she asked.

"Yes, for you," he replied huskily. Akeema felt her body flush at the compliment.

"If I let you have me here and now, everybody in the house would trip out!" she said, horrified.,

Belatedly, Joseph realized she'd taken him seriously and literally.

Playfully, he kissed her nose. "I know baby, don't worry about it. I'm hungry for food too. What's for dinner."

She was ready to chow down too. Together, they ate the salad and crescent dogs until Joseph was properly stuffed. Akeema's food discipline stopped her from eating more once she was no longer hungry. Her once rock-hard body was now softer, but not flabby. Her rehab four days a week wasn't enough to maintain her dancer bod, but she was well toned. After dinner, they did one last kitchen spruce-up so that Jean wouldn't have anything else to do. Before they joined the others, they silently decided to get one last kiss. Holding her close, Joseph said, "I am so glad that you are in my life, Akeema."

"Thank you, Joseph. I feel the same way."

They gazed at each other lovingly. They could feel each other's hearts beating. Joseph inhaled deeply, smelling the clean freshness that was uniquely hers. He wanted her. All of her.

"Daddy!"

First, they heard him, then he was with them. Joey came in with all his little boy energy. Akeema and Joseph took several steps backwards, putting space between them.

"Meemaw said I could have some cookies before we go home if you say it's okay. Is it okay?"

Joseph looked at his watch. It was a little after 8:30 at night. It was time to go.

"Sure, partner. Get a couple for me too!"

Without hesitation, Joey pulled a chair to the counter so that he could climb up to reach the cookie jar.

Under her breath, Akeema told Joseph it might not be a good idea to give him a sugar hit so late in the evening. He gave her a brief nod.

"Joey, get two for you, and two for me."

"Okay. She made sugar and chocolate chip. I like the sugar ones. How 'bout you?"

"I'll take one of each, thank you."

"Got 'em! How 'bout you, teacher Akeema?" Joey asked.

"No thanks, sweetie. I'm still full of dinner."

Knowingly, Joey responded, "That's 'cause you have a itty-bitty stomach that get full fast."

Charmed by his deductive reasoning, Akeema picked him up for a big bear hug. Joseph watched them, hoping and praying that they would always love each other like this.

Later, Akeema flipped through a magazine while she waited for Joseph to call her to say a final goodnight.

From her bedroom, she could hear her aunt and uncle conversing in the living room with the TV on. She heard Jean's girlish giggle again. Only her uncle had that effect on her. Akeema looked forward to the day when she had a husband that she would happily grow old with. Had she already met him?

Her ringing cell interrupted her thoughts.

Finally!

Feeling chipper, she didn't just say hello – she sang it!

"Wow! That's amazing! Your gifts just keep on giving, don't they?"

That wasn't Joseph's voice.

Stunned, Akeema held the phone, saying nothing. Now the caller was confused too. "Hello? Are you still there? Hello?"

Her brain and tongue slowly reconnected.

"Uh, yeah, I'm here. Who is this?"

He got it. She hadn't looked at her cell display to see that he was calling her. The serenade was for someone else. They were both single and not dating each other exclusively. He knew and understood that. Unfortunately, that knowledge didn't stop him from feeling a twinge of jealousy. It was a feeling he wasn't familiar with. He didn't like it.

"Akeema, it's Derek."

He heard her quick intake of breath. "Oh, hey! I wasn't expecting you, but I'm glad you called." He heard the sincerity in her voice. He relaxed. A little.

"I'm glad you're glad. Do you have time to talk?"

"Sure, until Joseph calls. I'll need to go then."

Ouch!

"Okay, I'll be quick then. Do you have plans for this Friday night?"

"Not that I remember."

"I'd like to take you out to dinner, a movie, or both."

"Do I get to pick the movie?"

"Yes, you sure do."

"Yay, I'd like that! But I'll eat before we go out. I prefer my aunt's cooking."

Derek paused, waiting for her to invite him to dinner at her house. No invitation came.

"Okay," he said slowly. "I'll make sure I eat before I come to get you."

"Good. I won't be ready until after Joey and I have dinner together."

"Joey? The little boy?"

"Yep. I want to spend time with him because he'll be at home by the time our date will be over." She wanted to spend time with Joseph's son…not Joseph. Derek smiled.

"Sounds good. Is seven a good time to come for you?"

"Perfect."

"If you remember later that you had made prior plans, will you call me so that we can reschedule?"

"Absolutely! Oh! Here's Joseph. Bye!"

Click. She was gone.

It was the first time that Derek ever wanted to be a fly on the wall.

CHAPTER 37

There she was again. The well put together middle-aged woman. She was dressed all in black, with pearl accessories. She even wore a black hat with a lacy see-through veil. To Akeema's knowledge, she rarely spoke. The work-out room for the rehab patients was comfortably busy, clean, and never over-crowded. The mysterious woman didn't seem to be there for anyone in particular. She stood, or sat, in a corner, content to watch people grunting, sweating, and working. Akeema wondered if she was in mourning for someone who once worked out in the facility. She never caught her smiling or crying; she was just there. Akeema didn't know who she was, but there was something vaguely familiar about her.

After her daily exercise, Akeema felt strong, but tired on her weak right side. As a precaution, she used her cane to move better. Each day was bringing her closer to being gainfully employed once again.

Before meeting Aunt Jean in the parking lot, Akeema stopped by the office to make a payment on her account. The cheerful cashier was surprised to see her.

"Ms. Sprite, what more can I do for you today?" Perplexed, Akeema asked, "What MORE can you do? What do you mean?"

"Your account has already had a payment on it today. Is there something else you need?"

She looked at the pretty young girl with the two thick, brown ponytails, braces, and too many freckles to count. She was a woman who looked ten years old. Akeema didn't know that the helpful young lady was 18 years old, and that this as her very first day on the job since graduating from High School. Her name tag read: Carol.

"No, I'm fine. My aunt probably paid on the bill for me. Thanks, and have a blessed day." Carol smiled widely, exposing all her oral hardware.

"Thank you, Miss Sprite, you too!"

This young person wasn't self-conscious about her braces. She graced Akeema with a beautiful farewell smile.

As Jean pulled out of the parking lot, she reminded Akeema, "We've got plenty of time before we have to pick up Joey, so if you want to stop by the house to change out of your exercise gear, we certainly can."

Alarmed, her niece asked, "Do I need to? Am I stinking up the car?"

"Chile! I don't know why your sweat doesn't smell bad, but it doesn't. I thought you might want to see Derek since you missed him the other day."

Akeema smiled. "I let those kids take all of my attention, didn't I? Let's face it auntie, if I set foot in that school, I'll be headed to the kids – not the man!"

Jean nodded her agreement. Truer words were never spoken.

"Auntie, I almost forgot! Thanks for paying on my hospital bill for me, but I don't want you to do that!"

"What?"

"You know my insurance pays 80% so that I only have to pay the remaining balance. I've got it covered. So, I want to pay you back. How much do I owe you?"

Jean gave her a quick look. "I don't know what you are talking about, sweetie. You don't owe me a thing."

Akeema rolled her eyes. "Auntie, give me a break, will you? I insist on paying my own doctor bills."

"That's fine, dear. If you find that you need help, don't hesitate to tell us."

Akeema wondered if she was taking a trip to the Outer Limits. "Did you pay on my bill today?"

"Nope."

"Are you serious?"

"Yep."

"Did Uncle Rick do it then?"

"Nope."

"How do you know?"

"We haven't talked about it," she said simply.

"Do you guys talk about everything?"

"Yep, pretty much."

"If you didn't do it, who did?"

Jean shrugged, "I don't have a clue. Have you checked with the boys?"

"Boys? What boys?"

"Joseph and Derek."

Akeema shook her head. "I don't think so. I can't imagine either of them doing this without first checking with me. This is an invasion of my privacy."

Jean heard the irritation in Akeema's voice.

"While the office is still open, it might be a good idea to see if the payment was made by check. At least we'd have a name to research." Akeema turned around to do just that. Having that done resulted in more questions, than answers. The payment was made with cash. Akeema kept digging.

"Carol, did you take the payment on my account?"

"Yes, ma'am," she answered promptly.

"Was the customer male or female?"

"She was a well put together woman."

Akeema wasn't clear on what that meant. She asked, "Was she pretty?"

"She was attractive, from what I could see."

"You didn't see her clearly? Why not?"

"For some reason she hid her face behind a veil."

Akeema didn't trust her own ears. She dared to ask, "Was she dressed in all black?"

"Yes, ma'am. She sure was. Do you know her?"

"No, but I think I've seen her around."

"Me too. I've seen her in the rehab area the last few weeks. But, if you don't know her, why is she paying on your account?"

"I don't know, but I plan to find out."

The next morning, Akeema had a hard time concentrating on her rehab. She kept looking for the mysterious woman, dressed in black.

By the end of her session, she was worn out and dejected. On her way out, Akeema looked around every corner, crook, and cranny, hoping to see the missing woman, but to no avail.

When Jean saw her coming out of the building, she knew her usually smiling niece, wasn't happy. She lifted up a silent prayer for some answers.

She rolled down her car window, preparing to greet her. From a distance, she heard a female voice. Akeema's head turned to the left. Jean's heart almost stopped when a woman dressed in all black approached Akeema. Without a second thought, Jean got out of the car, rushing to the woman.

When she reached the woman and her niece, they were staring at each other without conversing. Unable to endure the tension around them, Jean was about to say something – anything – to ease it.

Thankfully, Akeema rescued her.

"You called my name. Do we know each other?"

Behind the veil, Jean and Akeema saw the woman's eyebrows lift. "Are you jesting?" she asked.

In mute, Akeema shook her head.

The woman lifted her veil so that she could be more clearly seen. Steadily, she held the young woman's gaze. Akeema returned her stare with no recognition.

Finally, the strange woman announced, "I am Lucille Butler, Jake's mother."

"Oh, no!" Jean exclaimed.

Alarmed, Akeema zeroed in on her aunt. Why was she so obviously upset?

"Auntie, what is it? Do you know this lady?"

Jean prayed for calm. She couldn't afford to get overly excited. Akeema would feed off her reaction. She took several deep breaths before turning to Lucille Butler. "My niece isn't being rude or disrespectful to you, Mrs. Butler. Since her head injury, she's only recovered about 60% of her memory…so far."

The media coverage didn't mention that. This was the first time Lucille had heard this. She lowered her head in shame. This was another thing taken away from Akeema by her son.

Looking back and forth to the two women, Akeema wasn't liking the weird energy between them. They obviously knew something that she didn't. Waiting wasn't getting her any answers. She threw polite out the window.

"Did you pay on my hospital bill?" she asked bluntly.

Mrs. Butler gave one short nod of her perfect head that didn't have a single hair out of place.

"Why?"

"It's the least I can do."

"I don't know you. You owe me nothing."

Lucille looked at her steadily. "You know me, you just don't remember me."

Akeema briefly searched her memory for this classy woman and came up with zilch.

"Are you a parent to one of my students?"

"No, I am not."

"Were you a fan of my work on the stage?"

"Yes, you were a beautiful dancer."

"Thank you. Did I see you in a Meet and Greet?"

"Yes."

"Is that how I know you?"

"Not exactly," she hedged.

Listening to their exchange was driving Jean crazy. If this was the day that Akeema would get another piece of puzzle in her life, so be it. Her job wasn't to interfere at this point. She just needed to be there for Akeema to lean, or fall, on.

"Where else have we met?" Akeema asked.

Lucille hesitated, trying to find the right words. She didn't look forward to upsetting her. She'd been through enough.

"We met at my home."

Super surprised, Akeema replied, "Why would I have been inside your house? What exactly was I doing there?"

"Eating dinner."

"What?!" Akeema sputtered. "I only eat my aunt's home cooking. The only place besides her place is fast food, or a restaurant!"

"That you remember," Lucille pointed out."Touché.

"Why did you invite me to dinner?"

"I only cooked the dinner. I didn't invite you."

"Oh, was it a party that I came as someone's date?"

"It was a four-person dinner date."

"Do you know who my date was?"

Akeema saw Lucille's eyes fill up with unshed tears as she nodded her head.

"Who is he? Apparently, we're not still seeing each other. The only men that I've talked to are Derek and Joseph."

Lucille's voice trembled when she responded, "No, you don't see him anymore."

Eyeing her carefully, Akeema knew that the unnamed man was someone special to Mrs. Butler. It seemed he brought sad memories to her. Maybe he moved out of town or something. She felt bad for bringing him up to her. She kinda – sorta wanted to drop the whole thing, but she was very curious about the man who knew this woman so well that she entertained, and cooked, for them. Lucille was quiet, but Jean saw her bottom lip trembling. She also noticed that Akeema was shifting her weight back and forth. Her leg was getting tired. It was past time to finish this.

"Your date was her son, Akeema."

The words floated in the air, surrounding them. Suffocating them. In horror, Akeema turned to Lucille.

"Your son tried to kill me?"

A slight nod was all that Lucille could muster.

"Did he tell you why?"

"He said he couldn't live without you, and he couldn't let you live without him," Jean responded.

Akeema's eyes almost bulged out of their sockets! "You watched him shoot me?" she croaked.

Wildly waving her hands, Jean yelled,

"No! No! It was in the suicide note that he wrote!"

Lucille Butler uttered a strangled sob of grief.

"Suicide?" Akeema whispered. "He's …dead?"

"Yes, dear. He intended that the two of you die together. Yahuah, our Father, had other plans for you."

Now, Jake's mother was sobbing into her open hands. Her cries were heartbreaking. Akeema felt weak in the knees. It had nothing to do with her weak right side.

"I need to sit down before I fall," Akeema said in a flat voice. Her aunt hurried to her side, helping her sit down on the steps outside the rehab center. Lucille followed them as she softly wept.

New memories filtered through Akeema's mind in jagged pictures. She concentrated with all her might, desperately trying to make sense out of what she was seeing. Slowly, the pictures started blending. The dread that filled her almost made her blot out the image that she saw. Her need to know the truth was stronger. A movie was playing inside her head. A horror movie.

"I was sitting in my car, outside the rehearsal hall," she began. Her voice was low and unemotional. Jean and Lucille stepped closer in order to hear her. "We were going to get something to eat. I called Joseph so that he wouldn't worry about me."

Jean cast a doubtful look at Lucille. This was about to get rough for her. She reached over to touch her hand. Lucille took hers and didn't let go as Akeema told the sordid story…

CHAPTER 38

Akeema jumped when Jake lightly tapped on her car window. She lowered the pane a little so they could hear each other. She wanted to get rid of him quickly. Her posse would wait for her at the restaurant where they planned to eat a light supper. She wasn't afraid…yet.

"Hello, my fair lady," he said pleasantly.

"Hi, Jake. I'm afraid I have plans so I need to run."

Smiling sweetly at her, he asked, "Oh! Where are you headed?"

Without thinking, she told him. "The girls and I are having supper together."

"Oh, I see. So, I'm not interrupting a date?"

"Yes, Jake, you are. I just told you that…oh, you mean I'm not having a date with a man." He nodded.

Akeema was a little late in realizing that none of this was his business. Oops.

"I need to go now, Jake," she said firmly.

"It's been a long time since you and I had dinner together. Is there a chance that I could talk you out of going to dinner with girlfriends, so we can eat together?"

Akeema was reminded of that old saying about a wolf in sheep's clothing. He was being charming – on the outside. She knew firsthand how well he could mask his inner anger. Now, she clearly heard the warning bell ring. She needed to get away from him. Fast! She turned on the ignition.

"Goodbye, Jake."

"Isn't it a little rude to talk to me over the motor?" The smile in his voice didn't reach his eyes. Uh-oh.

As she shifted the gear to reverse, Jake's timing was perfect. His black leather-gloved hand smashed the window on the driver side. Shattered glass flew everywhere. Akeema closed her eyes before covering them with her hands. When everything quieted down, Akeema dared to look around her. What she saw made her blood run cold. His gloved hand had a gun in it. She wanted to scream and faint.

"Turn the car off. Now!"

With trembling fingers, she did as she was told. She thought of the mace in the glove box.

Jake took a few steps back. "Get out of the car. Slowly."

Akeema did as she was ordered. When they were standing face to face, her eyes found the gun that was pointed at her heart. Jake also had an eyeful. He gave her a long, lingering look from head to toe. Physically, she was perfect in his eyes. If he couldn't have her, nobody would. His heart ached at the loss of her affection for him. Maybe, just maybe, it wasn't too late.

Tenderly, Jake declared his love. She was shocked by his words and the fact that he was pointing a gun at her as he said them.

"I hate that I had to be this drastic to catch your attention. You are the first, and only woman, I've ever fallen in love with."

He paused, hoping she'd say something similar back to him. She didn't.

"I've tried to be patient, Akeema. I've waited for you to miss me during our separation. Every time my phone rang, I hoped it was you coming back to me. It never was," he said sadly.

"I watched as you grew closer and closer to that kid you're crazy about, and his father. I couldn't risk waiting any longer. I was afraid the three of you would become a family. If that little boy hadn't already lost a parent, I might have off'd his dad," he said casually.

Akeema's neutral – looking expression turned to shock and dismay. "Oh, no!" she whispered.

"Don't worry. I felt bad for the kid."

Akeema sighed. A glimpse of humanity, finally.

"Jake, why can't we just go on with our lives like other couples who have broken up?"

Her heart stopped as she watched his sad, sullen expression change to fury. She'd obviously said the wrong thing.

"Don't you think I've tried to get you out of my mind?" he roared.

His anger was so hot, Akeema felt it hit her body. She took several steps backward, trying to escape him. Jake raised the gun, pointing it at her again.

"Don't you take another step," he said through clenched teeth.

Akeema did as she was told, watching the gun that was aimed her way. She was past terrified. In a low, controlled voice, she asked, "What do you want from me, Jake?"

"Your heart!" he bellowed, "and your body and soul. Everything!" he demanded.

She swallowed the dry lump in her throat. She tried telling him the truth. "I've gone on with my life, as I hoped you had. My heart belongs to someone else now." She wisely didn't tell him that he NEVER had her heart, only her body.

"With a steely stare, Jake said, "Follow me to my car.

"Why?"

"Because I said so."

She thought of screaming for help. The cleaning crew were still inside the rehearsal hall. If even one of them called the police, she had a chance. As if reading her mind, Jake made her a promise. "If you scream out and someone comes to help you, that person will be killed."

She believed him. Nobody was going to lose their life because she once chose a sexual relationship over her heart. No way.

Jake looked on in grudging admiration as Akeema lifted her chin before turning gracefully to walk to his car. Her posture was regal, her stride long. He knew she had to be scared to death. He couldn't tell by looking at her.

His gray BMW, that she was formerly so fond of, resembled a casket to her now. Jake could tell that his prey was headed to the passenger side of his car. Behind her, Akeema heard Jake's clipped voice say, "You're driving tonight."

She changed directions without him telling her to do so. Akeema didn't want to hear his voice any more than she had to. It sickened her to think that she'd found his voice extremely sexy at one time.

Jake directed Akeema to a remote area of White Rock Lake. For the most part it was dark, with an occasional night light and benches here and there. Right now, they were sitting in his car, facing the water. Usually, they listened to the radio or CD's, but everything was quiet while they listened to the night life in nature, along with the subtle rustlings of the lake itself. Akeema couldn't help but think how romantic this would be if Jake didn't have a gun pointed at her. When at last Jake spoke, his voice was deceptively soft and controlled.

"I know I don't have to ask this," he began, "but I don't want to assume anything at this point."

Akeema said nothing, waiting.

"Is there any chance at all that I can repair your car window before we go back to normal?" Akeema had been looking straight ahead. Now, she turned to look at her captor.

"What do you consider normal?" she asked.

"You and me together, loving and making love."

"I'm involved with someone else, Jake. You know that."

He nodded. "Yeah, I do. I want you to break up with him so that you and I can try again."

"You and I don't work well together. I think you probably need to meet someone like your mom."

Animated and excited, Jake exclaimed, "You're absolutely right! That's why I knew you'd make a perfect wife for me!"

Akeema had no idea what he was talking about. The way she looked at him telegraphed her feelings. He rushed on, desperate to make her understand.

"My father showed me the way. You choose the right woman who takes care of the home front while the man works to provide financial stability for the family. The woman should be good to look at so that any children that come out of the union will look good. Everybody wins, and everyone is happy!" Jake had it all figured out. Jake was delusional!

"Everybody WON'T be happy, Jake! Why can't you see that? Me, Joey, and Joseph won't be together. We'll be miserable!" she wailed. This was one of those rare moments when Akeema had let Jake see her cry. She had the ominous feeling that more tears would follow before this night met its end. She faced the possible reality that SHE might be facing her end.

She saw the returning glum look on his face.

"But Akeema, if you tried it my way, I'll make you happy…I promise!"

She said a silent prayer that she be given the right words to say. "The first problem we'd have is that I'm not like your sweet mother. She is a homemaker through and through. But, I not only have a career, I've got TWO! I love what I do. It's part of who I am. Whoever I marry has to let me be me, and vice versa!"

"You've got other virtues that fill your life! I've been to your place, remember? It's neat as a pin! On top of that, you are a good cook!"

"Jake, those are things I can do, not things that I ENJOY! If I had to do those things every day of my life, I'd lose my mind!"

She noticed the gun was forgotten in his lap. With his long arms, he reached over to grab her hands. He squeezed them painfully. Akeema didn't flinch or give any outward sign that she was physically uncomfortable.

"Can't you give us a chance? We'll work out our differences so that we'll have a happy, successful marriage."

Gently, Akeema whispered, "I can't marry a man that I'm not in love with, Jake. I've always been honest with you about that."

"I know, but it will come. I'll love enough for both of us until you catch up with me." He had a sad, glimmer of a smile on his lips. For a moment she forgot she was being held a hostage. For a moment she felt sorry for him.

"Jake, I can't guarantee that I'll ever fall in love with you. I could lie to you about this, but I won't. I respect you too much for that." Their clasped hands were beginning to sweat. It gave her no consolation that her body fluid was mixing with his. Yuck!

"Listen, I know how crazy you are about kids. You can adopt as many as you want. I have plenty of money, so we can afford them," he replied hopefully.

Akeema felt trapped in this exercise of futility.

"Oh, Jake! That would be a terrific bonus IF we had a loving relationship! Can't you see that love has to come before anything else? It must!" she emphasized.

Lamely, he responded, "I promise not to rush you into loving me. As long as we're seeing each other while we learn more about each other. I'll be patient."

Ah, yet another example of a willing spirit with the weak flesh.

"You haven't rushed me, Jake. We've tried to be a couple not once, but twice! It's past time for you to move on like I have."

With that said, he dropped her hands. Akeema quickly rubbed them over her leggings to help dry them.

In a harsh voice, Jake snarled, "Get out of the car."

So much for his patience.

Obedient to her captor. Akeema did as she was directed, shutting the door behind her. Jake began scoping out the area, turning his head back and forth, looking for others. Finally, he was convinced that they were alone. Going to the trunk of the car, he pulled out a bundle that Akeema couldn't quite make out. She came to the conclusion that it was probably something to sit on when they got closer to the lake. Then, she feared it might be something to LAY on because he wanted to have sex with her! It was the first time that thoughts of sex and Jake didn't turn her on. However, if it took a slam-bam-thank-you-ma'am to get her off this lake and back home, she'd give it her best shot.

Knowing he could outrun her, Jake walked with Akeema at his side, no gun in sight. When he found the spot he wanted, he spread the, now visible, sleeping bag on the ground. Akeema wondered if they were going to spend the night here. She hoped not. Joseph, aunt and uncle would be crazed with worry. They sat down on the bag for what seemed like hours. Finally, Jake said softly and sincerely, "I don't know how to live without you, Akeema."

She scoffed, "Nonsense, you just haven't given yourself a fair shot. You're just a wee bit out of practice, that's all. As soon as you start going back to your old stomping grounds, all the women will come your way. You'll have to beat them off with a stick."

He gifted her with a small smile. "I'm not that care-free guy that I used to be. You've changed me forever, my love."

Hearing that endearment made her cringe inside.

"We're BOTH different, Jake! It's called being human. We change as we learn. Anybody that's been in your life for any length of time makes you different."

"I don't want to be miserable the rest of my life."

She couldn't believe all this doom and gloom she was hearing from him. Was it possible that she'd ever really known him? She chided herself for asking a dumb question. The person she THOUGHT she knew would never have pulled a gun on her.

"You'll only be miserable if you choose to be! Pick happiness instead, for goodness sake."

She was talking to him in a more forceful voice. Akeema was frustrated with him, and she was tired. So very tired.

"My happiness is attached to you. You'll take it with you if you go."

Akeema perked up. Did he say IF she left? Jake continued. "Thinking of you in the arms of another man makes me physically ill. What cure do you have for that?" he yelled.

"Time, Jake! Give it time! Everything is raw right now. It won't always feel like this."

He stared at her so long and hard that she felt uncomfortable. The next question he asked, caught her off guard.

"Akeema, do you still pray?"

"Yes, I do. Every day, several times a day."

"Do it now."

"What do you want me to pray for?"

"Your life."

Akeema doubted her own ears. She couldn't have heard what she thought she heard. No way. "I'm sorry, Jake, I don't think I heard you."

Unblinking, Jake stared at her. His look was ominous. He didn't repeat himself. He didn't have to.

Akeema started to sweat profusely. This time, it wasn't due to body contact, however. This time, she saw herself dead. Every nerve in her body was activated. She wasn't about to just sit by his side as a willing victim. He'd have to work for this murder.

Without saying a word, Akeema jumped to her feet so smoothly that Jake was shocked. Her dancer's body was graceful and swift. She suppressed the urge to scream, knowing it would use up energy that needed to go to her feet. She'd seen enough TV shows to know that she had to avoid being an easy target by running in a straight line. Behind her, she heard Jake calling her name and cursing her. Her goal was to make it to the park's entrance where, hopefully, she could get to the main road where traffic was beginning for the day. Right now, Akeema and Jake were in a secluded area, giving him the confidence to do whatever he wanted to do to her.

The first shot whizzed by her right side as she redirected to the left. Her athletic body was serving her well. She had stamina for days. Akeema wasn't breathing hard, and her focus was clear. She lifted up a prayer for strength and protection. Akeema thought of her loved ones…Joseph, Joey, her wonderful aunt and uncle, all filtered through her mind as she ran for her life. She wanted to make it back to them, but only if Jake was out of her life. She'd rather die than have any of them hurt on her behalf.

Behind her, Jake wasn't screaming at her anymore. However, she heard his footsteps inching closer and closer. Akeema prayed that if he shot her, it wouldn't cause excruciating pain. She asked the heavenly Father to forgive her for the many sins that she willfully committed against Him. She promised Yahuah that if He saw fit to spare her, she would try as hard as she could to do better. The next bullet was so close to her right ear that Akeema smelled it and felt its heat. That was too close. Adrenaline and fear shot through her. She kept on running and dodging. She faced the fact that she'd rather be dead than be with Jake Butler.

The top of her tank top was yanked back so hard that her throat was crushed, cutting off air to her windpipe. He flung her to the earth so forcibly that even more air escaped her. Rolling on the ground and clutching her throat, she took a breath right before Jake's foot glued her to the ground.

Standing over her with his chest heaving, Jake spat, "If you're not mine, you're not anybody's."

In an instant, Akeema heard the gun go off as a powerful force hit her head. She marveled that she didn't feel the pain. Then, darkness.

CHAPTER 39

"Heaven help us, heaven help us," wept Lucille Butler.

The full impact of remembering the gory details about the shooting affected the three women differently.

Lucille, Jake's mother, mourned her son but carried his guilt. If she hadn't given him Kyle Butler as a father, perhaps he would've grown up to be a better man. Jake grew up listening to his father berate and sometimes slap his mother whenever she dared to talk back or disagree with her husband. To Jake, women had to know their place behind the man. Women were to do as the man instructed them. Only after Jake was dead and buried did Lucille get brave enough to leave the husband that cheated on her while they were still on their honeymoon! He was so sure of Lucille's lameness that he didn't even bother with a prenup. Lucille and her high-priced lawyer enjoyed taking 50% of everything that Kyle had. The vile names he'd called her in court, cost him even more of his precious assets. Until

Akeema's full recovery, Lucille planned to pay all hospital bills. She'd set up a trust for her that Akeema didn't know about yet.

For Jean, her feelings were mixed. First, she was thankful to the Most High for sparing Akeema as He also blessed her recovery. She felt Mrs. Butler's pain, feeling empathy for her. Where Jake was concerned, however, she wished he was alive, once more, so she could kill him all over again. So far, she still couldn't forgive him. However, the Holy Spirit kept prompting her to pray about it. She had faith that, in time, she'd succeed. Akeema's feelings were bittersweet. Although her consequences for disobedience was hefty in her view, she understood. Only she and Yahuah, the Holy Father, knew how hard-headed she'd been. She was with the wrong man while they did the wrong things. During that time, she hadn't asked for help or forgiveness from Yahuah. She gloried in her sinful ways. It took something forceful to yank her back to Him. She was ashamed to admit that for a period of time, sexual pleasure mattered more to her than what the Father thought of her actions. Yikes!

Not only had Akeema suffered a gunshot wound to the head, she could no longer dance professionally. The Almighty had blessed her with a second chance to live a life that pleased Him. She knew that trials and tribulations were bound to come her way for as long as she lived. From now on, she'd always seek the Father's help and guidance.

Lucille gave Jean's han,d a final squeeze before letting it go. In a strange way, she felt like she'd made a new friend. The Most High worked in mysterious ways. When she spoke, her voice was soft, but firm. Her eyes found and held Akeema's. "I'm so sorry for the pain that my son inflicted on you. He was my very own, but what he did wasn't right. He paid for it with his life," she whispered. "If I had the power to take it all back, I would. Sadly, that can't be done. But, I can make your life a little easier by paying your medical bills and set-ting up a trust for you. You don't have to work ever again if you don't want to."

Akeema and her aunt stared at each other in disbelief.

"What?" Akeema croaked.

"I intend to use Jake's fortune to make your life financially easier. He was my ex-husband's only heir. When he died, his money went back to the family estate. When I divorced my husband, I got half the money. You will benefit from that. I'm going to see to it," she said adamantly.

"You're divorced?"

Lucille nodded.

"I'm sorry, Mrs. Butler," Akeema replied. She didn't know what else to say.

"Don't be, my dear. Except for the loss of my son, I've never been happier."

Again, Jean and Akeema doubted their ears.

"How so?" Jean asked before she could stop herself. She knew and understood that she was there as a spectator and emotional support. It was obvious to Jean that it was important to Lucille that Akeema heard her truth.

"My Jake grew up in a dysfunctional family. All his life he watched his father bully me and wipe his boots on me as his door mat. If I kept my place, there was peace in the house. If I dared to have a different opinion from my ex, the house would rock!"

Reflecting on her past, really upset Lucille. Tears streamed down her face again. Jean gave her more tissues and hand pats. As she gathered herself, Akeema and Jean quietly, and patiently, waited.

When Lucille continued, her voice was steady.

"So, you see, Jake's version of the perfect woman was a grossly-imperfect me."

In a hushed voice, Akeema exclaimed, "But, I'm nothing like that!" She turned to Jean, "Auntie, I know my memory isn't 100% yet, but was I EVER like the woman Mrs. Butler just described?"

"Never!" Jean replied with conviction.

Lucille hastened to console Akeema. "Don't you see that your strength and belief in yourself is what drove Jake crazy? He couldn't MAKE you do anything you didn't want to. That's why I was surprised you two were together for so long. I couldn't imagine why you were okay with his controlling ways."

Lucille and Jean looked at Akeema expectantly. They both wanted to know why she was with him.

Akeema felt her body flush with embarrassment. She wasn't about to confess to them that she was held hostage by his expert love making.

"At first, he was the perfect boyfriend. He was sweet-natured and good to me."

Now it was Jean and Lucille who exchanged looks of surprise and disbelief. Seeing that, Akeema hurried to explain. "But the day finally came when we disagreed. I can't remember what we disagreed over, but I can hear the meanness of his voice and the bad names that he called me."

Lucille lowered her head in shame. Jean clenched her mouth shut to keep from cursing him.

Akeema continued. "I broke up with him right away. But he used the Holy Scriptures to lure me back."

In unison, Jake's mother and Akeema's aunt yelled, "How?"

"Jake pointed out that Yahusha, our Savior, said we should forgive 70 time 7. All he was asking for was one chance to make everything right." Again, Akeema gave a glimpse of the truth. She got back with Jake for two reasons: she couldn't refute the Scriptures and she wanted his lovemaking. After their first break-up, she knew that Jake was not the right man for her. Akeema never felt close to him again in her heart. Her body, however, had a will of its own. She knew their reconciliation was temporary. Jake was getting more and more obsessed with her as their physical connection got deeper and deeper…pardon the pun.

Jean asked, "How well did y'all get along the second time around?"

"Just fine. It was just…different. We didn't exactly pick up where we left off."

"Explain that" Jean urged.

"Well, I didn't ever feel the same way about him, that's all."

Jean kept pushing for more information. "Before the first bust up, how did you feel about him?"

"I liked him a lot. I could see us possibly falling in love one day. Knowing how I love kids, he said we could adopt if we decided to be a family."

"My son said that?" Lucille asked, surprised.

"Yes, ma'am. He said we could have as many as I wanted because he could afford them. He even promised to make me a stay-at-home mom if I no longer wanted to work." Lucille could only mutter, "Impressive."

"I remember thinking that he was the man for me," Akeema sighed wistfully.

"Oh, my dear," Lucille said, "I know exactly how you felt. My ex made me feel that way. Now, I can't be happy with him. You were blessed to discover all facets of Jake's personality BEFORE you two were married."

Sarcastically, Jean said, "Oh, yeah, she was blessed by a gunshot to her head. Woo-woo."

Lucille blushed crimson.

"Auntie, please," Akeema gently admonished.

"Sorry," she whispered, ducking her head.

"Besides, I'm sure each of us are thankful for the biggest blessing of all – my life. I still have work to do, apparently."

Jean added, "That's true. We, also, can't overlook the many, many, prayers that were lifted up for you. I believe Yahuah heard them all as He decided to spare you."

"Yahuah?" Lucille asked.

"Yes, it's the Hebrew name for our heavenly Father."

"Are you Jewish? Jake didn't mention it. When he told me he was studying the Word with you on Saturdays, I assumed you were Adventists. I was so glad he was reading the Bibl, I didn't ask any questions. I was just so glad," Lucille admitted.

"We're spiritual Hebrews. We're thankful to be part of the fellowship that Moses led out of Egypt."

Lucille looked surprised. "Really? I never heard of this. Since Kyle and I split up, I haven't felt comfortable going to our old church. I've been reading a little from the Bible by myself, but there's so much that I don't understand."

Eagerly, Akeema replied, "You're more than welcome to join our study any Shabbat."

"Shabbat?"

"I'm sorry, any Sabbath, the day of rest. That's the seventh day."

Lucille nodded. "That sounds good to me. Can we start the lessons with me this Saturday?"

"Absolutely!" Akeema responded.

The three women looked at each other, feeling like kindred spirits.

All three of them stood up, preparing to go their separate ways, temporarily.

"Oh!" Akeema said, "When Moses led people away from Pharoah, he invited any and everybody to follow the Most High, regardless of their prior faith. That included Jews, Gentiles, foreigners, every human that breathed. They were destined to be a part of one fellowship. There wasn't a split between Baptists, Methodists, Lutherans, or anything else. All of the different congregations are man-made. Can you imagine making it to heaven only to see the east side set apart for Catholics, the west for Presbyterians, and so on and so on?"

Lucille shook her head. "Actually, no, I can't imagine that mess going on up there."

"Neither can I. Since the Bible teaches we are one spiritual family, we strive to live that way," Akeema responded.

Impulsively, Lucille grabbed Akeema for a heartfelt hug. When she finally let go, they were smiling through unshed tears. Forming a triangle, the women hugged each other in solidarity. Nobody felt like a stranger.

CHAPTER 40

Akeema's heart was fluttering nervously. She was getting ready for her first real date with Derek. Looking at herself objectively in the full-length mirror, she resisted the urge to change clothes. Her casual navy-blue pantsuit wasn't fancy, but it was comfortable. To add a little pizazz to it, she wore a deep red silk blouse with cuffs and an oversized collar. Determined to leave her cane at home, she had on a pair of plain navy flats. When Derek had asked her what sounded like fun to her, she'd promptly said anything that didn't use her legs too much.

"Akeema, your young man is here!" called Aunt Jean.

A sudden wave of nausea hit her out of nowhere. Except for wanting to upchuck the dinner she hadn't had yet, she was ready. "Okay, I'll be right there!" Akeema yelled. Closing her eyes, she took several slow, deep breaths to calm her body down. She remembered doing this before a live performance. Akeema smiled at the memory. Slinging her mini tote over her shoulder, she gracefully walked downstairs. At the bottom of them, Derek was waiting for her. If her mouth wasn't so dry, she would've whistled at him.

The first thing she noticed was the adoring way that he watched her. He obviously liked what he was looking at.

As far as Akeema was concerned, Derek Keith Wilson was one fine specimen indeed. By a happy fluke, he also had on a navy suit that fit his broad shoulders perfectly. Several buttons on his white shirt were open to reveal a small dusting of chest hair. His sparkling white tennis shoes relieved the severity of his look, adding a casual flair. His even white teeth were gleaming with his wide smile. Once again, she marveled at his long, thick eyelashes that no man should have.

"Hello, pretty lady," he said in a voice for her ears only.

"Hello, you yummy-looking man you," she said with a hungry gaze at him.

A woman had never complimented Derek like that before. Her admiring stare made him feel like he didn't have enough clothes on. He couldn't help wondering if she was this aggressive in bed. He immediately felt shame.

Akeema's aunt and uncle joined them at the stairwell for a proper send off.

Clucking over them, Jean announced, "You two handsome people look like you're going to take a family portrait."

The couple blushed, saying nothing.

Rick could tell they were uncomfortable. He tried to lighten the mood. "My missus has dinner on the stove. You're welcome to join us before you head out."

Derek inhaled. "Something sure smells good."

Rick gave his gently rounded stomach a pat. "As you can see, my lady is a good cook."

Everybody chuckled, enjoying the good-natured levity.

Derek left it up to Akeema. "Since I was going to let you choose what you wanted to eat, I'll leave it up to you."

Akeema smiled at him, liking him even more. Turning to Jean, she asked, "What's for dinner, auntie?"

Proudly, Jean answered, "Shepherd's pie and a salad. One of your favorites!"

Turning to Derek, Akeema asked, "Do you like Shepard's pie?"

He shrugged. "I've never had it."

"What?" Akeema exclaimed. "What kind of a childhood did you have?"

Derek quickly defended his people. "A pretty good one as far as I'm concerned. However, my mother was a career woman who rarely cooked."

"Well, you owe it to yourself to experience my aunt's culinary skills," Akeema boasted.

Derek grinned. "I know that your aunt can throw down in the kitchen."

Basking in her glow, Jean responded, "As I said, I've cooked so let's eat!" Turning on her heels, she briskly walked to the kitchen. Like dutiful little soldiers, every-body else followed her.

After dinner, Jean announced, "I have sugar cook-ies and vanilla ice cream for dessert. Any takers?"

Every stuffed person sitting at the kitchen island groaned and rolled their eyes in mock misery.

Looking at his watch, Derek chimed in.

"Akeema and I have the second part of our date to get through, so I think we should get a move on."

He extended his hand to her, grasping it gently when she placed her's inside his. Hand in hand, they walked to the front door. Derek opened it, then stepped aside to let his beautiful date hug and kiss her family goodnight.

Game on!

Derek deliberately had his car radio tuned into a classical station. The all-instrumental music played softly as background to their casual conversation. They were totally at ease with one another. Derek regaled her with funny stories about the children at school that they both loved so much.

During a slight lull in their conversation, Akeema asked wistfully, "Have you ever been in love, Derek?"

Surprised, he wasn't sure if he should give a date response, or be honest with her.

"No," he replied shortly. "Have you?"

"With my memory coming in and out, it's a little hard to tell. I feel I've come pretty close at least."

"Why?"

"Because I was engaged. I can't imagine pledging my life to someone that I don't love."Ouch! He'd forgotten about Joseph and Joey.

"Good point. How do you feel about him now?"

Derek wasn't breathing. Her answer mattered to him.

"I adore Joseph and Joey. They're like family to me."

Concentrating on his driving, Derek summoned the courage to ask, "How do you feel about me?"

Without hesitation, she said, "I like you a lot. You look good, you smell good, and you kiss good."

"Thank you, sweet lady. Pleases know that I like the way you look, smell, and kiss too!"

"I'm glad, Derek. I hope we get to know each other better."

"You hope? Is there a reason why we won't?"

"Well…how old are you, Derek?"

"I'm thirty-five. How old are you?"

"Twenty-seven."

"Why do our ages matter, Akeema?"

"It's kind of old for someone to never be in love before. I want to marry and have a family sooner rather than later. I approve of you taking your time to be sure you've found that special someone, but I don't know how you fit into my dream."

"Does Joseph?"

"Yes, I believe he does."

"Then, may I ask why you guys called off your engagement?"

"Because of you."

Derek's heart made a hopeful leap.

"How so?" he rasped. His breathing was challenged again.

"You're so good-looking that I was attracted to you at first sight. I didn't think an engaged woman should be lusting after other men."

"Lusting? You wanted to have sex with me?"

"Not at first. Only after the dreams," she said as a matter of fact.

Incredulous, he sputtered, "You've had erotic dreams about me?"

"Sure."

Derek looked at her open-mouthed.

"Watch the road, homeboy."

"Derek, look! There's the theater!" Akeema cried.

"Yeah, so?"

"Can we go in? Please?"

"We're not dressed right, are we?"

"I don't know or care! I'd like to see my friends dance! Pull in, please!"

Resigned to his fate, Derek did as requested.

"Your wish is my command."

As they entered the theater, a myriad of emotions flooded through her. Conflicted, she felt like she was home, yet lost on a desert island.

Glancing around the lobby, Akeema realized she was looking through the wrong end of the lens. She wasn't supposed to be part of the waiting audience. She wasn't supposed to be on the receiving end of people looking her up and down because she was wearing casual, instead of formal, attire. Her rightful place was backstage putting on too much make-up and skin-tight costumes. She needed to be here. She wanted to go home.

As they were led to their seats, Akeema continued to feel out of place. Derek felt her uneasiness.

After they sat down, he leaned closer to her as he whispered, "You look a little tense. Are you alright? Can I get you anything?"

Since she'd practically begged him to bring her here, Akeema wasn't about to blurt out that this was the last place she wanted to be.

"I'm okay, I guess. I'm just not comfortable being a part of the audience."

Her whole countenance was sad. He was surprised at the way she made him feel.

"We can go right now if you want. Just say the word."

With perfect timing, the lights went down, and the curtain lifted. They were stuck.

The beautiful symphony music filled the theater. Derek felt his entire body vibrate with the power of the orchestra. Every nerve in his body came alive. Classical music had never been his thing. He was going to re-think that. When the two principal dancers took center stage, he was mesmerized. Their leaps were so high off the ground that Derek found himself squinting to see where the high wires were that seemed to lift them to the ceiling!

Whenever the male dancer held his partner over his head, he seemed to do so without any effort at all. Derek felt like he was all alone and that the performers were dancing just for him. It was a life changing experience.

When he turned to look at Akeema, the smile on his face faded, replaced by one of concern. His beautiful date was crying! Tears were streaming down her face.

She was sitting very erect, her back not touching the chair. Her hands were in her lap, unmoving. She reminded Derek of a queen sitting on a throne. Except for the overflowing tears, her facial expression was completely composed. He wanted to know what was wrong, but something stopped him from disturbing her. He didn't want to intrude on her thoughts, he wanted her to share them with him.

At the last curtain call, Akeema sprang to her feet. She clapped her hands together loud and long. Derek was amused when she whistled so loud that heads turned in her direction at the noise that came from this elegant beauty. He wanted her to teach him to do that!

Sensitive to the other patrons, Akeema stayed out of sight during the meet and greet. She was aware that her presence might disrupt the proceedings.

As she watched the last man make it to the end of the receiving line, Akeema stopped hiding behind the huge plant that covered her and Derek. With her shoulders back, and her head erect, she walked directly to her friends and co-workers; desperately trying to hide her limp. Derek followed her lead, enjoying the rearview.

Kristen was the first to see her. Her high-pitched squeal of joy caught everyone's attention. Kristen, Chelsea, and Suzy ran to her with open arms. Hugs, kisses and tears were happening all at once. Derek stood outside the woman circle as he observed the ruckus.

Kristen exclaimed, "Akeema, you look great! You doing okay?"

Akeema replied, "Thanks, honey. Yeah, I'm getting better every day."

"Are you teaching again?" Suzy wanted to know. "How's little Joey?"

"No, I'm not teaching yet, but it won't be long now. Joey's doing great. I either see, or talk to him, every day."

The chatter went on and on. Other dancers came by to hug or shake Akeema's hand. At last, she was ready to go.

"Well, ladies, I need to go. My date has been as patient as he could be. You guys remember Derek, don't you?"

The ladies all nodded, smiling at her handsome date. It was Chelsea who had the courage to say, "If you ever decide to dump this guy, Akeema, please kick him in my direction. He's a cutie pie!"

Uncomfortable with overly forward women, Derek looked down at the red-carpeted floor, shuffling his feet. Akeema's friends thought his bashful ways were endearing. They fawned over him even more, causing even more embarrassment.

Having pity on her date, Akeema gave everyone one last goodbye hug before taking Derek's hand, leading him to the door.

Outside the theater, Derek opened the car door for Akeema. Instead of getting in, however, she stepped into his arms. He gently held her next to him. After a while, she looked him in the eyes before saying, "Thank you for tonight. You've been wonderful."

"So have you. I've had a good time."

"Oh, I see. You've got a thing for women who weep in public places," she teased.

"Not really," he replied honestly. "But I took it as a good thing that you knew you could be yourself around me. Tears or no tears."

Akeema could tell by the way he said it, that he meant it. Inching a step closer to him, she touched her lips to his. As he deepened the kiss, she let herself join with him. She decided to let HIM decide when the kiss was over.

It was a l-o-n-g kiss.

CHAPTER 41

The next morning, a fuzzy headed Akeema awakened after a fitful night's sleep. The house was quiet, and there weren't any wonderful smells coming from the kitchen.

Yawning loudly, she reached for the phone. She had only one man on her mind. She wanted to start her day hearing his voice.

"Hello, sweetness. You're up early. Is everything okay?"

"Yep, I just woke up missing you," Akeema said softly.

"Well, now. I think that's the sweetest, sexiest, thing I've heard all day."

"It's the ONLY thing you've heard," she pointed out.

He smiled into the phone. "When you are right, you are right! Have you had your breakfast yet?"

"No," she responded. "I need to tell you something first."

"Okay, let's hear it."

"I discovered something last night."

"What was that?"

"That I'm in love with you. Only you."

She heard his breathing stop for a while, before restarting. In awe, he asked, "Oh, baby! Are you sure?"

"Absolutely."

"I love you, too. I've never stopped. When did you figure it all out?"

"I haven't talked a lot about it, but it's been on my mind and in my heart. I've also done a great deal of praying about it."

"I'm glad to hear that. That means that both you and I were seeking the Will of Yahuah in our lives. It's pretty obvious that He has led you and me to each other. Hallelujah!"

Akeema giggle. "Ditto, homeboy! Am I going to see you today?"

"You bet. If your aunt and uncle are okay with it, we can do our Bible study and fellowship from there."

"I'm sure they'll be in on it. Jake's mother said she wanted to join us today."

"Really? Wow, I didn't see that one coming. Are you okay with that?"

"Sure. I'm always up for people to discover the love of our heavenly Father. She's also feeling lonely since she's no longer married to Jake's father."

"She isn't? Double wow."

"Yeah, I know. She shared with Aunt Jean and me that they had mutual friends as a married couple. She now feels out of place. I feel good about having her in our lives as a friend."

"Well, sweetheart, if it's good for you, it's also good for me."

"I like the sound of that. Come on over so you can give me a hug."

"Will do. See ya in a little bit."

"Cool. Give Joey a hug and kiss from me!"

Inhaling deeply, Akeema now smelled coffee and breakfast coming from the kitchen. Aunt Jean was busy working her special brand of food magic. Sitting on the steps across from the front door, Akeema was anxiously waiting for her boys to arrive. With a little extra time on her hands, she found herself reflecting on last night's date…

Derek's kiss seemed to go on and on. Akeema was thoroughly enjoying his technique. As she stroked his back, she enjoyed the taut muscles under his clothing. She liked the way he smelled. She liked the way he tasted. To date, she liked everything she knew about him. In the middle of this romantic moment, there was only one missing element: Joseph. In Derek's arms, Akeema had a nice warmth going on. But she was woefully aware that when she and Joseph kissed, every strand of her hair, and every single one of her toes, seemed red hot! When she was on the receiving end of his lovemaking, she couldn't think straight. The fact that she was comparing their kisses while she was being kissed, told her a lot. What an odd time to have a moment of mental clarity.

When at last the kiss was over, Derek was aroused and breathing hard. Akeema wasn't. Feeling the need to stay close to her, he began kissing her ear and the side of her neck.

"Would you like to end our date at my place?"

His invitation was delivered in a silky-smooth sexy voice. Instinctively, she knew he'd be a satisfying lover. There was only one thing wrong – he wasn't Joseph.

Akeema pulled back a little so that they could see one another. "No, thank you, Derek. It's kind of late. You should probably take me home." He was a little confused. Had he misunderstood their desire for each other? Maybe she just wasn't ready to take their relationship to the next level. He was disappointed, of course, but she had to make the call. The choice wasn't his. He kissed her smooth forehead, let go, then opened the car door for her. On his way to the driver's seat, Derek counted to twenty. By the time he started the car, his libido was under control.

They rode in silence for a while before Derek decided to clear the air.

"Akeema, you know that I respect your choice when it comes to our personal life, right?"

"Yes, Derek, I appreciate that. Thanks."

"No problem. So, we're cool?"

"The coolest," she said with a smile.

He glanced at her, before turning his attention back to the road.

"Derek?"

"Yeah, babe," he responded.

"If we keep dating, how does that work out since you're my supervisor?"

He sighed. "I'd have to transfer you to another school."

Akeema made an ugly face. "Yuck, I don't like that."

"I know, but I don't think it's ethical to date my employees. Do you understand?"

"Yes, I do. It's part of the reason that you are so respected. I'm glad you are my friend."

Derek sensed this conversation wasn't going his way. Her fresh scent was still clinging to his clothes. He could still taste her in his mouth.

"I'm glad we're friends too, Akeema. I hope we'll grow closer than that."

"We won't."

"Why not?" he shouted without meaning to.

"I'm not giving Joey up when I don't have to."

"You won't be giving him up. You'll still have access to him in your personal life. You know that."

Gently, she replied, "I'm not giving up Joseph either, Derek."

This made sense to him. After all, Joey was only seven or eight years old. Since he was a minor, naturally, she'd also see the dad.

"That's good. I don't expect you to give up any of your friends to be with me. In due time, we'll probably all hang out together."

Akeema knew he didn't know what she meant. He was so nice that she didn't want to hurt or disappoint him. Oh well.

"Actually, Derek, I think you and I are talking about two different relationships,"

Curiously, he asked, "How so?"

"It sounds like you're planning for you and I to have a romantic future."

He nodded. "Absolutely."

"Not really."

"What do you mean? I call what we were doing a few moments ago very romantic, don't you?"

"Yes, but…"

"But what, Akeema?"

"As much as I like you, there's someone else that I like even more."

He glanced at her, seeing the tension on her face.

"You're talking about Joseph?"

"Yes, I am."

"Look, we both know how much you adore his son. Don't you think you might be confusing how you feel about one, with the other?"

"Uh-uh," she said confidently.

"What makes you so sure?"

"A few things. I don't want to hurt your feelings, Derek."

He winced. If he was on the verge of being dumped, he wanted to know why.

"I'm all about truth, Akeema. If you and I are destined to be just friends, I'd very much like for you to be honest with me about it. I won't be angry or give you a hard time. I promise."

Her anxiety ebbed a little.

"I'm glad you said that. Thanks."

"No problem. Now, I'm listening."

"I got a little upset watching the dancer on stage tonight," she added.

"Yeah, I noticed."

"I knew you were there for me, but I sat there longing for Joseph's shoulder to cry on."

In spite of himself, that stung. Keeping the tone of his voice moderate, he asked what had upset her.

"For the first time, I was hit with the knowledge that I would no longer have a stage to dance on. A part of my memory chose that time to surface. I remembered my last dance, and what it felt like to have complete control of my body. I felt the rush of pleasure and gratitude when the audience gave me a standing ovation. I mourned the loss of all that."

"Wow."

"Yeah, right? I sat there blubbering like a fool when I was the one who'd insisted that we be there!" she cried.

Instinctively, Derek took a hand off the steering wheel to grasp her hand, consoling her.

Again, Joseph crossed Akeema's mind. She wanted to be in HIS arms, not her date's.

"I'm so sorry, Akeema," Derek said softly. He felt like he was on the brink of crying himself. His heart ached for the pain she was in. This was the kind of woman he'd always been looking for. It was just his luck – or lack thereof – that the woman he wanted, wanted someone else.

"Don't worry about it. It's just the Ying and the Yang of my returning memory," she lamented. "The more I remember, the more I know how much I've lost."

"Listen, on the upside of things, we know that your teaching job is secure. Have you talked to your doctor about your work release?"

Akeema smiled faintly. "Yes, I have. It's good news. This coming Monday I'm being evaluated. Since I'm getting along better without my cane, I'm feeling good about it."

"Good! I couldn't help but notice how well you're moving around this evening. You're doing great!"

"Thank you, kind sir," she replied pleasantly. Derek gave her hand a last reassuring squeeze. He then drove Akeema home in comfortable silence.

The insistent doorbell brought Akeema back to the here and now. She rushed to the front door, anxious to see her boys.

When she opened the door, she stumbled back a little as Joey threw himself into her arms. An always alert Joseph stepped in to steady them. All was right with the world.

After a hearty breakfast and kitchen clean-up, the house settled down for the holy day of rest. They still had about two hours before the start of the Shabbat service, so everyone took time to relax and be still. Lucille Butler had already called to reserve her spot for their Bible study. To everyone's pleasure, she'd agreed to stay for supper.

Rick was reading Joey a story from the children's Bible. Actually, he was the official page turner while Joey did an exemplary job of reading out loud.

It was a mild autumn afternoon, perfect to sit on the wooden swing in Jean and Rick's backyard. Akeema and Joseph were rocking back and forth, feeling like teenagers who were courting. At last, Akeema broke the silence.

"Derek and I are just friends now. We've stopped dating each other."

Pleased, Joseph said, "I'm really surprised. He seemed very interested in you."

"I know, but we talked about it, and he agrees with me."

"Oh, so it was your idea, not his?"

Akeema nodded.

Joseph pressed on. "Do you want to stop dating me too?"

"Nope."

"Are you sure?"

"Yep."

"Do you want to be good friends or something more?"

"Both."

"Okay, uh, do you want to date other men, or just me?"

"Just you for me, and me for you, Joseph." He turned to look at her. Then, he turned her face toward his with his finger gently on her chin. They smiled at each other. They felt connected.

"I love you Akeema Dawn Sprite."

"I love you too, Joseph Smith. And Joey, too."

"I'm glad. How do you feel about being married one day in the near future?"

"I feel really good about it," she responded promptly.

"Do you remember that we agreed to not have sex before our wedding day?"

"Yep."

"Are you still okay with that?"

"As long as you are. I also remember our kisses. They were different from Derek's."

"Better, I hope," Joseph said under his breath.

"Much," she said promptly. "Derek was a good kisser. I felt nice and warm in his arms."

A jealous Joseph kept his mouth shut.

Akeema continued. "But, when you and I are in each other's arms, I feel all tingly from my hair down to my toes."

Akeema shivered just thinking about it. Meanwhile, Joseph tried not to puff out his chest. He realized a show of pride just wouldn't be attractive. Humbly, he said, "I'm glad to know we ring each other's bells."

Akeema sighed. "You're such a gentleman. You think of nice, sweet bells when we get together, while I see an explosion!"

They both got a laugh out of that.

"Listen babe, we can't do any exploding until our wedding night! I don't let my mind go there."

"I admit you're better at staying in the safe zone than I am. You should hear about the dreams ...,"

"Stop!" Joseph interrupted her. "It's Shabbat, remember?"

"Oops! So sorry."

"It's okay, it just feels like we're pouring salt in the wound."

"You're right, so I'll watch it. But, one thing I want to make sure we agree on is the time of day that we marry."

"What do you have in mind?"

Akeema was animated, her eyes glowing.

"I want the ceremony to begin around 11:00 A.M."

"Eleven in the morning? Why?"

"Because I have zero intention of being horny all day and half the night on the day we say our vows!" she all but shouted.

Joseph laughed while shushing her, covering her mouth with his hand. Batting it away, Akeema continued her tirade. "Listen to me, I'm serious! Now, the ceremony will be over by noon, so we'll have a bridal lunch instead of dinner. Then, we'll do the first dance, throw the bouquet and cut the cake. At the very LATEST we'll be all done by 3:00 in the afternoon! After that, our time is our own. My aunt and uncle will take good care of our Joey, so we won't have a thing to worry about."

He loved the way she said 'our' Joey.

"Your aunt and uncle are tops with our little boy. Next to you and me, they're his favorite people."

"Isn't that great? We have a wonderfully blessed family."

"We sure do, sweetheart. Where do you want to go after our afternoon reception?"

"To the nearest, nicest, hotel."

Joseph laughed. "Seriously, what state or town do you want to go to?"

"I am serious!" Akeema said stubbornly. "I want to talk, eat, and make love for at least five days!"

"Do you mind if we sleep a little in between that?"

"Only if you insist," she said ruefully.

They locked eyes before they laughed and hugged, rocking back and forth on the swing.

Suddenly, they heard Joey's footsteps rushing toward them. To their amazement, he was carrying a plate full of warm sugar cookies. Akeema and Joseph couldn't believe how fast he was walking while balancing the plate.

"Slow down, son!"

"Careful, Joey!" they said as one.

Giggling, Joey reached them safely without a single cookie hitting the ground.

"Look what I have!" he sang.

Akeema teased, "Are all of those just for you?"

Joey's imp was alive and well. "Only if you don't eat any."

"Give those to me, you little rascal," Joseph said. He took the plate from his son's hands just as Akeema tickled his sides.

"Help, Daddy, help! She's killing me!" Joey cried. He was laughing so hard, that Akeema felt sorry for him. When he finally caught his breath, he started to hiccup over and over. Joey got a kick out of it. Over-stimulated, he was laughing, crying, and gasping for breath. How he managed to talk in the middle of all that was a miracle. "Can a guy (hiccup) die from being (hiccup) too happy?"

Akeema and Joseph smiled at the idea. It would truly be a blessing. Joseph gave his lady the cookie plate so that he could put his son on his shoulders. As he stood up, Joey yelled, "Don't leave (hiccup) Akeema!"

Joseph replied, "We'll never leave her. She's one of us now, right?"

"(hiccup) right!"

Together, they walked back into the house where Jean was anxiously waiting with a cup of water in hand to help calm the hiccups.

All for one, and one for all.

Forever.

THE END

www.ingramcontent.com/pod-product-compliance
Lightning Source LLC
Chambersburg PA
CBHW040851010826

48978CB00013BA/975